DAUGHTER OF RAVENS BOOK 1

THE EXILE'S CURSE

M.J. SCOTT

PRAISE FOR M.J. SCOTT

The Shattered Court
Nominated for Best Paranormal Romance in the 2016 RITA® Awards.

"Scott (the Half-Light City series) opens her Four Arts fantasy series with the portrait of a young woman who's thrust into the center of dangerous political machinations... Romance fans will enjoy the growing relationship between Cameron and Sophie, but the story's real strength lies in the web of intrigue Scott creates around her characters."
—*Publishers Weekly*

"Fans of high fantasy and court politics will enjoy The Shattered Court. Sophie is such a great heroine..."
—*RT Book Reviews*

The Forbidden Heir
"This story was packed with action, political intrigue, scheming, and high stakes."
—*Alyssa - Goodreads reviewer*

"This is a marvelous book. The world building is unique and complex. The characters are well developed and likable and there is intrigue for days. If you've read the first book in the series it only gets better in this one."
—*Lissa - Goodreads reviewer*

"'Forbidden Heir' is a great rarity: a sequel that I liked better than the original book."
—*Margaret - Amazon reviewer*

Fire Kin

"Entertaining...Scott's dramatic story will satisfy both fans and new readers."
—*Publishers Weekly*

"This is one urban fantasy series that I will continue to come back to...Fans of authors Christina Henry of the Madeline Black series and Keri Arthur of the Dark Angels series will love the Half-Light City series."
—*Seeing Night Book Reviews*

Iron Kin

"Strong and complex world building, emotionally layered relationships, and enough action to keep me up long past my bedtime. I want to know what's going to happen next to the DuCaines and their chosen partners, and I want to know now."
—*Vampire Book Club*

"Iron Kin was jam-packed with action, juicy politics, and a lot of loose ends left over for the next book to resolve that it's still a good read for series fans."
—*All Things Urban Fantasy*

"Scott's writing is rather superb."
—*Bookworm Blues*

Blood Kin

"Not only was this book just as entertaining and immensely readable as Shadow Kin—it sang in harmony with it and spun its own story all the while continuing the grander symphony that is slowly becoming the Half-Light City story. . . . Smart, funny, dangerous, addictive, and seductive in its languorous sexuality, I can think of no better book to recommend to anyone to read this summer. I loved every single page except the last one, and that's only because it meant the story was done. For now, at least."
—*seattlepi.com*

"Blood Kin was one of those books that I really didn't want to put down, as it hit all of my buttons for an entertaining story. It had the intrigue and danger of a spy novel, intense action scenes, and a romance that evolved organically over the course of the story. . . . Whether this is your first visit to Half-Light City or you're already a fan, Blood Kin expertly weaves the events from Shadow Kin throughout this sequel in a way that entices new readers without boring old ones. I am really looking forward to continuing this enthralling ride."
—*All Things Urban Fantasy*

"Blood Kin had everything I love about urban fantasies: kick-butt action, fantastic characters, romance that makes the heart beat fast, and a plot that was fast-paced all the way through. Even more so the villains are meaner, stronger, and downright fantastic—I never knew what they were going to do next. You don't want to miss out on this series."
—*Seeing Night Book Reviews*

"An exciting thriller . . . fast-paced and well written."
—*Genre Go Round Reviews*

Shadow Kin

"M. J. Scott's Shadow Kin is a steampunky romantic fantasy with vampires that doesn't miss its mark."
—*#1 New York Times bestselling author Patricia Briggs*

"Shadow Kin is an entertaining novel. Lily and Simon are sympathetic characters who feel the weight of past actions and secrets as they respond to their attraction for each other."
—*New York Times bestselling author Anne Bishop*

"M. J. Scott weaves a fantastic tale of love, betrayal, hope, and sacrifice against a world broken by darkness and light, where the only chance for survival rests within the strength of a woman made of shadow and the faith of a man made of light."
—*National bestselling author Devon Monk*

"Had me hooked from the very first page."
—*New York Times bestselling author Keri Arthur*

"Exciting and rife with political intrigue and magic, Shadow Kin is hard to put down right from the start. Magic, faeries, vampires, werewolves, and Templar knights all come together to create an intriguing story with a unique take on all these fantasy tropes. . . . The lore and history of Scott's world is well fleshed out and the action scenes are exhilarating and fast."
—*Romantic Times*

Wicked Games

"Extremely engrossing book with great world building, captivating characters and a sizzling romance to top it all off. The chemistry between the protagonists is very steamy as well. I NEED the next one!."
—*Cherylyn - Amazon reviewer*

"A little bit different to the norm in this genre. MJ Scott has

written a rattling good yarn that keeps you engrossed from start to finish.."
—*Andew - Amazon reviewer*

"'This book is a bit like Ready Player One with witches. The premise is really unique and fascinating and I fell in love with the characters. I really want the next book in the series right now..."
—*Lissa - Goodreads reviewer*

Published by emscott enterprises.

Cover design by Deranged Doctor Designs.

Interior Art by Etheric Designs and M.J. Scott

ISBN ebook 978-0-6484814-7-8

ISBN print 978-0-6452948-1-1

For those chasing those second chances...

CHAPTER 1

Chloe de Montesse pressed a hand to her stomach, trying to keep her face impassive as she watched the sailors maneuver the gangway into position. This close to the dock, the sway of the ship seemed worse than it had during the crossing from Anglion, and she wasn't entirely sure she wasn't about to disgrace herself. Though, if she was honest, the churning in her stomach was part excitement, part confusion, part terror. But easier to blame it on the swaying ship than try to untangle the swirl of her emotions.

Home.

She was *home*.

In Illvya. In Lumia. Where, until a few months ago, she had never expected to be again.

Her eyes stung and she swiped at them quickly. It was only the sea air, not emotion.

There could be no giving in to emotion here or she might drown in it. As surely as she would if she stepped off the side of the gangplank into the dark, cold harbor waters instead of proceeding down it in an orderly fashion when the command came to disembark.

To distract herself, she searched the faces of the people waiting on the docks.

Illvyan faces. There was nothing that should immediately identify them as such, but she felt the certainty of it in her bones as she drank them in. A sharpness to their features. Subtle differences to the tones of skin. Different fashions than the ones she'd been wearing in Anglion all this time. But she couldn't focus on strange faces and the fact that she was finally about to set foot back in the empire after ten years in exile.

Not when she was frantically searching for faces she knew. She'd sent word that she was returning to her father, including details of the ship the emperor had provided her passage on. But there'd been no time for a reply, and even though Sophie—one day Chloe might get used to the fact that the young Lady Sophie Mackenzie was now Queen Sophia of Anglion—had assured her that her father missed her and loved her and very much wanted her home, Chloe couldn't bring herself to entirely believe it.

Not when the last time Henri Matin saw her had been a few scant hours before Chloe fled the country in fear, tainted by her husband, Charl's, disgrace and leaving her family to face what consequences may come.

What if she couldn't find him in the crowd? Couldn't recognize him? Ten years was a long time. A span of years that scarcely made sense now that it had ended. She'd yet to turn twenty-five when she'd left. Now she was ten years older and her father closing in on sixty-five. So much time gone by had wrought changes on her face. It would have changed him as well.

But just as she was starting to think she'd been right to fear that no one would come to meet her, that no one truly wanted her to return, she caught a glimpse of gray hair and long limbs moving through the crowd with a gait so familiar it almost stopped her heart.

"Papa," she called, waving one arm wildly in the air, all concern with not disgracing herself gone. "Papa, I'm here."

He must have heard her somehow because his head swung

round and pale blue eyes caught hers and suddenly she was pushing through the other passengers and racing down the gangplank, heedless of the sailors shouting at her or the fact that it was barely fixed in place, and then her father's arms came around her and she was finally and truly home.

✧ ✧ ✧

Chloe didn't let go of her father's hand as they made their way through the crowd, and from the strength of his grip, she wasn't sure he ever intended to let go of hers. The feel of it, so familiar yet strange, so steady yet overwhelming, made her eyes prickle all over again. She had already made a spectacle of herself, dissolving into tears as she'd hugged Henri. Perhaps she should just accept that the next few days and weeks were likely to be messy and emotional—things she had avoided for a very long time.

In Anglion, her carefully regulated and arranged life had been simple. She'd kept her head down and not let anyone get too close. No risk that way. It had taken two years before she'd even let herself take the slightest risk of breaching the Anglion laws when she'd created the portal beneath her store. Technically refugees weren't supposed to have portals, but she'd wanted an escape route if she needed one in a hurry.

Perhaps the fact that she was concentrating so hard on not letting herself burst into tears was the reason she almost walked into a man who stepped unexpectedly into her path. As she half jumped backward, trying to avoid the collision, her eyes flew up to his face, a warning to be careful about where he was walking on the very tip of her tongue.

Where it dissolved into chaos and silence when she registered the face staring back down at her, storm-green eyes wide with shock.

Lucien de Roche. *Dear Goddess, no.* Where was that damn portal when she needed it?

The one man in all the empire she least wanted to see. The man whose continued existence had given her no little pause for thought when she'd been coming to her decision as to whether she would return home.

"Chloe," he breathed.

The word felt like a slap despite its softness.

Lucien.

She stared back at him, unable to think or come up with any sort of response. Once upon a time, Lucien had been Charl's best friend. Tall and quiet and blond in contrast to Charl's dark and dazzling. One of her best friends as well. They'd been a trio of sorts, a small gang of their own. Bright and glittering and full of the certainty that their futures would be blessed.

Until it had gone so horribly wrong.

Thanks to Charl. Who had been charming and irresistible and, as it had turned out, entirely incapable of making good choices when they were most needed. Pity she'd only learned that—or perhaps only let herself see it—after she'd married him.

Lucien, on the other hand, had always done the right thing. Solid as the earth. And just as unyielding, as it had turned out.

Lucien de Roche. The reason why Charl was dead.

The man who'd stood up in court and prosecuted his best friend, knowing the penalty for the charges Charl faced was death.

The man who'd ruined her life.

The man who'd maybe saved it. Lucien had come to her after Charl's execution, given her a warning that she was not entirely safe in the wake of Charl's conviction. Suggested she might want to make herself hard to find.

Presumably he'd meant just for a short time.

But she'd been young. Broken by grief and betrayal, and wild with fear that what had befallen her would yet engulf the rest of her family. So she had run, leaving Charl's body barely in the earth and all manner of trouble strewn behind her. Fled to Anglion, where no one from the empire could reach her. Where no one could hurt her again.

No one had come after her.

Least of all Lucien de Roche.

Who, no matter that he was apparently still one of the most handsome men the goddess ever foolishly allowed to walk the earth, could never be anyone but her enemy.

"I believe that is Madame de Montesse to you, Ser de Roche," she said, channeling all the control she'd gained hard fought from her years in exile and all the disdain she felt for him to ice her voice into something smooth and glittering and deadly as a blade. She turned away from him. "Papa, we should go. I find myself quite fatigued from my journey."

Henri's pale blue eyes studied her a moment, then flicked over her head to where she was all too aware that Lucien still stood. "Of course," he said, then offered her an arm to guide her away through the crowd and away from the past she was entirely unwilling to face.

When they were settled in a carriage and some distance from the port, her father said mildly, "You got his title wrong. He's the Marq of Castaigne now."

There was no reproach in his voice, but she wondered why exactly he was telling her. Warning her that Lucien had more power now? That she should at least be polite? Not that the man needed any more power. He was a Truth Seeker, wielder of a rare form of the Arts of Air that let him know, when he chose, if a person was telling the truth. It had seen him rise quickly in the ranks of the Imperial judiciary from the moment he'd left the Academe di Sages.

He hardly needed his father's title to elevate him still further.

Though she had been fond of Emile de Roche, who had been quick to smile and more like Charl than his own serious son. She should ask how he died. But that would only provide an opening for her father to continue talking about Lucien.

"I will remember," she said tightly. "Though I don't imagine our paths will cross often."

Not at all if she had anything to say about it.

Henri studied her a moment, wearing what she had once thought of as his maistre look. The one he wore when he was debating whether to use something as a teaching moment. Seeing it was both delightful—she fancied any expression that crossed his face would be delightful for quite some time simply because it had been so long since she had seen any of them—and a little alarming. She'd forgotten how imposing he could be when he was being Maistre of the Academe and not her father.

Was he about to deliver a lecture?

However, if he had contemplated doing so, he thought better of it. A smile replaced the serious expression, and he reached out and touched her cheek. "It is good to have you home, daughter."

She leaned into the caress a moment, then pulled back, scared she might cry once more. She didn't want to emerge from the carriage red-eyed and tearstained.

"Are we going to the Academe?"

Henri cocked his head. "No, I thought you'd be eager to be home. I've left Madame Simsa in charge for a few days. The Academe can do without me for a time while we all get...reacquainted." He squeezed her hand tighter. "Your mother can't wait to see you. She wanted to come to the docks, but we didn't want to overwhelm you."

Chloe's heart squeezed. When Imogene du Laq—the Duquesse of Saint Pierre now, but also Chloe's best friend—had told her back in Kingswell that her mother was still alive, it had been one of the happiest moments of her life. Ana Matin's health had never been good, and she had only just begun to show signs of recovery from the white-lung fever that had weakened her for several years when Chloe had fled Illvya. She'd always been worried her mother would die and she would never know.

"And she is truly well again?"

Her father squeezed her hand. "She is far better than when you left. She will never be as strong as some, but having you home with us again will only make her stronger still."

She hoped he was right. But there was no way to know for sure, so she just held his hand and watched Lumia passing by through the carriage windows with greedy eyes.

It took a long time to fall asleep. The reunion with her family had left Chloe both joyous and overwhelmed, and she'd passed into that state where she was almost too tired to sleep. Or too afraid, perhaps, half convinced that she'd wake again in Anglion, having dreamed the whole journey home. Having dreamed her father's embrace and the tears her mother had tried and failed to hold back.

But eventually she succumbed to exhaustion, and when she woke, she knew instantly where she was. Her room. In her parents' house. It wasn't much changed. The colors of the curtains and the bedcovers were different, but the furniture was the same.

The carved redwood bed and the dressing table and armoire were precisely as she remembered, down to the chip in the dressing table where she'd once dropped a teapot and the faint lemon smell of the furniture polish.

When she'd left here to marry Charl, her sister, Yvette, had taken the room. But she, too, was married now and gone from the house.

Whereas Chloe was widowed and had returned after so long away.

Home.

The thought still made her grin, but there was a curl of anxiety beneath the joy. She had to begin again. Find her way. Face the past.

Deal with the mess.

She didn't even have a clear idea where she stood legally. The emperor had declared her free of any culpability in relation to Charl, so she had nothing to worry about there. But Charl had been found guilty. Where did that leave her? The emperor hadn't declared his property forfeit. As his wife, by rights, some of his estate should have come to her. Not that it had been large. They had lived in a small townhouse owned by his father, and she imagined the family would have long since reclaimed it.

Had they returned any of her belongings? Returned them here? Her parents hadn't mentioned it yet, but she'd left clothes and books and other small things behind. She'd taken what jewelry she could when she fled—nothing that had belonged to the de Montesse family, not wanting to have theft added to any claims that might fall against her—but the pieces Charl had bought her and that she'd already owned when they'd wed. Along with the small reserve of coins Charl kept in a lockbox in his study. It had been enough for her passage to Anglion and to keep her safe during those first months of trying to establish herself anew.

She had returned home with a far healthier balance of funds, having sold her business in Anglion, but not many possessions. Carin, who bought the store, was planning to live above it, as Chloe had, and had paid extra for the furniture. So Chloe had left it and most of her other household items, bringing with her only a few favored vases and pictures and the mirror from her dressing table, which had been one of the first things she'd bought for herself in Kingswell.

Other than that, she returned with clothes, cash, her medicine chest, and notes from her years of working in her store—potions and remedies and such she'd learned or developed—and a few supplies that would be scarce in Illvya. At least until the emperor and the new queen restarted a more regular trade system between the two countries.

So her new life—or new old life—came with only a simple beginning in terms of belongings. Albeit with a somewhat more complicated one in terms of just about everything else.

At least she didn't have to worry about finding a place to live and immediate employment. She rather thought the opposite might be true, that her parents might just try to keep her as close to them as they could for as long as possible.

For now, she was happy to stay. To soak up the pleasure of being reunited without rushing to determine what her future might hold.

Time enough to worry about that in the days to come.

Today, she could just let herself be Chloe.

She smiled and stretched her arms above her head. The sounds of the house stirring below were familiar, as was the smell of bacon and fresh bread and the strong Elenian coffee her mother favored over the tea that was more popular in Lumia. She'd missed coffee like fire for her first few months in Anglion. No one drank it there. It wasn't grown on the island, nor was it one of the few rare imports exchanged with the empire.

Maybe she would have lost the taste for it. Or maybe not. The smell was making her mouth water.

So. She was home. Breakfast was waiting.

Time to begin.

Two days later, she was starting to think that simply beginning was not so simple when a note arrived from Imogene. Her mother handed it to her with a carefully neutral expression and took a seat on the sofa beside her. The small parlor was filled with sunshine and festooned with yellow flowers that made it feel like spring, but the sudden tension in the air added a chill.

Chloe opened the letter, scanning the contents with eager eyes.

"And what does the duquesse have to say?" her mother inquired. She didn't sound enthusiastic.

Back in Anglion, in the wake of the excitement of their unexpected reunion, Imogene had been strangely reticent to talk about Chloe's family. She had reassured Chloe that they were all well and provided some brief details, such as the fact that Chloe had brothers-in-law and nieces and nephews she'd never met. Having seen how her family, in turn, went quiet and stiff every time Chloe mentioned Imogene's name, she now understood why. Clearly things had become strained between them after Chloe left. It was time to address the issue.

"Mama, Imogene was my best friend. I'm hoping she will be again. Nothing Charl did was her fault."

Her mother winced, her dark eyes glancing away. Her hair had streaks of gray amongst the earth-witch red now, and she was still thinner than Chloe would have liked. Not as deathly thin as she had been at the worst of her illness, but not the strong and healthy mama of Chloe's youth. The peach tones of her dress added color to her face but not quite enough. "You met that man at Imogene's betrothal ball. You cannot deny that much."

She flicked her fingers dismissively, a gesture that struck Chloe as oddly Illvyan. But then many things had struck her as oddly Illvyan over the last three days. Even the language—though she found it returned easily enough to her lips—sounded both strange and familiar after a decade of the harsher sounds of Anglion.

"No. That much is true," Chloe agreed. "But Imogene didn't throw me into his path or force me to marry him." No, Chloe, smitten by Charl's looks and charm, had done the throwing and the reckless plunge into marriage all by herself. Imogene had actually suggested she take things more slowly. But Chloe, with her dreams of a career stymied by her mother's health and her head turned by the glamor of Imogene and Jean-Paul's rapid romance, had ignored that advice. Marriage had seemed a chance at adventure of another kind.

There had been many times that Chloe wished she could go back and change that moment. Take back the words and never ask Imogene to introduce her to Charl. But she had never blamed Imogene for what happened afterward. That was on Chloe's head. And Charl's. And, of course, Lucien's.

No. Do not *think of that man.*

She squared her shoulders. "None of it was Imogene's fault," she repeated. "You need to be kind to her. I doubt I have many friends left. And she did, after all, invade Anglion to find me." Granted, it had been part of a larger invasion, but Chloe knew it was Imogene—and her sanctii, Ikarus—who had focused on finding her during the craziness that had been the night Sophie returned to Anglion and became queen amidst rebellion and chaos. Her mother bowed her head a moment, then lifted it and smiled. The expression was somewhat strained, but her voice sounded genuine when she said, "If she has been a true friend to you, then I will be happy to see her again."

"Actually, she's invited me to tea at her townhouse," Chloe said. "So you can avoid her a little longer."

This time the wince that crossed her mother's face was impossible to miss.

Chloe reached out and took Ana's hand, the bones of it feeling fragile under the skin. "Mama, it is perfectly safe. Imogene will send a carriage for me and return me promptly. I promise no one is going to steal me away." No one had stolen her away the first time. She had taken herself away, in the dead of night.

At the time, she hadn't let herself think about the cost to her family. Even in Anglion, that was something she had tried not to dwell on. She was alive. Safe. She was fairly certain they knew that much. There were a few complicated channels of communication—both legal and otherwise—between Anglion and her sworn enemy Illvya, and news trickled back and forth. The captain who'd transported her across the sea between the empire and the island nation had promised to take word back that she was safe. But it was too dangerous to stay in contact with Charl's crimes so fresh. She had to hope it was enough that they knew where she was.

Safe but exiled was preferable to dead.

"I know, darling," Ana said. "It's foolish. But you were gone for so long a time. I haven't had my fill of you yet."

Chloe smiled. "Nor I of you. But I'm not going anywhere, and we must start to find a new routine. You have friends of your own and things that you must want to get back to."

"Nothing that cannot wait a while longer."

She kept the smile in place but hoped it didn't appear strained. She'd expected her family to be happy to have her home. Had imagined hours and days alone with them. She'd thought it would feel nothing but joyous.

It *had* been joyous. But there was an edge of worry to her mother's attentions that made her uneasy. She didn't want to cause her mother any more pain or, Goddess forbid, cause a relapse of her illness, but she couldn't let Ana keep her at home forever.

But she could indulge her for another day or so. Ana's fears would lessen once she accepted that Chloe really was home. At least she hoped so.

CHAPTER 2

Imogene waited until her very correct seneschal had left the room before embracing Chloe in a hug so tight, she nearly couldn't breathe.

It was a long time before either of them let go. "You're finally *home*." Imogene smiled so wildly, blue eyes sparkling, that she looked about sixteen again. Far less regal than a duquesse should despite her expensive gown and the pearl-and-sapphire combs taming her dark hair.

It was impossible to stop an answering grin. "So it seems."

"And is it wonderful?" Imogene asked. She plopped herself down on one of the spindly legged sofas dotted around the room, patting the pale green velvet in invitation.

The grin faded a little. "It is...disorienting," Chloe said after a pause. "Things are different." Nothing stood still in ten years, and it seemed she was constantly noticing changes—small and large.

Take, for example, Imogene's parlor.

The du Laqs still used the townhouse in Coteau-Arge, near the Imperial Palace where they'd lived when they'd first wed rather than the grander home the old duq had favored. But the last time Chloe stood in this room, it had been awash in pale blues and grays, all low velvet divans and watery-sheened wallpaper, with crystal light fittings and lamps shimmering light everywhere.

Now it was a confection of light greens and yellows and pinks, the furniture light and airy, the fabrics floral. The walls were now white with a border of tiles also painted with tiny flowers. Real flowers graced the tables in tall white porcelain vases, filling the warm afternoon air with scents she'd half forgotten. Anglion and Illvya shared some plant life but not all of it. She thought of her notebook tucked safely back in her dressing table at home and her stores of Anglion herbs. She would have to go shopping. Round out her collection with some of the Illvyan remedies she had been unable to obtain in Anglion.

Imogene lifted an eyebrow, then shook her head, patting the sofa again. "I suppose they must be. But your family must be so happy to see you safe."

"They are. And I am exceedingly happy to be home. But I will confess it was nice to leave the house. They all keep watching me like I might vanish into thin air if they look away." Chloe sat beside Imogene, wondering if she sounded crazy.

"You all just need time to adjust," Imogene said. She cocked her head. "You've been through a lot."

That was the goddess's own truth. But Chloe was worried that it was perhaps too much to truly recover from. That she would never fully understand what it had been like for her family left with the aftermath here in Lumia, and that they would never fully understand what her life had been in Anglion. Or how Charl's betrayal had changed her. "I hope so."

"I find time solves many problems," Imogene said sagely.

Chloe giggled. "That was very duquesse-like of you."

Imogene stuck out her tongue in a very un-noble fashion. "You try being one for years and see how you sound."

"No, thank you. No more dabbling with the aristos for me."

Imogene's face fell. "Dearest, I didn't mean—"

Chloe patted her knee. "It's fine. Charl has been dead for ten years now. As you said, time is...useful." Useful but not a cure-all. Sometimes the memories of her marriage seemed like a distant dream. Sometimes the grief of what he'd done still cut through her like a knife. And, sometimes, so did the memory of the times they had been happy.

"Have you had any word from his family?" Imogene asked.

"No. I'm sure they want nothing to do with me."

"Perhaps. But there must be legal matters to see to. You were his wife."

Trust Imogene to get straight to the point. Her family, so far, had not raised the subject. Waiting for her to broach it, perhaps. But she wasn't ready for that. Easier to speak her fears to Imogene. "The wife of a traitor. The wife who ran away." The thought of approaching the de Montesse family made her stomach twist. Charl's parents had been kind to her on the whole, but they'd been fast to distance themselves when their son fell afoul of the law.

Imogene straightened, frowning. "But you need money, dearest."

Chloe wrinkled her nose. "I have money enough to rent an apartment when I am ready. My shop in Kingswell was quite the success."

The frown lightened to something closer to curiosity. "One day you will have to explain to me how you convinced the Anglion dominas to ignore an Illvyan selling magical supplies."

"Better to sell the supplies than practice the magic," Chloe said. "By the time I bought the store, I had been assisting Ginevra for several years and causing no trouble. Keep your nose clean long enough and you become boring. Besides, everything I sold was for earth witches. Perfectly respectable." If not the most exciting way to spend her days. Yes, the herbal lore and such healing as the average Anglion earth witches used were interesting, but they limited themselves with their taboos and rules. She knew her skills were nothing close to an Illvyan healer's. Or even a strong Anglion one. The temple trained those, and while they had tolerated Chloe, they wouldn't have welcomed her showing any interest in learning more magic.

One of Imogene's perfect brows arched. "From what I've seen of the Anglion temple, they're very willing to stick their noses in, even if you're boring. But you'll tell me more another time," she said. "So, you can afford to rent an apartment when you're ready, and thus the de Montesse family can wait. Which brings us to the question of how you intend to fill your days."

Chloe huffed out a surprised laugh. Imogene had never been the shy and retiring type, and becoming a duquesse had only made her more direct with time. "That's not an easy question. And I don't know the answer yet. Papa wants me to spend a semester at the Academe. Refresh my theory, as it were. It is a reasonable enough plan." Even if she wasn't sure she wanted to comply. The need to reconnect with her magic, she couldn't deny. The familiar strength of Lumia's ley lines had been humming through her veins since she stepped off the ship, but she'd been too nervous try her magic again. Not even the small earth magics she'd allowed herself back in Kingswell, let alone the water magic she hadn't touched for so long.

"That seems a sound idea," Imogene said. "A way to accustom yourself to being back in Lumia. The Academe doesn't change much, even if the students do."

No mention of the fact that Chloe needed the practice, which was kind.

Imogene chewed her lip briefly. "Jean-Paul and I are holding a small ball next week. I would love for you to come."

Alarm pricked down Chloe's spine. *A "small" ball?* She'd been to a few of their balls before Jean-Paul had become the duq. They'd hardly been "small" then. Doubtful they would have shrunk now that he was one of the highest-ranking men in the country. "I'm not sure if I'm quite ready for that—"

Imogene held up a hand. "The emperor asked me to invite you," she said. "He seems quite adamant that you should take your place in society again."

The prick of alarm turned to a shiver. Why should the emperor care if she attended balls and parties? "I don't really have a place in society. I'm the common-born widow of a mere younger son. One who did a terrible thing. I have no desire to return to court life or be in the public eye."

"I understand," Imogene said, her tone sympathetic but firm. "But Aristides wishes it to be clear that you are in favor and not tainted by what Charl did. That can't happen if you hide yourself away."

That was definitely the duquesse talking. Chloe needed to remember that Imogene had changed, too. For one thing, she was now close enough to the emperor that she called him by his first name. He had always been fond of her, of course. Imogene had foiled an attempt to poison the empress before she was even married to Jean-Paul. Imogene and Jean-Paul had both increased their rank and influence since then. Not to mention that Imogene had designed the flying ships—the navire d'avions—that were going to be an invaluable tool to the empire as Chloe understood it.

"Am I to take it that this invitation is more a command?"

Imogene hitched a shoulder. "Close. I suspect you could refuse this particular invitation. But if you do, they will only keep coming. Both from me and whoever else Aristides chooses to involve."

Hardly likely anyone from Charl's former circle would be enthusiastic about the idea of inviting her to a gathering. But Chloe had other friends from court back then. Younger women like herself. Now less young. And, of course, there were whole other circles of society centered around the Academe and the parliament. The latter she would be avoiding. It had been a parliamentarian who had lured Charl into his idiocy, amongst others. Though the full extent of the conspiracy had never been uncovered. Charl had confessed, but he hadn't known all the other parties. A pawn, not an instigator. Lucien had told her that much. She might hate the man, but she knew he wouldn't lie.

He didn't need to.

His powers as a Truth Seeker were unrivaled. And his reputation, even then, still early in his career, impeccable. The de Roche family was more powerful than the de Montesses, and he was the heir. He'd had nothing to gain from condemning his best friend. He'd done it because he believed in law and duty and the truth more than friendship, it seemed.

Rationally, she understood. But she loathed him still for the role he'd played in everything she'd lost. When her father had told her that no other conspirators had ever been unearthed beyond the first three who'd confessed with Charl, that loathing only deepened. What use was truth seeking if it couldn't even bring those who'd corrupted Charl to justice?

So no, no parliamentarians. But she suspected Imogene was correct. If indeed the emperor wanted her to join in, then join in she would. Yet another thread of oddity wrapped around her return, tugging her more off-kilter. She may have been in exile in Anglion and may have had to obey the rules of Anglion society to a degree, but she'd had a far freer life there than she would if she was to step back into the life of a society lady in Lumia.

Imogene took her silence for indecision. "I understand that you may not wish to deal with the court. And with what comes with it. The gossip and nonsense and people intentionally misunderstanding what happened. You will have some hard moments, yes. But those moments will come regardless. If you take the initiative and show them you are not ashamed—because you have nothing to be ashamed of—and that you still have the friendship of not only Jean-Paul and me but the emperor, then there will be far fewer such moments. Many of them will be expecting you to be an apologetic mouse, hiding from scandal. Don't give them the satisfaction. Show them you are not their prey, and they will find someone else to toy with."

She made it sound simple. But such things rarely were. However, refusing wasn't an option. But if she agreed in the interests of getting the worst of it over and done with and then being able to slowly fade out of view, there was another problem. If she wore her Anglion clothes, the Illvyan courtiers would think her mouse-like indeed. A peculiar mouse at that.

"I don't have any ball gowns." She'd brought the dress she'd worn to Queen Sophia's coronation back with her. A reminder of one happier moment in Anglion. But Anglion court dress was oddly old-fashioned. The dresses were beautiful but ornate, with huge, stiffened skirts and myriad wide petticoats. Definitely not what an Illvyan might wear to a friend's ball.

Not that she knew what an Illvyan would wear to a ball now. Fashions had changed. Skirts were narrower but more draped, and the colors and patterns were different to her memories. Imogene's glorious sapphire-blue silk dress was embroidered with vines of black flowers and was, as her clothes always were, a triumph of the clothier's art.

There'd been no need for ball gowns in Kingswell, and Chloe mostly stuck to deepest green or dark gray or midnight blue for practicality—mixing potions could get messy—and to ensure she drew no additional attention. But wearing such somber colors in Lumia would do precisely that. No point in reminding everyone where she'd been and why she'd been there. "Though perhaps Mama kept some of my old ones," she finished.

That brought a contemplative expression to Imogene's face. "Ten years out of date? You might as well wear an Anglion gown. But perhaps there are some that can be made over in time. But for now, no. We need a gown that no one can fault. Which will be no problem. I know all the best clothiers." She tilted her head, dimples flashing. "They will be falling over themselves to make you a wardrobe."

"I expect that your clothiers are out of my price range. I need to pay for rent, not gowns."

"You are ignoring the fact that I have ten years of missed birthdays and Fete de Froi presents to make up for," Imogene said triumphantly. "I will buy you some dresses."

Chloe shook her head, laughing. She should have expected that offer. "Is there any point in me arguing about this?"

"Jean-Paul claims there never is," Imogene said, with a smile.

Jean-Paul was probably right. Imogene had always been single-minded in pursuit of whatever she set her mind on. "All right. You may buy me a gown."

"*Gowns*," Imogene corrected.

"A few," Chloe said, throwing up her hands in defeat. "Not an entire flock. I have no need for a wardrobe as large as yours." Imogene had had an entire room devoted to her wardrobe when Chloe had last been in Lumia. And even then, those were only the clothes she kept in the city. Given she spent half her days in military uniform, it made Chloe tired to think of how many outfit changes palace life must require for her to need so many.

"We'll see," Imogene said. But she smiled, clearly pleased, then looked across the room. "Ikarus, would you tell Lili that we would like some tea, please?"

"Ikarus is here?" Chloe asked.

She had forgotten about Imogene's sanctii. In Anglion, the familiaris sanctii were strictly taboo—considered demons of the darkest, vilest kind. Queen Sophia would change that slowly, given she came with a sanctii of her own. But before she had come to power, sanctii and water magic had been forbidden for many, many years. Chloe might have snuck in a little earth magic here and there in Anglion where she had need, but she hadn't been even slightly tempted to try water magic in a country where it might just get her killed.

But in Illvya and the other parts of the empire where water mages were common, there were sanctii. Not all water mages bonded with them. The required rites took a degree of skill and power that not all could attain. Nor the willingness to spend one's life joined to a companion from a race completely different to one's own. A healthy regard for the potential for destruction embodied in the sanctii's powers also deterred some from trying.

Some but not all. Enough tried and succeeded that she would

have to learn once again to guard her tongue and consider the fact that there might be an invisible listener to any given conversation involving a water mage. The skills at dissembling she had gained in Anglion in that regard would continue to serve her well.

"He's nearby," Imogene said with a careless flick of her fingers. "He can always hear me anyway."

"And you use him to convey messages to your servants?"

"Not always. But he doesn't mind. He quite likes Lili."

A sanctii became part of a household over the years. Her father's, Martius, had been part of her life since birth. He had seemed happy to have her home again, as much as any sanctii expressed emotion. It made sense that Ikarus would make his own relationships with the people in Imogene's life.

Chloe had been on what she considered friendly terms with him when Imogene first bonded with him, though he had tended to stay out of sight. She'd met Sophie's Elarus a time or two as well, but the female sanctii—an even rarer thing—was less communicative and more focused on Sophie. Which made sense given the situation in Anglion. The young queen was leading an overturning of centuries of schism in the temple there, not to mention trying to root out the seeds of a plot that had led to her gaining the throne. She needed her sanctii to be focused on keeping her safe.

"I see," Chloe said. She would regain her former ease with sanctii other than Martius in time.

Imogene smiled again. "So, that takes care of clothing. What of your jewelry?"

"I have a few pieces. But in truth, I sold much of it in Anglion."

The smile disappeared. "What of the de Montesse stones Charl gave you?"

"I left those behind. I didn't want to be accused of being a thief as well as a traitor's wife."

Blue eyes blazed. "No one thinks that."

Chloe shrugged. She appreciated Imogene's loyalty, but she had to be pragmatic. There would be those in Illvya who didn't wish her well and would have been perfectly happy if she'd lived out her years in exile. "I guarantee you that some people do. And his family suffered enough."

"They truly haven't contacted you?"

"No, but I did not expect them to. I don't know how much of an estate there was," Chloe said. "Charl was, after all, just a second son of a second son. He claimed to handle the money himself and never gave me reason to think matters were difficult. But then again, he never gave me reason to think he was conspiring against the emperor either, so who knows what he was really doing?"

She looked away for a moment, regretting the bitterness that had crept into her tone. She was supposed to be convincing everyone that she was fine. Ready to embark on a new life.

Imogene squeezed her hand. Chloe squeezed back, willing away the bite of anger.

"Were that man not already dead, I would throttle him myself," Imogene muttered, voice fierce despite the softness. "I know you loved him, but—"

"You would have to form an orderly line behind several other people," Chloe said.

"Including you?" A dark eyebrow arched.

"Possibly," Chloe said. "I was angry for a long time. Now I am mostly just sad for a waste of a life." A waste of *their* life.

"All the more reason not to let anything make you waste another second of yours," Imogene said.

She looked up as the door to the parlor opened and one of her footmen appeared bearing a tea trolley. He was followed by Albeir, Imogene's seneschal. Imogene stayed quiet as the tea service was set up, then took up the pot when the servants left them alone again. "Still sugar and lemon?"

Chloe nodded and took the delicate china cup gratefully. The scent of the rich black Sisiian brew was wonderful. Once they both had tea and had investigated the plates piled high with enough artfully arranged frou-frous masquerading as cakes to feed them for at least half a day, Imogene settled back on the sofa.

She sipped tea, dispatched several tiny cakes, then faced Chloe once more. "You do need to deal with the de Montesse family at some point."

Why was she so concerned with the estate? Maybe it was an aristo thing. The obsession with inheritance ran deep in the noble families. "Possibly. But, as I said, there is no urgency to the matter."

"A smart woman does not give up resources that belong to her."

Chloe narrowed her eyes at her. "A smart woman also does not stir up old troubles for no good reason. I don't need their money."

"Let me at least task Jean-Paul's lawyers with doing a little investigating as to whether there was an estate," Imogene said. "They are fiendishly effective and utterly discreet. No one will get wind that you're looking."

She wasn't going to drop the subject. Chloe wrinkled her nose. "You have become more ruthless as a duquesse."

"Did you not become more ruthless in Anglion?"

"I survived."

"Being a duquesse is something of a game of survival, too. There are ample opportunities to do good with the power it grants me, but only if I am able to wield it with authority. And seize opportunities." Imogene sipped tea again and reached for a cake glazed with pale green icing and violet-shaded sugar flowers. "I should hire a worse cook. Eat some of these so my ball gown does not grow too tight."

"Are you bribing me with cake to let you have your way?" Chloe asked, rolling her eyes, as she took a gold-and-aqua cake of her own. It smelled like lemons and somehow, also of summer.

"I would give you cake regardless," Imogene said. "I will also continue to try to convince you to let me help."

Chloe took a tiny bite as a delaying tactic. Her father would, she had no doubt, say much the same if she asked him. That she should pursue the matter. He would be willing to pay for a lawyer, too. Her family were not poor. Henri's position at the Academe had seen to that. However, her mother's illness had been expensive. Knowing her father, and her mother's ongoing need to dote, they would insist on contributing to her expenses for some time as well. And her father would never hear of her repaying him. Whereas Imogene, on the other hand, might eventually allow her arm to be twisted in that direction if Chloe insisted. So Imogene was, perhaps, the more palatable option. For now.

"If I eat the cake and give in now, am I less likely to wind up with indigestion?" she said with a smile.

Imogene swallowed the last of her cake. "I never gave you indigestion," she said indignantly.

"Only tried to turn my hair gray a time or two before I was even twenty," Chloe said.

That earned her an eye roll. "Your hair is no more gray than mine. And you are a young woman still. No reason you can't do whatever you want with your life. A new career. Another husband and children—" She held up a hand as Chloe began to protest. "If they are what you choose," she finished. "Do not give me that look. No one is going to force you to have babies. You have enough earth magic to avoid that as long as you wish."

"Is that what you've been doing?" Imogene and Jean-Paul had been married a long time. The lack of an heir to the duq's estates couldn't have gone unremarked upon.

Imogene's expression turned thoughtful. "It has never seemed quite the right time. For either of us. We have discussed it, of course. I told Jean-Paul he was going to have to support me if we decided to delay. Otherwise, all the nosy old biddies at court would be saying I was barren and a terrible choice."

"But you do intend to have children?"

"Yes, Goddess willing. I knew that when I agreed to marry the man. Now that my navire project has reached a degree of success and the Anglion issue has been resolved, we may have peace enough for a time to do something about it." She smiled at Chloe. "And, of course, you are home to be an aunt to them now."

Chloe had had her share of dealing with younger brothers and sisters when Ana had been ill. She'd met her nephews and nieces over the last few days, but she didn't intend to become one of their minders, as adorable as they were. "I have forgotten all I know about babies," she said firmly and took another cake. This one was pale peach and blue, but inside was seila berry jam that burst across her tongue.

"I'm sure it will come back to you," Imogene said with a satisfied smile. "Now, let us discuss your gowns."

CHAPTER 3

"Does that sound reasonable, my dear?" Henri asked two days later.

Chloe started. She'd been thinking of her morning with the clothier and had completely lost track of the thread of the conversation. Given the topic at hand was how she might refresh her studies at the Academe, it was somewhat mortifying to realize her thoughts had drifted. Perhaps it was only that she was hungry, having spent most of the morning standing in the middle of a fitting room, being assessed and measured and pinned.

Imogene worked fast. Chloe didn't want to know what she had done to secure an appointment with one of the most famous clothiers in the city so quickly.

Helene Designy had been fascinated by what Chloe had been wearing and keen for detail of the fashions of Anglion. Her brother Marx had delicately dug for gossip while looking slightly askance at the serviceable gray wool of Chloe's dress. But they were professionals and whirred into action when Imogene mentioned the deadline for the ball gown.

Two more days. Imogene still claimed it would be only a small ball. Chloe still wasn't certain that she wanted to go. At least she would be well dressed.

"Chloe?" Henri prompted.

She grimaced apologetically. "I'm sorry, Papa. It is a lot to take in. Perhaps you could write down your recommendations so I can think on them some more this week?" His initial suggestion of a semester at the Academe to refresh her skills had somehow expanded to a year's worth of studies, and her head was whirling.

His smile was approving. "Of course, my dear. There's no rush. Your mother won't thank me for stealing you away from her any sooner than necessary."

No, but it might be better for her mother if he did. Better for all of them, if they could find some sort of balance in this new life quickly. Which would be easier if she knew what her new life was to be. But she needed to give herself time. And her parents the same grace.

She rose from the chair by her father's desk and nodded to Martius, his sanctii, who was standing by the fire, as she gathered her purse and gloves. The sanctii nodded back, his dark eyes as inscrutable as ever. But his mottled gray skin had been cracked by a slow smile the day she'd returned home. Which was likely as close to an admission that he was pleased by her return as she was going to get. Somehow, the sanctii's calm acceptance was easier to take than her family's delight.

"Are you returning home?" Henri asked. "Or did you want to stay? We could lunch together. I believe those lemon cakes you like so much might be on the menu."

That could hardly be a coincidence. Just as her mother had been trying to keep her close, her father had been bringing up the subject of her to returning to the Academe for a year or so of study with not-so-subtle regularity. Lemon cakes—one of her favorite things—were a bribe. But as tempting as they sounded, her mother had been stuffing her with Illvyan delicacies for days, and if she returned to the Academe, she would be able to eat the lemon cakes regularly.

"Perhaps another day. I promised Mama I would be home to help her in the garden this afternoon."

Henri smiled. "Well, I dare not keep you from that."

Chloe nodded. "We can talk more this evening. Bring the list of classes home with you." Nerves stirred in her stomach. She needed to brush up her skills, and Henri's enthusiasm for magic was always infectious. But a year seemed a long time and, she suspected, another unintentional manifestation of her father's desire to protect her. The Academe was half-home to her and, with the number of sanctii residing there with their mages, one of the safest places in the city.

She'd loved being a student, but she didn't think it was what she wanted to do forever. Teaching was Henri's passion, not hers. But until she did know what she wanted, the Academe was a good place to begin.

Lucien de Roche strode down the corridor of the Academe di Sages, mind still mostly on the stacks of paperwork awaiting him back in his office. He had spared a few hours, as he did twice a year to come and address the students who showed an affinity for the Arts of Air about his abilities as a Truth Seeker. His was a rare talent amongst illusioners. There were only ten Truth Seekers currently in the emperor's service, and it had been several years since a new one had been found. They could always use another.

But he held no strong hope that there would be a student in this year's class who might hold the spark. If he was honest, it was always a mixture of relief and resignation when no one displayed the talent. Truth Seekers, once discovered, really didn't have much choice in the matter of their careers. It was the law and the service of the emperor. There had been, in the past, a handful maybe who had refused that call. Most of those had ended up choosing to serve the temple. Professing a religious calling was one of the few acceptable ways to avoid the long arm of the Imperial family.

Not one that tempted him.

No, he'd been happy with the law. Maybe it was from growing up watching his father settle disputes on their estate and seeing the very real stakes of such matters.

A talent for the truth was invaluable in the law. But it was unlikely that he'd be unearthing a new Truth Seeker today. Which left his mind free to contemplate other things. So he wasn't paying particular attention to his surroundings when he turned a corner and came face-to-face with Chloe de Montesse hurrying in the other direction.

He stopped dead. So did she, her eyes flaring wide with what he thought might well be horror before her expression snapped into a coldly distant blank.

He bowed, manners drilled into him since birth difficult to overcome, though these days he outranked the daughter of the Maistre of the Academe by more than several degrees. But he owed Chloe courtesy, at the very least, having caused her no little chaos in the past.

"Madame de Montesse," he murmured even as his mind corrected the thought. It was Chloe's husband, his former best friend, Charl, who had caused the chaos and destruction rather than Lucien himself. He had only done what duty and honor and his goddess-sworn oaths of truth had forced him to do. It had given him no pleasure and endless grief to do so, though he had buried that in order to do his duty. He doubted Chloe saw it that way though.

"My lord," she said in an icy tone that sounded nothing like his memories of the laughing, vivid woman who'd been one of his closest friends.

It seemed, someone—Henri, presumably—had informed her of his change in status.

"I am here to address the students," he offered when she continued to stare at him, dark brown eyes opaque. With her black-streaked red hair braided around her head and color staining the golden skin of her cheeks as she stood ramrod straight in a simple dark gray dress, she looked formidable. Older than the Chloe in his head, which was confusing. Not happy to see him. The rejection felt like a slap, though it wasn't unexpected. She'd made it clear on the docks that she wanted nothing to do with him.

Careless of him to not consider that she might be at the Academe. He'd expected her to be tucked at home, enjoying the family she had so recently returned to, what, less than a week ago?

His heart had nearly stopped when he'd seen her on the docks. He'd had wind of the news that she was returning from Anglion. With relations between the two countries tentatively returning to something more open, there were plenty of ships filled with Illvyans being ferried back and forth to assist in the emperor's plans to assist Anglion's young Queen Sophia to solidify her reign, and they all carried news. But he hadn't known she was returning that day. It was pure chance he'd gone to discuss a matter with the captain of one of the ships in the de Roche fleet.

And suddenly there she had been. Where there had been a lack of her for ten years. Ten years where he had only known that she had fled to Anglion, and no more news than that had ever reached him. Ten years when he had never dared to entertain the hope that he might see her face again.

"I would not like to keep you from your task," Chloe said, still cold.

He nodded and stepped back, intending to bow and be on his way, but instead he found himself unwilling to leave as she stared him down.

Heart-stopping, indeed, that face. He had seen it for the first time the night of Imogene and Jean-Paul du Laq's betrothal ball. Imogene and Chloe had been standing across the room, Chloe laughing while Imogene had looked vaguely nervous under her immaculate makeup. As well anyone marrying into one of the highest families in the empire might. Chloe's dress was a blaze of red that had caught his attention against Imogen's betrothal-white. Imogene was a beauty, her face and vivid blue eyes the stuff of painter's dreams, but she had faded into the background once he'd seen Chloe. She had looked so purely joyful that it had caught him like a lure, leaving him dazzled as though he had stared too long at the sun.

And then, minutes later, the two of them had crossed the ballroom, and Imogene introduced Chloe to him and to Charl standing with him. It had not taken very long to realize it was Charl who had caught Chloe's interest. Charl, who was always charming and handsome and attracted women like bees to a flower. It had taken a little longer to see that Charl was, unusually for him, interested in return. That had been the point where Lucien had to turn away from the light.

Charl was his best friend. He would be happy for him. He had schooled away any yearning his heart had in Chloe's direction and been a friend to them both. Or he had tried to. It had been difficult to watch them fall in love and marry. But watch and welcome and support he had.

Then Charl had ruined everything beyond recovery through sheer idiocy.

He'd died for his folly.

Chloe had fled.

And Lucien had been without either of his best friends for ten years.

Now Chloe had returned, but he feared the woman who had been his friend was gone for good.

There was no sign of warmth or light in her now. No sign there might be a way to slip inside the barriers she had so clearly erected. He could not blame her. He imagined if he had lived in exile for ten years, he might have some walls of his own. And he must leave her to hers and not do her the discourtesy of trying to batter his way through them like a lout. Things had changed. He would accept that fact.

"I will bid you good day, then, Madame."

He thought for a moment that he detected the faintest of winces before she regained her steely composure. He had never been so strongly tempted to send a whisper of his power toward her, to find out, if she spoke to him again, if she spoke true. But that would only add another layer to his betrayal. Not to mention go against all the oaths he had sworn to the emperor and himself. Truth seeking wasn't an easy talent and not one he would have asked for, given the choice. All he could do was try to use it for good. And even that sometimes led to unbearable choices.

And betrayal.

"Farewell," he said. This time he completed the bow and made himself step around her. There was work to do. His answer had always been to work. Work ceaselessly, and with a focus that had earned him a fearsome reputation within the judiciary and the Imperial mages. Until his father had died a year ago and he had become the marq and had to return to a life that required more of him than the work of a Truth Seeker.

The way titles passed was unfair, passing the burden of responsibility that came with them at a time when the recipient was also reeling with grief for the loss of a father. But he had shouldered the load and taken up his duties. In the last few months, he had even been listening to his mother's increasingly broad hints about heirs and grandchildren and starting to look at the women of the court with a different eye.

He hadn't been entirely alone for ten years. There had been stolen nights and short affairs along the way. But he hadn't found a woman who lit the world for him as Chloe had.

But he didn't need that in a wife. He would choose a woman

who he liked and respected and who offered him the same in return. That was enough for a family. A foundation that had carried many of the noble families of Illvya far through the centuries. Making heirs and protecting a heritage didn't require passion. It required commitment and friendship and a shared sense of duty. Marrying such a woman was the sensible thing to do.

But then he'd seen Chloe on the docks, and all the sense in his body had dissolved into dust and blown away.

Goddess help him, she was more beautiful than ever. He clenched his fists against the urge to turn back and look at her once more. He hardly needed to. The memory of her just now was still vivid.

Whatever had happened to her, it had polished her to brilliance like a diamond. Her face had lost the remnants of girlhood, and now the cheekbones had angles that only drew attention to the curving mouth and dark eyes fringed with thick lashes. Eyes that held no hint of the laughing besotted wife of his best friend. Well, it would be impossible think that ten years in exile had not changed her. But he hoped that same joyous spirit was still there somewhere inside.

Not that he believed he would be given a chance to find out. She had looked as though she would rather smite him dead than speak to him.

But he wanted the chance.

The stupid male part of his brain whispered that death would be worth it.

But it had been a very long time since the stupid male part of his brain ruled him. He would not let it do so now. He might want to ease the pain she still so clearly carried, but he would not add to it.

He had nearly reached the end of the hallway when he thought he heard her say, "Good day, my lord." It was another effort of will not to turn back, to see if possibly his ears were playing tricks on him and it was only his imagination conjuring the sound.

He'd had plenty of conversations in his head with both Chloe and Charl over the years since things had gone so horribly wrong. Long detailed conversations and arguments and rationalizations with the versions of the two of them who lived in his memories. Some might call it irrational, but he didn't think so. It was simply a way for him to make sense of how it had all gone so terribly wrong. And maybe it was his magic, wanting to find the truth that lay at the heart of the disaster. But he never had. Perhaps he never would.

A regret he would carry to his grave along with the regret that Chloe had not forgiven him.

✦ ✦ ✦

Damn the man.

Chloe marched down the hallway, no longer entirely sure where she was headed but determined to put distance between herself and Lucien. She hadn't expected to see him here at the Academe. She'd not expected to see him anywhere, quite frankly.

He'd been perfectly polite. Regretful, even. But that didn't change the fact that seeing him was a lightning strike, carrying in its wake a storm of memories deadly as a flood.

Of her life before. Of the young woman who'd had hopes and dreams and had seen them all smashed to dust.

No. She wasn't her. And she wouldn't let memory rule her.

She turned right blindly and pulled up short when she found herself facing one of the outer doors. One shove and she was out in the sunlight, breathing hard, wanting only some air. And a chance to wrestle her feelings back under control.

If Lucien was addressing the students, he would be there for some time. She'd told her father she was going home, but now she couldn't. Not until she had herself back under control. Her mother would notice if she was upset, and that would only lead to questions.

She didn't want questions. Right now, they might break her.

So she walked, trying not to think, trying only to feel the sun on her skin and the sounds of the city around her. The students were in class, so she should be safe enough from any more unexpected encounters. She followed the cobbled path around the corner of the building, thinking to seek out one of the gardens, and almost knocked over the person coming in the other direction.

"Watch where you are—Chloe Matin? Is that you?"

Chloe blinked and focused on the woman whose robes she had grasped in a desperate effort to keep them both upright after their collision. "Madame Simsa! My apologies, Venable. Are you all right?" She loosened her grip and stepped back, surveying Madame Simsa with a quick glance, happiness at seeing her warring with embarrassment that she'd almost knocked her over.

Madame Simsa was thinner than the last time Chloe had seen her, a little more stooped perhaps—she carried a carved black cane in her right hand—and the wrinkles on her face had gained some friends in ten years. But her blue eyes were bright and sharp as she gazed up at Chloe, expression intent. She tapped her cane on the earth. "I will survive, I expect."

Chloe bobbed a curtsy. She'd spent too many years in Madame Simsa's classes to lose the instinct to offer respect to one of her favorite teachers. "Again, I apologize, Venable."

"Where were you going in such a hurry?" The older woman looked her up and down, lips pursing briefly. "And what has you all stirred up?"

Chloe gritted her teeth. Madame Simsa was more than just her teacher. More an honorary sort of great-aunt. She'd taken an interest in Chloe from the time she'd first toddled the Academe's halls in Henri's wake, years before she became an actual student. They shared the same affinity for earth and water magic, and once it had been Chloe's dearest wish to grow to be just as skilled and formidable. So far she had fallen miserably short of that goal.

And she wasn't going to admit to Madame Simsa that it was Lucien who had thrown her off balance.

Madame Simsa had been married a long time ago, but her husband had died of a sudden illness when they'd both still been quite young. She hadn't remarried, seemingly content to carry on alone. She had never shown the students any sympathy if they let romantic entanglements get in the way of their studies, and Chloe suspected she had never much liked Charl. So no, she wasn't going to tell Madame Simsa that an encounter with a man had upset her.

"It is just...just unsettling being home," she said. "Part of me keeps expecting to wake up and find myself back in Anglion."

"I imagine it does," Madame Simsa said. "You were gone a long time." Her expression turned speculative. "Tell me, have you used your magic since you returned?"

Damn. It had only been a matter of time before someone asked her that. There was no need for her to use magic at home. They'd made changes to the house when Ana had been sick so she wouldn't tire herself using her magic to light earthlights and such. They had gas lamps and a number of ingenious gadgets to make daily tasks easier that required no power. So far no one had noticed that Chloe wasn't using her magic at all.

Henri hadn't asked about it. Chloe suspected it had never occurred to him to check. Magic to him was like breathing. But Madame Simsa had always been able to see into the heart of a matter. And she always pushed her students to hone their abilities. Chloe had been one of the students she'd pushed hardest, once. But her mother's illness, her marriage, and what came after had left her potential untapped. To Madame Simsa, Chloe's return would be a second chance.

"No, Madame. The need has not really arisen."

Madame Simsa snorted. "Since when does there have to be a

need to use your magic here? I imagine you had little opportunity over in *that* country, given their backward views, but all the more reason to use it now." She tapped her cane again, three quick staccato beats. "By the look of you, it would do you good. Come, young lady, we will go to the practice rooms. I will put you through your paces."

"I am not so young anymore," Chloe said. "Nearly thirty-five."

"Bah. Talk to me about your lost youth when you reach eighty or so. Earth witches age slowly. Plenty of time for you to do...whatever it is you wish to do."

"I hope so, Madame," she said. "But I don't want to keep you from your students."

"I would not offer if I did not want to do it, or if I needed to be elsewhere, you know that. Besides, you can tell me some tales of Anglion. I learned something of it from young Sophie, but she was biased, being Anglion herself. You have an outsider's view. You can tell me more of how they differ from the way we do things."

"I'm not sure I can tell you much. The temple didn't let me in on all their secrets," Chloe said.

"Just as well. It doesn't sound like much good would have come of tangling with that Domina Skey. Trying to control the crown. Bad business."

"Not so much for Sophie," Chloe pointed out. "She's queen now."

"Waste of talent, if you ask me," Madame Simsa said. "She is strong, that one. We could have taught her much more. And now, no doubt young Aristides will be pestering us for staff to send over there to teach the Anglions what they have been denied all these centuries." She peered at Chloe. "I don't suppose you wish to go back there and help with that?"

Chloe shook her head. "No. I've had quite enough of Anglion for now. I would like to see Sophie and Cameron again and some of my friends, but I have no desire to live there for any length of time. Illvya is my home."

"In which case, you need to reacquaint yourself with the most important part of it." She tapped her cane again, as though striking down to the ley line that ran beneath the school, then turned on her heel and headed back in the direction she had come from. "Let us not waste time."

CHAPTER 4

Madame Simsa might be old, but she moved fast when she wanted to. Chloe had to half jog to keep up with her. "How is Belarus, Madame, and...Riki?" Belarus was Madame Simsa's sanctii and Riki her petty fam, a monkey. Petty fams were an earth thing. Not many mages who bonded with a sanctii also had a familiar. The small boost in magic that a petty fam offered became somewhat superfluous to a water mage who had a sanctii to work with.

Though sometimes it was more a case of the animal choosing the mage than the other way around. Madame Simsa claimed Riki had chosen her, and Sophie said the same about her raven, Tok. Riki was as smart as the Academe's ravens—the birds were a common choice for petty fams—and she had the extra advantage of fingers and toes and being able to climb far out of reach after stealing whatever object caught her attention. She didn't care much for human views of ownership. In fact, she seemed to delight in causing mischief. The ravens weren't above stealing shiny objects or begging for tidbits but were far less likely to make off with one's shawls or books or shoes. Though maybe Riki had grown more sensible while Chloe had been away. Petty fams lived past a normal lifespan, bolstered by their mage's powers, but they still died eventually, and Riki had been with Madame Simsa as long as Chloe could remember.

"Both are well. Riki will be happy to see you again. She always did like you. How is Sophie's Tok doing?"

"He's learning to talk." She smiled at the memory. "The Anglions aren't entirely sure how to take him. I don't think talking crows are common over there."

Madame Simsa grinned as they rounded the corner and passed onto the long oblong patch of grass that lined the front of the sturdy stone buildings that housed the Academe's practice rooms. "I dare say he is less startling than Elarus."

Chloe laughed. "Yes. I think it's going to take years before most of them are anywhere approaching comfortable with a sanctii in their midst. What they're going to do when more people start practicing water magic is anybody's guess. I don't envy Sophie her task."

"She is a smart girl. She will win them over. Or that husband of hers will bash some heads together until they listen to her."

"He does tend to loom menacingly in the background and glare at people who are being difficult." Sophie's husband, Cameron—formerly Lord Scardale but now the Prince Consort of Anglion—was tall, dark-haired, and blue-eyed like many Anglions who hailed from the north of the island. He didn't waste much time with small talk, and he was, as far as Chloe could tell, 100 percent focused on keeping his wife safe and happy in her new role. He wouldn't hesitate to do what needed to be done to protect her.

"The best ones do, child."

She didn't respond to that. Charl had tended to try to charm, not loom. He, too, had had dark hair and bright blue eyes, but he'd laughed a lot more than Cameron did and talked a mile a minute, his emotions running close to the surface. Or so she'd thought. But it had, it seemed, been an act, or at least partially so. There had been secrets he'd kept hidden beneath the charm. Secrets she'd learned too late.

No. Best not to think about that.

They reached the first practice room, and Madame Simsa opened the door, sweeping a hand to usher Chloe forward. "After you."

Crossing the threshold was like stepping back in time. She reached by habit to lift the student robes she wasn't wearing to walk over the threshold, then twitched her hands away, shaking her head.

The practice rooms were small and low-roofed, built from stone and reinforced with magic to withstand student mages losing control.

"Light the lamps, girl," Madame Simsa said from behind her.

Chloe hesitated. Lighting the earth lights was the job of any student with even a hint of earth magic. And there were few, no matter how heavily their talents might lean in other directions, who couldn't manage even that tiny spark. It should have been as instinctive as lifting her robe to step inside.

Illvyans used magic casually to make life easier when it came to things like lighting lamps or warming water or themselves. Blood mages and even some illusioners—though they were schooled to be cautious, as their powers could be amplified by strong emotions—could nudge a stray object out of the way. Water mages had less magic that was useful for small daily tasks, but most had at least some talent for one of the other arts. That was another thing the Anglions had wrong, the idea that people could only use one kind of magic. But it seemed the years she'd spent being so careful to not use magic anywhere anyone could see her had broken her of being careless of her power. She hesitated, one hand half raised toward the lamp before she dropped it back down.

"You are in a bad way," Madame Simsa said, moving around to face Chloe. She waved a hand and the earth lamps came to life, warming the gray walls to something more cheerful. "Tell me, when was the last time you actually used your magic?"

"Before I returned," Chloe admitted. "But only for simple

things." She'd gotten used to hiding her powers. Barely dared to use even the odd trickle of earth magic to add strength to some of the potions and medicines and teas she'd sold at her store. A hard habit to break, even after Sophie had taken the throne and rescinded some of the temple's more ridiculous strictures. She'd had no need for water magic in Anglion, anyway. No desire to scry for the future when she'd spent most of her time trying to avoid thinking too far ahead. No need for a sanctii nor any illusion that she had enough control over her powers to bond one anyway.

"Lighting earth lamps is simple enough," Madame Simsa said. "Why the hesitation?"

"Spend ten years stifling the urge to use your powers and you learn to be careful," Chloe said. "I've grown used to doing without magic."

"Sounds like a dull sort of life," Madame Simsa said with a brisk shake of her head. "Well, then, best we reintroduce you to Illvyan magic. Start with the ley line. I am guessing it will remember you. Or you, it, rather." She smiled. "Or both."

Chloe shook her head. Madame Simsa was one of the few mages who thought the ley lines were more than just a source of power. That they might have an awareness of a kind of those who tapped into it. True, there hadn't ever been a recorded case of the ley lines rejecting a mage. In Anglion she'd tapped the lines a time or two, limiting herself to the least amount of power necessary to achieve her aims. Once when she'd created her highly illegal portal to give herself an escape route, should she ever need one, and once when she'd caught a fever that had left her shaking and sweating and half delirious, scared she might die. In the end, the portal had served Sophie and Cameron better than her, but knowing it was there if needed had been a comfort.

Even though she knew Madame Simsa was being whimsical, it was hard to shake the fear she might be proved right. What if

Chloe tried to use the ley line and nothing happened? What if her powers had withered and faded through disuse?

Once she'd planned to try to bond a sanctii. Imogene had managed it, and Chloe had been, if anything, the stronger of the two of them.

But Imogene had honed her powers in the diplomatic corps before she'd tried and been schooled by the best. Whereas Chloe had left the Academe to look after her mother and the family. There was little need for grand workings to run a household. And even when she'd married Charl and been free again, she had focused on being a good wife and hadn't tried to return to her studies and her ambitions straight away, thinking she'd have plenty of time.

She'd been wrong about that. Foolish to sacrifice everything for love, even though, at the time, it hadn't felt as though that was what she'd been doing. Maybe she was being foolish again now to try again.

"You'll never know if you do not try," Madame Simsa said. "I understand that you have been through a lot, child, but trust me, reconnecting with your magic might make you feel more like yourself than anything else can."

Would it make her feel like Illvya was home again? That would be true magic.

Perhaps beyond her reach. But she hadn't survived ten years in Anglion by being timid. She might have denied her powers, but she'd used her wits, her brain, and the strength of her body, and she had survived. She had never backed away from a challenge. She was hardly going to do so now, in front of one of the mages she respected most in the world.

So. The ley line. Running far beneath her feet through the depths of the earth. A river of magic, light, and song that once had been a constant reassuring refrain in her head. She could hear that again.

If she let herself try.

Habit and memory came to her rescue again. Madame Simsa

teaching her younger self the forms for connecting with a ley line. And the first time she had actually touched the ley line after her Ascension and her birthday rites.

Feet on the earth. That was how it began.

She bent and untied the laces of her half boots. The stone floor was cold through her silk stockings, but the sensation grounded her, stilling her mind. Madame Simsa watched silently. Chloe took silence as approval and continued.

Spine held straight. Breathe deeply. Concentrate. A breath in to fill her lungs. A breath out for longer still. Repeat as many times as it took to feel a sense of calm. Of control.

Then she reached for the spark inside her that she thought of as her power and sent it seeking down to find the ley line.

It felt as though she had plunged after it. She knew she still stood in the room, but she was also plummeting headlong toward a deep dark sea. As though she'd thrown herself from a cliff, arcing through the sky to whatever fate awaited her in dangerous waters below.

As she fell, the song filled her head. Soft at first, then louder and louder until it was all she heard. And the light rushed with the sound. She'd always seen the ley line as a drift of pinpoint lights. Like stars scattered across a country sky, blazing and brilliant, a thousand glimmering points. But this was more like the flare of the sun, dazzling and overwhelming. The power rushed over her and through her, and oh, Goddess, it felt good. The sheer luxury of letting herself fairly bathe in power. Unthinking, she threw her arms wide, and there was a sudden series of small explosions as the earth lamps all cracked and blew apart.

"Chloe!" Madame Simsa said, reaching for her arm. "*Enough!*"

She came back to herself with a jolt, cutting off the flow of power, breathing hard.

"It seems we can cross off connecting with your power as a potential problem," Madame Simsa said, her eyes wide as she looked at the shards scattered around the edges of the room.

Chloe imagined she must be a little wide-eyed herself. "But we may have to work a little more on control."

Chloe stared down at her, heart pounding, skin tingling. She wanted to laugh or spin around or run. Anything to use the rush of power. She'd never felt anything quite like it, not even when she'd first connected to a ley line. She knew it could happen, of course, that some people got almost intoxicated from the contact with so much magic. And, in truth, that was the closest thing she could compare this to. The giddiness of having drunk too much campenois. Or of falling in love, perhaps. The feeling of being able to do anything and goddess damn the consequences.

Rumor had it that it was that exact thing that had led to Queen Sophia—or Lady Sophie, as she had been back then—and Cameron's hasty and unexpected wedding. Some mishap on the morning of her twenty-first birthday, when they'd been away from the palace after it had been attacked.

But she was no new-to-magic fledging witch. She shouldn't be so easily affected.

Though perhaps, after ten years, she might as well be a new witch.

"Chloe?" Madame Simsa said, patting her hand softly. "Are you all right, child?"

"Yes, Madame," she replied. She pulled her wits together with an effort of will, turning her mind away from the enticing song of magic and back to reality. And the mess she had just made. "I'm sorry, that was careless of me. I will fetch a broom."

"I imagine someone will be along with one soon enough," Madame Simsa said, the side of her mouth lifting in a familiar half grin. "You made quite a noise just now." Her tone was a mix of satisfaction and amusement and...pride, perhaps. She wiped at her cheek, where there was a tiny bead of blood.

Goddess, did one of the shards from the lamps hit her?

"Your cheek," she said.

"Pffft. It is nothing. I've had worse scratches from Riki's

whiskers. I am old, but I am not fragile. Unlike these lamps, it seems." She surveyed the room, looking amused.

"The lamps...," Chloe said. The practice rooms were built to withstand precisely this kind of accident. Students who destroyed property through poorly controlled magic were not blamed—unless they had been deliberately breaking a rule when they lost control—but they were expected to clean up and help put any damage to rights.

"We have plenty of lamps. Why do you think we use earth lamps in these rooms? Easier to replace those than anything else. And less messy than oil lamps. Exploding oil lamps is more excitement than anybody needs. Let alone those newfangled gas fabrique ones." Madame Simsa waved dismissively at the mess on the floor. "I think we should turn our attention to control rather than cleanup. I recommend some of the beginner exercises. Breathing. Small magics. Light a candle or two. Make a soothing tea. Coax an ailing plant. You know the kind of thing."

"Earth magic," Chloe said. "I can do that. Though I don't need to practice teas. I did plenty of that in Anglion. I owned a store where I sold magical supplies and herbal remedies."

Madame Simsa's silver eyebrows lifted. "An interesting profession for one trying to avoid attention."

"I had the knowledge of plants. Well, the ones that are common both there and here. I didn't need to use my magic. I was an assistant at first, and the temple used to check on me. But they lost interest when I didn't break any rules."

"That must have been a challenge. You and Imogene were never particularly good at staying between the lines. Though she has learned to be more so now that she has to be a duquesse. And I guess you have, too." Madame Simsa peered up at her. "All right, no teas. But earth magic. Small things. I think we should leave the water magic until you have regained some finesse." She smiled. "Come to think of it, the last student I had in here who made a complete mess was Sophie. Broke a scrying bowl clean into pieces the first time she attempted to see. Ink everywhere.

You should be thankful that earth lamps are less messy to clean up."

"Yes. Stone doesn't stain." She ignored the stinging on her hand where one of the shards must have grazed her. "I could try and close that scratch for you." She half expected the older woman to refuse. Offered a treatment by any healer who had just exhibited such a loss of control, she would definitely decline. "I know a lot about healing. Ginevra, the woman who took me on, the one who owned my store before me, she was an earth witch." There was no other choice for Anglion women. They weren't taught blood magic or the Arts of Air. In fact, they were taught that they couldn't have talent for that kind of magic. Outside the royal family and the nobility, most women only received minimal training, and most of them had what, by Illvyan standards, were small powers. "She never let me use my magic, but she did teach me a lot about what she did. And I helped her when people came to see her with small hurts."

"You don't need to convince me," Madame Simsa said. "I taught you earth magic in the first place. I know your power and your skill." She smiled with a flash of surprisingly white teeth. "And now that I know what to expect, I can control you well enough if need be."

She lifted her chin, presenting the scratched cheek to Chloe. "Go on, then. Show me that you can still manage some precision."

Chloe sucked in a breath. She'd done it now. No backing down. Perhaps that was what Madame Simsa had intended.

Control. Finesse. It wouldn't do to get it wrong and do something that would leave the oldest teacher at the Academe scarred.

"May I?" Chloe said, stretching a hand toward Madame Simsa's face. She'd been taught to always ask permission before touching any patient, whether she intended to use magic or not. On that matter, the teachings of the Academe and Anglion seemed to be in accord. Or at least Ginevra's beliefs. She hadn't really spent much time with temple healers. Other than the fever that had made her so ill early on, she'd been fortunate to not suffer any serious illnesses or injuries in Anglion. Any small ills she'd been able to treat herself—or with Ginevra's help—well enough.

"Of course," Madame Simsa said, not moving. If she was nervous, she didn't show it.

But she'd had many years' experience in letting inexperienced earth witches demonstrate healing skills. Learning to act outwardly composed no matter what one was feeling inside was a useful skill for a teacher. Just as it was for royal courts or navigating life in a hostile country.

Chloe laid two fingers on either side of the tiny cut. It was barely a scratch. If it wasn't for the small smear of rapidly drying blood, she might not have even been able to find it.

Madame Simsa made an encouraging noise, but she didn't move her head.

Chloe closed her eyes and took a breath, focusing on her heartbeat. And on the sense of magic that had strengthened since she'd touched the ley line. She wouldn't have to call on it for something as small as this. She opened her eyes again, let herself see the glimmer of magic around Madame Simsa and, there, for the first time in a long time, around her own fingers. And she listened for the song. It came, too loud at first, and she made herself push it back, narrowing the connection until it faded to a trickle rather than a flood.

She pictured the light sinking into Madame Simsa's skin. Felt for the sensation of wholeness, of completion. Of life being in order, as the goddess intended. Then she let her power free, concentrating on releasing just a little at a time. There was a tiny bright spark followed by a sensation that felt cool under her fingers before she lifted them. The tiny cut was gone.

"There, child," Madame Simsa said. "Nicely done. Perhaps you have not forgotten as much as you feared."

CHAPTER 5

The day following their practice session, Madame Simsa had sent Chloe a note with a list of suggested reading materials and invited her to another session the next day. It didn't matter that Chloe hadn't yet decided to return to the Academe; Madame Simsa seemed to have taken her on as a project anyway.

Lacking any good reason to refuse, she had accepted the invitation. It would take her away from the house, a respite from her mama's efforts to hide the fact that she was still hovering and gave her something to do with the restlessness dogging her.

She arrived early for their lesson, eager to start. But after three hours of Madame Simsa drilling her in small earth magics, her head ached like fury. Controlling the flow of magic that wanted to rush through her down to a whisper was exhausting. And yet, somehow, the fatigue did nothing to dull the restlessness.

She should go home. It was nearing the dinner hour, and Imogene's ball was tomorrow. An early night seemed called for. But instead of seeking out her father to see whether he was ready to leave, her feet took her in a different direction.

To the far west corner of the Academe, where the Raven

Tower stood sentinel, climbing several stories higher than the rest of the buildings. Its lower door was closed, as was usual. With the light fading, the ravens would be returning for their evening meal, and Mestier Allyn, the Master of Ravens, fed them himself. During the day, students spent time in the tower. Learning raven lore and helping to clean the tower were part of life at the Academe. Those who manifested strong earth magic and had an interest in bonding a petty fam at some point would often spend more time there to get to know some of the ravens better.

But Mestier Allyn alone cared for the ravens at night. Though sometimes during breeding season he recruited an assistant for a few weeks to help him deal with hungry mothers and broods of fledglings. Chloe had done it one season when she'd been about fifteen. And she'd spent plenty of time here as a child. She'd always liked the crows. And they seemed to like her.

She pushed the door, with its inlaid brass raven flock, open and slipped inside, closing it behind her. Mestier Allyn wouldn't thank her if she allowed one of the birds out when they should be settling for the night. It was a game to some of them to see if they could escape and harass the kitchen maids or students into handing over extra scraps to supplement their dinners. They were big birds, protected and cared for from birth, and having one perch beside you and squawk a demand for food was hard to ignore.

Inside the tower, the cool air smelled like stone and feathers. The earth lamps lining the spiraling staircase were alight as always. No open flames near the birds. She trailed her hand along the brass banister as she climbed the stairs, the smooth metal familiar beneath her fingertips.

When she reached the door at the top of the stairs, she paused, listening. The soft sound of Mestier Allyn's voice, combined with various squawks and grumbles, told her dinner was in progress. But the ravens weren't too loud, so likely not all of them had returned yet. She wouldn't be causing too much of an imposition if she interrupted. She knocked, heard a surprised "Come in," and opened the door carefully, keeping the gap just wide enough to step inside.

"Chloe!" Mestier Allyn said, bushy brown eyebrows flying upward. "I heard you were back—"

A squawk from the raven sitting on his shoulder interrupted, and he pulled a piece of raw meat from the bowl he held and handed it up to the bird

"I am," Chloe said, smiling. "But I don't want to interrupt. I just felt the need for some air." She pointed past him to the closest of the tall windows that studded the walls of the tower.

Mestier Allyn nodded and fed the raven another piece of meat.

She smiled her thanks and hurried over to the expanse of glass. Her hands found the clasps without thinking, and she pushed the windows open and stepped through the gap onto the narrow walkway that ringed the tower. The crenelations were nearly as tall as she at their highest, but the lower parts were chest height, offering a sweeping view of Lumia through the gaps. Chloe gripped the stone and peered down at the city, something she couldn't quite name still nipping at her heels.

The tower had always been one of her favorite retreats. She'd probably been only five or six the first time she crept up the stairs, escaping from her father's office when he was busy teaching and she'd grown bored. Instead of shooing her away, Mestier Allyn had welcomed her to the tower, introduced her to the birds, and let her help him for an hour or so before showing her the view of the city from the walkway and sending her back to her father. She'd loved the tower ever since.

And it, at least, seemed unchanged in the years since she'd last climbed the stairs.

Years that had been stolen from her.

Her fingers curled over the edge of the stone. She couldn't dwell on the differences or the lost time. Samuel, the captain who'd taken her to Anglion when she'd fled, had taught her it was useless for an exile to play "what if." Useless to long for what might never be hers again. She'd fought hard to learn that lesson and find some peace in Anglion.

But the win had cost her. And now, when she was finally *home* again, too many of those long-ignored emotions were surfacing to toss and turn her like one of the gusts of winds that rolled around the tower and made it dangerous for the unwary.

But she wasn't unwary. She knew this place. The lights blinking into life below her made the city gleam, and she could recite the names of each street and alleyway they illuminated. Lumia was in her bones. So why did it feel as though she no longer fit there? Like her feet couldn't quite find a solid place to stand. It had been a week and a day already. When would she start to feel normal?

The granite bit into her fingers. Curse Charl to whatever hell he burned in. He had stolen this from her with his stupid need to play politics he clearly hadn't been skillful enough handle.

And curse Lucien de Roche for exposing that failure. For being so sure of what was right and wrong and for doing the former even at the cost of his friend's life.

And *damn* it. Why was she thinking of Lucien again?

The lights of the city blurred beneath her as tears stung her eyes. She swiped at them furiously.

No tears.

Tears wouldn't help. She just had to find her footing. Like after a sea voyage. Anglion was the ship she had ridden for close to ten years, and now she just had to learn to walk on Illvya's solid ground. She would do it.

No one was going to take her choices from her again.

"Hello!" A grumbling voice came from behind her, and she swung around. A raven perched on the top of the window frame, gazing down at her through curious eyes. A female, she thought, though, in truth, she was out of practice with judging the sex of a raven. Or the age. Though this one was sleek and shiny, and its eyes were dark. Young but not a juvenile.

"Hello, yourself," she said softly.

The raven bobbed its head, stretching its wings. A pale flash caught Chloe's eyes. One of the pinion feathers was white, a flare of light amongst the shimmering black. Unusual, but it happened from time to time. According to the records, there'd even been a pure white raven or two amongst the tower's residents over the centuries. They were supposed to be a good omen. But there'd been none in Chloe's lifetime. Maybe that explained why her life had gone so wrong. Or maybe the one white feather was a sign of hope that now it could go right again.

"Food," the bird said.

Chloe spread her hands wide to show they were empty. "If you go on inside, Mestier Allyn will have your dinner, same as always."

That earned her a disgruntled squawk, as though the raven wanted to her to know that humans who couldn't produce tasty tidbits on demand were disappointing. Chloe laughed.

The bird tilted its head again. "Who?"

Chloe blinked. She'd forgotten how clever the birds were. Crows that bonded as petty fams could develop quite extensive vocabularies over their magically extended lifespans, but even those who didn't serve a mage could learn to speak. Not all did, but this one clearly had.

"Chloe," she said, touching her chest.

The black beak clacked once, and the crow cawed again. Then it launched into flight, swooping down over Chloe's head before executing a tight turn and flying past her again and straight in through the window, calling, "Food."

Amused, Chloe followed. The light was dying and the air turning cold. Birds were not the only ones who needed their dinners. She had choices to make, yes, but freezing to death on the tower's walkway wouldn't make them any easier. Nor did she want her father to come looking for her.

By the time she had drawn the windowpanes closed behind her and locked them into place, the raven was sitting on Mestier

Allyn's shoulder, grumbling in his ear as he loaded a plate with strips of meat.

"She's a feisty one," Chloe said.

"Yes. But, so far, fussy about the company she keeps. Perhaps she will become one of my breeding girls. She's from Issey's line."

"Like Tok," Chloe said. "Who is doing very well in Anglion. Sophie asked me to let you know."

"Your father mentioned it. Well, he knew what he wanted, that one. Now he's petty fam to a queen. Hopefully he'll live a good long life." Mestier Allyn's expression turned speculative. "Perhaps Queen Sophia would like some breeding stock eventually. If she changes the minds of those stubborn Anglions about magic, they may start to want petty fams."

"They have ravens in Anglion," she offered.

"Not as smart as ours."

"No," she agreed. "They haven't had the chance to be." She watched as the crow sidled to the left and snatched a piece of meat off the plate before retreating to the top of one of the night cages. She giggled. The ravens were usually fed in their cages to make it easier to keep them safely in at night. "What's her name?"

The master rolled his eyes at the bird, his expression fond exasperation. "Mai. It should be Trouble."

Chloe laughed. "If we named all the ones who deserved to be called Trouble, Trouble, it would get very confusing."

Mestier Allyn smiled. "I cannot argue with that." He crossed to a cage and opened the door, sliding the plate into the slots built to hold it. The bird peered at him. "That's where you get the rest, young lady," he said. "Stop misbehaving or Chloe won't come to visit us again."

That turned the crow's eye in her direction. "Clo."

"Clo-ee," Chloe corrected. "She's quick. Tok is learning to speak fast, but he has the benefit of his bond. It's entertaining to see the faces of the Anglion courtiers when he talks to them." She smiled at the memory, then shook off the sense of disorientation that came in its wake. Just then the memory of Anglion felt like a memory of home. The place where all was familiar. But Lumia was home.

She could only hope that it would stop feeling so strange sooner rather than later.

"I hope you will be visiting us more often," Mestier Allyn said. "The Academe has missed you."

"Thank you. I missed you all, too. I'm sure I will be here. My father is keen for me to refresh my skills. As am I," she added hastily, not wanting it to seem that, were she to return, it would be under sufferance.

Mestier Allyn grinned. "Heard you already started on that. Cost us some earth lamps already. Some things don't change."

Chloe rolled her eyes. Gossip traveled around the Academe faster than a raven pouncing on a worm. "I didn't blow anything up today."

"I'm sure Madame Simsa will be glad of that. Just as well it's not both of you back again. Not sure the Academe could take it."

He meant her and Imogene. They'd had some escapades in their time. She smiled. "The duquesse has other things to occupy her now. But I'll tell her you remember her. I'll be seeing her tomorrow."

He nodded approval, then clicked his tongue at Mai, pointing at the cage door. The raven decided that dinner won over rebellion, hopped neatly onto his hand, and then made another short leap into her cage.

"Good night, Mai," Chloe said as Mestier Allyn closed the cage door. He turned back to her, and she curtsied. "Thank you for loaning me your window."

"They are always there, Chloe. Should you feel the need to find your bearings."

✦　✦　✦

Chloe couldn't fault Imogene's clothier. She couldn't remember the last time she'd worn a dress as beautiful as the one Helene had produced at such short notice.

Possibly her own wedding.

Though her dress for that particular day, while lovely, had been the result of compromises between her taste and that of her mother. And Charl's mama. Who had had very particular ideas about what was appropriate for a woman marrying into the de Montesse family to wear.

Chloe had watched Imogene go through a quick-fire course in how to be a duquesse-in-waiting, fulfilling her duty as best friend to hold Imogene's hand and let her vent when the rules and protocol surrounding her future had become overwhelming. Charl, however, was not an immediate heir. Chloe hadn't anticipated the same level of oversight of her own nuptials. But Babette de Montesse had been determined that a commoner shouldn't disgrace the family, and she had a bossy streak a mile wide.

It had been entertaining, once she was no longer the focus of Babette's attention. Charl didn't really care for all the pomp that went with court life. True, he enjoyed the benefits of his family's money and privilege, but she had always liked the fact that he had shown little desire for snobbery and formality in their day-to-day lives. He'd certainly been keen enough to prove his love to her, to convince her that he did indeed want to marry the daughter of the Maistre of the Academe and not one of the many girls from families far grander who would have been happy to snap up even a younger son.

He had only a small amount of blood magic. Just enough to warrant him toying with the idea of joining the Imperial army but never quite follow through. He'd had an equally small talent for illusion. Mostly good for conjuring sparks of light to amuse or to summon the pretense of her favorite flowers when he'd been trying to win her favor. Nothing like the startling strength of magic his best friend commanded.

And there was Lucien, in her thoughts again.

She scowled into the mirror. She was about to walk into an Illyvan ballroom and face an Illvyan crowd of what had once been her peers for the first time in ten years. She needed to keep her wits about her, not get lost in the memories and regrets.

Imogene had promised a small, relaxed affair. But 'small' and 'relaxed' were relative. And no ball thrown by a duq and his wife could ever be entirely free of court games.

Games she had no desire to play.

She intended to enjoy the music and the spectacle, drink some campenois, avoid dancing as much as she could, and lurk around the outskirts of the party before leaving at the earliest possible hour she could achieve without being rude. It was a waste of a magnificent frock, perhaps, but it was all she felt she could manage.

She took a breath and smoothed her face into something calm, contemplating her dress rather than the event it was for. Imogene had tried to talk her into bright red, but she'd chosen something more subtle, having no desire to stand out any more than she had to.

The dark green silk was sumptuous and the cut magnificent. Helene Designy hadn't been in business when Chloe married, but, gazing at her reflection, Chloe understood exactly why Imogene paid her so well. The woman was a genius with fabric. But still, the dress was cut lower across her chest than anything she'd worn in Anglion in years, and she had to resist the urge to try and tug it higher.

Imogene had lent her a necklace of amber and peridots that would at least draw the eye up to her neck. And there was a fan in matching silk that would also provide distraction. Not that she should. She had no need to try to avoid the temple's attention here. There would be no disapproving dominas at Imogene's ball. Not that an Illvyan domina would be disapproving.

No, the problem would be the attention of all those people who'd known her before—and those who'd known Charl and what he'd done. She wasn't entirely sure that she wouldn't prefer the scowls of even Domina Skey rather than subjecting herself to the scrutiny of the Illvyan court. But Imogene had promised her it would be smooth sailing, and she had to trust that.

Besides, Imogene was right. Hiding away wouldn't convince people that she was innocent. She'd watched Imogene learn to stare down gossip and petty politicking when she'd first become engaged to Jean-Paul. No one had expected the heir to one of the most powerful duqdoms in the empire to marry a commoner.

A water mage at that. One who had a sanctii.

There had been plenty of upper-class noses put out of joint and plenty of gossip and spite because of it. She'd had her own turn at that when Charl chose her. Which, come to think of it, had put her in good stead when she'd endured a different kind of suspicion and rumor and scrutiny when she'd arrived in Anglion.

She could do it a third time. After all, with the emperor's declaration of her innocence behind her, there was not much that any of them could throw in her face that would do her any real harm. And once they realized she wasn't hunting for a second husband amongst the courtiers, that she was happy to fade into the background and just be the formerly scandalous friend of the Duquesse of Saint Pierre who appeared in their midst now and then, they would leave her alone.

She lifted her chin. Let them stare a night or two. She had nothing to fear from their judgment of her clothes, at least. And she wasn't going to fear whatever else they might judge her for either.

CHAPTER 6

"It's a Kharenian Rill," Imogene said. "You know the steps. They haven't changed. Jean-Paul will partner you to begin."

Chloe stared out at the small dance floor, working hard not to bite her lip. She used to love to dance, and the music had been tugging at her all night. But so far she had refused every man who had approached, out of nerves. After the first four were turned away, no one else had tried.

Imogene was looking faintly exasperated. Chloe couldn't blame her. She needed to appear normal. Unconcerned. Hiding in the corner with a few familiar faces was cowardice.

She'd faced her fear with Madame Simsa. Reached for her power. It had felt shocking in both its strength and the excitement that had turned her veins to pure bubbling joy in its wake. The kind of joy she hadn't felt for years. Possibly not since Charl died.

Maybe more of it waited for her if she could face this fear, too.

She could manage ten minutes on a dance floor following patterns that had been ingrained in her muscles since she was a young girl.

"Go on," Imogene said. "You know you want to. I know what

you look like when you want to dance, Chloe. It's all right. You are allowed to be happy. And it's perfectly safe here."

A servant appeared at Imogene's side. She leaned away, listening to whatever message he was conveying. Nothing good, judging by the frown that flashed briefly over her face as she turned back. "I have to attend to something." She waved a hand at Jean-Paul, who was talking to some friends a few feet away. He excused himself and came to join them.

"Chloe needs to dance," Imogene declared. "Take her onto the floor, my love. Make sure her toes don't get trodden on for the first few minutes of the set." She smiled up at Jean-Paul. "Apparently there's some crisis in the kitchen and Albeir needs to speak with me. I won't be long."

"We have our orders, it seems," Jean-Paul said, smiling down at Chloe. "Shall we?" He offered his arm and she took it, smiling back.

No one would be rude to her while she was dancing with him, at least. She knew how to read a crowd of courtiers, even if her skills were rusty, and she'd been watching the flow of the ball since she arrived. The du Laqs were respected. She'd known on an intellectual level what it meant that Jean-Paul held the title now, but that was different to seeing it. He'd always been imposing, not only due to his sheer size but his military bearing and being the heir. But now he wielded an invisible level of command. People melted out of their way as they walked to take their place on the dance floor, clearing the center of the space as though it was his rightful place. Once he reached it, there was a small rush as people moved to be in the first set with the duq.

"Does that get tiring?" Chloe asked as they took their positions, joined hands crossed, and waited for the musicians to begin.

"Mostly I don't notice," Jean-Paul said with a half shrug. "This isn't court proper, so there's little point to currying my favor." He gazed over the line of men and women forming beyond them. "Just ignore them. This is supposed to be fun, remember?" He grinned, the expression teasing. He was a mountain of a man, tall and dark-haired, with shoulders that strained the seams of his beautifully tailored jacket. When he smiled, he was also startlingly handsome. And he'd always been her friend. "Now, do I need to remind you of the opening measure?"

"I remember."

Fun. A simple dance with a friend. Nothing to worry about.

The musicians began to play, the strings moving through a series of notes that she knew by heart.

"Good. Imogene will be displeased if you don't. So, Madame, let us dance."

She smiled and let him swing them into motion. Jean-Paul was a surprisingly good dancer for a man of his size and height, and she'd danced with him often enough that they moved easily together.

As she gave herself up to the dance, her smile turned to a grin. Her feet and hands remembered what to do, and she didn't have to think. When the time came to change partners, she reached out her hand automatically. To her relief, the man who took it was one of the Imperial mages, someone she'd known from the Academe.

A friendly face. She relaxed and let herself just dance. Through her second partner and a third and a fourth until she spun around, hand outstretched to reach for the hand of the fifth, only to realize it belonged to Lucien.

She almost stumbled to a halt, but his hand closed over hers as his other went to her waist and guided her back into motion before she knew what was happening.

"Madame de Montesse," he said. His face was fixed in a pleasant court smile, but from the tension in the shoulder under her hand, he was as startled as she.

"What are you doing here?" she hissed, making sure her own smile didn't slip. This was exactly the kind of encounter she'd wanted to avoid. A feast for the gossips if she had a fight with the Marq of Castaigne in the middle of a du Laq ball. "Imogene didn't mention you were invited." And it would hardly have slipped her mind. Imogene had sat by Chloe's side when Charl was arrested. When he'd been condemned. She knew how Chloe felt about Lucien.

"I wasn't," he admitted. "I tagged along with some friends." He stared down at her. "I didn't expect you to be here."

Damn aristos. She'd forgotten that for the smaller balls and parties, groups of them would just show up, drifting from entertainment to entertainment as the night took them.

"Imogene is my best friend," she said. "Did you think she would shun me, my lord?"

A wince flickered over his face. "No. I can't see any of your true friends wanting to give that up," he said. "But you've only just returned. I thought you would be spending time with your family still."

"I'm a grown woman. I am hardly going to sit at home with my parents every night." Was it her imagination, or did his eyes flicker down over her dress and the neckline she suddenly regretted?

Regardless, his hand tightened over hers. "I should have known. I apologize."

It was the third time they'd met since her return, and his third apology.

She should tell him that it wasn't his fault, that it was inevitable they would encounter each other, but she didn't want that to be true. And she couldn't bring herself to do the thing she should do and offer him forgiveness.

If a true friend would not give up her friendship so easily, then there was no way he could have considered himself a true friend. Not and do what he had done. And that was a wound far from healed despite all the time that had passed.

Even if theirs had been a light and airy friendship—or as light and airy as Lucien, who was always minded toward seriousness, could be. She'd often wondered if he'd been drawn to Charl, who was the very definition of light and charm, to balance his own darker calling. To cling to the part of light that she had thought must become very distant when one dealt too frequently with the darkest sides of people's hearts and minds and deeds.

Had he been so serious before he manifested his powers? She hadn't known him then. He was three years older than Charl, four years older than her. He'd been in his final year at the Academe the year she'd manifested, and she hadn't known him by more than sight and reputation. She had no real skill for illusion and therefore not a candidate for the advanced training that might have led to their paths crossing. Her few memories of him from the Academe were of a serious face above the black robes, illusioner silver at his collar.

"It's only another measure or two and the dance will be done," he said. "It would be better for you to stay with me until then. Anything else will only draw attention."

"I'm well aware how to behave, my lord," she said, resisting the urge to tread on his feet. He was nimble enough to dodge anyway.

"That's not what I meant," he said, mouth flattening briefly as he guided her through the next turn.

How were her feet still moving? She'd danced with Lucien plenty in the past, and he'd been a perfect partner, as graceful as Jean-Paul. She couldn't remember a single time when Lucien had stumbled or put a foot wrong during any of the many dances they'd shared. It had always been fun to dance with him, her teasing him gently and he offering back his own wit and smiles.

But now he felt foreign, and every word he spoke hit her exactly the wrong way, scraping at raw nerves. *Only a minute more,* she told herself. Her heart was pounding, and her face felt hot. Every muscle screamed to leave, but he was right. A scene would be worse.

The last notes sounded and she made herself leave her hand in his, waiting for him to release it, rather than rudely tugging it away.

When he did, she muttered, "Good night, my lord," as she curtsied faster than was strictly polite. Keeping her smile fixed, she turned and made her way from the dance floor. It was an effort to walk, not run. The room was stifling and suddenly too small as she headed for the doors. She left the ballroom and moved on instinct, toward the rear of the townhouse and the garden that lay beyond.

There was no guarantee the garden would be empty, but anywhere would be an improvement over the ballroom.

But when she stepped through the back door, no one was in sight. She moved deeper into the garden, hand clenched too tightly on the sticks of her fan as she tried to cool herself down and not give in to the urge to loosen the back of her dress so she could catch her breath.

She could breathe perfectly well. She wasn't foolish enough to lace too tightly.

Besides, if she did manage to undo the damned buttons, there was no way she'd be able to do them up again. Being discovered in Imogene's garden half undressed was not the way to avoid a scandal.

But her breath still came too fast.

Lucien. *Damn* him.

She'd been doing well. Thinking it was possible that Imogene was right and she could become part of life in Lumia again. But the truth was it wasn't going to be so easy. She had been Madame de Montesse, Illvyan refugee and therefore automatically suspect and strange in Anglion. Here she was Madame de Montesse, either tragically fooled widow to those who believed the emperor's declaration, or likely traitor who had managed to get away with it to those who didn't.

That would change over time. She could live quietly and people would lose interest, as they had in Anglion. But that was exhausting to contemplate. She'd lost so much time already. Why did she have to fight again, here, where things had once been simple? She wanted to be somewhere where things could be simple again. Or at least where she had no reputation preceding her. Where people judged her on who she was and the skills and qualities she had to offer.

People who saw just *her*.

But she had no idea where that might be.

A sob caught in her throat.

"Chloe?" Imogene's voice came softly from behind her. "What's wrong?"

She didn't turn to face her friend. Didn't want Imogene to see her so close to undone. They'd cried back in Anglion, when they'd finally been alone together, after the shock of the rescue attempt and the assassination of Queen Eloisa and the upheaval that had followed in its wake. She'd been determined not to cry again. She was home. She should be happy.

"I'm all right," she managed.

"Jean-Paul told me Lucien was here," Imogene said. "I'm sorry, love. I didn't invite him. And I didn't imagine that he would just appear. He isn't a regular at our parties."

Just her luck. The one night Lucien de Roche decided to kick up his heels was the night she took her first tentative step back toward society.

"I don't care about the Marq of Castaigne," she said savagely.

Imogene snorted. "I hardly need to share his talents to know that can't be true."

"I don't want to talk about Charl," Chloe said, whirling to face her. "I can't change what happened."

"Of course you can't," Imogene said. "But that also means you can't change the fact that it still affects you. That what he did altered your life. But you can control your reaction."

Chloe clenched her jaw, anger chasing away some of the distress. She had been nothing but controlled for *years* now. "Maybe I shouldn't have come back."

Imogene's eyes widened. "What? That's ridiculous. You're Illvyan. You belong here, with the people who love you."

"The people who love me can't see me as who I am," Chloe

said. "You don't know who I am now. You love me, I know that. I love you, too. But to you, I'm still the idea you used to have in your head of me. I want to be the person I am now. And I don't know how to become that here in Lumia. With all of it hanging over my head." She snapped the fan out in frustration, flapping it back toward the townhouse. Maybe it would cool her temper along with her face.

To her credit, Imogene didn't flinch or try to argue. She just regarded Chloe for a moment, the moonlight glinting off her diamonds, then asked, "Who do you think you are?"

Chloe blinked. She'd been expecting an argument. More protests that she should just give herself time to adjust. That she'd find her feet. That she'd fit back in. But why should she fit back in? Maybe there needed to be changes.

"I wanted to join the mages, once upon a time. Travel. See the world a little. Do some good. Like you did."

She hadn't realized until she spoke the words that they were true. Or still true, perhaps. Joining the mages was a dream she'd made herself let go of when Ana had fallen ill. And then she'd buried it entirely in Anglion. Holding onto it would have torn her apart. To survive there, she had to be small. It sounded strange to say it out loud. But it didn't *feel* strange.

"Well, you could still join," Imogene said in a matter-of-fact tone.

Chloe blinked. That wasn't the answer she'd expected. "I'm too old," she said. Most mages joined the army straight out of the Academe.

"Not for the diplomatic corps, if that's what you want. Diplomats need brains, not muscles." Imogene smiled. "Not that you're not capable of defending yourself. But the corps looks for other skills than the ability to wield a sword. You'd be an asset. You can't deny you have unique experience to bring with you."

"Don't they also want skilled mages? I'm rusty. Very rusty." Madame Simsa still hadn't let her try her water magic.

"Rust is polished away easily enough. What matters is

whether the metal beneath is still strong. And you were always strong. You've proved that by surviving Anglion for a decade. You can do this, if it's what you really want to do."

"It might kill my mother," Choe said, naming another fear. "I'm not sure she'll cope if I announce I want to go traipsing all over the empire."

"Your mother is no longer ill," Imogene said, waving her fan dismissively. "And yes, perhaps she will be upset. But she'll forgive you if she sees it makes you happy. And she wouldn't forgive herself if she realized you were staying in Lumia and hating every second just to make her happy."

"I'm not so sure about that. She hasn't wanted to let me out of her sight."

"Also a natural reaction. But one that will ease with time. It might even speed things up if you went on a short mission and returned safe and sound. It would set her mind at ease to know you aren't going to vanish again."

The tightness in her chest was easing, the night air cooler now against her skin. Imogene made it sound easy. And that it was normal that she should want to attempt this. Was she right? "What if I hate it?"

"Well, then, you return and try something else. Nothing is set in stone."

Easy for Imogene to say. Her life had followed a steady path after that one unexpected fork when she met Jean-Paul. She had money and power, and no one would gainsay her if she decided to take up an eccentric interest.

She didn't have to earn a living. And she hadn't lost ten years of her life.

But Chloe didn't know how to explain the lurking sense of time slipping away from her. "I guess. It all seems so daunting. How would I even apply to the mages now? Recruiters aren't looking for people like me."

Imogene grinned. "No. But they listen to their officers. Like me. I can promise a glowing recommendation. And they listen to generals from the regular corps. Like my husband, who adores you like one of his sisters. But in your case, love, if you truly want to move things along, I recommend starting at the top. Ask Aristides for his blessing, and no one else will stand in your way if he grants it."

Aristides. The name rolled so easily off Imogene's tongue. Chloe had met the emperor in Anglion, but she wouldn't have dared to address him as anything but Your Imperial Majesty. He had been kind to her, but it was hard to forget the power he wielded. With a word, he'd offered her the pardon and the means to come home. With a word, he could take that away again. He held the power of life and death over all the empire's citizens. Hardly a man one could regard casually. But apparently Imogene felt differently.

"And if he doesn't?"

"Well, then, you try things the regular way. Work at the Academe for a month or so to brush up whatever skills you are worried about, then go to headquarters and make your case. But I don't think the emperor will refuse to help. He brought you home. He wanted me to help you rejoin society. He seems to have taken an interest in you."

Was that a good thing or a terrifying one? "Why do I have the feeling that if Aristides orders them to take me on, that will come with its own set of problems?"

Imogene shrugged. "There may be some degree of resent-ment, but I doubt it would go much beyond that. Raw recruits get set some odd tasks, testing their mettle, so to speak, but I doubt they'd tease you too much. You're bringing more to the table than some fresh-out-of-school Academe student." She grinned suddenly. "Trust me, I was one of those. You know far more than I did back then."

Imogene had been a star pupil of her class. She could have had her pick of positions in the Imperial mages. Or any of the civilian mage guilds. Or even the Academe itself. But like Chloe, she'd wanted to travel and had chosen the diplomatic corps.

She'd been twenty-two. Fresh from school. Surely Chloe could manage it now?

She took a deep breath. Imogene, too, had suffered through a scandal early in her career. Her very first mission had been a failure that set relations between Illvya and Andalyssia, the most northern country in the empire, back severely. It hadn't been Imogene's fault, but everyone on the mission had been caught up in the resultant disgrace, and she had to fight her way back to a second chance.

"You're thinking very hard," Imogene said. "You don't need to decide everything tonight. Come back and dance. Lord Castaigne has left, so you don't have anything to worry about. Or I can call for a carriage and you can go home. I'll tell people you have a headache."

"No," Chloe said. She straightened her shoulders. If she disappeared into the night, then it would just start rumors all over again. "I'll come back inside."

Imogene looked relieved. "Good. Supper will be served soon, and our cook made seila berry pies for dessert in your honor."

Seila berries had always been her favorite. Tiny and sweet with a burst of tartness at their heart. They didn't grow in Anglion. "Are seila berries even in season?"

"We have miles of greenhouses at Sanct de Sangre. We always have a few delicacies available to grace our tables all year. And your homecoming seems like a good reason to use some of them."

"Thank you," Chloe said. Seila berry pie might chase away the last of her anxieties. "I'm sorry I got upset."

"No need to apologize, I can only imagine it must be very strange. But I am on your side—don't ever forget that. And never hesitate to ask for help."

It was strange indeed to think she had people to call on now after fending for herself for so long.

"I won't," she promised. "Starting with now. Because I don't need to think about it. I would like to join the mages. Do you think you could get me an audience with Aristides?"

Imogene grinned. "That, love, will be even less of a problem than the seila berries."

Chloe laughed.

"What's so funny?"

"That Imogene Carvelle, my friend who once almost set her hair on fire trying to curl it, can now call on the emperor's favor. Life is strange."

"It is. But it's also an adventure. And yours is just beginning again."

CHAPTER 7

"My lord Truth Seeker?"

Lucien looked up to find his junior grefiere, Kristof, hovering in the doorway.

"Yes?" he said, then regretted the sharpness of the tone when Kristof flinched. He was new to the role but had the makings of a good steward, and Lucien had no reason to be short with him. Especially when the irritation rising in his veins at the interruption was purely his own fault.

"A note from the Imperial office, my lord." Kristof moved to the desk and offered an envelope. "The courier said it was urgent."

"A new case?" Lucien asked, turning the envelope over, ignoring the throb in his temples at the thought of more work. The headache bedeviling him was of his own making. After he'd blundered into Chloe's path last night and she'd fled the damned ballroom as soon as possible to get away from him, he'd taken himself off to one of the salons he and his friends sometimes frequented, planted himself by the fire, and drunk most of a bottle of Ilvsoir, trying to drown out the memory of her face.

Goddess, she loathed him.

He didn't want to think about how much. It was just salting

wounds that he should know to leave damn well alone. The resultant headache was the reason he had chosen to work from his office in his house in Arge-Nor rather than the one at the headquarters of the Imperial judiciary.

That and the fact that both his seneschal and his senior grefiere, Fidel, who handled the business of the estate for him when he couldn't do it himself, had been dropping tactful "you are spending too much time on the judiciary" hints for the last few weeks. He needed to spend a day or so where they could ask him all the things they wanted to ask and brief him on everything he needed to know and get him to authorize more damned bank drafts.

He'd already growled at Fidel that it was too damned early to discuss the breeding lines of pigs earlier that morning, which was probably why Kristof had been tasked with bringing him the message. He was clever—Fidel wouldn't have taken on anyone without the brains for the job—but perpetually cheerful and seemingly delighted to be learning the business of a grefiere. All of Lucien's household seemed to regard any sign of ill temper toward the lad as equivalent to kicking a puppy.

He turned the envelope over and frowned. It wasn't the Office of the Judiciary's seal on the back. It was the emperor's.

Damn.

He couldn't think of any good reason for Aristides to write to him. The trail on the Anglion scandals had largely run dry. They were looking for new leads on who the Anglions had hired in Lumia to attempt to kill Queen Sophia and her husband but so far had come up short. Likewise, they were yet to find the connections in Anglion. That was the only active case of his that the emperor had taken a direct interest in.

"That will be all," he said to Kristof. "I'll let you know if there's an answer."

Kristof nodded, his hand snapping a salute.

You could take the man out of the army, it seemed, but not the army out of the man. The judicial corps didn't really stand much on ceremony. Kristof hadn't served that long with them before the chief clerk had dropped a word in Lucien's ear that Kristof had perhaps more talent for the civil side of the law, given he seemed to delight in contracts more than the criminal code. The cases the Truth Seekers got involved in were rarely pleasant, and some people just didn't have the stomach for the work.

It had been timely. Fidel had been not so subtly hinting that he needed an assistant. Fidel had interviewed Kristof, and after that, it had been easy to free the lad from his service. But Kristof had been through basic training and a year or so in the regulars and couldn't quite break himself of the habit of saluting a man who was a major, a Truth Seeker, and a marq. He would relax in time. Lucien's talent was rare, and he had always been pleased to use it to serve the empire, but when he was home, he wanted to be Lucien, not the soldier. Definitely not the Truth Seeker. He didn't want a household of staff who were in awe—or fear—of him.

He glared down at the envelope as Kristof closed the door on his way out. Tempting to toss the damned thing in the fire and pretend it hadn't arrived. He was in no mood for new tales of betrayal or thievery or dishonor.

Not when the remorse snaking through his stomach with poisonous persistence kept telling him he was guilty of all three.

But he served the truth. It was the only way he could reconcile the power the goddess had seen fit to damn him with. To make good of it.

It was the only way he could remain human. Men weren't supposed to know what other men were thinking, to see into their deepest hearts.

He'd caught a glimpse of Chloe's as they'd danced, those big dark eyes full of anger, and he hadn't had to use his power. She was never going to forgive him. And they were destined to cross paths and simply hurt each other more every time they did.

He couldn't avoid court. She was the best friend of a duquesse. It was inevitable.

So he needed a strategy for how best to handle those occasions. Definitely not as he had last night. But then again, simply abandoning her on the dance floor would have caused a scene. She didn't need scandal. He had let her go at the end, even though he had to force his hands to release her. He was a gentleman, and he would bloody well behave like one and leave her alone. His heart would get over it eventually.

He hoped.

Damn it. Maybe a new case from Aristides was a distraction he needed after all.

He flipped open the envelope and tugged the heavy white paper free. The note was short. He was to attend his emperor. No explanation. Another sign that the matter could be nothing good.

And, Goddess, he felt like ten levels of hell. His head pounded, and his eyes had looked like he'd boiled them when he'd shaved earlier. The shave itself hadn't been his best attempt. His uniform was clean, and he'd drunk equal gallons of coffee and minted tea to attempt to clear his head and freshen his breath, but neither had helped overly much. They certainly hadn't dealt with the self-disgust.

He had a tiny skill for earth magic, but not enough to magic away a headache of this proportion. At the Academe, they'd told him his talent for illusion was so strong and his Truth Seeking so rare that his other magics were never going to amount to much. At the time, before he'd truly understood what being a Truth Seeker meant, he'd been proud. But there were days now—more of them each year—where he'd happily trade his power for some middling talent for blood or water that no one particularly cared about and settle down to running his estate.

He hadn't yet asked Aristides for a reduction of his caseload, but he could tell he was stretching things too far since his father died, even without the commentary from his staff. He owed the

Castaigne holdings and their people more attention than he was currently giving them. He had no desire to be an absent, neglectful lord. It was just that he hadn't yet worked out how to avoid that and also avoid neglecting his duty to the empire and the truth.

Frustrated, he yanked open the top drawer in his desk. He kept tinctures his mother made him there for days like these. She was an earth witch to be reckoned with, and one of her remedies would ease his head. It would also taste dire and chase away sleep for a night. He was short on that, too, but he would take tired over feeling like someone was running a dull blade through his temples.

The cork in the vial yielded easily, and he downed the contents in one fast gulp. His mother told him she made the taste unpleasant so no one would be tempted to use them too often. Unpleasant was underselling it. The stuff tasted like socks that had been worn for a month by someone with a dire foot disease and then perhaps pissed on by an angry cat. He chased it down with water and the now cold half mug of mint tea on his desk, which made his mouth somewhat happier.

Then he opened the door and told Kristof to call for a carriage, as he had to go to the palace and see what fate awaited him there.

The emperor was in one of the open, grassed parts of the palace grounds near the stables, studying a very expensive-looking chestnut filly when Lucien was ushered into his presence thirty minutes later. The horse's finely drawn lines and dished nose suggested Kharenian stock. Expensive indeed. She watched Aristides with big curious eyes, ears flicking back and forth as he stroked her neck. The saddle on her back and Aristides's breeches and relatively subdued jacket suggested the emperor had been putting her through her paces. He looked up as Lucien approached.

Lucien bowed as Aristides nodded at him. "You wished to see me, Your Imperial Majesty?"

"That is a very formal tone for such a sunny day." The emperor peered at him with assessing eyes. "You look tired, my lord Truth Seeker."

"I am fine, Your Imperial Majesty." He resisted squinting. Sunlight sometimes pained his eyes, and the lingering edges of his headache definitely didn't appreciate it. But while smoked-glass spectacles had become fashionable in Lumia a few years ago, he'd never been convinced that they didn't look somewhat ridiculous. And they definitely weren't acceptable to wear at court.

Aristides handed the mare off to a waiting groom. "A present for my daughter. Cecilie," he added, which was helpful. The man had a flock of daughters, after all.

"Is it her birthday soon?" Lucien tried to remember the court calendar. He didn't always have time for every social event the palace held, but as marq now, he had to attend more of them. And Imperial anniversaries and birthdays and such celebrations were more important than most. Or so his father had told him. Lucien was still making his own assessment of priorities, but it was true that it was hard to avoid being missed at such events when the majority of the court turned out in force.

"She will be sixteen," Aristides said. "Goddess protect us all."

Cecilie had a reputation for being strong-willed. His mother kept telling him she was going to be a beauty. He'd made it plain that he had no intention of marrying someone less than half his age, even if the emperor defied all reason and decided to waste an Imperial princess on a mere marq. He grinned at Aristides. "At least it's another five years until you find out if she has any magic."

Aristides winced. "Perhaps I can arrange for an extended

tour of the empire around that time. I could leave straight after her Ascension, should it come to pass." He nodded at the groom. "Take her back to the stable. She will do nicely."

"I think the empress would hunt you down and drag you back," Lucien said with a grin.

"You are possibly correct," Aristides said, smiling ruefully. "Well, five years is a long time. No need to borrow trouble."

Not when the empire produced enough of it for the man to deal with now.

"Ah," Lucien said. "Which brings us to business. How may I be of service?"

"Walk with me, Lucien," Aristides said. He led them through the grounds to a section of his private gardens that Lucien knew. Its main feature was an outdoor dining pavilion, shaped in finely carved wood to echo the lines of the palace. The emperor seemed to enjoy spending time outside the palace when the weather was fine and often discussed business there. Given the man's schedule and obligations were more suffocating than Lucien's—he wouldn't trade places with Aristides for the world—Lucien couldn't blame him for wanting to escape the palace walls as often as possible.

Aristides took a seat at one end of the long table that sat square in the center of the pavilion, beneath a replica of the Imperial seal picked out in gold and enamel on the wooden ceiling. "Sit." He pointed to the chair on his left.

Lucien sat. Aristides called for tea, then made maddening small talk until the servants arrived with it.

The tea was at least hot and strong and, in combination with his mother's tincture, made progress in chasing away the last edges of his hangover. Which was almost worse, in a way. Without the pounding head to distract him, the memories of the ball and Chloe were far too clear.

"How are your cases progressing?" Aristides asked eventually after he, too, had drained his cup and devoured some of the small works of art masquerading as cakes that the servants had brought with the tea. Lucien left those alone, not quite trusting his stomach yet.

"They are in order, Your Imperial Majesty. You have all the latest information in the Anglion matter."

In fact, Aristides might know more than Lucien. The emperor had, like Chloe, recently returned from Anglion. He'd sent Lucien a briefing, as it was pertinent to his investigation into the attempts against Sophie and Cameron in Illvya, but a report wasn't the same as a firsthand account.

"Yes, well. We will see how that progresses. Queen Sophia has work to do, and it will not help her if we go hunting for problems too soon. But Domina Skey must have had contact with someone here to have access to scriptii."

"Or else they have a water mage in Anglion who no one knows about," Lucien countered.

Aristides shook his head. "I do not think so. Their fear of water magic is real. I cannot see Domina Skey sanctioning such a thing. Too much risk to her power. I think part of the reason that she viewed Queen Sophia as a threat is that she may have sensed the potential in her. And without her being bound to the temple in the usual way, she was a risk." He considered Lucien a moment. "Speak to Edouard. He will tell you what impressions he gained from the court there."

"I will, Your Imperial Majesty." Edouard had been a Truth Seeker longer than Lucien, and his skill was subtle and impressive.

"Do so," Aristides said. "But as Anglion must be left a while to find their feet, allow me to present you with another matter." His face twisted a little, which was probably about as close to an apology as Lucien would get for whatever mess was about to be dumped in his lap. "I know you have a lot on your hands, Lucien. And I would not add to that if I could avoid it."

"But?" Lucien said. The emperor was clearly not going to avoid it. He might respect his tools and give them leeway when he could, but he would never hesitate to deploy a tool when he needed it.

"But we will be sending a delegation to Andalyssia. It requires a Truth Seeker."

"Andalyssia?" Lucien was too startled to be polite. Truth Seekers did travel sometimes for cases in other parts of the empire, and he'd been to Andalyssia once before, briefly, in the wake of an assassination attempt on the empress. Located in the northernmost part of the empire, it was freezing cold most of the year, and the people were strange. And unforgiving. They'd shown no love for Illvya. Not that he could blame them when the Illvyans at the particular time had been upending one of their noble houses with proof of treachery. He had no desire to go back. Such a trip would take—he tried to recall the geography and distances—at least two months. He could scarcely afford to be away from his estates for so long. "Your Imperial Majesty, my estates need—"

"I understand the ramifications," Aristides said, cutting him off.

Lucien's stomach dropped. He wasn't going get out of this.

"I know it is inconvenient. I will provide you with adequate compensation. You can hire as many land stewards as you require."

He had an excellent land steward already. But he couldn't expect Fidel to run the estate for months in any other way than what his father had already set in motion. Lucien had ideas of his own. Things he wanted to change. Not to mention it was early autumn. Most of the hard work of summer harvest was done, and the tenants were planning the coming seasons. They needed access to their lord. As would his staff. Traditionally this was the time of year when he would be at home, to meet with his people. Local problems and requests were dealt with by the lord if they didn't need to be dealt with by the judiciary. He was depriving them of that. His younger brother was married and living half the country away on his wife's family lands. His sisters were married, too. He could hardly expect them to step in for several months.

But the emperor was unlikely to be swayed by those arguments.

"Has there been an incident that requires a Truth Seeker in Andalyssia, Your Imperial Majesty?" he asked, carefully controlling his voice to remove any hint of frustration.

"Not an incident as such," Aristides said. "But the king is about to marry. He has made a petition for us to consider restoring House Elannon early."

"What?" Lucien wasn't sure he'd heard correctly. House Elannon had been behind the attempt on the empress.

Aristides grimaced. "It is a matter of their bloody balance," he said. "The priests are claiming it would be inauspicious for the king to begin his wedded life without a full council. Or, rather, they have said it would be inauspicious for the queen-to-be to be crowned in such circumstances."

"They didn't argue that when the king was crowned."

"Less time. They crown a new king within days of the old one dying. There was no time to ask, though I am sure it crossed the council's mind. But the queen's coronation will not happen until the month of marriage rites is up."

Which left time for negotiations. And an opportunity to force a matter that was a wedge between the two countries. He put down his tea. He couldn't immediately recall the particulars of Andalyssian wedding traditions, but he'd butted heads with their concept of balance when he'd been there to oversee the Ashmeister Elannon's trial. Andalyssians believed the goddess wanted the land to be in balance in order for it to thrive. And that idea permeated their lives. It affected how they used magic and how they structured their society. The king ruled, but he had the council—the sixteen largest noble houses each appointed an Ashmeister to advise the king—the priests, and the seers to advise him. Each year one of the Ashmeisters was appointed to rule the council, and that role rotated through the cycle of houses until it began again.

When the Ashmeister Elannon had been found guilty, part of the punishment—part of the agreement which had saved the house from being annihilated—had been the removal of House Elannon for one full cycle of the council. Sixteen years. Long enough for the older generation to lose their grip on power and the younger members of the house to reflect on the consequences of treason. Long enough for the whole country to reflect.

It had only been thirteen. They were asking for the emperor to forgive them early. Which sat uneasily in Lucien's gut.

Balance or not, this was politics.

"What happens if you refuse?" he asked.

"That is difficult to predict," Aristides said. "I like Mikvel. He is young, but he is forward-thinking and shows signs of being a good king. But he needs the council's support."

Which he could well lose if he couldn't at least get Illvya to agree to discuss an early end to House Elannon's disgrace. That might mean a wedding turned to a coup. And if the royal house lost power, then the Ashmeisters would fight. Some of them were still very traditional. Possibly some of them shared the views of the Ashmeister Elannon about breaking up the empire to restore balance. Andalyssia was cold and grim, but it also controlled the mountain ranges where a lot of the empire's iron and gold—not to mention other precious stones and metals— were mined. Illvya needed it to be ruled by a man they could work with, not an enemy.

"So you want me to go and what—see if Elannon has learned their lesson?" And if they had, tell Aristides to back King Mikvel and allow a house that committed treason to step back into power? Or, if they hadn't, face potential chaos in one of the richest countries in the empire. He was glad he wouldn't be making the decision.

No, just finding the evidence to help Aristides make it. Goddess damn it.

"Something like that. But not just you. We were sending a delegation to the wedding anyway. Both to attend the ceremonies and to discuss the mining treaties."

There were always discussions of the mining treaties.

"You don't want to attend to this yourself?"

"No. At this point, if I go, it can only be interpreted as Andalyssia being back in favor or me being there to tighten my fist. Neither would be useful to the matter at hand. Better to see if we can resolve this quietly. You have a high enough rank that you can represent us at all the wedding festivities as well as determining whether Elannon can be trusted to rejoin the Ashmeisters."

The Ashmeisters. His memories of them were of a group of seriously grim and ruthless men. The passing of the old king had been unexpected, and his son was young. In Andalyssian history, there was more than one instance where that set of circumstances had led to one of the Ashmeisters taking the throne.

He could understand why Aristides was keen for them to not stir up trouble again, but he had to ask, "Are you sure I'm the right person? After all, I was there for the Ashmeister Elannon's trial."

Aristides smiled, the expression fierce. "If they protest, I will claim it would be balance for you to be there. They are unlikely to be able to argue with that."

Maybe not, but they would want to. There had never been an Andalyssian Truth Seeker. Favoring one magic over the rest so strongly was against balance. They did, however, have seers who exercised quite some influence in the court, with their odd mix of ritual keeping and foretelling and other things he'd never entirely gotten straight. He'd been able to tell that the seers spoke what they believed to be true when they made their pronouncements of the future, but given the Andalyssians professed not to use straight water magic and it was usually water magic that leaned itself to prophecy, he'd been unsure whether their pronouncements often came true. He hadn't stayed long enough to find out.

"Is there any point in me trying to convince you to send someone else?"

"No. You solve my problem neatly. Your cases are all in a position where they can do without you for a few months, or so the clerk of your division informs me. The advocate general agrees."

Dammit. If Maxim had agreed, then this was already a done deal.

"How long?" Maybe it would only be a week or so actually in Andalyssia, which would make the whole thing more bearable.

Aristides grimaced. "The wedding rites begin a week before the wedding itself. And continue until the queen's coronation."

"Five weeks?" Lucien sputtered. Goddess damn it. Factor in travel time and that would be more like three and a half months away freezing his bloody ass off at the top of the world. He resisted the urge to bang his head on the table. Marqs did not bang their heads on tables. Not in public, at least.

"How soon will the delegation be leaving?" he asked.

"In a few weeks. The wedding rites begin at the end of the month. They need them to be completed before winter sets in and no one can travel back from the mountains. I am putting a navire at the disposal of the mission. That will cut down the travel time to something like a week each way, I believe."

Well, that was something. He'd only lose two months, not closer to three and a half. He made himself nod, though he couldn't summon any further expression of enthusiasm.

"So you have some time to prepare and put whatever you need in place to assist you in the management of your estate while you are away. Send the bills to me if you have costs."

"I am not destitute, Your Imperial Majesty. My father left the estate in good standing."

"I know. But more money is always useful. And I am inconveniencing you."

"I am a member of your judiciary. It's my job to go where you send me."

"You are also a peer of my empire," Aristides said. "Which means our relationship is slightly different to the way it was before. Truth Seekers may be deployed as I wish, true, but I have duty to your people not to deprive them of their lord unnecessarily. They are my people, too, Lucien. Do not forget that part. I want them to prosper as much as you do."

He hadn't thought of it in exactly that way before. Or realized that the emperor viewed him differently now. They'd spoken immediately after his father died, but it hadn't been spelled out in so many words. Or maybe it had and Lucien had been too caught up in the fog of grief and sudden unexpected responsibility to understand. "Thank you, Your Imperial Majesty."

"Good, that is settled. You will be given more details as we have them." Aristides paused as though considering something. "On another matter, you are aware that Chloe de Montesse has returned to our shores?"

Goddess, was the emperor determined to hit him everywhere he was vulnerable today? He gritted his teeth, willing his voice to indifference. "Yes, Your Imperial Majesty."

"You understand what it means?"

That he was damned and making a fool of himself at every turn? That maybe two months away might be exactly what was needed? "That it may stir up old memories? Yes." Charl had been guilty of treason, but he hadn't named all his co-conspirators in the matter. Hadn't known them all as far as Lucien had been able to determine. Nor had the other men condemned with him. Whoever organized the plot had been cunning enough to hide themselves. If any of them were still alive and still had ambitions of that nature, Chloe would possibly be a rallying point or a reminder. Or a symbol.

"Exactly. So we will be careful. I would prefer that she is not caused further distress in this matter."

"So would I."

Aristides regarded him steadily. "You were friends with her and her husband, I recall."

"Yes."

"You were also the one who took her husband's confession? And informed her of his admission of guilt?"

Why was he asking when he knew the answer very well? The man had a mind like a steel trap. He forgot very little. Definitely not the details of trials involving treason. "Yes, Your Imperial Majesty. I didn't tell her to flee to Anglion, if that is what you're asking."

He had only wanted to warn her to perhaps put herself out of sight for a few months so Charl's co-conspirators couldn't reach her if they tried. He still regretted that he had bungled that message and Chloe had fled.

"I cannot imagine that you did," Aristides said. "My apologies, my lord Truth Seeker, if I am causing you pain. Lady de Montesse—"

"She prefers Madame de Montesse," he said automatically. "Charl didn't use his title." It had only been a minor one, after all. His uncle had died without heirs, and Charl's father had become the marq not long after Charl and Chloe wed, but his older brother was the heir.

One of Aristides's dark brows lifted. "That does not change the fact that she is entitled to use it. I know she used 'Madame' in Anglion, but she is home now. Perhaps you and Lady de Montesse will be able to find some degree of friendship again."

"I don't expect so, Your Imperial Majesty. I condemned her husband. I can only imagine she loathes me." He wasn't going to tell Aristides that he had already seen Chloe and knew that to be fact. Not if Aristides didn't bring it up. He owed his emperor his loyalty, but he didn't see what his feelings about Chloe or hers for him had to do with that.

Aristides watched him with serious gray eyes, and Lucien tried not to look away. The man had an uncanny way of making Lucien feel like he was talking to his father. More than twenty years reigning as emperor added gravitas beyond his actual years.

"A difficult situation," Aristides said eventually. "But perhaps there can be a better outcome than you anticipate. People change with time. And they have a remarkable capacity for forgiveness. Or some of them do," he added.

Lucien didn't think Chloe did. Why should she forgive him? Some things were unforgivable.

"But, of course, this is a matter for the two of you to navigate. So let us return to Andalyssia. Do you have questions?" Aristides asked.

Lucien straightened. Frankly, talking about Andalyssia with Aristides and contemplating a long and complicated journey to the frozen ends of the empire was more appealing than discussing Chloe. "Yes, Your Imperial Majesty. I have a few."

CHAPTER 8

"Lady de Montesse, please, sit," the emperor said, indicating the chair opposite his. He sat by a small table, where a porcelain tea service was laid out. A half-full cup sat by his right hand, the faint floral scent of the tea drifting through the air.

Chloe moved toward the chair. Imogene had worked fast. Two days after the ball and she had an audience with the emperor. It seemed impossible, and she wished Imogene had stayed with her instead of merely escorting her to the audience chamber so she had a friendly face to steady her nerves. But if she wanted to seize a new life for herself, then she had to seize this opportunity first.

She sat, smoothing her skirts into place. She'd worn one of her nicest Anglion gowns, a silk in so dark a green it was nearly black and held a little of the rainbow sheen that the Academe robes had. "I prefer Madame de Montesse," she said. Well, actually, she wasn't entirely sure she preferred being Madame de Montesse, but it was better than "lady." She was used to it. In Anglion, she'd stuck to "Madame" to establish her widowhood and offer no clue as to her real social status. In Kingswell, "Madame" was exotic, adding a small dose of mystery to entice the curious into her store.

Aristides quirked an eyebrow. There were a few silver threads in his hair now, but they somehow only emphasized the authority in his steady gray gaze. "You are entitled to the title. You should use it. Imogene tells me that you wish to join the Imperial mages. Are you eager to leave home again so soon?"

She barely stopped the flinch. She'd rehearsed an answer to this question, expecting him to ask, but those words now sounded too practiced in her head. How to explain when she didn't entirely understand herself?

"Not eager, Your Imperial Majesty. But—" She broke off, frustrated. She curled her fingers into her palm, then clasped her hands so she wouldn't fidget like a nervous child. "It is difficult to explain. I lost ten years of my life in Anglion. I survived them, yes, and even made a life for myself, but it wasn't the life I once wanted. And I am afraid that, if I do not take steps to see if some of those old dreams might still be mine, I will lose the courage to try."

Aristides blinked, lifted his teacup, and sipped before putting it down. It was a delicate thing, the porcelain almost translucent where it wasn't painted with tiny golden suns. The emperor's fingers held it gently, but she couldn't help thinking he could crush it with a careless squeeze.

"You have never struck me as someone who lacks courage. As you said, you achieved something most others in your place have not. You built a life for yourself in quite unfavorable circumstances." He poured tea into one of the empty cups and passed it to her.

"A life now left behind," she said, accepting the tea. "Which leaves me back where I began."

The emperor tilted his head. "When I was a child and my father was emperor, there was a man at court who had been there since my grandfather's time. A former Lord of the Faithless Isles. My grandfather brought him to Illvya when he conquered the Isles. One of the hostages, I suppose. Though those conditions were eventually revoked, I believe. I asked him once why he did not return home, and he said to me that exiles sometimes live under a curse of a kind. When I asked what kind of curse, and could a mage not fix it for him, he laughed at me. Not many people dared to laugh at me in those days. Not the young crown prince." He smiled somewhat ruefully. "When he stopped laughing, he told me the curse was not a magical one, just one imposed by life itself. And that the home he dreamed of, after so much time, lived only in his head. And that, if he returned, he was afraid he would lose even that, if he found his home had changed completely in the years he had spent in Lumia. Which it may well have done."

Chloe sat very still, an unwelcome prickle of recognition stinging her eyes. No. She would not cry in front of the emperor. She was here to convince him she was capable and worthy of serving him, not to garner sympathy. She swallowed and said, "I imagine it would, Your Imperial Majesty."

He nodded. "Yes. And I imagine you may have found some degree of change here. Enough to be unsettling."

His tone wasn't quite a question, but she found herself nodding anyway.

Damn the man, he was charismatic, if nothing else. But an emperor who couldn't learn to charm and convince people to do his bidding probably didn't last long. And Aristides had been emperor for twenty-odd years.

"Things are different," she admitted. "I am different, too. I cannot slot neatly back into life here. The life I left—" She stopped then, fearing she was straying into dangerous waters. "Well, I have to make a new life for myself. See who I will become. And besides, I have traveled little in the last ten years. Your empire is large, Your Imperial Majesty. I always wanted to see something of it."

He smiled over his teacup. "I can sympathize with that urge. I spend too much time in Illvya these days."

The emperor's family had cemented their control of the

continent two generations ago. The wars were largely over and the empire ran smoothly, barring the odd snarl here and there.

Aristides ruled mostly through governors and ambassadors who represented him and operated alongside the governmental structures of the individual countries, be that nobility or clans or whatever system of rule they favored.

There were only a few places, like the Faithless Isles, where the existing governmental structures had been removed completely. Places where the wars for territory had been vicious and the treaties severe. But even those were mostly peaceful now. The diplomatic corps represented the emperor when necessary, and he seldom traveled far beyond Lumia's borders. Select trips to the various reaches of the empire to be seen at intervals, but those were all pomp and ceremony, carefully planned and full of politics. A junior diplomat might have some freedom to explore a foreign land, but emperors didn't roam freely.

Not least because it put them in danger. Aristides was a target. He had been targeted here in Lumia and would be again. He would be targeted wherever he went.

"I do not wish to be chained to one place," she said. "Not so soon, anyway." Eventually she might want to settle down. She couldn't imagine getting married again. The young and eager Chloe who had said yes to Charl after a few short months seemed like a figure from a story, barely remembered. But a house of her own, work to do, friends, security. Those were all things she wanted.

But she couldn't settle with this itch under her skin, with this feeling that she didn't fit the old Chloe-shaped hole the city and her family wanted her to fill.

"I understand chains," he said. "I also understand responsibility. And duty."

She stiffened. Was he referring to Charl or merely to her family? "I would serve you well, Your Imperial Majesty."

"Ten years out of practice with your magic," he countered. "What makes you think you have the required skills?"

Another question she had anticipated. "I was near the top of my class at the Academe," she said. "And I have ten years of surviving in a country where most of my magic was taboo. Where I could have been put to death for using it. Where I arrived with very little. Yet I prospered. And rest assured, I did not completely abandon my powers in that time, Your Imperial Majesty. I believe I have every skill a diplomat requires. I know how to get along, how to learn a place fast, how to observe. How to be invisible when needed. And what magic I may have forgotten will come back quickly enough with a little study. I have access to excellent teachers. I am, after all, my father's daughter." She raised her chin.

Aristides nodded, then smiled. "Well argued." He considered her a moment. "Very well, Lady de Montesse. I will speak to General Vincent, and we will see what can be found for you."

She ignored his use of her title, too happy to be annoyed. She wanted to leap out of her seat and squeal with joy as she and Imogene might have when they'd been at school. But ten years in Anglion, watching her words and behavior near constantly to ensure she didn't make a fatal error, had taught her too well. She merely nodded with a smile and said, "Thank you, Your Imperial Majesty. I am most grateful."

He lifted his cup again, sipped, and put it down, dark eyes serious. "Of course, if you fail in whatever they set you to, I will not intervene on your behalf again. I do not second-guess my army."

She doubted that was true. At least not when push really came to shove. But she was not an empire-in-peril-level problem. When it came to her, he would, indeed, let her be shoved with no regret. "Of course, Your Imperial Majesty. I would expect no less."

✦ ✦ ✦

The emperor worked even faster than Imogene. The invitation to attend the barracks and meet with representatives of the diplomatic corps came the next morning. Early. Before her father left for the Academe. His expression was sober as he handed her the envelope, his thumb rubbing over the unmistakable seal of the Imperial mages.

"Something to tell us?" he asked, glancing back over his shoulder toward the dining room where Ana was finishing her coffee whilst reading the morning's newsheet.

Chloe took the envelope, opened it neatly, scanned the paper within, then folded it all back up again and slipped it into the pocket of her skirt. She wasn't ready for her mother to know about this yet. But it seemed she was going to have to tell Henri. "I'm thinking of joining the mages," she said softly. She hadn't wanted to tell them until after her appointment with Aristides. Not until something actually came to fruition.

Henri was quiet a long moment. "Keen to leave us already?" His pale eyes were steady, but sadness lurked in their depths.

She sighed, heart twisting. "Papa, you know that's not the case. But I have to make a life for myself again. This is something I always wanted to do, you know that. If...if what happened hadn't happened, I would have ended up trying to join the mages at some point." She and Charl had been frivolous and light-hearted for those first few years of their marriage, but she'd known deep down that she hadn't wanted children yet. She would have grown bored eventually, would have turned back to work and magic. But she hadn't had the chance. "Can't you understand?"

He winced. "I do, darling. Your mother will be less easy. She has longed for you to be home."

"I am home. But that doesn't mean I can sit in the parlor doing embroidery all day. And I don't expect you and Mama to support me. I'm used to working. Used to making my own way. I need to *do* something."

"What corps?" Henri asked.

"Diplomatic," she said. "It's what I always wanted to do, the same as Imogene."

"Haven't you spent enough time in far-flung places?"

She lifted her hands in a helpless gesture. "I've spent time in one far-flung place that was hardly of my choosing. It's not the same thing. Surely you can see that? Is it wrong of me to want to see something of the empire?"

"No. It just feels...fast? You've only been back two weeks." His tone was wistful.

Chloe nodded. "I know. But it's not as though I would leave tomorrow, if they do decide to let me join. It was months and months before Imogene ever joined a mission. I'll have to do some training. And most of the missions given to junior officers aren't that long. You'll barely notice I'm gone before I'm back again." She hoped that would appease his concerns. Months sounded far too slow for her liking. Not that she could control the timeframes. But slow or not, she didn't want to hurt her parents more than she had to. "I need to know that I can go where I want, Papa. Anglion may have saved me, but I was trapped there. You don't know what that's like."

"You might be surprised," Henri said. "When you get older, when you have a family and obligations, it also narrows your choices."

"I understand that. But it's not the same. You and Mama could travel wherever you wanted. She's well enough now, and any Academe in the empire would be happy to offer you a job for whatever length of time you chose. You have options. Choosing not to take them is not the same as not having them to begin with."

"You have options, too," Henri objected. "You can return to the Academe. Once you have your magic steady in your hand again, you could do anything."

"And what I want to do is this," she said, her temper sharpening. "At least, it's what my heart tells me to do. Maybe I'll hate it and I'll be out at the end of my first deployment. But regardless, I have to try. I love being back here, love spending time with you and Mama and the others, but it's not enough for me, Papa. You didn't raise me to be idle. And all that time in Anglion taught me to work, to be busy." If only to maintain her sanity. Throwing herself into the store and the fine details of running her business and making it successful had kept her mind occupied. Stopped her from thinking too hard about Illvya in the beginning, and then, as Anglion had started to feel more familiar and without any hint that she might return one day, the focus had been what she needed to feel whole.

She dipped her hand into her pocket, fingers rubbing the wax seal on the envelope. "I have to do this or I'll never know who I can be. I've had too many choices taken away from me already. I intend to drive my own fate from now on."

Henri sighed again. "I should have coddled you more," he said, one side of his mouth quirking. "Made you into one of those home-loving daughters."

She smiled. "Well, you didn't. And you can't change me now."

"I've never wanted to do that, darling. And I still don't. I only want you to be happy. And safe. But I know you're sensible, so I will focus on the happy and ignore the portion which involves gadding about the empire."

"The empire is hardly a hotbed of danger now," Chloe said. "It's not like diplomats are sent home headless anymore. I'll be surrounded by soldiers. And mages. And sanctii." There were wild tales from the early days of history, when the emperors had still been building their empire. Back then, diplomacy had been a chancier venture. Now it was more focused on keeping things running smoothly. In truth, it was more the travel and going to other countries and seeing how people lived there that interested her over the actual diplomacy part. But she would take the less interesting parts to go with the challenge of being able to move around as she wanted.

"Do *not* mention headless diplomats to your mother," Henri said. "In fact, could you wait to tell her until you know for sure?

I fear she's going to be upset, and it might be easier to present her with a deal that is already signed and sealed. Otherwise, she'll try to talk you out of it. She won't be able to help herself.".

"Of course," Chloe said. She'd had no intention of telling her mother one second before it became necessary. It had been easy to see that Ana would indeed try to convince her to change her mind. Better to not upset her any sooner than she had to.

"And you will still come back to the Academe, take lessons with Madame Simsa when you can?"

"I expect that it will be a condition of me joining up," she said. She didn't intend to deceive the army and lie about her magic. That would be pointless. She'd been found out. The Imperial mages had their own schools, of course. Imogene had learned how to bond her sanctii from the army, but Chloe wasn't considering that option just now. She couldn't imagine how her mother might react if she arrived home with a sanctii in tow.

Perhaps a petty fam one day. Something for company once she had a place of her own. Petty fams were also acceptable to the army. Her mind flew back to Mai, in the Raven Tower. Sophie's Tok was a character, and she'd always liked the ravens.

A petty fam would be company in an unfamiliar world. But it wasn't the right time to add another new thing to her life. If she was destined to have a familiar, the right one would present themselves at the right time.

"Are you unhappy about that?" Henri asked. "Have I been pushing you too hard to return?"

She shook her head. "No, Papa. Don't be silly. I love the Academe, and I know I need to reacquaint myself with my magic. Madame Simsa has been helping me already. I was just thinking of something else. Nothing of any import."

Henri smiled somewhat ruefully. "I wish your love for the Academe had let me convince you to stay here and teach. I think you would be good at it." He held up a hand. "But I understand your reasoning. I can't say I'm entirely happy about it, but I know you need a life of your own. And that you have to find your way again after so long."

"I didn't know I would feel this way," she said softly. "When I returned, I thought I would be perfectly happy."

"It would be strange if you were," Henri said. "Change is never easy. But you know that better than most, I expect. And so I will be a good parent and help you do what you need to do."

CHAPTER 9

It seemed ridiculous to be more nervous to be meeting with the diplomatic corps than the emperor. But Chloe's palms were clammy and her pulse jittery as she walked through the halls of the barracks, following a black-clad ensign who looked barely old enough to be out of school.

Maybe that meant she was too old to be there.

No. This was the last hurdle. No time for doubt.

She swiped her palms quickly over her skirt and straightened her shoulders. Curious faces looked up as the ensign led her into an outer office, two rows of two desks arrayed like small gates before another inner door. The ensign ignored them all and went straight for the door. Chloe followed.

"Come in," a voice called out.

"Madame de Montesse to see you, sir," the ensign said.

"Show her in."

The ensign flicked his hand at Chloe, herding her forward.

She pasted her most confident smile on her face as she walked into the office.

A tall, blonde woman dressed in Imperial black sat behind a huge desk, signing a document. She put the pen down and looked up. "Madame de Montesse. I am Colonel Brodier."

Technically, as a civilian, and a minor member of court, she didn't need to curtsy to an officer, but the colonel's voice was commanding, and Chloe had to fight the urge to bend her knee. "Colonel. Thank you for seeing me."

The door snicked shut behind her as the ensign left, leaving them alone.

"Please, have a seat," Colonel Brodier said. No additional colors ran through her hair. Not a mage. But the diplomatic corps used both regular soldiers and mages.

Two spartan-looking wooden chairs sat in front of the equally plain desk. Chloe chose the closest, giving the desk a quick once-over, trying to get a sense of the person who sat behind it. It was clearly well used, but the papers were all neatly arranged, stacked in piles or in wire baskets separated by pieces of heavy paper. No clutter.

Colonel Brodier, it seemed, was one for order and discipline.

She resisted the urge to wipe her palms again them. Why was she so nervous? People didn't defy the emperor's will very often, but the military had its ways and they could turn her down, or they could take her on to please the emperor and keep her chained to a desk, filing papers, if they didn't think she was ready for anything more.

"You can call me Honore for the moment," the colonel said. "While you're still a civilian, we may as well take advantage."

While she was a civilian? Did that mean that status may change? "Thank you. Please, call me Chloe."

"Very well." The colonel studied her a moment. Northerner blood somewhere in her ancestry with that hair and eyes an icy pale blue. Illvyans tended to be swarthier and darker haired— shorter too—though in truth, over time, the empire had led to enough travel and immigration that Illvyans and the people in most countries closest to Illvya itself had a wider range of skin and eye colors these days than may have once been the case.

"You know Major du Laq, I believe?" Colonel Brodier asked.

"Yes. Imogene and I have been friends since the Academe."

"You didn't follow her into the mages after you graduated?"

Did Honore not know her background? Or was this a test to see if Chloe would be forthright? "Imogene was a year ahead of me. My mother fell ill in my last years at school, which delayed my ambitions to join. Then I fell in love, and I suspect you know very well how that ended."

Honore nodded. "I do. Which is why I was somewhat surprised to find myself receiving a direction from the emperor suggesting I should add you to my unit."

Colonel Brodier wasn't going to simply accede to the emperor's will, then. Chloe raised her chin. "I am not my late husband, Colonel. I had nothing to do with what he did." She didn't soften it to "what he was accused of." Charl had confessed. Lucien's power had acknowledged that confession to be true. She might hate Lucien for what he'd done, but she didn't doubt his power. Or believe he would condemn Charl if it wasn't true. She'd never asked Charl directly, of course. She'd been allowed to see him once, briefly, after he'd been condemned, to say goodbye. He had spent most of that time crying and asking her to forgive him. There had been little chance for anything more than that.

"So I am informed. By both my emperor and Major Du Laq. You have friends in high places, Chloe."

"I have friends, yes. I don't know about in high places. Imogene and I have known each other a long time. She is my friend. His Imperial Majesty is...my emperor. He has granted me the courtesy of believing I'm innocent. But I would not call him a friend. And he was very clear that if I mess up here, he will not intervene. His favor may have been the reason you're seeing me today, but I intend to succeed in the mages on my own merits."

"And they are?"

"I am my father's daughter. I graduated close to the top of my class in the Academe. I'm a water mage and an earth witch. And I have navigated a life in enemy territory for nearly a decade. Survived and thrived there. I think I have some skills that would be useful in a diplomat."

Honore smiled briefly. "Well, you are confident, at least, and that's a useful trait. As long as one knows when it's warranted. Ten years is a long time away from home. I assume you didn't use your magic often in Anglion. Are you certain you have the control required of an Imperial mage?"

"I've been working with Madame Simsa," Chloe said. "A refresher, if you will. If you talk to her, I believe she would give you no cause for concern." She hoped that was true. Madame Simsa was pleased with the amount of power Chloe could wield, but she had no idea if her teacher would vouch for her control yet. "But I will be happy to undertake any course of study or examinations you consider necessary. I'm not expecting to join and be immediately deployed. I understand how the Imperial army operates. As you said, Imogene du Laq is my friend. As is her husband and a good number of the mages I went to school with." Lucien was one of them, technically, but she wasn't going to mention him. "The Academe teaches all the students military history and some basic strategy. Blood mages get more, of course, but they give us all a grounding. They know a certain number of their students will follow this path."

"I am aware," Honore said drily. "I was an Academe student myself. I didn't manifest in the end, but I studied there before I joined up. I remember Madame Simsa. So, yes, I will speak with her and consider her recommendations. But skills aside, why is this a path you want to follow? I would have thought you would want to stay close to home after so long away."

"I thought so, too, at first," Chloe said. "But I have come to realize that I need something more. You're not the first to ask me why. I expect you won't be the last. Everyone thinks I should just slip back into life in Lumia and continue on as though I never left. But that conveniently ignores the fact that I did leave. That I'm different now. I worked to survive in Anglion, and I've grown accustomed to it. Being of use is something I enjoy. I would rather pursue a career that means something to me than one I stumbled into out of necessity. And having spent so long away from the empire, I find myself minded to see more of it."

"You could travel. I'm sure your father could afford to support you."

"Assuming I was willing to let him. Which I'm not. I will stand on my own two feet. And I want to do some good in the world. Anglion is an example of what can happen when politics and power go wrong. It warped generations of Anglions and eventually upturned the entire country. I believe it is better to not let that happen elsewhere. That the emperor's power does good rather than only benefitting Illvya. That is what interests me in the corps. I would like to help the empire become better."

There was curiosity in the colonel's eyes now. "That is not a small ambition."

"Are women supposed to have only small ambitions? You are a colonel in the Imperial mages. I can't imagine you got here by lacking the will to succeed. I wouldn't say Imogene has small ambitions either. She invented a ship that can fly through the air. Something that will change the empire, I think. But it needs to change it for the better. So it will take care and consideration to spread that idea safely. And that's just one invention. There are changes and developments every day that could aid everyone. And there are disagreements and squabbles and people who would seek to use power for their own ends. Those need to be kept under control, lest we end up with death and disruption like Anglion."

She fell silent, a little surprised at her speech.

Honore regarded her with something like approval. "That was a good answer. Too many people view politics as a path to power rather than a way to help. If you said as much to His Imperial Majesty, then I can see why he likes you."

"Thank you," Chloe said, unsure what else to say. Perhaps she should have said the same thing to Aristides, but they had spoken of chains and fate instead. Found an unexpected moment of understanding. Not that she wanted to share it. A conversation with the emperor was private.

"It's not all excitement and adventure," Colonel Brodier said. "The travel can be long, tedious, and uncomfortable, and, if I'm honest, so can some of the diplomacy."

"I am not looking for sword fights and skullduggery, Colonel," Chloe said. "And I am good at detail and seeing things through. I think I could serve the empire well, should you give me the chance."

"And if you don't like it?"

"Well, I imagine I would do what many soldiers have done before me. Give my service until the end of my term, then part company and find another path. You needn't worry that I would go running to the emperor, asking to be released from duty. I don't know him that well. And I believe in paying what I owe and keeping my word. I wouldn't shirk."

Honore's brows were only a few shades darker than her hair, but they arched nicely. "No, I don't think you would. All right, Madame de Montesse. Let me speak to the Academe, see how they assess your skills. If I am happy with what they have to say, and if you are happy to do whatever remedial training is considered necessary, then I believe we can come to an agreement. You'll be a lieutenant. A junior one. That's the best I can offer you. There will be some grumbling that you're taking a spot in the corps without time served elsewhere as it is, so giving you a higher rank would only add to the problem."

Chloe pressed her lips together to stop the smile that wanted to spread across her face. The colonel didn't need to be grinned at. Save the excitement and celebration for when she was safely away from the barracks. "That is perfectly fine with me. I had no expectations of a high rank. I'll work hard for you, Colonel. I want to earn my place."

Colonel Brodier nodded. "Good. I will see that you do."

✧ ✧ ✧

Chloe looked at the message one of the clerks had just handed her, and her stomach tightened uneasily. It was only her third day in the mages. Only a little more than three weeks since her meeting with the emperor.

The time had passed so quickly the days had blurred together. She'd spent most of her days at the Academe, practicing with Madame Simsa and several of the other venables, and her nights at home, studying more about the history of the corps, except for a few dinners spent with Imogene and Jean-Paul, where she had thrown politeness to the winds and grilled them both relentlessly about life in the army.

And then, in the blink of an eye, it had been her first day. She'd spent most of it, and most of the two days since, completing paperwork of her own and then filing paperwork for one of the captains, in between listening to one of the older lieutenants give her several well-rehearsed speeches on the basics she needed to know as a new recruit.

There hadn't been time for her to mess up yet.

So why was she being summoned to Colonel Brodier's office?

Hoping she didn't look as worried as she felt, she smiled her thanks at the clerk, poked her head in to tell the captain she had to go see Honore, and then, when he waved her away, headed for the colonel's office. She'd only gotten about halfway when she met Honore coming in the other direction.

"Ah, Lieutenant de Montesse, there you are. Walk with me."

"Good afternoon, Colonel. Where are we going?" She quickened her pace as Honore set off again. The colonel was moving fast. She looked as though she'd had a busy day, some blonde hair escaping her neat crown of braids to curl around her face, her fingers smudged with ink.

"We have a meeting with Major du Laq."

Imogene? "We do?" The question popped out before she could stop it.

The colonel glanced at her, smiled briefly. "Don't look so nervous, Lieutenant. You're not in any trouble. How have your first days been?

"Busy, sir," Chloe said. "But interesting."

"Good. You'll be happy to know they are about to become more so. You are being assigned to a mission."

Chloe gaped at her. Then recovered and snapped her jaw shut again. "Sir?"

Honore's mouth quirked. "I'm sure I don't have to tell you that this is unusual."

"No, sir."

"Good. Then I will get straight to the point, as we have no time. We're sending a mission to Andalyssia."

Andalyssia? Chloe managed not to gape with an effort, clenching her jaw shut. But some of her shock must have shown on her face.

"The king is getting married," Honore said as they reached Imogene's office. "Illvya needs a presence at the celebrations." She opened the door without knocking.

Chloe followed her into the room, mind racing. Andalyssia didn't have a permanent ambassador. Elenia, the country which lay at the base of the Eissgora—the vast northern mountain range that constituted most of Andalyssia—did. But Andalyssia, one of the last countries to join the empire, had negotiated not to have one.

Imogene stood to greet them, moving out from behind her desk, not all surprised to see them. How long had she known about this? "Colonel. Lieutenant. Good morning." Her mouth quirked briefly in Chloe's direction.

"Major, thank you for seeing us. I appreciate your assistance."

Assistance? Was Imogene coming, too?

"I'm happy to help, Colonel. Why don't we sit and talk about what needs to happen?"

The three of them arrayed themselves around the small table tucked in one corner of the office.

"So, Andalyssia?" Imogene said. "It's true?"

"The king is getting married," Honore replied. "That's no secret. The emperor needs to be represented."

"The Elenian ambassador can't attend?" Chloe asked.

"The Elenian ambassador will attend the wedding itself. But he is needed in Elenia, and the celebrations go on for over a month. Besides which, this is a wedding of a king. Illvya wishes to indicate its respect."

Meaning, Chloe thought, that there wasn't a chance that Aristides would travel to a country that had tried to assassinate his wife, so instead he would send a herd of diplomats to make the king feel important.

"Is it more than just the wedding?" she asked.

Colonel Brodier raised an eyebrow.

Imogene laughed. "You're getting the hang of this. Illvyan and Andalyssia have mining treaties to renegotiate. Always a touchy business."

If anyone knew about the touchiness of Andalyssia, it was Imogene.

"The wedding means there will be a number of rites and ceremonies and parties where someone with your experience at court will be valuable, Lieutenant," Colonel Brodier said. "We don't have any other junior lieutenants available right now who hold a title."

"Mine is barely a title. A courtesy honorific. If you want a title, Imogene should go."

Imogene shook her head. "Oh no. They need me for the navire project. I can't head off into the wilds just at the moment."

"Whereas you were married to an aristo and are familiar with royal protocols," Honore cut in. "We can, presumably, rely on you not to fumble the social events where we will be out of uniform. The Andalyssians take protocol quite seriously."

Chloe wanted to protest that she knew nothing of the Andalyssian court, but she clamped her mouth shut. Qualified or not, she wasn't going to ruin this chance for herself before she even began.

"Which is where I come in," Imogene said. "You'll need a wardrobe. There isn't time to have it all made, so Helene is going to alter some of my dresses for you."

That implied there was going to be either an inordinate number of gowns or that they were leaving soon. Or maybe both. "How long until we leave?" Goddess. Her mother was going to have a fit.

"In four days," Colonel Brodier said. "Short notice, I know, but that is the nature of the job sometimes. The major tells me you're a quick study, and you clearly have a talent for adapting to countries where things may be more...old-fashioned. So, you have what we need. Quite the opportunity to show us what you can do."

"I—"

Honore held up a hand. "I realize you have barely begun your training. We can continue while we travel, but you're going to be thrown in somewhat under prepared. Which is also the nature of the job. There will be a number of background briefings over the next few days, but as Major du Laq says you will need to be present for these wardrobe shenanigans, she has kindly offered to teach you about Andalyssia herself. That way your time won't be wasted. I'll have the other briefing papers sent to your home—you haven't moved into quarters, if I recall?"

"No, sir." It wasn't compulsory for officers to live at the barracks, and the Matins' house in Haut Charmant was a quick enough journey via portal. Chloe had decided that staying at home for at least a few more months might make it easier for Ana. So much for that plan.

"Good. So we'll send those, but you can report to Major du Laq in the morning. Tomorrow afternoon, you'll have to come back here for the reveilé, but otherwise, you're under the major's command temporarily."

Chloe nodded, still slightly stunned.

"You don't have a problem with a reveilé, do you?" the colonel continued.

Chloe shook her head. "No. I hadn't really thought about it." Where they could, diplomats usually studied languages. Chloe knew Anglion and Illvyan and had a smattering of Kessian, the language spoken in Kesseret, one of Illvya's largest neighbors. She had intended to work on improving that first and then decide which others to add. But sometimes, like now, it seemed, there wasn't time for the old-fashioned way. When there was a need to learn a language fast, then a reveilé was the answer. A sanctii who understood something of the language shoving that knowledge into a mage's brain via magic. A process she had never before needed to undertake. A process she understood to be somewhat painful.

"If time allowed, we would give you a chance to get the basics an easier way," Honore said. "But unless you have an exceptional skill for language that you failed to mention, then I'm afraid you'll be joining most of us in using the reveilé." She shrugged. "We are fortunate that we have two sanctii who have spent sufficient time in Andalyssia to have learned the language well enough to make it possible. Their experience is a few years out of date, but Andalyssia is not a society that changes rapidly, so it should be enough to get us by. We'll have language practice on the journey, too. That will have to be enough. Most of the Andalyssian nobles speak Illvyan, so we will be able to make ourselves understood. But we also need to be able to understand the things they don't want us to."

Chloe nodded. That was a lesson she'd learned from Anglion. It had been frustrating and scary to be surrounded by people speaking a language she knew little of, and she'd worked hard to learn Anglish as fast as possible. "I understand, sir," she said. "Is there anything else?"

"No. You have your orders, Lieutenant. And an opportunity. I expect you to do well with both."

In other words, don't complain and don't fuck it up and this will be good for your career. She caught Imogene's eye, and her friend nodded encouragingly.

"Yes, Colonel," she said. "I understand. I won't let you down."

CHAPTER 10

"**M**y lord, another briefing packet has arrived."

Kristof hovered in the doorway of Lucien's office, looking somewhat disheveled. Lucien knew how he felt. Since Aristides had ordered him to Andalyssia, he had spent far too many hours locked in this room, trying to organize the estate for three months, file any outstanding paperwork with the judiciary, and reread his case notes from the trial of the Ashmeister Elannon as well as everything else about the history of Illvyan-Andalyssian relations he could get his hands on.

It added up to a mountain of reading and sending Fidel and Kristof in all directions to deliver orders, fetch various other servants, field questions, and help him pack. None of the three of them had slept more than six hours a night in a good week or so.

At least Colonel Brodier hadn't insisted on him having a reveilé. He'd learned Andalyssian that way once before. Luckily, he had a good head for languages and seemed to have retained most of it. Which had come in handy when he'd discovered some documents in the palace's archives relating to the mining treaties that were actually written in Andalyssian.

Even Kristof's good humor seemed to have slipped as he stared down at the leather-bound bundle of papers in his hands.

"Did the messenger say it was urgent?" Lucien asked. He wasn't sure he was capable of reading another word. And he only had about twenty minutes before he'd promised to present himself back in his bedroom so his valet and Fidel could finalize his packing.

"No, my lord," Kristof said.

Well, that was a relief. It could wait until he was onboard the damned navire. He intended to spend as much of the journey as possible in his cabin, finishing his preparation and, hopefully, catching up on his sleep.

"Put it in the valise that's going to my cabin, then," he told Kristof. "Then you can take the rest of the night off. I don't think there's anything more to be done here. Just make sure you do what Fidel tells you while I'm away, yes?"

"Yes, my lord." Kristof smiled at him. "I will."

The lad had been disappointed that Lucien wasn't taking any servants with him. But he could tie his own damned cravats, and the palace at Deephilm would provide him any services he needed for laundry and such. And Colonel Brodier would have plenty of junior officers and ensigns eager to assist.

He watched Kristof do an about-face and leave. Then he sat to check his notes again, making sure there was nothing he absolutely needed to deal with before he departed. Ten minutes later, he was satisfied there wasn't. He shoved the papers back into a neat enough pile. Fidel would tidy up his office while he was away.

His hand froze as he reached automatically for the heavy bronze paperweight to lay on top of them. The stylized raven had been a birthday present from Chloe and Charl. The one reminder he'd allowed himself.

He'd considered sending Chloe a note to inform her he would be out of town for a time and that she was perfectly safe socializing in the capital and moving around the barracks at the palace—he'd made sure not to go there since he'd heard she'd joined the mages—but common sense had thought better of the impulse. He doubted she'd appreciate any sort of contact from him. And the rumor mill would inform her that he was away soon enough.

Perhaps two month's distance was just what he needed, and when he returned, he would have regained some sanity when it came to her. By then she might also be away on a mission, giving him even more time to deal with his unruly heart.

Perhaps. But somehow, he knew that was as unlikely as the brass raven taking flight.

Chloe gazed up the gangplank of the navire d'avion, stomach turning uneasily. The steep boards were no different to any ship she'd ever boarded, but this one didn't sail on water. Four days was barely enough time to reconcile herself to the fact that she was actually going to Andalyssia, let alone to traveling on a ship that flew through air to get there.

One of Imogene's creations. She trusted her friend's abilities, and Imogene had reassured her several times that the navire was safe, but the reality was still daunting.

The navire would save them weeks of travel. The alternative was travel by charguerre. Magically powered iron carriages drawn by magically powered iron oxen were designed to be tough and fast, not luxurious. Bone-rattling was the politest term Imogene used for them. So a month of discomfort versus a week trusting her best friend's skills as a mage ingenier and the strength of the mage and sanctii teams who would power the flight. She'd wanted adventure. She was about to have one.

An ensign bustled up and started checking the labels pasted on her trunks. There was an embarrassing number of them.

Gowns took up far more space than uniforms, and the frantic work of Helene's team of seamstresses meant Chloe now had more dresses fit for a royal wedding and its associated festivities than normal clothes. But apparently there must have been advance warning of the amount of baggage she would be bringing, as the ensign didn't bat an eyelid, just ticked the trunks off, asked which one she wanted taken to her cabin, and pointed her toward the gangplank.

She hefted the bag on her shoulder and tightened her grip on the other small leather case she carried—full of medicinal herbs and other sundry magical supplies. Overkill, perhaps, when the mission had any number of fully trained earth witches, but she liked to be prepared.

Besides, she still had the lingering edges of the dire headache caused by the reveilé, and she'd rather treat that herself than ask one of the others.

The gangplank swayed slightly beneath her feet but seemed sturdy enough. Still, she tightened her grip on her travel case. It contained, amongst other things, a small fortune's worth of Imogene's jewels. She didn't want those tumbling into the water.

That would hardly be an auspicious start to her journey to Andalyssia.

Andalyssia.

It still seemed unreal. Imogene had told her as much as she knew of the place while Chloe was engulfed in a whirlwind of fittings. Though Imogene had tried her best to stay neutral, occasionally Chloe caught a worried expression on her friend's face, and her commentary had leaned heavily to the history of Illvya's tense relationship with the Andalyssians.

Of all the countries that made up the empire, the Andalyssians had been the most fractious for over a decade now. They hadn't outright rebelled since one of the Ashmeisters had attempted treason, but they still did their best to maintain as much secrecy and autonomy over their country as they could.

She didn't blame them for that. Empires came from

conquest, after all, and even if that conquest had been long ago, and even if the empire did seem to operate to benefit everyone these days, she understood the resentment that came with having choices taken away or life turned on a whim so that the ground crumbled beneath your feet.

When it came to a whole country, she could understand that that hurt would not dissolve quickly. Particularly if there were those within the country who still wanted to keep it fresh, as apparently the older generations of Andalyssians did.

"Lieutenant de Montesse, welcome aboard," Captain Theisse said as she crested the gangplank and stepped onto the deck itself. "You're in cabin 10. You're sharing with Lieutenant Olivier." He pointed behind him at an open doorway situated beneath the upper deck where, like on a ship, the wheel used to steer the navire was housed.

The sight of it set a fresh wave of nerves loose in her gut.

Goddess. She didn't even know all the terminology for a ship's parts. What was she doing? But too late to change her mind now. "Lieutenant Olivier. Yes, sir."

She'd met Giane Olivier on her first day.

A fresh-faced twenty-three-year-old, who'd only been in the mages six months herself. She'd seemed smart and keen and boundlessly cheerful.

Chloe had once been smart and keen and boundlessly cheerful, too. Maybe Giane would rub off on her. She was going to have to get used to bright young things in the mages outranking and out-experiencing her at every turn.

"You're not scheduled to be one of the navire crew," Captain Theisse continued. "Colonel Brodier wants you focused on learning the briefing materials. So get yourself settled and stay put while we get underway. That's scheduled for about an hour from now. Once we're underway, dinner will be in the mess hall at six."

In other words, make herself scarce until then. Fine with her. She had no particular desire to watch the ship lift off. Something about it just seemed unnatural, despite Imogene's reassurances.

"Yes, sir," she said again.

Skirting around him, she made her way across the deck, moving carefully as the navire swayed slightly in the water. They were designed to land in water or on land, and the changes to their keels to enable that meant they sat heavy in the water. Or so Imogene had said.

Chloe had been too busy with everything else she'd needed to do in the last four days, not to mention fighting her headache, to take in the technical explanations. She'd just nodded at Imogene and focused on not being stabbed with too many pins while trying to practice Andalyssian in her head.

Having a language poured into one's mind by magic was an odd experience. Strange words floated across her thoughts regularly, but she didn't know what all of them meant. She had the vocabulary but not yet the context.

Which seemed to also neatly sum up her current feelings about the mission overall. She knew some of the theory of what she was supposed to do, but she was about to sink or swim when it came to putting it into practice.

If only Imogene was coming with her.

But no. Imogene had her own duties, and Chloe had wanted adventure and to see the empire. A journey all the way across it met that definition, even if she hadn't been expecting to cover so much of the continent at once.

She made her way across the deck, avoiding the black-clad crew who all seemed intent on doing various tasks with practiced efficiency.

Chloe's experience of ships was limited, most of it gained on her journeys to and from Anglion. Her father had taken them on vacations over the years, but they'd usually traveled overland to Kesseret or Sasskine. And that had been before her mother fell ill. There'd been no pleasure travel after that. Ana had been too frail. There had been trips to various temples and retreats for treatment, but those were accomplished by slow, cautious carriage rides rather than by ship.

Imogene warned her that some people could get airsick as they did seasick. Chloe's stomach hadn't much been bothered by sea travel, but she'd prepared some stomach soothing teas just in case. And hunted through her earth magic textbooks for the section on charms against such things.

The door that led below deck was narrow and not much taller than her. The men on the mission would spend half their days ducking to go in and out. Inside, the ceiling was low and the light came from earth lamps, which was one reassuring thing. Safer than naked flames on a wooden ship flying through the air. She followed the stenciled signs on the wooden walls down a steep short staircase to the first of the lower decks and, from there, along to her cabin.

Cabin 10 was small, with a set of small bunk beds. Giane wasn't there, nor was there any sign of any of her things, so Chloe claimed the lower bunk. Let the younger woman clamber up and down. She might have more time in the corps than Chloe, but Chloe had the experience to know that sometimes it was better to take what you wanted.

She unpacked her bags into one of the wooden chests bolted to the floor by the foot of the bunks and hung a few things in the small armoire likewise bolted to the wall. There was a small table similarly fastened to the floor with lockable drawers underneath the single round window, or porthole, maybe. She put her notebook and leather folder of briefing papers into the top one, locked it, and pocketed the key.

There being little else to do, given she didn't want to look out the window and her trunk was still somewhere else, she sat on the bed and tried to calm her nerves.

The journey wasn't going to take more than a week, if the winds cooperated. They would make several overnight stops for rest and to deliver mail and other official news and such before they eventually landed in Elenia, the country bordering Andalyssia.

Elenians were more friendly toward the empire than the mountain nation, so it had been deemed safer to leave the navire there. The last stage of the journey into the Eissgora would involve the charguerres Imogene disliked so much.

But now, best not to think of that. One step at a time or she would be overwhelmed.

The cabin didn't offer much scope for entertainment. It seemed risky to pull out the briefing papers until they were safely in the air. Otherwise, she might just end up chasing them around the room, should the takeoff not go smoothly.

But she had brought a few novels in her travel bag, so she retrieved one of those and retreated to the bed, stomach twisting. Imogene had recommended the author when Chloe first returned, and she'd enjoyed the first book—a satisfying mix of adventure and romance—she'd tried, so she'd purchased more to bring with her for when she required distraction. Like now. She wanted to be a diplomat, but that didn't mean she couldn't be a little daunted until she found her feet. It was normal. It was no different to the first few days after she'd agreed to marry Charl or the few days before her wedding or the first few months in Anglion. Nerves would fade with time as she became familiar with her new circumstances.

She'd only read a few pages when Giane arrived. They made small talk as she unpacked. She, too, retreated to her bunk for the takeoff, after reassuring Chloe that there really was nothing to worry about. As she had done this before, Chloe made herself try to believe her. Imogene had created these things, she reminded herself sternly. The emperor had flown in one. It was safe.

In the end, it was uneventful. The navire jerked a little, and then there was a sensation not quite like anything else Chloe had ever experienced as they rose into the air. And once they stopped climbing, the shallow angle of the vessel becoming flat once more, there was little besides a gentle bobbing from time to time, the same as a ship on a relatively smooth sea.

"See, nothing to worry about," Giane said, climbing back down from the bunk. She walked over to the window and peered out, one hand fiddling with the long braid that hung down the back of her uniform. "Come and see."

"I'm fine," Chloe said. Better to take some time to get used to the thought of all that empty air beneath her before she actually saw it.

"You don't like heights?" Giane inquired, turning back.

"I'm not sure. I've rarely had to deal with them."

"You never climbed the Raven Tower at the Academe?"

"The Raven Tower is slightly less than fifty feet. And it's solid. And there are quite substantial parapets preventing one from falling off the edge." She'd never considered the Raven Tower to be too high, that much was true. So maybe it wasn't so much the height but the lack of anything between the navire and the ground far below that was so unsettling. But it was another thing she would get used to.

"The navire has railings," Giane said with a smile. "And if it gets rough, there's a harness and rope system. No one's fallen over the side yet." Her expression softened. "Sorry, I won't tease you. At least you're not puking like the last lieutenant I shared with. That wasn't fun. Of course, the weather was rougher, but still...."

Chloe didn't want to think too hard about puking. So far her stomach seemed untroubled, and she hoped it would remain so. It wouldn't do to be "the new lieutenant who vomited all the way across the empire." That wouldn't convince anyone who was already skeptical about her being included on this mission that she was qualified to be here. "I'm feeling fine. It doesn't bother you?"

Giane shook her head. "Not so far. And my head no longer hurts after that bloody reveilé, at least." She shivered. "I'm not sure I'll get used to that any time soon."

Chloe nodded in sympathy. "Me either. But it's part of the job. And I have teas and things if your head bothers you again. Or your stomach." Giane was a blood mage with some skill in water as well, judging by the black streaks in her brown hair, but there was no hint of red to indicate any strength in earth.

"Earth witches are handy that way," Giane said, smiling again. She peered out the window again. "Are you sure you don't want to look?"

"Where was your last mission?" Chloe asked, firmly changing the subject. If they were to be bunkmates for days, they might as well get to know each other a little.

"The Faithless Isles," Giane replied. "Somewhat warmer than where we're headed now."

"Just about everywhere in the empire is warmer than Andalyssia," Chloe agreed. She'd been provided with winter uniforms, including an impressive wool cloak lined with fur. Imogene had advised her to wear layers and presented her with woolen and silk underthings that were finer than anything the army provided. Along with extra woolen socks and advice on warming charms. "The weather in the north will be interesting."

Giane shivered a little. "I grew up in Sasskine. I'd hardly seen snow until I came to Lumia. I'm not looking forward to freezing half to death in Andalyssia. The temperatures are dire. And it's still only autumn. At least we'll be out of there before winter proper hits."

"Yes, but it's Andalyssia." There was no farther north to go in the empire and few countries as mysterious. Though why they wanted to hold a royal wedding at a time of year where the weather would be growing increasingly worse was part of that mystery. But traditions were hard to argue with. Apparently their seers set the date. Seers. More mysteries. "We're lucky to be chosen."

"I guess," Giane said. "We just better hope we're more successful than some of the previous missions. No one wants to come home in disgrace. And a royal wedding in a country so...traditional seems rife with chances to break some obscure point of etiquette and cause a scandal."

"We just have to pay attention and listen to what the others tell us to do," Chloe said firmly. "Junior lieutenants aren't expected to be front and center." She didn't know if that was going to be strictly true in her case. Not if Colonel Brodier had been serious about Chloe attending all the wedding festivities. "I know there was a less-than-ideal mission a long time ago, but there's no reason for that to happen again. From what I heard, the captain in charge was an idiot and dragged all the others down with him. Colonel Brodier is not an idiot."

She wasn't going to mention that she knew one of the people who'd been on that mission. Most of the delegation knew she was friends with Major du Laq, but she didn't intend to bring the subject up if they didn't. Imogene didn't like talking about her ill-fated early mission, so it wasn't as though she knew much about it anyway.

Lucien had been to Andalyssia, too, in the wake of the Elannon scandal. He'd been tight-lipped when he'd returned. And he was the last person in the empire she would seek out for advice now.

She'd avoided him successfully in the army's section of the palace complex as well, so far. The judicial arm of the mages had its own building closer to the palace than most of the other barracks. Closer to be at the emperor's beck and call perhaps. Or maybe to be summoned to the dungeons at a moment's notice.

She shivered a little at the thought, then pushed it away. She had no reason to ever become familiar with the dungeons and no intention of ever getting to know how the judicial corps did their work. She'd had enough experience of courts and trials for a lifetime. Diplomats rarely had to give evidence in public. And if they did, it would be a ranking officer. The rest of them wrote reports and stayed out of sight. Which suited her perfectly well. And now she was far above Lumia and putting miles between her and Lucien de Roche with every passing hour. That was a cheering thought.

"Tell me about the Faithless Isles," she said to Giane. "Tell me everything."

They managed to pass the time from the navire ascending until the bells started to ring to signal the change of the hour on this subject. In fact, Giane's descriptions of pristine beaches and handsome dark-skinned men and warm nights had been delightful. Though also underscoring that their current destination was likely to be a quite different experience.

"Dinner," Giane said happily when the bells fell silent. "Good, I'm starving."

Chloe's stomach was starting to rumble, too. Her nerves had mostly gone now that she was underway and knew she could get along with her roommate. She'd spent so little time sharing living quarters with other people over the last ten years that she wasn't sure how she'd react to sharing such a small room. But Giane was funny and easygoing, and it seemed likely that they would get along well enough.

They made their way to the mess hall, Giane leading the way with confidence. The Imperial army still only had a few navires, and so far all of them had been built to Imogene's initial design, which in turn had been based on the medium-sized courier ships the navy used for ferrying small delegations or important passengers around in the past, or so Imogene had informed her.

"Know one of them, know them all" had been her exact words. Giane had repeated them as she'd led the way from their cabin. Which was useful, to know it was true. It made it simpler to think that if they changed vessels, Chloe would still be able to find her way around. A small piece of confirmation to start building her own confidence in this new venture.

But that pleased sense of hopeful confidence only lasted as long as it took to step through the doors of the mess hall and realize the man seated to Colonel Brodier's right at the head of the dining table was Lucien.

CHAPTER 11

Her first instinct was to turn on her heel and run. Swiftly followed by the realization that there was nowhere to run *to*.

She could hardly fling herself over the edge of the navire. The mages who kept the damned thing aloft couldn't catch her midair and save her. Instead, she froze in place, staring at Lucien like a rabbit who spotted a fox.

What in the name of the goddess is he doing here?

He didn't notice her at first, his attention on his plate as he buttered a roll. Until Colonel Brodier said mildly, "Don't stand there blocking the doorway, Lieutenant de Montesse. Take your seat and eat before it gets cold," and Lucien's head snapped up a shade too fast.

Their eyes met, his flaring wide for the blink of an eye, the wild green of them piercing. He held her gaze a few seconds too long before he composed himself and looked away. Somehow she managed to make her legs move and walked to the closest empty chair, sat, and tried to remember how to behave like everything was normal. Her hands moved by rote, laying her napkin over her lap and then reaching for water as her mind whirled.

Lucien? Lucien was on this mission. On this navire. How?

And why had nobody mentioned it to her? She racked her brain for whether there'd been a full list of the personnel in any of the briefing notes. But no, they'd been full of Andalyssian political history, not logistics other than information about when to report to the navire.

She hadn't really thought about who she would be working with on the mission, too swept up in the unexpectedness of being chosen at all, and too new to the corps to make any educated guesses. She hadn't even met most of the corps yet.

It had never occurred to her that Lucien might be going. He wasn't even in the corps. Imogene couldn't have known either. She would have told Chloe.

Long years of practice at hiding her feelings got her through the dinner. The food was hot, but beyond that, she didn't notice anything about it, eating only because it would draw attention not to. Giane sat on her right, and the senior lieutenant, Bertrand Rennie, opposite her. She concentrated on them, avoiding any reason to look to the head of the table. She pretended to drink the wine served but mostly sipped water, wanting to keep a clear head as her thoughts continued to reel.

What the hell was happening? Lucien here? On this mission? Why?

As one of the Truth Seekers sent to Andalyssia after the Ashmeister Elannon incident, it seemed unlikely that he would have won himself many friends there. So why was he included in what was supposed to be a goodwill mission to show the new king support?

Was there more to the mission than she'd been told? It was entirely possible. She was brand-new and wouldn't be told everything. But if she was going to be doing more than merely the usual junior lieutenant things of note-taking and organizing and being a dogsbody as needed, if she was to attend the balls and ceremonies and speak with the members of the Andalyssian court, shouldn't she know if they had another agenda?

Maybe she was yet to be briefed.

Or had Aristides had a hand in this? She had no idea why the emperor would be keen to throw her into Lucien's company, but neither could she imagine that the emperor didn't know the precise history between them. Truth Seekers were rare, and they almost all worked for him.

Illvyan aristos committing treason were rare, too. So, no. She had no doubt that Aristides knew exactly who had prosecuted her husband's case.

Was he trying to mend fences between them? Or was there something else at play? Some connection to Charl?

She sipped water again as the next course was served, her throat dry.

Maybe she was being ridiculous. Maybe Aristides couldn't care less about her, and he had needed a Truth Seeker on this mission, and Lucien had been the one who was available. Regardless of how he had come to be on the mission, he was. And she had to spend the next few months in close quarters with him.

That was going to go well, considering it had taken approximately fifteen minutes at Imogene's ball for his company to nearly undo her.

She risked a glance in his direction, keeping her face turned toward Lieutenant Rennie opposite.

Curse her luck, he was looking her way. She flicked her attention back to her plate. Had he noticed? Surely he had. Ugh.

He didn't miss much, Lucien. Of the three of them, he had the best mind for detail and precision. A natural inclination, honed by his Academe training and his choice of profession. Now he was a marq, too, who had to remember the intricate details of an entire estate to look after it and his people. He never did anything halfway, so she could only imagine he'd worked even harder on improving his organization and attention to detail. Useful traits for a diplomat, she supposed.

Damn the man.

What was he doing here?

Why did a mission to Andalyssia require a Truth Seeker?

Thankfully the colonel didn't drag the meal out for much longer than was necessary. She made introductions, which Chloe was grateful for. Putting names to faces was helpful. Though there were also more of the delegation who were currently above deck, on duty. The teams of blood mages paired with water mages and their sanctii who powered the navire's flight stood watch in three teams at a time. So at least six faces missing from the table, all of them ranking officers. The Imperial mages didn't really have enlisted men, their lowest rank being ensign. When the mages needed muscle, they drew from the regular army.

After dessert, Colonel Brodier dismissed them back to their freedom for the evening. Chloe had planned to explore the ship, but now that she knew she might randomly bump into Lucien, that idea had lost any appeal. Tempting to claim an upset stomach and retire to her cabin, but that was complicated when she'd just eaten an entire meal, not to mention sharing a room. Giane would see through a ruse soon enough, and then Chloe would have to deal with questions she didn't wish to answer.

Dammit. She was going to have to find a smaller group and socialize and hope Lucien didn't join them. But who?

While she dithered, most of the others cleared the room. If she didn't move, she was going to be alone with Colonel Brodier and Lucien anyway. She turned and hurried out of the dining room, listening to see if she could determine where the others had gone.

She hadn't gotten very far when she heard footsteps behind her.

"Lieutenant, wait."

Lucien. *Damn it.* Not only could she not avoid the man, but he also outranked her. She couldn't ignore him and keep walking. She took a moment to compose her expression and then turned. "My lord Truth Seeker."

In the low-ceilinged corridor, he seemed too large. Too solid. Imperial black shouldn't have suited him, but somehow it always had. It highlighted the planes of his face and the depth of green in his eyes. Just then it also highlighted tense shoulders and a tight mouth. "Am I to guess that you didn't know I was on this mission?"

"Am I to guess that you didn't know *I* was on this mission?"

"I didn't," he said shortly. "I'm not in the habit of checking on the junior officers. Besides which, I'm not part of the corps. Personnel is Colonel Brodier's job. I've worked with her before, so I saw no reason to inquire." He looked down at her, and she wasn't entirely sure if it was frustration or irritation tightening his jaw. "I had heard that you joined the mages."

He had? Goddess. Army gossip and court gossip. Both moved faster than a sanctii.

"But that was barely a week ago," Lucien continued. "It's unusual for such an inexperienced officer to be chosen for a long mission so soon." His mouth flattened briefly. "But I guess the emperor would see your experience as useful to get us through this damn wedding."

Did that mean he didn't think her experience was useful? "Are you questioning my abilities, my lord?"

"Technically, it's Major," he said. "When I'm doing this, rather than directly working on a case, it's less confusing if we stick to ranks. And no, I do not question your abilities, Lieutenant. I know you, remember?"

"You knew the girl I was long ago," Chloe said tightly. "Do not think you know me, my—Major de Roche."

"Well, it seems we will be getting to know each other again, to some extent, during this mission," he said, his voice equally tense. "We have to work together. So we have to be civil. I will not seek you out, but I can't avoid you entirely. If you're not going to be able to work with me, then you need to let me know. I can speak to Colonel Brodier. We will be landing in Bonaroi tomorrow with some mail. You can be excused from the mission. It would only take you a few days to return to Lumia via the mail carriages if there's no official transport heading for the city."

She stared at him. Did he truly think that was an option? "If I leave this mission, it is unlikely I will ever be given another. I'm already considered an oddity because of my history, and the fact that I joined the mages so late. Not to mention, as you so kindly pointed out, I'm brand new in the corps. If I throw away this chance, I'm done. Perhaps you should return home." That was bordering on rude. And was definitely insubordinate. A lieutenant shouldn't be hissing at a major in such a small space. If anyone saw them, rumors of the exact kind she did not want would ensue.

"I was requested to join this mission by the emperor," he said. "Short of me breaking both my legs, I'm not going to be given permission to leave."

"That could be arranged," she snapped before she thought.

Lucien burst into laughter.

Oh *no*. She didn't want to see him laughing. He'd always been far too handsome when he relaxed and smiled. Once, she had made an effort to coax smiles out of him whenever she could. He was serious by nature, and his career only increased those tendencies. She hadn't like seeing him grow so solemn. His smile had always been her reward. Knowing she had reminded him that he was more than just his powers.

But that had been Lucien before. And she should take no pleasure in a smile from him now.

"Now, that," he said when he got himself back under control, "is precisely what I was talking about. Diplomats—and junior lieutenants—do not tell their comrades that they will break both their legs. At least not very often. And usually not when there is no alcohol involved."

She scowled, but he was right. She wanted to be a diplomat. She needed to control her emotions. There would be plenty of times where she had to deal with difficult people, and she needed to show them nothing she didn't want to reveal. Win them over and make them think they delighted her, if necessary.

"I can't imagine I will need to make a similar offer to

anybody else," she said. "But I apologize, that was rude of me. Perhaps, Major, if you would give me permission to retire, I can remove myself from your presence and go practice my self-restraint."

He nodded and, not wanting to give him the chance to say anything more, she turned and hurried away.

The next morning, the navire descended into Bonaroi after a breakfast during which Chloe kept her attention firmly away from the end of the table where Lucien sat with the other senior officers.

She wasn't going to quit or ask to go home, but it was something of a relief to touch down and know there would soon be more than the space afforded by the navire between the two of them.

The stop in Bonaroi was to give the mages who powered it a night of rest and to allow for the delivery of mail for the small garrison stationed in the portside town. The next leg would be longer, only one more stop before they reached Elenia and their destination. The town was in Kesseret, one of the small eastern countries closest to Illvya. It was busy and bustling, and Chloe, tasked with accompanying the colonel and Captain Theisse to speak with the commander of the garrison, drank it all in with curious eyes, an odd sort of peace descending over her.

Different streets. Different stores and houses. Different people.

Nothing with any memories of family or marriage or Anglion tied to it.

If Lucien hadn't been on the mission, it would have been just about perfect, but the unwanted awareness that he was made a small dark spot in her enjoyment of the day. All she could do was ignore it and focus on doing her job. Which was mostly to listen as Colonel Brodier and Captain Theisse spoke to the commander and discussed mundane things like provisions and the quality of roads and handed over directives from the various imperial officers.

Chloe scribbled notes and also worked on storing the information in her head. She'd been cramming on the geography and politics of the empire, and the grounding she had from her studies at the Academe had come back easily enough, but a seasoned diplomat like Colonel Brodier had to know the empire intimately. Know things like the ai-fish catches being lower than usual, as the commander was relaying, and what that meant for the farmers here who apparently used the parts of the fish discarded from human consumption for fertilizing crops.

So she paid attention.

They finished with the commander after lunch and walked back to the navire.

"Thank you, Lieutenant," Captain Theisse said as they stepped on deck. "Make sure you have a copy of those notes by the time we reach Elenia. We can send them back to Lumia then. But for now, you should head to language practice."

Damn. She'd forgotten about that part. That they would all be drilling on Andalyssian, trying to cement the language acquired by reveilé. "Will you be joining us, sir?"

He shook his head. "I've been to Andalyssia before. I had a refresher rather than the full reveilé. And I have duties to complete before we take off. But I will be joining the class for the next few days while we fly. So pay attention today."

Lucien regarded the door before him with something akin to distaste. And he was rarely troubled by such things as doors.

But today, he was troubled by many things. He'd been thankful when there had been no message for him upon landing, requesting the services of a Truth Seeker, and he'd been able to stay in his cabin for most of the morning and attempt to get his temper back under control.

He'd been trying—and failing—since the previous evening.

Not that he was angry, precisely. But he hadn't expected Chloe. Though, once he'd checked the final packet of briefing papers that he'd ignored back in Lumia, her name had been on the list of personnel the colonel had sent. So it was his own damned fault that he had been sandbagged by her presence.

He didn't blame anybody else for that.

But what was needling at him was why she had been included. The emperor, goddess damn it, was meddling. Either he was trying to put Lucien and Chloe together because he thought they had unfinished business between them or he was doing it because he thought it would be useful in another way.

Neither option sat easily. Chloe appeared to have no desire to mend fences, and he had to respect that. And if there was another reason Aristides wanted them together, then it would have been useful to know of it in advance.

But he had agreed to come on this mission. His emperor had asked, and he had, as usual, chosen to serve. Aristides owed him no explanations about personnel choices.

So, he needed to take control of himself and think of Chloe as just another junior lieutenant.

Which would be easier if Honore Brodier hadn't informed him after breakfast that Chloe would be one of the mages attending all the wedding ceremonies with him as Aristides's proxies. It made a horrible sort of sense. There weren't that many officers in the mages who were noble born. There were plenty, of course, who were experienced with courts and protocol, but given the nature of diplomats, most of them were out in various parts of the empire at any given time and not so easily recalled. Chloe was the most experienced of the younger officers when it came to courts. She was also a widow, rather than an unmarried woman, which was helpful in Andalyssia, where unmarried women were subject to more rules than married ones, and she was Lady de Montesse, for better or worse.

He suspected that she, like he did, viewed it as worse.

An opinion that wouldn't change when she learned that he would be escorting her to the balls and other celebrations surrounding the weather. Making conversation with her. Dancing with her.

The last time she'd stepped into his arms, she'd ended up fleeing the room afterward, and the stupid senseless male part of him had wanted to chase her down and not let her go, so that didn't bode well.

He gritted his teeth. He was a gentleman. A nobleman. He would respect her feelings. He could look at her dressed in whatever silks or satins or jewels she chose to drape herself in and still treat her as just another lieutenant.

He wouldn't enjoy it, but he would do it.

Two months. It wasn't forever.

Two months of frozen northern wilderness in a court of nobles who didn't welcome Illvyans and the woman who hated him.

It would just seem like forever.

He suppressed a sigh. Goddess damned duty.

Some days it was easier to bear than others. Today it was a choke chain at his throat. But he was sworn to serve, so he went where he was sent, he did his work, and he did it well.

A Truth Seeker. One of the emperor's hounds of justice, on watch for prey.

It was a speech that Maxim Girarde, the advocate general, liked to give to younger members of the judiciary. Leaning heavy on the glory and righteousness of the law. Of the rewards of being a faithful servant of the empire.

Well, Lucien had been that, but he was no dog to obey his master unthinking. And Maxim's speeches left out the reality of the work. That it often wasn't easy, and it was the very opposite of glory when his skills were truly needed. There was justice, perhaps, and the service of truth, but the tools at his disposal, the means by which he could uncover the truth if someone tried to hide it, were hardly glorious. More brutal and efficient.

He would have preferred not to have to use them at this damned wedding.

Given that he was going to have to wade back into the mess wrought by House Elannon and figure out who amongst them might be trustworthy, what he preferred didn't matter.

What mattered was securing the treaty with Andalyssia and the rule of the king. Who had been a small boy the last time Lucien set foot in his country. The old king had been a tough and ruthless mountain man who had no trouble smiting his own internal enemies, a fact proven by his holding the throne for thirty-odd years unchallenged.

But even tough and ruthless mountain men weren't immune to the vagaries of fate. King Berlund had fallen from a horse and died, and his twenty-three-year-old son had been crowned a little over a year ago. So far he had survived, but if he was to continue to do so, and to thrive, he needed a council who supported his power. The father of his bride was one of the Ashmeisters, which would help, but not enough if the priests and the seers continued to agitate about balance and House Elannon couldn't be restored.

It could all go very horribly wrong despite Lucien's magic.

The power was rare, and he still didn't know exactly why the goddess had gifted it to him when other illusioners had, it seemed, far more entertaining lives using the Arts of Air. He could do those things, too, of course, conjure illusions to delight or conceal or confuse. But he could also see truth. Not just the awareness that allowed illusioners to see through another's illusion but actual truth.

And in Andalyssia, the truth was complicated.

As was the fact that Chloe was here.

Today he wasn't so sure about where the truth lay. Aristides had requested him to join this mission, and his orders to board the navire on the appointed date had arrived shortly after.

Last night, at dinner, she walked into the room, and Lucien had been undone all over again.

He was a thousand times a fool when it came to this woman, it seemed.

Months they had to spend now. In proximity that he was perfectly clear she didn't desire. Just as he was perfectly clear that his own preference would be different.

Which was why he was still standing outside the dining room like an idiot, regarding the door as though everything would be just fine as long as it stayed closed. During the day the room became a working part of the ship, and today he was taking his turn teaching the junior members of the delegation some of the finer points of Andalyssian.

One of whom was Chloe.

Who was going to be loathing him every moment.

He fought the urge to bang his head gently on the still new wood of the door. He had refrained from using his powers on Chloe. He didn't use them when he wasn't required to in service to the law.

But he didn't need to use them to understand how she felt about him.

He could feel the sting of her dislike in the blaze of those dark eyes and in the lines of tension in her body every time they met.

Goddess knew why they kept meeting.

But there was nothing to be done about that.

He couldn't go to Colonel Brodier with the whole troubled history he and Chloe shared. For one thing, she was probably already well aware of it. Of who Chloe was and who her husband had been and Lucien's own role in what happened to Charl. She hadn't already raised the subject, so Lucien could hardly do so.

Instead he had to find a way to do his duty and minimize the pain for both Chloe and himself.

And given he had no good answer about how he might do that, he would instead open this damn door, go inside, and see if trying to teach the snaky, smoky syllables of Andalyssian might prove a distraction.

CHAPTER 12

Of course it was Lucien.

Chloe had assumed the language classes would be led by one of the mages whose sanctii had done the reveilés. Apparently not.

That would be far too simple.

Lieutenant Plesse, who had served in the corps for several years already, stood as Lucien entered the room and threw a salute. Everyone else copied him, bumping chairs and rustling uniforms.

"Major de Roche, my lord Truth Seeker. Welcome," Lieutenant Plesse said. He sounded nervous, and for a man who had a sanctii at his side, that was unusual.

But sanctii, while not exactly common, were more common than Truth Seekers. Most people didn't cross paths with them often.

Lieutenant Plesse, Chloe had discovered last night after dinner, was, like her, from a non-aristo background. His parents owned a cloth factory in Neimes, one of Illvya's smaller cities. They'd had a few mages in the family in earlier generations, but Theo's abilities had been something of a surprise. Even more of a surprise when he turned out to be a water mage and had chosen to join the army rather than return to the family business.

Not a history which would have given him much cause to mingle with Lucien or any of his colleagues. Most of the more experienced members of the delegation would have dealt with the judicial branch from time to time, but even they looked nervous. Maybe it was because most of them weren't from noble families.

Truth Seekers, aristo or not, tended to move in the higher court circles when they weren't working. Their talent was rare enough that forming an alliance via marriage with one was an attractive proposition to a great family. Or, at least, a great family who thought they might be able to sway a Truth Seeker to work in their favor. Truth Seekers who weren't aristos like Lucien found it easy to marry well when they chose to do so.

From what Chloe knew of Lucien's unswerving allegiance to his work and the truth he had sworn to pursue, she doubted those marriages worked out as the noble families expected in terms of gaining sway over a Truth Seeker. Or future Truth Seekers, perhaps. But given there weren't many of them alive at any one time, the families seemed to think it was worth continuing to try. Lucien, born to inherit his father's title, had no ladders to climb. And he didn't use his talent for personal gain.

Or he had never done so when she had known him. She'd met a few of his colleagues, and while not all of them were as serious as him, they all seemed scrupulously honorable. And none of them complained about the burden of responsibility they bore.

Then again, they did somewhat cultivate an air of mystery about their work that made whining in public counterproductive. Or so Lucien had informed her one night when they'd all had too much campenois. He'd been embarrassed about that confession, but that didn't stop him being able to play the role with aplomb when required. And he'd had ten years to refine it since she'd last seen him at work.

Lucien's green gaze swept over the class, a smile of "relax, I'm not intending to read your minds just this moment" resting on his lips. His public face, intended to put people at ease. His eyes met hers for a moment, then moved on.

"Thank you, Lieutenant Plesse," he said. "Good afternoon, everyone. Colonel Brodier has asked me to take the lesson today. I'll admit, my Andalyssian might be a bit out of date, but I can certainly help you with the pronunciation and some context."

He looked back at Lieutenant Plesse. "Colonel Brodier also said you were the one who knew where everyone's skills are, Lieutenant. Perhaps you could give me a summary?"

Theo stood and started to do just that. Not everyone was as new to Andalyssian as Chloe. The diplomatic corps valued language skills. Illvyan had spread throughout the empire as the language of trade, but most countries retained their own languages as well. And understanding a language required more than just having it stuffed into your head by a sanctii. The fluency to navigate delicate situations required practice. So diplomats had lessons in the languages they wanted to use and studied the countries and cultures they would be working with. Chloe, who had always loved to learn—too much her father's daughter to be otherwise—had been happy to realize this when she first joined up.

A sanctioned reason to indulge her thirst for knowledge that had been somewhat stifled in Anglion. She had focused on the herb lore and medical knowledge that Ginevra had taught her and supplemented that with some history and geography when she had begun to read Anglion well enough and had money to spare for books. But she hadn't been able to dive deep into anything that might draw the temple's attention.

But now she didn't need to stay invisible, and she was, in a strange way, looking forward to the mountain of information she'd be learning if she stayed in the mages.

But that learning had barely begun. And when it came to

Andalyssian, "barely begun" was too strong a term when she could still remember the headache from the reveilé.

In Anglion, she'd learned the hard way, stumbling over words, listening to people, and reading with a notepad at hand so she could ask Ginevra for help.

Samuel, the sea captain who had taken her from Illvya to Anglion, had taught her some basics of Anglish and given her a translation of a very sparse vocabulary that had been built up from his experiences and contacts with the refugees he ferried over his years of doing so.

Over time, she'd met one or two other Illvyan refugees and learned a little more from them before she'd been able to get her hands on a dictionary. Some Anglions—mostly the military or certain members of the court—learned Illvyan, so there were books translating one language to the other to be found.

Having learned a language that way, she was curious to see how the reveilé impacted the process. How quickly would practice let her find some order to the unfamiliar words crowded into her head so she could put them to work as she was keen to do? She was less keen to find out by spending hours in a small room with Lucien. But she had no choice, so she bent her head and took notes as he ran through some practice exercises.

His voice sounded odd speaking Andalyssian, though there was something about the depth of it that suited him. It was a language of contrasts, with the drawn-out sibilants and the more pointed harsher consonants. The deeper tones of Lucien's voice smoothed out some of the contrast somehow, taming it into something slightly more familiar.

And Lucien, damn him, was a good teacher.

Of course he was. He was good at most things.

He explained the connections in the words and the rules of Andalyssian grammar easily. And after warming them up on some basics, he moved them into more advanced concepts to do with laws and contracts.

The kinds of things that diplomats needed to know. The kinds of things that were complicated enough to learn about in Illyvan, let alone understand in another language while also trying to understand how the laws might be subtly altered by a culture. The empire imposed some standard rules on its citizens, but, like languages, there were still local laws in each country based on their traditions.

The Illvyan emperors had not tried to turn an entire continent into one country, recognizing, perhaps, the futility of such a task.

But with choice came complication.

Complexity.

And a lot of words in any language to understand it all.

Lucien moved them through the lesson smoothly, and she found herself both intrigued by what he taught and distracted by the sound of his voice.

It was odd that his was the presence that kept tripping her up. Her first few weeks at home, it had been a surprise to hear her family's voices around her, but she had mostly gotten over that by the time she'd left.

But every time she heard Lucien, it was a moment of dislocation.

Perhaps because for him to be familiar, for things to be easy with him, it required Charl to be there, too. Part of the trio. One corner to the angles, the three of them supporting each other.

And Charl was gone forever. Leaving them awkward and lopsided, a gap between them too raw to mend.

Even before she considered the reason for the gap.

"Lieutenant de Montesse?" Lucien said, and she realized she had missed the question he'd asked her.

Goddess damn it.

She didn't want to make a mistake in front of him on top of everything else.

"I'm sorry, Major," she said, not quite meeting his eyes. "Could you repeat the question, please? I was busy with my notes, and I missed what you said."

"I asked how you would say 'This clause is not acceptable,'" Lucien said. His tone was mild, no hint of rebuke, but she felt herself bristling anyway as her brain raced to put the translation together.

She spoke the words, trying to wrap her tongue around the sibilants that made the language tricky. Lucien's brows lifted as she spoke, and others around the table smiled.

"What did I say?" she said, resigned to the fact that she had gotten it wrong somewhere. She was learning, she reminded herself. She was allowed to make mistakes, as much as it tweaked her pride to do so.

"You said 'This teacher is unacceptable,'" Lucien said. "I will take your review on notice, Lieutenant, and endeavor to do better." It wasn't a reprimand and was delivered with a half-smile that told her he was trying to put her at ease, but that didn't help.

"The fault is mine, Major. What should I have said?"

Lucien spoke the phrase again. "The accent on the third syllable is what is letting you down, Lieutenant. That is a tricky sound."

She repeated the phrase, and he nodded. "Better. Keep practicing, Lieutenant. Time and effort always improve things, I find."

Was he talking about her Andalyssian or the difficulty of having to deal with each other? She'd bite off her tongue before seeking clarification on that matter. So she turned her attention back to her notes and tried to pretend that Lucien was nothing more than a teacher.

✦ ✦ ✦

The class continued for nearly two hours, and Lucien seemed to be preparing to dismiss them when the door opened and Colonel Brodier and Captain Theisse walked in.

"Major," Honore said. "How go the students?"

"Well enough, Colonel. A few more days' practice and we won't be embarrassing ourselves in Deephilm."

Honore flashed a smile at that. She walked to join Lucien at the far end of the room. "All right. Practice will continue at this time each day whilst we are traveling. Anyone not without other specific duties will be here." She studied the group a moment. "And given most of you are here, I'm going to take a few minutes to brief you on something else."

A murmur of surprise—or speculation—rippled briefly around the table before everyone fell silent.

"As you know, we are attending the wedding of King Mikvel as the emperor's representatives, and we will be meeting with the Ashmeisters and the king and others to discuss the mining treaties. But we also have another task to attend in Deephilm."

Chloe's skin prickled with sudden nerves. Another task? What exactly? Lucien looked completely unsurprised by Honore's words. Was this why he was going with them?

"King Mikvel is a young king and a new king. He is dealing with his own politics as he approaches this wedding. And there are certain factions in Andalyssia that are, perhaps, taking advantage of that fact. But we don't know all the details yet. What we do know is the king has petitioned the emperor for House Elannon to be restored."

This time it was more than a murmur.

"Three years early?" Theo blurted.

"Yes. They are citing balance, making it a matter of religion as well as politics. Given what you all know from your briefings, I'm sure the difficulties become clear, and we will discuss them more as we continue our journey. But for now what you need to know is that the emperor has asked us to assess the situation and whether House Elannon has been...rehabilitated, shall we say.

We do not have overly long to come to a decision, given the religious angle. There is some danger that the priests will refuse to complete the king's marriage rites if the house is not restored. After that, all hell could break loose." Honore held up a hand before anyone else could ask another question. "This is, of course, confidential. We do not know how widely the king's request is known in the Andalyssian court. We can assess that when we get there. But until I say otherwise, you are to say nothing of this to any Andalyssian or anyone else you encounter on this trip. This particularly applies to those of you attending the court ceremonies and celebrations. Understood?"

There was a chorus of "Yes, sir" and "Yes, Colonel."

"Major de Roche will be taking the lead on this part of the mission. After we arrive, I will assign some of you to assist him as necessary. Now, I'm sure you all have things to be doing, so I will see you at dinner."

The iron fer-taureaus who pulled the charguerres waiting to take them into the mountains steamed gently in the cool morning air, the mist rising around them softening their harsh line. After a week of air travel, Chloe was glad to be off the navire, but she wasn't sure the next part of the journey was going to be particularly pleasant.

She shivered and pulled her cloak tighter as she waited with Giane. The delegation's luggage was being loaded into the charguerres, and the courtyard at the front of the Elenian embassy was organized chaos. But even with what seemed like a hundred people to-ing and fro-ing and small iron braziers set up to warm the air, it was colder than Lumia would be in the depths of winter, let alone autumn.

It would be colder still in Andalyssia, and the fact that they were proceeding with a convoy of charguerres and a squadron of soldiers was a reminder that the weather was not the only possible threat.

But her shivers were not entirely due to the weather. No, some of it was anticipation. Andalyssia was going to be strange and possibly dangerous, but it was also a challenge. Something new. A chance to find out who she was now.

She had to keep fighting a smile off her face as she stretched her hands toward the brazier. They'd arrived at Haalbrod, the Elenian border town, just before sunset the night before, so there hadn't been any chance to explore. When she'd opened the curtains in her room earlier, the view over the town to the mountains beyond had been breathtaking. The mountains were larger than any she'd ever seen. Snow-capped and mist-laden even in the morning sun. It seemed impossible that there were roads through them, let alone towns and cities nestled amongst them, but there were.

And she'd be in the largest of them by nightfall. If they ever left. They were running late, and Colonel Brodier, who stood speaking to the Elenian ambassador at the front steps of the building, was beginning to look tense. If they left too late, they'd hit darkness before they reached Deephilm, and the mountain roads at night were icy and treacherous.

But after a week on the navire, Chloe wasn't keen to immediately climb back into an even smaller box on wheels and sit for hours, so she didn't entirely mind the delay.

Eventually, the hubbub around them slowed and they were ordered into the charguerres.

"Thank the goddess," Giane said as she climbed inside the charguerre designated for the lieutenants and some of the clerks. "I hope it's warmer in here."

"It should warm up eventually, I suppose," Chloe said, settling in after her. She was mostly thankful that the seating assignments in the charguerres seemed largely based on rank and she was safely with other junior officers. Six hours bouncing in an iron box through a mountain range was one thing, but doing it with Lucien sitting across from her would have added a whole new layer of discomfort.

She was too aware of the man. Like a burr in her skin. A burr she couldn't quite pluck free, no matter how she tried. Each language class, each briefing session about House Elannon—and that was a tangle she was glad she wasn't in charge of undoing— that she spent with him only made the sensation worse.

The charguerre moved off slowly. Everyone huddled into their cloaks, the chatter that had accompanied breakfast and the preparation for them leaving dying off. Thin-skinned Illvyans, used to warm weather. Only Captain Theisse had looked mildly comfortable while they'd waited to climb into the charguerres. He claimed to enjoy the cold.

Chloe did not. Kingswell had cool winters, but not much colder than Lumia. Plenty cold enough for her. She'd piled every blanket available to her onto the bed last night and still felt the chill in the Elenian air despite the fire in her room. She would need furs or a permanent warming charm to survive Andalyssia.

Which made it a good a time to practice. She'd been too tired the previous night to try and connect with the Elenian ley lines. But she searched for them now, sending her senses down to the earth. They felt distant and slow moving, the song of them icy and distant, but after a few minutes, the chilly note changed slightly, softening somehow. Enough to let her draw a thread of power up to faintly ease the chill as the charguerres rumbled out of town.

It was good practice, too, to try and keep the connection running as they moved over the roads that were not as smooth as one might wish. But with savage winters, maintaining roads was an expensive exercise. That was one of the things that had been discussed at dinner with the Elenian ambassador.

The tone of the conversation had been that this was a familiar topic, one that came up regularly enough to be expected. It had been couched in tactful language. The complaint registered, but no action promised precisely. She had paid attention, trying to follow the dance of what wasn't being discussed as well as what was. It boiled down to a request for more money from Illvya—or perhaps a reduction in taxes paid to the empire, which would amount to the same thing—to assist with road maintenance. The Elenian ambassador was passing on the request from the Elenian Clan Hall, but Chloe got the feeling she was keen on her own behalf as well. Understandable if the woman spent a lot of time on the roads of Elenia and the mountains beyond.

She'd made an eloquent case, which Colonel Brodier had listened to gravely and then neatly avoided promising anything more than relaying the message. Lucien hadn't spoken much during the meal, though he'd played the part of attentive dinner guest well, seated between the ambassador and Honore. The Elenians had all eyed him warily, as though the black of his uniform somehow drew their eye, though it was no different to what any of them wore. Or maybe it was the raven on his collar tabs rather than the usual imperial sun, proclaiming what he was.

He hadn't seemed to notice. Perhaps it was just normal to him now, after all these years. That must grow tiring. She'd been a subject of suspicion in Anglion. Knew the scrape of unfriendly eyes across skin. The hairs that rose on the back of your neck when your instincts told you someone was watching. Worse in Anglion, where reaching for her magic to defend herself—if it had ever come to that—would have meant death.

So she could sympathize with Lucien over that. Or could if she chose to. But she wasn't going to so choose. He had been fending for himself for years. Not to mention he had the protection of his rank and power. He didn't need her to worry about him.

She snuggled deeper into her cloak and looked out the slotted window of the charguerre. The narrow sliver of glass showed only a small slice of the world outside, but a fascinating one. One that made her wish for an ordinary carriage. Not just because it would be more comfortable than the charguerre, which was built for strength and speed, not luxury, but for bigger windows to let her see this brand-new part of the world.

The charguerre moved faster than a normal carriage. That was the purpose of them. The fer-taureaus—iron bulls—that drew them were tireless, their metal bodies fueled by magic. She had never quite been able to grasp how the mage ingeniers gave the fabriques they created the spark that kept them moving, no matter how many times Imogene tried to explain it to her. Apparently she didn't think about magic in the same way as an ingenier did. And hadn't been raised by an ingenier of the non-magical kind like Imogene either.

Still, tireless wasn't the same thing as perfectly comfortable. They were winding their way over roads that climbed farther into the foothills of the Andalyssian mountains. The border between the Elenia and Andalyssia was a narrow plateau, just after the first rise of the hills. It seemed to Chloe that it would be more sensible to place it at the base of the hills instead, but no doubt there was some military advantage to where it was. She didn't like the feeling of not knowing. Preparation and a healthy degree of caution had kept her alive in Anglion.

Though perhaps a diplomat could never be truly prepared for a new place. Not on a short-term mission, at least. So she would have to learn to live with the discomfort. It was going to be part of the job, as far as she could tell.

The charguerre jolted abruptly, and Chloe winced as she bounced again Giane, seated to her right. "Sorry."

Giane shook her head. "We'll spend the entire journey apologizing if we do it every time there's a bump in the road. And this road appears to be mostly bumps."

"I guess it's hard to carve a road through mountains," Chloe said. "Maybe they sent us this way to prove the ambassador's point about maintaining the roads."

"They sent us this way as it's the only road big enough for the charguerres. But I assume they wouldn't mind if the other is demonstrated, too." She leaned forward, peering past Chloe to try and look out the window. "Anything interesting?"

"So far mostly grass and rocks," Chloe said. "If you tilt your head back, you can just see the start of the mountains above the hills."

The Eissgora were the highest mountain range in the empire. The most forbidding and deadly. Beyond them lay mostly frozen land that was largely empty. One very small clan of tribes hunted the ice lakes for fish and waternahls. They ignored the Andalyssians, who, from the empire's view, owned the land, and the Andalyssians, it seemed, mostly ignored them apart from a small amount of trading. There were no other resources in the far north to be squabbled over. Just the wealth that lay beneath the mountains, enough to keep Andalyssia powerful. They were the ones with the secrets of working the depths of the earth in the freezing cold.

Illvya needed some of what they produced. Strange to think that she was going to help make sure the treaties were working. But after Honore's announcement back in Bonaroi, it was clear that the treaties were the lesser of the two problems they'd been set.

House Elannon. Imogene had been the one to foil their attempt on the empress. It had changed her life. Now Chloe was going to be part of the next shift of that cycle. And Lucien. It felt almost inevitable, in a way. Though also near impossible. And dangerous. If House Elannon hadn't changed, if there were those within who still hated the Illvyans, then who knew what might wait them in Deephilm?

They'd tried to kill an empress. What else would they risk?

CHAPTER 13

The walled entrance to Deephilm looked ominous in the dying rays of sunlight, but Lucien was too pleased at the thought of getting out of the damned charguerre and no longer being rattled around like a child's toy to worry overmuch about a chilly reception from the Andalyssians.

He'd seen the city before, and the vast granite wall hung with the white-and-gray mountain-and-moon banners of King Mikvel Surayov looked the same. There was probably some subtle difference in the runes curving over the moon now that Mikvel was king rather than his father, but Lucien didn't read Andalyssian runes, and he was too tired to care.

If the new king had a new motto, it would be buried somewhere in his briefing papers and he could find it if needed. What concerned him was what changes had occurred—or not—behind the walls since he'd last seen those banners.

His job to find out. To make a decision that could, perhaps, start a war if it didn't fall the way the Andalyssians wanted.

It wasn't the first time in his career that he'd faced a task he didn't relish, and while he was prepared for the work, now that he had arrived, the weight of it settled over his shoulders.

The gates swung open slowly, and a squad of gray-clad guards strode out to escort them through the city. The streets still bustled with people on their way home before the darkness and cold set in for the night, and the convoy drew plenty of stares as it wound up the hill to the palace. Carved into the side of a mountain, it, too, looked ominous, oppressive, and frankly, damned cold. It had been high summer the last time he'd been here, and even then the palace had been heated to ward off the chill.

Torches burned around the forecourt, warding off the fading light. A horde of palace servants dressed in various shades of gray and black and white waited on the wide, steep steps that led up to the main entrance. He'd learned the various uniforms on his previous visit and their meanings would come back to him. For now, he looked for the man in charge as he climbed out of the charguerre behind Honore.

There. On the top step. A man dressed in the silver and white of House Surayov. Not the king himself. They wouldn't be meeting with Mikvel until morning, when there was to be a formal audience of welcome. No, this was the king's Wardmeister. Head of the palace guard and seneschal rolled into one. A role both ceremonial and practical. Mikvel didn't have a younger brother to take on the role as would be traditional, and his father had no surviving brothers, so he'd chosen the youngest of his mother's brothers. Roland Zatry, who technically belonged to House Zatry, as the dowager queen had before she married Mikvel's father, but who, as Wardmeister, was now Surayov by duty.

Lucien had a vague memory that they had met before, but Roland hadn't held any particular position of power under the old king's rule, so he had no strong recollection of the man.

Roland's face was serious but not hostile as he descended the stairs to greet them. He was fifteen years older than the king, a few years older than Lucien himself. His braided blond hair reflected the red from the torches, and the light caught the silver of an old scar across one eyebrow.

"Colonel Brodier," he said as he reached them and bowed. "Welcome to Deephilm." He spoke Illvyan, which was a relief. After six hours in the charguerre, Lucien wouldn't have been surprised if all his knowledge of Andalyssian had been rattled out of his brain entirely.

"Thank you, Wardmeister," Colonel Brodier said. "Illvya is glad of your welcome."

They continued the formalities, and Lucien listened with half an ear while he discreetly scanned the surroundings. And resisted the urge to turn around and see if Chloe had made it through the journey in one piece. Of course she had. The woman wasn't made of glass, and none of the charguerres had plunged over the edge of the mountain. She was perfectly safe. Or at least as safe as any of them were inside these walls.

She wouldn't thank him for looking.

She might thank him to mind his own business and make sure he was doing his part in this mission. Well, perhaps not thank him, but at least she would have no further reason to be disappointed in him.

If he did his job here well, that would keep her safe. Hopefully. He still wasn't entirely sure what might happen if he discovered that House Elannon weren't trustworthy. The extra squadron of soldiers they'd brought with them wouldn't save them should the Andalyssians truly turn against them. The sanctii might manage to get some of them out alive but not all.

Not that that was really any different to the reality of any diplomatic mission. Far from home and outnumbered.

He had to have faith in the power of the empire and the goodwill of the man Roland served.

Colonel Brodier finally said, "And this is Major de Roche, the Marq of Castaigne."

"My lord Truth Seeker," Roland said. "Welcome back to Andalyssia."

It seemed he was remembered. He sharpened his focus.

"Thank you, Wardmeister. My congratulations on the upcoming happy occasion."

Roland's face was about as expressive as the stone walls of the palace, giving no clue to his feelings. Presumably he was privy to the real reason Lucien was here. "Thank you, my lord." He looked past Lucien to the rest of the Illvyans. "We appreciate Illvya's support of the king." His expression lightened slightly. "Now, I think it's best if I show you all to your quarters. The journey from Elenia is never easy. And none of you are used to our weather."

In other words, "come inside, soft southerners, before you freeze to death." Though whether there was duty or concern or the desire to demonstrate that northerners were tougher behind the words was anyone's guess. Lucien wasn't going to argue. A warm room, food, and a good night's sleep and he would be a far happier man.

The Surayov palace was something of a maze, as all palaces were. Though none of the other palaces Chloe had ever been inside were carved into the side of a mountain, giving the impression that they might go on forever and ever into depths of stone and earth.

The walls were hung with tapestries and the stone-flagged floors, once they got past what she assumed were the ceremonial parts of the building and further into the private areas used for everyday things like living quarters and such, laid with layers of rugs and carpets to ward off the chill. The Wardmeister—handsome in a grim sort of way, as Giane had whispered to her back in the forecourt—escorted the delegation through the palace to the wing where they would be staying. A bevy of servants waited as Roland gave a quick explanation of the communal areas of the wing, a private dining room and several areas set up like parlors for relaxation and meetings, before handing them over to be shown to their rooms.

A short and wiry girl with ice-blonde hair and eyes the colors of grassberries came over to Chloe and Giane, introduced herself as Allita, and led the way to their rooms, moving swiftly, the heels of her gray leather boots tapping on the floor. The bedrooms ran along two corridors, and Allita took them right to the end of the longest hallway before producing two keys and handing them one each.

Chloe smiled and took hers, thanking Allita in Andalyssian. Individual rooms. A luxury she'd hoped for but hadn't expected. After a week sleeping in a tiny cabin with Giane snoring gently over her head, it was a relief to know that she would have some privacy during their stay.

Allita used another key off the ring hanging from her waist to open the second-to-last door at the end of the corridor. She held it open, ushering Giane inside and telling her she'd be with her shortly. She then unlocked the very end door and held it open for Chloe.

The air that wafted out was warmer than the corridor, and Chloe stepped inside quickly, not wanting to let the heat escape. The room had plastered walls painted dark green and lined with more tapestries. It seemed Andalyssian needleworkers must be kept busy. The floor was slate, but there were plenty of rugs. Maybe in summer the stone underfoot would be cooling, but she was glad to see she wasn't going to have to pad across it in bare feet.

There was a large double window in the far wall and lamps already burning on each wall. A fire crackled in the small grate, throwing out a surprising amount of heat. Allita crossed over and fussed with the curtains, drawing them tight across the window, hiding the last rays of light. Chloe took quick stock of the rest of the room. A large bed framed with wrought iron and piled with layers of blankets and feather quilts with a dark fur draped over the end stood in one corner, positioned out of any drafts from the window. Against the other wall sat an armoire that looked like it would just be large enough to fit all the damned gowns.

"Once your luggage is brought up, I will help you unpack," Allita said, stepping back from the window. Chloe was pleased that she could follow the girl's Andalyssian, though she suspected Allita was speaking a little more slowly than usual to be kind to a foreign guest.

"This is the bathroom," Allita continued, opening a door between the bed and armoire.

Chloe stepped through, keen to wash her hands and face after the long journey. The bathroom wasn't huge, but it was more luxurious than expected. Tiled in a riot of colors partially obscured by plants in woven hangers, it was dominated by a large tub sunk partway into the floor.

"It's warmer here than in the other room," Chloe said, puzzled. "How?"

Allita smiled. "There are hot springs beneath the palace. Under parts of the city, too. The hot water gets piped through the palace, which helps keep it warm. The bathrooms tend to be warmer. They have the most pipes."

With that, she excused herself and went to help Giane, leaving Chloe to contemplate the empty room. It was the first time she'd been truly alone in a week, and after washing, she made a beeline for the hearth to soak up the heat. Hopefully there might be time before dinner to test out the bath and soak some of the charguerre-induced aches from her body, too.

Because tomorrow the real work began.

✦ ✦ ✦

"Someone should tell them that 'hearth' is supposed to mean something cozy," Giane whispered as they waited for the welcome ceremony to begin the next morning.

"Shhh," Chloe hissed back. She didn't disagree. The King's Hearth, as the Andalyssians called the throne room, had nothing welcoming about it. She'd been in the throne rooms of the emperor's palace and the Anglion palace at Kingswell, and while those were both ostentatious and dazzling, displaying power through wealth, this one was brutal.

Dominated not by the throne but by the massive fireplace it was named for. A rough-hewn gaping space that could have easily roasted a team of the fer-taureaus within its depths, it looked like it had been drawn forth from the heart of the mountain. If not for the fire blazing within, Chloe wouldn't have been overly surprised to see snow on the rough-hewn wall above it. The flames were a curious golden color, too uniform to be entirely natural. Illvyans burned salt grass anointed with oils to make offerings to the goddess, and those burned blue or green. Perhaps the Andalyssians had a similar tradition.

Or perhaps it was something more.

Whatever burned in the fire, the air was permeated with the scent of smoke and incense and something damper and greener that reminded her of some of the mosses Ginevra had used to bind wounds. Not entirely unpleasant but strange, like the slow, icy song of the ley lines below her feet, even cooler and deeper than they had seemed on the journey up the mountain.

For someone used to the emperor's palace, which was all glass and gold and white marble and vivid colors, the King's Hearth felt like stepping into another world.

Everything was shades of gray and silver. Sharp edges and angles to the arches and columns supporting the roof conveyed rock and mountains and strength and threw odd shadows over the assembled court.

The throne was as unforgiving as the hearth. Tall slabs of pale gray granite formed a rough chair shape that protected the king from the heat of the fire behind him but couldn't be comfortable. No furs or cushions padded the stone, only the king's robes providing any barrier between him and the stone.

Perhaps that explained the elaborate layers of court robes the Andalyssians wore. Pleated into shapes as angular as the stones, overlaid with embroidery in intricate geometric designs that somehow only added to the severity. There was symbolism in those lines of color. Statements about houses and loyalties and history. But deciphering the subtle details was beyond her. Difficult enough to try to recall the key colors of the sixteen houses, let alone their lesser vassal families and everything else the embroidery conveyed.

The large room was cool despite the fire roaring in the hearth. Perhaps that was the other reason for the heavy structured robes. A convenient way to hide the layers of clothes needed to avoid turning to icicles.

But the Andalyssians showed no sign of feeling the cold. Predominantly pale-skinned and pale-haired, they might have been carved from stone, too.

The eyes in those pale faces ranged from ice-pale green to leafy to something near the color the darkest heart of a forest. There were a few other shades, pale grays and blues, and the odd more coppery head of hair, but on the whole, the assembled court seemed cut from a single mold. No streaks of deep red or black in their hair to indicate a strong connection to earth or water. But Andalyssians used magic differently. Their devotion to balance demanded that no one strength was used dominantly, with few exceptions for healers and their priests and seers. But even they used magic woven from all the strengths.

Andalyssians didn't bond sanctii. Which was one reason the empire had an upper hand. All the mission's sanctii stood with their mages, possibly more sanctii than any of the Andalyssians had seen in one place before.

How they reacted remained to be seen.

Colonel Brodier stood closest to the throne, back straight,

her blonde hair pinned around her head in coils. The Andalyssians favored looser styles, their hair falling halfway down their backs, the pieces around their faces picked up in groups of thin braids in a variety of configurations as complicated as the embroidered robes.

At the front of the court stood fifteen men in robes more elaborate than the others. Eight to the king's left, seven to his right. All of them older than the king, though two of them looked as though they had, at best, maybe five or six years on him.

The Ashmeisters.

Only fifteen. They had deliberately left a gap in the row of seven. A space where an eighth man would have stood. House Elannon. Their colors were green and orange, and so far, she hadn't spotted anyone wearing them.

King Mikvel had shown no emotion as they'd entered the room, merely watching their approach with vivid green eyes. Unlike the rest of the court, his robes were a gray so pale it was near silver, the designs picked out in silver and white threads that shimmered in the flickering light from the fire and the oil lamps hanging from the ceiling. His hair was unbraided, held back from his face by a silver band studded with diamonds that glittered like his robes.

The king finally nodded at Honore, acknowledging her presence. She stepped forward and bowed. Well rehearsed, the rest of the delegation did the same. When they'd all straightened again, Colonel Brodier launched into her greeting, her Andalyssian sounding effortless to Chloe's ear. The words provoked no reaction from the court, at least. Though stony silence could be good or bad.

"Thank you, Colonel Brodier," the king said after Honore fell silent. "You are welcome at my court. And my thanks to the emperor for sending you to share in my joy."

His voice was deep and low and his Illvyan near flawless. The *s*'s were perhaps stretched a little too long, as they would have been in his native tongue, but otherwise there was no hint of an accent.

Hopefully his proficiency was shared by most of his court. Her Andalyssian was improving, and she would use it where she could, but she didn't want to make a fool of herself.

"It is His Imperial Majesty's pleasure, Your Majesty," Colonel Brodier replied. "He wishes you and your bride-to-be every happiness."

King Mikvel nodded thanks, and Honore launched into a longer speech in Andalyssian. The king's face was serious as he listened, his expression still. Which, in Chloe's experience of courts, was the way of things. Kings and queens and emperors didn't show their hand until it was useful to do so.

Now that the speeches were underway, she risked sneaking sideways glances at the court. But unlike the Illvyan court, where there would probably have been a courtier or two making whispered remarks, the Andalyssians were remarkably focused on the throne. Perhaps they were reserving their commentary until they saw whether or not Honore made it through her speech without stumbling. Or maybe they were quelled by the presence of the sanctii.

Right now, faced with a court silent as stone, she wished they'd brought more sanctii with them. But some had stayed with the navire, bonded to the water mages who would be taking it to the next stop. The emperor didn't have enough of the vessels yet that he could afford to have one sitting idle for five weeks while the delegation was in Andalyssia. So the navire would carry out some smaller errands in the region and return every week to make sure things in Andalyssia were running smoothly.

There were contingencies in place if something went wrong. Ways for sanctii to contact sanctii if there was need, but they may have to retreat to Haalbrod and wait if something went truly terribly wrong.

Which it wouldn't. Honore was smart and experienced, and

Lucien was no slouch at navigating political situations either. It would be fine. It was a wedding, not a treaty negotiation.

Though all royal marriages were treaty negotiations to some degree. It just wasn't a treaty negotiation with Illvya.

Rather between the man on the throne and his stone-faced court.

Who, she hoped, would prove somewhat less stony during the festivities. Or else it would be a very long five weeks indeed.

Honore finally fell silent, drawing a deep breath before bowing again to the king and then stepping back to stand beside Lucien.

Mikvel inclined his head once more, then turned to look to his left. Chloe couldn't help following the line of his gaze. In the far wall of the room, a door she hadn't noticed before opened and a woman strode through, her footsteps striking the stone floor with a confident rhythm, accompanied by the tap of the tall black staff she carried in her right hand, and deep red robes flowing around her.

She reached the king in seconds, though she didn't seem to be moving overly fast, bowed to him, then turned to face the Illvyans.

CHAPTER 14

Chloe's spine prickled, and she fought not to step back a pace. Something about the woman's posture reminded her of Domina Skey, back in Anglion. A woman perhaps too comfortable with her own power.

Or maybe that was Chloe being paranoid, having trained herself for too many years to avoid drawing the attention of the temple. Not that this woman was a domina. The Andalyssians didn't worship the goddess exactly. The dominas in Lumia had always said that other religions were just acknowledging the goddess in one of her many aspects, but whether or not the people who worshiped those other gods agreed was not always clear. But Andalyssian priests wore green, not red.

No, this woman was something else.

A sejerin, unless Chloe was mistaken. One of the mysterious Andalyssian seers.

Maybe it was the firelight, but the shade of her robe was too close to blood, deep and bright, for comfort. It was unadorned other than the hem, which had a border several inches deep embroidered with densely clustered Andalyssian runes in white, forming a triangular pattern that resembled the stylized mountains on the king's banner.

The seer regarded the Illvyans steadily, hand easy on the twisted and carved staff. Unlike Madame Simsa, it didn't seem as though she particularly needed the staff. It was too tall to be a useful support anyway. Ceremonial, then.

Or else she was going to lay into someone. The blood mages back home trained with staffs to build strength and agility, and Chloe's experiences in the training ring had given her a healthy respect for the staff as a weapon.

Easy to picture this woman striding into battle with one.

Her eyes were eerie. So light as to be nearly colorless. In contrast, her hair was a pale shade of red gold. Faint lines at the corners of her eyes suggested she was older than she first appeared. Unlike the rest of the court, the sejerin was using her magic.

Chloe watched warily. Better to be overly cautious than foolish. The song of the seer's magic echoed with a sound like a rush of cold feathers underscored by the deep heart of a bell tolling. For a moment she was suspended in time, as though icy chilled air surrounded her, the sun sharp in her eyes and the song of the mountain hawks piercing the air. Almost as though she stood on the mountain rather than within it.

But then she blinked and she was back breathing smoke and mystery, staring at the seer. Who glowed from more than the firelight, the edge of magic around her a misty rainbow shine that Chloe hadn't never seen before.

She blinked again, but the glow didn't fade.

The sejerin struck the ground with the staff and began to talk. Or declaim, perhaps. It was clearly a formal speech, the syllables measured and rhythmic. It was also clearly not Andalyssian. This was harsher and stranger, the sound of Andalyssian ground beneath stone and echoed back.

Compelling, but also frustrating not to know what she was saying.

Neither Colonel Brodier nor Lucien nor any of the others

who had been here before seemed alarmed, so she had to assume it was a ritual speech, not some sort of spell.

Evoking balance, most likely. The obsession with balance had struck Chloe as an odd choice, perhaps, for a people who lived in a place of extremes. Or maybe not. When you lived on a knife's edge of ice and snow where bad weather could potentially obliterate the world, maybe the idea was appealing. Something to strive for.

The words rolled on and over them, and the whisper of the sejerin's magic underneath them remained steady rather than flaring as it would if the woman was drawing on extra power.

The inability to understand the words scratched at her brain. Parts of them sounded almost Andalyssian, but the sounds together made no sense. The Andalyssians were watching with expressions she judged to be more polite than concerned, which was reassuring, but she would have given her arm for a proper translation.

Eventually the sejerin stopped speaking and struck the stone floor three times again with her staff before turning to bow to the king.

"Thank you, Sejerin Silya," Mikvel said. Chloe noted the name and added it to the list in her head. Doubtful she'd have any trouble remembering this one after such a dramatic introduction.

Clearly Sejerin Silya was important, so it seemed likely they would cross paths again. Whether or not that was a good thing remained to be seen.

She couldn't quite shake her initial impression. She'd grown more wary of people since Charl died, reluctant to fall for dazzle or charm. In Anglion, she'd honed her instincts for those who might be ill-intentioned. Running a business alone as a woman had made her a target for certain kinds of opportunistic fraudsters or thieves who were bold enough—or stupid enough—to ignore the fact that she was Illvyan. Or maybe they had just assumed she'd be prevented from using her powers by fear of the temple.

They'd been right about that part, but none of them had ever succeeded in stealing more than a few silver coins' worth of supplies. And the men looking to con a woman out of her money always tried to deploy the kind of bright and bountiful charm that Charl had naturally. Given most of them were nowhere near as handsome as Charl had been, and she had no longer been a love-struck girl, she remained unmoved by their efforts.

Chloe doubted that Sejerin Silya would try to charm anybody, but still, until she found reasons to either confirm or allay her instincts, she would be careful.

"What do you think that was all about?" Giane whispered through the side of her mouth, not looking at Chloe as Sejerin Silya walked back toward the door she'd entered from.

"Well, none of us has turned into a frog, so I'm going to guess some sort of welcome ritual."

Giane snorted softly. "Maybe it's delayed frogs."

"Shhh," Chloe said, willing her mouth not to smile. "Pay attention." The king was rising from his throne now, standing for a moment while regarding the court with an expression that seemed almost a challenge.

But then he clapped his hands together once, a gesture that made him look more like the young man he was. "And now," he said, finally smiling, "dinner."

The dining hall was, thankfully, built on a more intimate scale than the King's Hearth. Though intimate was always relative when it came to palaces. It still seated several hundred people, but the walls were plastered and painted and draped in tapestries rather than being bare rock, giving it a human touch. The tables, draped in white and set with gold-rimmed china, silvered goblets, candles and tiny white flowers, looked welcoming.

The king's table was at the front of the room, raised on a small platform. Colonel Brodier, Lucien, and Captain Theisse were seated at a table in the first row facing it. The rest of the Illvyans were scattered across several tables in the third and fourth rows. Not insulting but emphasizing that they were less important. At least they had the tables to themselves and wouldn't have to make polite dinner conversation in Andalyssian just yet. Honore and Lucien and Captain Theisse were less fortunate. They were seated with Andalyssians in a bewildering array of colored robes. She didn't think any of the men were Ashmeisters, but they must still all be senior members of the court.

Lucien seemed at ease, speaking to the man beside him. She made herself turn her attention elsewhere. She wasn't going to spend the evening staring at Lucien. Not when there were far more interesting people in the room.

King Mikvel was seated beside a young woman dressed in silver trimmed with white and pale blue. From the quietly happy looks they exchanged as they waited for the servants to fill their glasses with wine, Chloe gathered this was Lady Katiya, his fiancée. Either that or he had no interest in hiding the fact that he was in love with somebody else and only marrying for political reasons.

But Andalyssians had conservative attitudes to marriage vows and fidelity. Their women, like Anglions, were supposed to remain virgins until they wed. Loyalty was an important trait, which made sense when the king had to work with the Ashmeisters. Lady Katiya brought with her House Uleniska, one of the strongest of the sixteen houses and it seemed unlikely he'd offer insult to her at so public an occasion. So no, the pretty blonde whose pale green eyes were fixed on Mikvel had to be the queen-to-be.

Chloe had less idea who the others seated with them were. Relatives of the king and his fiancée most likely. Roland sat at the far-left end of the table and another man of similar age at the right.

There was no sign of the sejerin or anyone else wearing red robes, which was a relief.

The seers were, most likely, less formidable to anyone familiar with them, but they supposedly held the power of foretelling, and that was something Chloe had never been hugely comfortable with. An aspect of water magic she'd never shown much talent for at the Academe, and she had little desire to know what lay in her future.

Life could be difficult enough without spending your time braced for something you had been told might come to pass.

Besides, seeing the future was a vague art at best. There had been few water mages truly strong in that talent over the years. They were rarer than Truth Seekers, even, and had, according to the Academe's histories, tended to be somewhat loosely connected to sanity.

Knowing the future, or perhaps seeing too many options to be able to see clearly at all, was a burden that didn't rest easily. There were no such water mages in the Illvyan court currently. But there were always water mages who dabbled with scrying and foretelling with some success, and others of smaller powers who made a living bilking people who wanted to believe out of their hard-earned money with vague predictions and insights that were, on the whole, not. She'd crossed paths with a few in her younger days, when it had been fashionable to ask frivolous questions about love and such.

She hadn't always enjoyed the experience, and seeing a seer was unexpectedly disconcerting.

As a distraction, she watched Katiya sip deep red wine and talk quietly with the king until her own glass was filled and the Wardmeister stood to make a toast. After that, the room broke into conversation, and she turned her attention to the meal, suddenly starving.

Dinner didn't last for hours as court meals sometimes could.

All too soon, the servants were removing the dessert plates, and members of the court began to leave. Colonel Brodier and Lucien didn't move from their table, so Chloe and the others stayed where they were. The room was halfway empty when Honore beckoned to Chloe.

She pushed back her chair and went to see what the colonel wanted. There wasn't room to stand by Honore's side thanks to a group of courtiers gathered around the next table over, so she was forced to stand next to Lucien, muttering, "Excuse me, Major," as her uniform skirt brushed his shoulder.

"No apology needed, Lieutenant," he said softly.

She didn't look down. Didn't want to see what was lurking in those green eyes.

"You need me, sir?" she asked Honore.

A nod. "There's to be a smaller gathering for drinks and to meet Lady Katiya after dinner. You're invited."

"Invited" in this case seemed likely an order. "Me?"

Honore lifted an eyebrow. "We named you as one of the people attending all the formal wedding ceremonies, so yes."

Captain Theisse—or Gilles, as she should try to remember to call him at the wedding celebrations—had no title, but he and Honore were the senior members of the delegation, so it made sense that they would be included. Still, she hadn't expected the "navigating the court celebrations" part of the mission to start tonight. She could have used another good night's sleep and more time practicing her Andalyssian. But the ceremony was in five more days, and royal weddings waited for no woman, apparently. "Of course, Colonel."

"Apparently we'll be escorted once the king leaves." Chloe looked toward the high table. King Mikvel was holding out his hand to Lady Katiya. Chloe turned in place so she could, as protocol required, face the king and bow with the rest of the court. She turned back only to find herself face-to-face with Lucien.

Too close again.

Just like at Imogene's ball, she could feel the heat of his body, and his scent—soap and man and the cool green cologne he wore—filled her nose. After the strange smoky incense that lingered over the court, it was like taking a lungful of clean, crisp air, and she wanted to move closer, take a deeper breath.

Her cheeks heated. She would do no such thing.

She stepped back hastily. Lucien's mouth quirked in a half-smile that vanished as quickly as it appeared, making her wonder if she'd imagined it altogether. But before either of them could say anything, a young woman clad in white and gray, the king's mountain embroidered around the collar and cuffs of her dress and the trim of the long vest she wore over it, arrived by Honore's side.

"Colonel Brodier," she said with a quick curtsy, "if you and your companions would follow me, I will take you to His Majesty."

"Thank you," Honore said.

Chloe saw Giane, still at the other table, watching them curiously.

"What's going on?" Giane mouthed.

"Business," Chloe mouthed back before Colonel Brodier said, "Let's go."

The servant turned, her pale blonde braid swinging, and they followed her out of the dining hall and down a confusing series of corridors—really, parts of the palace seemed to be modeled after a rabbit's warren—before they arrived at a doorway flanked by two guardsmen. The door was partially ajar, and the sound of voices speaking Andalyssian came from within. Not too loud, but enough to suggest there were quite a few people inside. After the delicious meal and long day, she'd rather return to her room than deal with protocol in a foreign language. But this was what diplomats did. They developed relationships and forged them into new or strengthened alliances. Sleepy or not, out of her depth or not, this was what she was here to help do.

Hopefully there would be tea.

The reception room was warm and not too large. A small fire burned in a grate in the far wall, but even near the door, the temperature was pleasant, making her think it must be warmed by the pipes as well.

There were only about twenty other people in the room, a mix of men and women of various ages. That much was a relief. Fewer names to remember after the inevitable introductions. And if these were people important to the king, it would be a head start on learning who was who in the court, putting faces to the names she'd been studying since being assigned to the mission.

King Mikvel stood with Lady Katiya near the fire, talking to an older man whose robes were a deep blue with pale green embroidery. The king looked over and smiled, beckoning them to join him.

They did so, which necessitated another flurry of bows and greetings. She hadn't realized how out of habit she'd grown with the niceties of a court. Somewhere along the way she'd lost the feeling that it was completely normal rather than an odd waste of time, even though the ritual and moves of it still came automatically. But she was going to have to get used to it again. Diplomats lived in protocol.

"This is my betrothed, Lady Katiya Uleniska," King Mikvel said. "Katiya, here is Colonel Brodier, Major de Roche—also Lord Castaigne—Captain Theisse, and...." He paused for a moment, studying Chloe. "I believe this is Lieutenant de Montesse, also Lady de Montesse." He raised a brow at Chloe.

She nodded and curtsied again. "Yes, Your Majesty. An honor to meet you and Lady Katiya."

He smiled at her, his pale eyes warming. "Welcome to Deephilm, Lieutenant. I trust your stay will be enjoyable."

"It already has been, Your Majesty," she said.

Katiya smiled at her, which only made her more beautiful. Her eyes sparkled, as though she, too, found it all faintly ridiculous.

The king introduced the older man as Georg Uleniska, Katiya's uncle, but before they could start any further conversations, Lady Katiya said, "Lieutenant de Montesse, let me introduce you to some of the other women." Her Illvyan was nearly as good as the king's.

Startled, Chloe could only nod and, after Colonel Brodier offered no objection, followed Katiya across the room.

"My uncle will bend their ear for hours if Misha lets him," Katiya murmured as they walked. "It will be very dull, and tonight is supposed to be enjoyable."

Misha. That would be the king. And, if Katiya was annoyed by the serious tone of the evening so far, did that mean it wasn't entirely usual for the court? Was the matter of House Elannon causing additional tension? Hardly questions she could ask when she had just met the woman.

"You speak Illvyan very well," Chloe said, replying in Andalyssian and hoping it was right. "But we can use your language if you prefer."

Katiya shook her head. "No. Let me practice. You will have many more opportunities in the next few weeks to speak Andalyssian than I will Illvyan."

They reached the opposite side of the room, where a young woman in the same blues and greens as Katiya's uncle stood near drawn curtains embroidered with stars and moons and strange flowers. She was trying, as far as Chloe could tell, not to look bored. Her eyes lit as they approached, and she stepped forward. "Katya, hello. Did you escape, then?"

Katiya smiled at her, the expression faintly exasperated. "Lieutenant de Montesse, this is my little sister, Irina."

"Hello, Lady Irina," Chloe said. Little sister explained the pet name. Katya, not Katiya. She filed that away for reference, along with Misha for the king. Not that she expected to grow close enough to either one to use them.

Irina nodded and bobbed a quick curtsy. "Lieutenant de Montesse." Her hair was more coppery blonde than pale like her sister's. Back home, Chloe would have thought her an earth witch.

"You're from Illvya. Is it exciting there?" Irina spoke Illvyan with a similar ease to Katiya.

Something in her tone reminded Chloe of herself when she was younger. And her own little sisters. By the color of her hair, Irina must be over twenty-one but perhaps not that far over. Katiya was only twenty-three, just two years younger than her husband-to-be.

"It is, like most places, interesting sometimes, dull others, and mostly quite nice in between," she said.

Irina grimaced. "Deephilm is just dull."

Katiya laughed. "Irina! My wedding is not dull."

Her sister rolled her eyes. "Well, no, I am happy that you and Misha will be married at last, and that you get to be queen, of course. But then you will be doing terribly important things all the time, and I will be back to—" She broke off as a servant approached bearing a tray of short glasses filled with a light green liquid that Chloe assumed was some form of liqueur.

"Kafiet," the servant said, offering the tray.

Katiya and Irina both took one, so Chloe did, too. Kafiet meant something like "cold-fire," if she was translating correctly. "Pretty," she said, raising the glass to inspect it. It was faintly warm to the touch. Not like tea, but as though the alcohol, if that was what it was, had been set somewhere to warm before being served.

"It's delicious," Katiya said. "But it has, do you say, 'a kick' to it." She raised the glass and added, "Zvodoya," then downed the contents of her glass in one gulp.

Chloe knew that one: "health." The toasts at dinner had been plentiful, and she'd already had more wine than might have been strictly wise. She didn't really need more alcohol, but it would be rude to refuse at least one toast.

"Zvodoya," she said, then tipped the glass back and gulped.

At first all she sensed was warmth. But then her mouth filled with a sensation like ice on fire, mint burning sugar and light and heat over her tongue and down her throat. Her stomach warmed with a glow almost immediately before the sensation spread down her legs and through her arms. She blinked, startled by the intensity. A kick indeed. Something to be wary of.

She handed the glass back to the servant, the taste still singing in her mouth. "That is delicious," she said. Delicious and dangerous. "How is it made? I taste...some sort of herb?"

"Miyata," Katiya said, nodding. "It's a kind of alpine plant. Related to mint. But cold-hardy."

"And something else?" Chloe ventured. "Ginger, maybe? There's warmth with the cold."

Irina looked delighted. "Yes, and a kind of pepper we use here. Are you interested in herbs, Lieutenant? You're an earth witch?"

"Earth and water are my strongest talents," Chloe said. "And yes, I've learned quite a bit of herb-lore in my time. Are you interested in healing, Lady Irina?"

Irina exchanged a look with Katiya. "Our father wants me to get married. And I am supposed to use all my talents." Her cheeks flushed, the pink bright against her pale skin, though Chloe couldn't tell if it was passion for her subject or perhaps the effects of the kafiet. Her own cheeks were hot, too.

"Irina," Katiya said. "You have to finish your studies."

"But why should I study things I have no talent for?" Irina said, sounding exasperated. "I'm strong in earth. I like earth." She turned an inquisitive expression on Chloe. "Don't you agree, Lieutenant de Montesse? It makes sense to work to one's strengths."

"Well, in Illvya they make us learn the basics of each of the four arts," Chloe said, trying for a diplomatic explanation that wouldn't offend Katiya's religion if she was a believer. Clearly Irina wasn't resigned to the strictures of balance, but Irina wasn't the future queen.

"But then you—" Irina broke off as the door to the room

opened inward. Her face twisted into a grimace briefly as Sejerin Silya walked through it. "Oh, smelt, that's all we need." But she smoothed her face into a polite expression as her sister frowned at her.

The seer swept a glance around the room, taking in the king still talking with the other Illvyans and Katiya's uncle, and then, to Chloe's dismay, headed toward her instead.

She bowed to Katiya when she reached the group, but it was briefer than what would be strictly polite. "Lady Katiya, your health this evening." She spoke Andalyssian. Did that mean she didn't understand Illvyan, or was she making some sort of point?

"And yours, Sejerin Silya," Katiya responded in Andalyssian. She slid a sideways glance that seemed part apologetic at Chloe. "It is kind of you to join us."

Irina had gone quiet beside Chloe, the flush on her cheeks fading. Seeing her turn from animated to wary did nothing to quell Chloe's earlier uneasiness with the seer.

"Irina," Silya said.

Irina just bobbed a curtsy, murmuring, "Sejerin Silya."

"Katiya, perhaps you would introduce me to the Illvyan," Silya said.

Well, that was rude. Or did the seer not imagine that Chloe spoke Andalyssian?

"Sejerin, this is Lieutenant de Montesse. Lieutenant, this is Sejerin Silya, currently senior of the sejerin council."

Had she stressed that "currently" slightly? The sejerin council advised the king, like the Ashmeisters. So Sejerin Silya had power. It was interesting, in fact, that there was a seer here but nobody from the priesthood.

Chloe curtsied as rapidly as the sejerin had and said hello in Andalyssian, hoping her accent held up to scrutiny.

The seer regarded her with narrowed eyes, then said something to Katiya in the same language she'd used for her ritual back in the King's Hearth.

Katiya looked somewhat surprised, then annoyed, as the seer turned on her heel and headed over to the next group.

"Good riddance," Irina muttered in Andalyssian. "Katya, when you're queen, can you send her to the outer peaks for several years?"

Chloe hid a smile, but curiosity won over amusement at Irina's obvious dislike of the seer. "If you don't mind me asking, Lady Katiya, what was that last thing she said? I know Andalyssian but not whatever language that was."

"It's seer tongue," Irina said.

Katiya shook her head at her. "It's an older form of Andalyssian," she said to Chloe, switching back to Illvyan. "Ancient, in fact. The seers use it in their rituals."

Irina snorted. "It's seer tongue. They make us learn it at school, but no one but seers ever uses it. They just do it to seem more mysterious than they are."

"Irina!" Katiya said, but the word was half a laugh.

"You know it's true. If the priests can talk normally, why do the seers need to be different?"

"Tradition," Katiya said firmly. She turned to Chloe. "And to answer your question, Lieutenant, she said, 'So this is the daughter of ravens.' I'm assuming that's a reference to your father?"

Chloe blinked. As much because Katiya knew who her father was than the phrase itself. Though the former was foolish. Katiya was to be a queen. Of course she would be as well briefed on the foreigners visiting her court.

"Who is your father?" Irina asked, eyes bright again.

"Henri Matin. He's the Maistre of—"

"The Rookery," Irina said, clapping her hands. "I know who he is." She glanced down at Chloe's hands. "You do not wear a wedding ring, Lieutenant. But you are not Lieutenant Matin?"

Ah. This was a question she had expected. She'd stopped wearing her ring after her first year in Anglion. Her widowhood was, by then, accepted in Kingswell, and she'd hated the reminder of Charl greeting her every time she glimpsed it. But Irina's query, as genuine and lacking malice as it seemed to be, still caused a pang. "My husband died," she said gently. "A long time ago."

She risked a glance at Katiya, wondering how thorough her briefing had been. She would have been a child when Charl was executed, and though it had been a scandal in Illvya, she wondered if it had been news in the farthest reaches of the empire. The Andalyssians would still have been dealing with the repercussions of the Ashmeister Elannon's plot, so maybe they wouldn't have been focused on the ins and outs of what was happening in Lumia.

"Have you not returned to your father's house, then?" Irina asked.

Chloe lifted a brow in query at Katiya.

"Childless women who lose their husbands sometimes choose to rejoin their own families," Katiya said. "Take back their old name." She looked at her sister. "I don't think it works the same way in Illvya, Irina."

"Not exactly," Chloe agreed. "Sometimes women might change their name back if they get divorced, but most widows don't." She didn't think muddying the waters by explaining that she actually was living with her parents again, made much sense. And she'd noted that Irina had assumed she must not have children to be a member of the army. So she might chafe against the balance, but Chloe needed to remember that Andalyssia was not Anglion. She wanted to ask more about the seers, but it didn't seem to be quite the moment.

"So you went to the Academe in Lumia?" Irina asked.

"Yes, I went to school there as a child and then completed my magical studies after my Ascension."

"See, Irina, everyone has to study. Not just you," Katiya teased.

Irina frowned. "But why must I study the useless parts? My earth sense is strong. I want to use that."

"Earth sense?" Chloe asked.

"Irina has an unusually strong talent for earth," Katiya said softly. "Most of us are more in balance. Earth sense is helpful here in the mountains. It helps to find caves or warn of cracks beneath the ice. It's mostly used in the mines, to follow the seams."

"But a daughter of Uleniska can't be a miner," Irina muttered. "They leave that to the men."

Chloe hadn't heard of earth magic being used in that way before. How would it work? An extension of the senses a mage used to sense the ley line? More specifically attuned to the earth itself? But given Irina's sour expression, she didn't think it was the best subject to pursue. "Perhaps you can be a healer?" Chloe said, returning to their earlier conversation. "Plenty of married women are healers in Illvya. It's a handy skill in a family."

Katiya looked grateful for the change in topic. "Yes. Healing is one of the professions where it is acceptable to weave one band of talent more strongly in your power. We have stillrooms and a dispensary here in the place the healers use. I enjoy spending time there." She cast an assessing glance at her sister, who still looked somewhat disgruntled. "But, Lieutenant, why don't you tell us more of Illvya? Is it true the Academe has a tower of magical ravens?"

Chloe laughed. "Well, they're not magical as such. They're very intelligent birds though, and some earth mages bind them as familiars. Do you do that here?"

Katiya shook her head. "That would be out of balance to the creature, to bind it so."

"They benefit, too," Chloe said. "They live longer, for one thing. Do you not use bindings here at all, then?"

"Sometimes," Katiya said. "Between two people. That way it can be equal."

That was nice in theory. But no two people were perfectly evenly matched in power.

"Do you have a raven?" Irina asked as another servant

appeared with a second tray of kafiet. She took one after glancing at Katiya, who, sighing, nodded permission. She took a second herself and gestured the servant toward Chloe. She was still warm and tingling from the first one, but maybe another would help her sleep. She took the glass and downed the kafiet in a quick gulp. Mint fire spun through her again, hitting faster this time. Definitely the last one for the evening.

"No." She shook her head, remembering what Irina had asked as the sting of the kafiet faded. "No raven. Maybe one day. I've always liked them. Do you have ravens here?"

"In summer," Irina said. "Most of our birds travel with the season. It's too cold in winter. Not enough food. There are snow eagles year-round. They're big enough to survive the storms and can fly down to Elenia to hunt in the worst of the weather."

Chloe wasn't sure she wanted to meet an eagle big enough to survive the kind of storm Andalyssia was reputed to have. "They sound impressive."

Katiya nodded. "Apparently people used to hunt with them. These days some of the men still use smaller birds. Hawks and such. Misha has a sun falcon who is quite beautiful."

"Bad tempered though," Irina said. "He bites."

Katiya didn't correct her, so presumably it was true. Having been nipped a time or two by an overenthusiastic young raven, not to mention having developed a healthy respect for what their talons could do, Chloe had no desire to tangle with a true bird of prey.

"I'll remember that," Chloe said, "should I chance to meet him."

"Well, there will be a hunt two days after the wedding," Katiya said. "The men will use their birds if the weather permits." She glanced over her shoulder. "Does Lord Castaigne hunt?"

"Well, not with birds, but he's a very good rider," Chloe said before she could think.

"Oh? Do you know him well?" Katiya asked, curiosity lighting her eyes. "Outside of the army, that is?"

"We're...acquainted," Chloe said, trying to be vague. Her cheeks were heating again. Damn Kafiet, making her careless with her tongue.

"He's very handsome," Irina said. "Is he married?"

"No-o," Chloe said, casting a wary glance at her. She didn't think, from what Irina had said before, that she was on the hunt for a husband, but she didn't want to cast Lucien to the wind as it were and declare it open season on him. Though perhaps his occupation—not to mention the fact that he was Illvyan—would make him less appealing.

"You should marry him, if you need a new husband," Irina said with a grin. "He has nice eyes."

"'Rina!" Katiya said. "That's hardly respectful. Nor is it a sensible thing to say when Silya is around."

"Why? They are nice. He looks kind. I didn't say I wanted to invade his bedchamber and have my way with him. *That* would be disrespectful." Irina grinned at Chloe. "Though perhaps fun."

For one horrifying moment, Chloe found herself thinking idly that Irina might not be wrong about that. Then she came to her senses and wrenched her thoughts away from the idea of Lucien lying on a bed, clothes rumpled and eyes hot and fierce. "I don't need a new husband," she said firmly. "And Lord Castaigne is perfectly able to find a wife should he want one. He and I wouldn't suit."

"No more kafiet for you," Katiya said firmly to her sister. She waved away the servant who was heading for them again. "In fact, I will call for some tea."

CHAPTER 15

The tea the Andalyssians served, robust and earthy as it was, was not quite enough to counteract the effect of two glasses of kafiet on top of several glasses of wine. Chloe did her best to pay attention as Katiya introduced her to everybody else in the room, but the evening began to take on a dreamy quality she recognized as her being both tired and having, as her mother would phrase it, more to drink than was ladylike.

Fortunately, it wasn't enough to make her do anything too embarrassing. Her laugh was possibly a little too fast, and she wished she could shed her uniform jacket, or throw open one of the sets of curtains and stick her head out into the cool night air, but she didn't disgrace herself. But names and faces blurred together, which meant she had to work hard to remember who was who and not make a mistake.

Finally Katiya delivered her back to Lucien's side and wished her a good night. Chloe concentrated, determined not to let him see she'd overindulged.

"Lieutenant," he said, sounding vaguely amused. "Have you had an enjoyable evening?"

She looked up at him, determined to keep her face serious. "Yes, Major." Trouble was, Lucien had been with her too many times before when the three of them—Lucien and Charl and her—had indulged in too much campenois. He knew her tells.

Damn the man.

And damn Irina for being right. He *was* handsome. And in the firelight, the green of his eyes was wild and tempting.

Goddess, that was another thought she wasn't going to indulge.

She looked around, seeking a distraction. "Did the colonel and the captain leave?"

"Thirty minutes or so ago. The Wardmeister wanted to go over something about tomorrow's schedule," Lucien said. "Didn't you notice?"

If she hadn't already been too warm, she would have blushed. She hadn't noticed. Damn it. Losing track of one's senior officers wasn't a good thing. "I was busy."

"So I saw. You seemed to be getting along well with Lady Katiya. The colonel said to leave you to it."

Was that a compliment? Perhaps it was. She suppressed a pleased smile. "But you're still here."

"Well, it's a big palace. I wanted to make sure you get back to your room safely. That green stuff they were serving is, er, potent."

"It's delicious."

"I don't disagree. But it would be easy to overindulge by accident, I think." Green eyes smiled down at her.

"Are you accusing me of being scuppered?"

His brows lifted. "Scuppered? No. A little merry, perhaps. And you never did have the greatest sense of direction."

She scowled at him. "It's not polite to point out a lady's faults." But she couldn't argue. She had improved her sense of direction a little over the years, but she'd need Irina's earth sense or whatever it was to find her way through the maze of hallways tonight.

"No," he agreed. "But it's also not polite to let her get lost in a strange palace either. So, Lieutenant, shall we return to our rooms? The party seems to be over."

So it was. There were a few people left in the room. Katiya and Mikvel stood, smiling at each other, near the fireplace. Irina lolled on one of the couches, yawning, clearly waiting for her sister to be done.

"All right," she agreed. "If it's not out of your way."

"My room is in the same corridor as yours," he said drily.

"It is?" She hadn't realized.

He nodded. "There are only two corridors of rooms, after all. It was a fifty-fifty chance."

He gestured toward the door, and she moved forward before he could offer her his arm. And before she did anything stupid like take it. Kafiet or no, she would keep her distance.

Lucien watched the swish of Chloe's skirts as she headed for the door, then threw a hasty bow in the direction of the king and his fiancée, who were too busy gazing at each other adoringly to pay him any heed, and followed her.

She may not be drunk, but the kafiet had added a glow to her cheeks. Hells, he suspected it had added a glow to his own. It had a kick like a mule—or maybe a rogue fer-taureau—and he'd had to down three glasses of it while he'd been talking with the king. He suspected Georg Uleniska had been trying to see if he could play a game of "coax the foreign dignitary into an alcohol-fueled faux pas." But he'd had kafiet on his last visit here and was well aware of his limits. He'd forewarned Colonel Brodier about the stuff.

Watching Chloe walk ahead, her line of progress an oh-so-subtle snaking line rather than a straight one, he wondered if Honore had had time to warn her. Kafiet was expensive due to the rarity of its ingredients. Not the kind of thing served at general palace dinners, but he'd known it would appear at the more intimate celebrations.

Perhaps even at the wedding ball itself. Serving several hundred guests a liqueur worth its weight in gold was a kingly thing to do. Andalyssia was many things as a kingdom, but it wasn't poor.

He realized he was paying far too close attention to the sway of Chloe's hips and jerked his head up. The palace corridors were quiet and dimly lit, only a stray servant here and there moving through them. In other circumstances, it would be an intimate stroll back to their rooms.

But this was Chloe, and he was all too aware that the kafiet had heated his blood and he could very well say something stupid. Or *do* something stupid. But he wouldn't. Cold-fire or not, he'd never once touched a woman who hadn't invited him to do so, and he wasn't about to start with a woman who had done precisely the opposite of that.

They reached the first intersection in the corridors, and Chloe swayed a little farther right. They were going left.

Seemed he was going to have to take charge to some degree.

He hastened his steps so they were side by side. "Other way."

Chloe paused and looked up, eyes slightly narrowed. "I am aware." Her mouth quirked a little. "But lead on, Major." She waved an imperious hand in the direction of their rooms.

His breath caught. Not drunk, but definitely more relaxed in his presence than he'd seen her since before Charl's arrest. The curve of her mouth and the silly gesture hinted at the Chloe he remembered.

Back then, if the three of them had been wandering home, slightly drunk, he wouldn't have hesitated to offer his arm. In fact, she probably would have already slipped hers through both his and Charl's, walking between them and trying to coax him into singing for her or telling terrible jokes to get him to laugh. Some of his favorite memories were of their adventures.

But that was then. Now she was no longer his best friend, and Charl was not here to be a choke chain on his hunger for this woman who would as soon skewer him on the nearest sharp object than let him take her arm.

So he would be sensible. Think of something innocuous to discuss for the remaining time it would take to reach their rooms, then leave her at her door.

"What did you and the ladies talk about tonight?" he asked as they turned left. "That was Irina Uleniska, wasn't it? Lady Katiya's little sister?"

"It was," Chloe agreed. "She's an earth witch."

"Well, not strictly," he said. "They don't really have those here. Not as we do."

She frowned. "She is though. And it seems wrong that she has to deny it." The frown deepened. "I thought I was done with countries where men tell women what to do with their magic."

He didn't disagree. The way the Andalyssians thought about magic had never sat easily with him. What would have happened to him if he'd been born in such a country? His power discouraged? Or suppressed? Or feared? "To be fair, they tell everyone what to do with their magic. It's not just the women. And change comes slowly."

"Sometimes it comes fast," she said. "Like Sophie."

"Well, we're here to support the king, not overthrow him, so let's leave the Andalyssians to do things their way. Lady Katiya seems content and well able to protect her sister's interests should they need protecting. Irina seemed lively enough from what I could see."

"She is." Chloe's frown disappeared. "I like her."

He tried not to show his relief that she had accepted his change of topic. The politics of man versus woman versus magic and religion in the empire's various countries was nothing he wanted to debate with her in the corridors of Deephilm.

"She thinks you're pretty," Chloe added.

Startled, he stopped walking. "She does?"

"Yes," Chloe said. She studied him a moment. "It's probably the blond hair and green eyes. You almost blend in. Maybe if you avoided the sun for a few years, you could pass as a native."

His skin was more gold than pale like hers or the Andalyssians. And Andalyssians didn't like Truth Seekers. "I like the sun," he said firmly. "And being warm." *And avoiding marriage-hungry sisters of foreign queens.*

"Don't worry, I don't think she's marriage minded." She smiled suddenly, and from the familiar looseness of the expression, he knew she was perhaps more intoxicated than she had seemed back in the king's parlor. Kafiet was sneaky that way. Burned in the blood for a long time before it finally caught fire.

He couldn't risk letting his own blood burn.

"Well, that's good," he said.

"Yes," Chloe agreed. "She suggested that I should marry you."

"What?" He almost stumbled again, shocked by both the idea and the fact that she had mentioned it. Hardly a suggestion that could have pleased her.

She laughed as he caught himself. He stared at her, and she went still. In the dim light, her pupils were wide, but there was amusement lurking in the depths. Amusement and—his breath caught again. He'd seen her smiling at Charl like that many times. Dark-eyed and happy and not entirely hiding the fact that she intended to drag her husband off to bed at the closest opportunity.

Why was she looking at him that way?

She wasn't was the short answer, merely intoxicated. He tore his gaze away, tried to ignore the heat coiling through him, and started walking.

"Don't worry," Chloe said. "I told her we wouldn't suit."

Oh, they would suit. He knew that much. Had always known it. But he couldn't say it. He'd never been able to say it. And he wasn't going to take advantage of this small moment when she was—kafiet influenced or not—warming to him ever so slightly to make a fool of himself now.

"Good," he said. "They take marriage seriously around here. Let's not start any trouble. What else did you talk about? What did the seer say?"

The amusement faded from Chloe's face. "Not much. She called me 'daughter of ravens' and then wandered off again. I'm not sure I like her much. She reminds me of Domina Skey."

Daughter of ravens? Well, that was apt. But a strange thing to call somebody upon first meeting. "In what way?"

"She likes power," Chloe said.

"Many people do," he countered. "I would think you'd be pleased that a woman can hold a high rank here."

She shrugged. "It depends how they got it. It's odd that we haven't met any of their...what do they call the priests?"

"Svasyas," he said. "King Mikvel said they undertake some sort of ritual prior to commencing the wedding rituals. He mentioned ice water and prayer. It didn't sound appealing. I'm sure we won't be able to move without tripping over one in a day or so."

"Is Deephilm like you remembered?" Chloe asked as they turned another corridor.

"Mostly. More cordial, which is nice. Though still somewhat wary. At least I'm not actively prosecuting one of them for treason this time. That helps." Though still hunting for signs of it.

That made her smile slowly. "I would imagine so. Though I got the impression that Katiya thinks the wedding is...solemn. I don't know if that's usual or if I imagined it."

"Solemn?"

"She made a comment that the gatherings should be enjoyable. But the matter of House Elannon must be making things more difficult, perhaps."

"Possibly." Chloe was new at this, but he had never doubted her instincts. He hadn't detected any hint of falsehood in the king's welcome or during their discussion after dinner, but he was yet to meet any of the Ashmeisters, let alone representatives of House Elannon. The first of those was to be held tomorrow. He wasn't entirely looking forward to it, though it would, at least, give him some idea what they were facing in navigating the Andalyssian court.

It was part of the reason he'd wanted to walk Chloe back to her room. A small part, perhaps but it was still there lurking in the back of his thoughts. He would keep her safe in this palace carved into a mountain, no matter what else happened.

"You've gone quiet," she said.

"It's late," he said. "People are sleeping." They'd reached the end of the corridor where their rooms were located. Chloe's was at the far end, whereas his was second from the turn of the hallway. A wise man would leave her to walk the remaining few hundred feet on her own. There was no one lurking in the corridor.

But he didn't want to bring this to an end any sooner than he had to. In the morning, she would wake and no longer feel any kafiet-fueled kindness toward him. And he would have to miss her all over again. Forget this glimpse of his friend and bury his feelings deep.

Tonight though, he had maybe a minute more. Chloe stretched her arm out, running her hand over the tapestries that lined the walls between each door. She was smiling again, relaxed and open.

"Pretty," she said.

"Yes," he agreed, though he wasn't talking about the tapestries. "Very. Practical, too. Makes it warmer."

"Maybe I should take up needlework," she said. "Something to do on long journeys."

"You used to say needlework was dull," he said.

She tilted her head to look at him over her shoulder. "I used to say many things. Many of them foolish." Her smile was lopsided, and sadness flashed over her face.

He didn't like seeing her sad. "It wasn't foolish to love Charl," he said. "Or, if it was, then we are both fools. He didn't start out the man he ended up being."

The smile died. "Someone changed him."

"Yes."

"Do you know who?" She was moving again, heading for her room. He hurried to keep pace.

"No." It was one of the few failures of his career. They'd arrested two other men, both of whom had killed themselves before they could be fully interrogated. Which shouldn't have been possible. But short of Aristides freeing the Truth Seekers to interrogate everyone at court, and in the parliament and beyond, that had left few trails to follow. "But I will. Eventually." He hadn't given up on the case. He never would.

Her expression turned savage. "Good. Because I would like to have words with whoever it was."

"So would I."

She flashed a smile that was closer to bared teeth than amusement. "Perhaps we have something in common still after all, Lucien."

They'd reached her room, and she fitted the key into the lock while he stayed silent, not sure how to respond.

Lucien. She'd said his name. Not Lord, or Truth Seeker, or Major. Just Lucien. As she used to.

Kindly meant, perhaps, but another prick to his heart that he didn't let himself respond to for fear of ruining things.

"Sleep well, Lieutenant," he said at last.

She blinked at him, and there was something, for a moment, in her expression that made him think she appreciated him not pushing her.

"Good night," she said and slipped into her room, closing the door.

He heard the lock turn again.

There. She was safe.

He'd done his duty.

He could go to his own room and pray for sleep himself. He'd earned that much.

But instead he stood there, in the dark hallway, wishing he could have said something more, hand flexing against the urge to knock. To ask her to let him in. To hold on to the moment a little longer. And it was many long minutes before he was finally able to turn away and leave.

CHAPTER 16

"All right," Honore said as the appointed hour for breakfast was coming to an end. "We have a change of plans for this morning. Lady Katiya has seen fit to invite the women in our party to attend a ceremony with her."

Chloe's ears pricked up. She had been late to breakfast, and despite guzzling tea and eating her fill of fried bread and eggs and the soured cream with preserved fruit that the Andalyssians had served, her head still reminded her that she'd had too little sleep and too much of that goddess damned kafiet. Not hungover precisely, but not looking forward to spending the morning sitting in the back of some meeting room taking notes while Honore and the other senior officers talked trade with the Andalyssians.

A social event might not be much easier, but Katiya had been friendly and her sister entertaining. There would be, at least, less chance of disgracing herself by dozing off. She poured herself another mug of tea as Honore continued.

"I expect this won't be the last such unexpected invitation. Nor do I think it prudent for us to refuse at this point. Not until we have a better view of how things lie and what parts of these things we can avoid without giving offense." She tilted her head, spreading her hands before flattening them on the table with a huff of a breath.

Understandable that she would view the invitation as somewhat frustrating. She had more pressing tasks. It was a mark of respect that Aristides had chosen her to deal with such a complicated mission. But perhaps he hadn't factored in the more...traditional nature of the court and the fact that some parts of this wedding would be segregated by sex. Hopefully not too many, or Colonel Brodier was going to have to choose between offending the king's fiancée or failing her empire.

She didn't know when Lucien was meeting with House Elannon, but he and several of the others had left breakfast early. She'd been relieved not to be assigned to his team. Their late-night walk had been too comfortable for a moment or two. Better to stay away from him.

"I'm given to understand that our uniforms will be acceptable," Honore continued, "so no need to change. The ceremony begins shortly. Someone will come to fetch us." She turned her attention to Captain Theisse. "You will take charge of the treaty meeting until I can join you."

Captain Theisse nodded. "Of course. You will miss some of the boring preliminaries, but we'll take notes."

Colonel Brodier looked as though she'd rather not miss any of the preliminaries, boring or otherwise.

"Do we know what the ceremony involves?" Chloe asked.

Honore shook her head. "The message called it the tscherov. I haven't had time to ask more than that. I only received the invitation as I was leaving to come to breakfast."

"Tscherov," the Andalyssian in the Chloe's brain suggested, meant something like twine or braid or string. Which left her none the wiser.

"It wasn't mentioned in any of the information provided by the Elenian ambassador or the Andalyssians," Honore continued. "Which means it's probably something they weren't expecting us to be involved with. But the invitation was for us to watch, so hopefully we can't go too wrong with that." She looked across at Chloe. "You spoke with Lady Katiya last night, didn't you? Did she mention this?"

"No," Chloe said. "She was very kind though. And seemed interested in Illvya." Her memory of the previous evening was slightly blurred thanks to the kafiet, but she was certain she hadn't forgotten an invitation.

"Well, you must have made a good impression," Honore said. "Well done, Lieutenant. Of course, the other possibility is that they're throwing us into something complicated to see if we will make idiots of ourselves, but let's hope that's not it."

That thought hadn't occurred to Chloe. Time to begin thinking like a diplomat. Katiya seemed unlikely to play political games—though appearances could be deceptive—but Sejerin Silya or one of the Ashmeisters might try. "If they wanted us to do that, surely it would be one of the important ceremonies they'd try to sabotage?"

"Depends whether they wanted to get rid of us or just embarrass us," Honore said. "But let us take the optimistic view for now and assume Lady Katiya is merely being welcoming."

That gelled better with the impression she'd formed of Katiya and Irina. Irina was obviously headstrong, but Katiya also clearly loved her sister and had been, as far as Chloe could tell, quite genuine in her gentle curiosity about Lumia. Chloe had spent enough time with noblewomen to have a fair sense of when one of them was faking friendship or kindness. "Perhaps one of the Wardmeister's staff could tell us more about the ceremony?"

"There's no time for that. We will just have to see what happens." Honore pushed her chair back. "So, keep your wits about you."

✦ ✦ ✦

The tscherov was held halfway across the palace. There had been little chatter as the ten of them followed the servant through the hallways. Chloe had focused on spotting landmarks along the way that might help her find her way back again should the need arise.

Some of the hallways had windows that gave glimpses outside. The palace was built into the mountain in tiers, and the outer edge of each was given over to gardens and terraces. A clever way to give the inhabitants access to outdoor spaces. There seemed to be more small trees and shrubs than flowers, some of them turning gold and red, some bare-branched already. In such a cold climate, flowers might be difficult any time other than high summer.

Maybe Irina would know more about that. Chloe was looking forward to seeing her again. She and her sister had, so far, been the bright spots in the trip. They were strangers, yes, but it had been pleasant to speak to women who didn't know her history. Or at least showed no sign of it. As the servant showed them into a small but airy sunny reception room, she hoped she would get to speak with them again, diplomacy or not.

Despite the sunshine, the room was cool. The far wall had two glass doors leading out to a garden, and one of them was partially open.

The cold didn't seem to bother the Andalyssians. Katiya sat on a dainty gilded chair in the center of the room with about thirty other women milling around her. A number of them wore the blue and green that Irina had worn last night—including Irina herself. Her copper head was easy to spot amongst all the blonde. She stood with an older blonde woman who looked enough like both Katiya and Irina that Chloe assumed she must be their mother.

Some of the other women wore the silver and white of the royal family and the rest a mix of other house colors. Three or four of them were younger girls—maybe fifteen or sixteen—and one of the women in yellow and pale green held a baby wrapped in a white cloth embroidered with flowers in the same colors.

No red though. No sign of any seers.

But given the small size of the gathering, maybe the women were those Katiya actually liked rather than people she was obliged to include. Which begged the question why she'd suddenly decided to involve the Illvyans. In their uniforms, they looked like a flock of crows amongst the colorful Andalyssians. The women's dresses were less elaborate than the court robes, but the long vests they wore over their dresses were still embroidered with intricate patterns.

Tables laden with covered baskets flanked Katiya, but Chloe couldn't tell if they held food or something else. Katiya rose with a smile as they approached.

"Colonel Brodier, welcome." She flashed a brilliant smile at the rest of them. "Ladies. I'm pleased you could join me this morning."

She was going to make a good queen. She seemed to like people. And had the knack for making them feel comfortable.

"Thank you for the invitation, Lady Katiya," Colonel Brodier said. "I will confess I am intrigued."

"We're just waiting for the seer," Katiya said. "Then we'll begin. This is a less formal ceremony, a blessing of the bride, as it were." She paused, as though struck by an idea, then turned to call over her shoulder. "Rina, come over here."

Irina's bright head lifted, and she bounced over to join them. "You bellowed, sister dearest?"

Katiya reached out and tweaked one of the blue-ribbon ends hanging from Irina's braids. "Queens do not bellow."

"You're not queen yet," Irina said. But then she bobbed a curtsy. "Colonel Brodier, it's nice to see you again."

"Would you mind standing with the ladies here until it's your turn?" Katiya said. "You can explain to them what's going on. I'd better go back before Mother has a fit. If Sejerin Neni doesn't arrive soon, she's going to go on the warpath. The schedule is tight today."

The woman Chloe thought was Katiya's mother did look tense, though she was mostly hiding it. She, like her daughter, appeared too palely pretty to ever go on the warpath, but Chloe knew better than to judge a woman on looks alone, and this one had raised a daughter who was going to be a queen.

"Yes, yes," Irina said. "Shoo on back to all of them." She made a small "go away" gesture at Katiya, who just laughed, kissed her cheek, and made her way back over to the chair.

As she settled her skirts and vest around her, the door opened and a short plump woman with hair the color of a cloud on the edge of sunset curling around her shoulders came bustling through. She wore white and a vest like the others. But hers was embroidered with runes in red, the way the sejerin's robes had been last night. But against the white, they looked cheerful, not ominous.

This, then, was the Sejerin Neni who Katiya had mentioned.

She hurried over to Katiya, bent to kiss both her cheeks, then straightened. "My apologies for being late. There was a—" She broke off. "But no, that explanation is too boring, and I'm sure it will be more fun just to begin."

Katiya nodded agreement, a smile lighting her face. The seer stepped back and looked around. "Lady Greta, do you wish to begin? As mother of the bride-to-be, you can set the order if you wish."

Katiya's mother smiled, the expression half relief, and came around to join her daughter, standing by her shoulder.

Irina said softly, "The first part is just a blessing. Then the tscherov will start."

Sejerin Nene, beaming, spoke a few short sentences in seer tongue. Unlike Silya, her voice was light and happy. There was a faint glimmer in the air around her, like sequins sparkling in the light, and Chloe detected an icy chime at the edge of hearing. Whatever magic the sejerin was using was gentle at best.

She finished speaking, still smiling, and stepped back.

"Now," she said. "Lady Greta, you can begin." She waved a hand at one of the nearest women. "Uncover the baskets."

Women moved to follow instructions, and another of the women in blue and green placed a short wooden stool in front of Katiya, who was rolling back the long sleeves of her dress. There was some sort of symbol on her right forearm, but Chloe couldn't see it clearly. Lady Greta sat down on the stool and then hunted through the baskets as each of the six was presented to her, pulling a long length of colored thread from each.

She handed one end of each thread to Katiya to hold and then began to plait them together with a deftness that spoke of much practice. Around her the other women began to half sing, half hum a melody.

"This is the tscherov," Irina said. "Each guest will make one. The song is about marriage and joy and such things. But the maker of the tscherov puts her own good thoughts into her work. Those with power add a little charm for good luck. For those without, the sejerin will add that. Watch."

Chloe leaned forward, curiosity piqued. Now that she was looking for it, she saw a faint glow around Lady Greta's hands, but any sound of magic was blocked by the singing and laughter coming from the group of women. They were repeating the first verse of the song by the time Lady Greta finished her braid, a fine length of cord now about half the width of Chloe's little finger and perhaps a foot long. From a distance it was hard to determine all the colors, but there was definitely blue and green.

She and Katiya both knotted their ends. Then Lady Greta held it up to the sejerin, who laid her own hand on it briefly before nodding and passing it back to Greta, who looped it several times around Katiya's right wrist and tied it off. It looked loose enough to slide off if Katiya wanted. Lady Greta stood, kissed her daughter's cheeks again, looking pleased, then nodded at the woman who'd placed the stool.

"That's Aunt Vilna," Irina said. "She'll go next."

"Is there any particular meaning to the order?" Honore asked. She looked intrigued.

Irina shrugged. "We start with the mother, but then it can be each woman who picks the next, or the bride might. Katiya is letting each of us choose. She doesn't like anyone to feel left out." She shook her head fondly.

"And what about the colors?" Chloe asked.

"For a wedding, we use six strands. It's supposed to be four colors to represent the four strands of magic—there are a couple choices for each of those—and then two to represent the weaver's blessing. Here at court, usually that means the two house colors. Mama did our blue and green"—she gestured down at her vest—"as you saw."

"Will you?" Chloe asked.

Irina shrugged. "I haven't decided. I'll see what song the earth sings to me."

"You hear magic?" Chloe asked. "Most people just see it."

"We are taught to listen," Irina said. "But not all can hear. I think I do because of my earth sense."

Much as she wanted to know more about earth sense, Chloe didn't think now was the time to ask. It was clearly something slightly out of the ordinary for a woman, and with a seer present, she didn't want to risk causing offense by discussing something not strictly in accordance with balance.

"You said for a wedding," Giane asked, saving Chloe. "Do you do this for other events as well?"

"Babies," Irina said. She jerked her chin toward the woman with the child. "Wee Ivan over there will have one. Those are simpler. Two strands for family, two for good wishes, usually, as no one knows what magic a baby might have. His mama would have received some from her friends and family after she gave birth. That's the only other one with a proper ritual to the weaving though. People make them for friends, too. Children mostly. But sometimes if a friend is sick or sad or for birthdays, people will make them. Especially in the smaller towns. There are different patterns that belong to particular towns or families."

"It looks complicated," Chloe said.

"Not really. Well, some patterns might be, but at the heart of it, it's just a braid." Irina glanced up at Chloe's hair, where she'd wrapped two braids around her head as a quick and simple option to keep it out of the way. "If you can do that, you can do this."

Chloe looked at Irina's braids, which were arranged in a far more complicated manner than any Illvyan hairstyle she'd ever seen, involving not only a plethora of fine braids but ribbons and glass beads. Or perhaps they were gems. Many of the women had jewels sparkling at their throats and wrists and ears. Showing off their kingdom's wealth, perhaps? "I think Andalyssians might take braiding more seriously than we do."

Irina snorted. "Small children make these. Just watch, you'll see how it's done."

She subsided back into silence, and they watched the next few women take their turn. The song changed a few times, and as Chloe studied each woman, she could see that each moved her fingers in slightly different ways. After five bracelets, Katiya held up her hands, laughing and flexing her fingers. "Time for a break. And wine."

Chloe glanced at Honore. The colonel was starting to look less interested and more like she was thinking of the no doubt long list of things she should be doing rather than watching thirty women repeat a ritual thirty times. According to the clock sitting on the mantel, they'd arrived a little over half an hour ago. At this rate, the ceremony would take at least three hours. It would be midday before they got to the treaty talks.

She shifted her feet and rubbed her hands together, glad of the chance to move. The room was warmer now that everyone had been standing around for some time, but not by much. Time for that warming charm again. Servants were circulating with glasses of wine and cups of what smelled like tea. No sign of kafiet, thank goodness.

Tea in hand, she wandered over to the window, ignoring the cooler air as she took in the view. From this side of the palace, she could see only a slice of the city below, and if their schedule continued to be as busy as it had been so far, she doubted she would be seeing much more than that. Perhaps after the wedding itself. The month of ceremonies to follow was less frantic. Of course, they would still be focused on their mission. But to make up for her frustration at not being able to get to know the city, there was, at least, a breathtaking view of the mountains. Their lower reaches were wooded, and there was the odd patch of green here and there above the tree line which must be valleys or small plateaus, but the peaks seemed to stretch forever into the distance.

"Enjoying the view?" Katiya asked, coming to stand beside her.

"It's beautiful," Chloe said. Beautiful and wild and not a little intimidating. There was a harshness to the mountains. An unmistakable air of "enter at your own peril." As she had no intention of venturing farther into them on her own, she could ignore that and merely enjoy the spectacle.

"And the ceremony?" Katiya said with a smile.

Chloe turned back from the window. "It's very interesting. We don't have anything like it back home." She gestured down at Katiya's arm, where the five tscherovs she'd acquired hung in a rainbow band of color. "What do you do with them afterward?"

Katiya giggled. "Traditionally, I'm supposed to hang them on the bedposts on my wedding night. But Misha's bed is carved from stone. It doesn't really have bedposts."

Chloe raised an eyebrow but refused to be drawn into the subject of how familiar Katiya was with the king's bedchamber. "Is that a tattoo on your forearm? If you don't mind me asking?"

"I don't mind." Katiya held her arm up, shaking the bracelets back toward her elbow. "It's my zaka. We get them on our Ascension to mark our connection to the goddess."

The design was a stylized tree and moon in shades of blue and green that were very dark against Katiya's pale skin.

"Does everyone get the same one?"

"No, there are variations for house and personal taste. Most people use elements from their house marks to work into the design. You've seen some of those on our robes. Each house has a few key motifs but plenty of other symbols, so very few zaka are the same." Katiya smiled. "They're not the first we get. Those are the keya." She dragged a finger across her left bicep. "Around our arm here when we turn thirteen and pledge loyalty to the House. Those tend to be more similar."

Intriguing. There'd been nothing about tattoos in the briefings. "Are there more tattoos?"

"Well, the marriage mark," Katiya said. "That one goes here." She touched her chest above her heart. "First drawn in indigo dye. Then, once the marriage month ends, it is made permanent and tattooed if the couple don't change their minds."

"You can do that?" Chloe asked, startled.

Katiya laughed and sipped her wine. "Well, it would be a vast scandal if I did, so it's just as well Misha and I know we suit. But in the towns and villages, sometimes a couple will realize something isn't right. That's why we have the month. Here in the palace, it's full of ceremony and ritual now, but out there, it's mostly for the newlyweds to spend a lot of time together. There are a few simple ceremonies over the weeks, but it gives them time to be alone and know they've made the right choice."

And have plenty of sex, Chloe imagined. That would be a luxury in a small village where everyone worked hard. A month to spend just with your new wife or husband would be a break from the hard work of day-to-day life. Particularly in such a climate. "What about people who change their minds after a longer time?"

Katiya frowned, shaking her head. "We don't have divorce as

you do. If there is cruelty or violence, then the priests will some-times grant that the marriage be dissolved. But it can be hard to marry again after that. It's not balanced to do it. And it rarely happens in the sixteen houses." She grimaced, as though the subject was uncomfortable.

Time to change the subject back to something lighter. She was spoiling Katiya's fun.

"And other than the marriage mark, are there more?"

"Some people get more. Men, in particular. Some women get them for children or when somebody dies. The seers and the svasyas have their own traditions, too, but some of them are secret."

Of course they were. "Sejerin Neni seems...more approach-able than Sejerin Silya."

"Neni is a sweetheart," Katiya agreed. "She's my second cousin. Or maybe it's third. I lose track. Between the houses, sometimes it seems like everyone starts being a distant relation somehow or other. The House Namenmeisters keep track to make sure no one is marrying too closely."

She'd never thought about that in the aristos back home. Illvya was, of course, a much larger country, and there were more of them, so maybe it wasn't a problem.

"I suppose you would have to," she said, fascinated despite herself.

Katiya smiled. "Is this why you like to do what you do, to learn about others?"

"It's part of it," Chloe said.

"It is a long way to travel. So far from home to find out about tattoos and silly braids."

"Not so far. And not forever. I like to see the world. If I didn't leave home, I wouldn't get to see this." She gestured at the towering snowcaps, blazing white in the sun.

"I've been to Elenia but no farther." Katiya smiled lopsidedly. "The houses keep their daughters close."

"But you'll be queen soon. Will you and His Majesty see

more of the world then? You have other neighbors to deal with besides the Elenians. Near and far."

"Perhaps. In time. I think Misha has more concerns with those at home right now." She took another sip of the wine. "To be a young king is not always easy."

Was that a subtle way of raising the subject of House Elannon? Not the place for such a discussion. But perhaps it was acceptable to reassure her that they didn't want Mikvel to fail.

"He was raised to the job. From what I've seen of him, he is strong and clever. Well suited for his task. And he clearly has good taste to want to marry you." Katiya had a spine of steel beneath her snow-maiden exterior, Chloe suspected. If she didn't, she wouldn't be risking the slightly disapproving looks some of the older women were directing their way because they'd been talking so long. Irina was still chattering enthusiastically with Giane a few feet farther away.

"I'm not sure it's a matter of taste. Our families came to this arrangement when we were young. But we were fortunate. We were friends as children and, over time, came to find something more." Her smile was more relaxed now, more natural. "I will marry the man, not the crown. I think, perhaps, that is a good thing."

"I think, perhaps, you are right," Chloe said. "It is the man who matters, not titles and trappings." Though it might not always be entirely possible to separate the two when the man was a king. Politics was part of that life, and Katiya would need some of that steel to see it through.

"Have you never been tempted to marry again, Lieutenant?"

Chloe still wasn't sure what Katiya knew of her history.

"No, not so far. I loved my husband." Which was true, if not the entire truth. Better to be thought the long-grieving widow than a betrayed one.

"I am sorry." Another sip of the pale green wine, making the row of woven bracelets slip down her arm in a flutter of color. "It is a long time to be alone." Her mouth quirked again, and the glance she gave Chloe was somewhat wicked.

"I think, perhaps, that is a conversation I'm not supposed to be having with the king's bride-to-be," Chloe said. She wasn't about to discuss any other aspects of the few men who'd passed through her bed in Anglion with an Andalyssian who was supposed to be a virgin. She and the king seemed genuinely in love, so who knew if she had managed time alone with him before their wedding, but given the gaggle of women surrounding her today, it seemed unlikely.

Katiya snorted. "I'm not ignorant, Lieutenant, of what happens between men and women."

Chloe glanced back over her shoulder. "Again, I think perhaps this is a conversation not to have in a crowd. And if you're going to ask me about these things, I also think you should call me Chloe." And that Katiya should stop drinking wine and switch to tea.

But then again, Chloe wasn't the one about to marry an ice king. If the wine and some risqué conversation with a foreigner eased any nerves Katiya might be feeling, then all well and good. There would be nerves, of course, no matter how in love Katiya was. Chloe herself had nearly thrown up the night before her own wedding, despite the fact that she'd been certain marrying Charl was the right choice. Perhaps she should have listened to her stomach after all. Imogene, too, had threatened to flee Lumia and make a run for it two days before her marriage with Jean-Paul after a particularly fraught exchange with his mother.

Katiya had to be nervous, no matter how she felt about Mikvel. She wasn't just getting married, she was also becoming a queen. Chloe hadn't been present when Sophie and Cameron married, but she and Imogene had kept Sophie company in the days before her coronation, and there'd been wine and tea and more required to keep the young queen on an even keel. Sophie hadn't been raised to know she would take on the crown as Katiya clearly had, but the responsibility—and the risks—were the same. Royalty was no guarantee of love and happiness and a long and healthy life.

"Katiya, we need to keep going," a voice called from behind them.

Katiya nodded at Chloe, then turned to take her place back in the chair.

CHAPTER 17

The ceremony went on for most of the morning. Katiya stood after every five or so braids and mingled with her guests but didn't come back to speak to the Illvyans until what Chloe calculated should be the last break. Irina still hadn't taken her turn, and she stepped forward to study her sister's arms.

However the magic bound into the braids worked, the colors of the threads almost glowed in the sunshine. Katiya was glowing, too, smiling, cheeks flushed. Irina gestured to the nearest servant and pressed a cup of tea into her sister's hands.

"Drink that. Any more wine and you'll fall asleep, and then I'll get in trouble for not watching you." For a moment, she sounded like the responsible older sister rather than a younger one. "I don't want to spend the rehearsal this afternoon being lectured by our mother and Sejerin Silya. They'll give us that speech about queenly responsibilities again."

Katiya laughed but took the tea, the tscherovs sliding down her wrists. Chloe leaned in to examine the patterns.

"Would you like to try?" Katiya asked.

"Is that allowed?" Chloe asked, surprised. "Isn't this for your friends and family?"

"It's for people who wish me well," Katiya said. Chloe

noticed Honore listening a few steps away. "You wish me well, don't you, Lieutenant de Montesse?"

"Of course," Chloe said, meaning it. Whatever troubles Illvya and Andalyssia had had in the past, she had no desire to see them spill back over into the present. Katiya deserved as happy a life with her king as it was possible for royalty to have. Joy to offset the duties and protocol that would rule a lot of her time. She glanced over Katiya's shoulder at Honore, who raised one eyebrow slightly but didn't shake her head or give any other indication that she thought Chloe should decline. "I'd be honored to try."

"Good," Katiya said, smiling. "You can go second last, before Irina. She can help you."

Chloe gestured at one of the more intricate patterned braids. It was striking, weaving two shades of pale blue, a deep brown, white, a deep green, and red into an almost sinuous repeating wave of color. Chloe had no idea how the pattern was achieved with mere braided thread. "Well, I can't guarantee I'll produce anything as complicated as that, but I'll try my best. And the good wishes part will be easy, Lady Katiya."

Katiya laughed again, shaking the braids back up her arm. As she did so, the light caught the colors again as the circled cords shifted and, Chloe realized the red she'd been admiring was actually a variegated blend of red and orange. The sunlight highlighted the latter, spotlighting a patch where the orange ran against the green for an inch or so.

Chloe blinked. Green and orange. House Elannon. Maybe it was just a coincidence, but it slid a thread of unease down her spine.

As Katiya walked back to her chair, Chloe stepped a little closer to Irina and lowered her voice. "That one I was admiring. Do you know who made it?"

Irina nodded absently, watching her sister. "Lady Cela. Over there in the pale blue. But she won't tell you how she did it.

Some of the patterns are used by certain houses. It's bad manners to copy."

"What house is hers?" Chloe asked, trying to sound casual.

"Reynavik," Irina said. "Well, her husband's house. She was a Daskyev before she married." She frowned. "She's Silya's cousin. Their grandmother was an Elannon." She almost whispered the last word. "But that's not her fault."

If she thought it was strange that Lady Cela had used colors that skated close to House Elannon, she didn't mention it. So maybe Chloe was being paranoid. But she made a mental note to keep an eye on Cela. Hopefully she was friendlier than her cousin. She had the same silvery blonde hair, the pale blue of her dress and vest setting it off nicely. The embroidery on her clothes had no colors resembling those of House Elannon. Only the hint of a pale orange in places and a leafy green that didn't have the same acidic edge to it as the Elannon green.

But Chloe couldn't shake an edge of unease, even if Irina seemed unconcerned. She looked for Honore. The colonel was currently talking quietly with Katiya's mother, and they both looked serious. Not a time to interrupt. Time enough to tell Honore later.

She turned her attention back to the tscherov and hoped she wouldn't make an idiot of herself when it came to her turn.

It probably wasn't a good sign that the meeting had only been underway for a few minutes and Lucien already wished it was kafiet, not tea, in the cup before him. He'd been told his initial meeting with House Elannon would only include a small number of people. So he'd brought only Lieutenant Plesse and Ensign Bretain with him for support.

Apparently the Andalyssians had a different interpretation of small. Or maybe they were putting on a show of strength. He didn't know. The king seemed genuine in his desire to resolve this matter, but Mikvel was only one man. He sat at the head of the table with Roland opposite him. Three men in Surayov colors, who had not been introduced, sat against the wall behind Mikvel, notebooks at the ready. Lucien and his party were seated to the king's right, and across the broad granite table were no fewer than four representatives of House Elannon, the current senior Ashmeister from House Reynavik, Sejerin Silya, and two men in deep green robes who had been introduced as Patrarch Federov and Svasya Meloskya, the two ranking priests of the kingdom.

If they'd thought to overwhelm him with numbers, they shouldn't have bothered. He didn't need anybody else in order to exercise his powers, after all. If he wanted, he could know within seconds if anyone in the room was lying. But he wanted to start the meeting in good faith despite the fact that, so far, the behavior of House Elannon was not reassuring. Their expressions were stony, and they had wasted five minutes in determining who should sit where until Mikvel had given them an exasperated look and told them to take their seats. To their credit, they had followed that order. Not ready to outright defy their king, it seemed.

Mikvel lifted a hand. "All right. We all know why we are here today. Major de Roche, why don't you begin?"

Go first before his people could start ranting? Lucien squared his shoulders. "Of course, Your Majesty. The emperor received the king's request that House Elannon be restored early. While he is respectful of your beliefs, he wishes me to reiterate that there was a reason for the conditions imposed on House Elannon and that he needs to be satisfied that the house has learned from its past before he will agree to lift them."

He watched the faces of the Elannon men. While the two younger men, one of whom—Andrej—was the current head of the house who would have been the Ashmeister, were Elannon still afforded one, looked serious and attentive, the older two were more remote. The oldest, Uli Elannon, was the youngest brother of the Ashmeister who had led them into disaster. He hadn't been part of his brother's plot, but if Lucien had to pick someone who might still hold the seeds of rebellion in his heart, he would choose him. His eyes were ice green and showed no hint of remorse.

Lucien pointedly turned his attention back to Andrej. "Which is why His Imperial Majesty has sent me. He wishes to see true change, not platitudes and pretense of reform. Now, do any of you wish to deny the emperor's authority in this matter? Because that would shorten this process considerably."

No one spoke, though Uli's mouth tightened fractionally.

"No? Good. Then we can begin. Now, today is just a preliminary meeting. I will need to speak to a number of people from House Elannon and the other houses and—"

The patrarch held up his hand. "If I may, Major. We must make sure that you understand the ramifications of this decision. The kingdom must be in balance for the king's wedding to be blessed by the goddess. While the Ashmeisters are not whole, the balance cannot be whole."

He'd been prepared for this line of argument. Which was prevarication at best and religious posturing of the kind he had little time for at worst. After all, they'd crowned their new king without the full council. In fact, they'd done everything for the last thirteen years without a full council, and the country had not yet fallen off the side of the mountain, lack of balance or not. He bit back the urge to say just that. "I am clear. But merely restoring House Elannon is not the path to true balance. Unless I am mistaken, for there to be balance, there cannot be treason at the heart of the kingdom. Treason against the emperor is treason against your king as well, as it can only harm him."

The patrarch looked like he had bitten into something sour, but he didn't offer a counterargument.

"The emperor forgives treason which he chooses," Uli

Elannon said. His voice was low, gravelly. It had been that way when Lucien was last here, and age had only added to the effect.

"Does he?" Lucien asked.

"There is one among your party who was married to a traitor, isn't there?" Uli continued. "Clearly the emperor has forgiven her."

Lucien's stomach tightened. Chloe? He was bringing Chloe into this? For what reason? "If you are referring to Lieutenant de Montesse, she had no knowledge of her husband's actions. She is in no way a traitor and continues to serve her emperor faithfully."

"Convenient," Uli said.

"Uli—" Andrej began in a warning tone, but Lucien held up a hand.

"My lord Elannon, I will answer, if I may." He stared at Uli while Andrej nodded and sat back in his chair.

Lucien leaned forward in his. "It is truth, sir. Not convenience. I do not serve convenience, and I never will. I do, however, serve the truth. As I am sure you remember. And, like Lieutenant de Montesse, if House Elannon has done as it should and removed those who would place rot and dissent over the well-being of its members and its country, then you have nothing to fear from the truth."

"Are you so sure of the daughter of ravens, then? Trouble likes that one. It's not finished with her," Sejerin Silya said.

What in the name of the goddess did that mean? But he didn't want to get into an argument with the seer. "Lieutenant de Montesse is loyal. I know that to be truth."

"So certain. Those the goddess touches are not so simple, Illvyan."

He flattened his hand on the table to stop it curling into a fist. "I know, I am one of them, Sejerin. The goddess gave me my magic. I use it at her will." Hers and the emperor's. So far, she hadn't objected to anything Aristides had ever tasked him with.

Or as far as he could tell. He still had his magic, after all. "The lieutenant is not part of this matter."

Silya looked amused for a fleeting moment. "And how shall you know the truth? Using your power?"

The power the Andalyssians thought unbalanced. "The power granted to me by the grace of the goddess. Yes, where necessary. But it will not be necessary for everyone. And I will seek permission before using it. I do not use my power on the unwilling or the unwary other than when it is required for a matter of law. This is not yet a matter of law." A reminder that it could become so should they defy the emperor.

The sejerin looked no happier with him than Uli. He was winning no friends around this table. Not that he had expected to.

King Mikvel cleared his throat. "Thank you, Major. I am happy with your approach. I am eager for this matter to be settled." His voice was calm, steel behind the words.

He cast a look at Uli Elannon that was not entirely happy. He might be young, but it seemed House Elannon were underestimating their king if they thought he was simply going to roll over and do their bidding. Or let them take his throne.

"Andrej, you will assist Major de Roche in his discussions. Starting now."

Chloe didn't get the chance to speak to the colonel before the evening's functions began. Honore had been determined to make up for lost time after the tscherov, and the afternoon had turned into a blur of meetings and appointments where she sat in the back and took notes.

After the meetings, there had only just been time to change for dinner. A more formal affair tonight, followed by a ball. As there would be every night between now and the wedding. Once Mikvel and Katiya were safely married, there would be some breathing space to focus on actual diplomacy. There would be fewer wedding-related demands on their time. Only in the final week did the schedule look crowded again in the lead-up to the king and Katiya making their wedding marks final and Katiya's coronation.

Provided she didn't change her mind—unlikely, if Chloe was any judge—or that things didn't go completely sideways with Lucien's investigation of House Elannon.

At dinner, Chloe wasn't seated with Honore. She was at a table in the second row with Gilles Theisse. Honore and Lucien, thankfully, were seated in the first row again, as a reflection of their rank. Honore wore a silver-blue gown that matched her eyes. She and Lucien could almost be Andalyssians.

But not quite. Lucien's evening jacket was black, his shirt and cravat snow white. He looked like night fallen amongst the rainbow Andalyssians. The choice of plain black and white was severe even for Illvyan evening wear, where the men sometimes wore colors. The only way he could have stood out more would be to turn up in his uniform. Besides his eyes, the only spot of color he sported was the bloodred ruby in the heavy gold Castaigne signet ring he wore on his right hand. Lucien had never been showy in his choice of clothes, but his outfit tonight seemed to be intentional. A reminder of his profession rather than his rank?

None of her business, and she had been watching him a shade too long as it was. She turned her attention back to her dinner companions, taking each mouthful with care to avoid spilling anything on her gown. The dress was drawing enough attention without her adding to it through clumsiness.

Left to her own taste, she wouldn't have chosen this precise shade of scarlet. It was a tad too bright with her red-and-black-streaked hair and not designed to blend into the background. But it had been one of Imogene's gowns that Helene Designy had deemed to be easy to alter quickly, and that had been the end of that discussion. It was lovely, made from a heavy silk and beaded with a spray of flowers that clustered the bodice and spilled down the skirt in a glittering fall. It wasn't, however, very Andalyssian.

Allita had done her best with Chloe's hair, working a number of fine braids into it that were going to be a nightmare to undo on her own. It was a nod to Andalyssian fashion, but the braids emphasized the differing shades of her hair, drawing attention to her magic.

Imogene had lent her jewels, but she had restrained herself to only a pair of ruby earrings. The dress was enough. The balls were only going to be more and more elaborate as they approached the wedding, and then there was the wedding itself and the coronation. She needed to keep something back for those.

Dinner passed quickly. It was easier to follow the conversations, her confidence with Andalyssian growing, but she still had to pay attention to make sure she didn't miss anything. Or offend anybody. But it was exhilarating to know she was starting to be able to hold her own, and she was smiling by the time Captain Theisse offered her his arm after dinner to accompany her to the ballroom.

She was tempted to tell him about Lady Cela, but it was too risky when they were surrounded by Andalyssians who understood Illvyan perfectly well. She hadn't yet seen Cela tonight, but it seemed unlikely she wouldn't be at the ball if she had been invited to the tscherov. Maybe she could get Irina to make an introduction, then see if a conversation with the woman might ease her doubts.

The ballroom was almost as big as the King's Hearth, though decorated in a more intimate manner. There were, inevitably, tapestries, but here they were narrow columns of white and silver velvets hanging floor to ceiling between expanses of white plastered walls studded with small jeweled tiles that dazzled the eye. It wasn't as large as Aristides's ballroom, and it lacked the mirrors that made the emperor's room appear almost infinite, but it was breathtaking in its own way.

A reminder that Andalyssia's riches came from the mines beneath their feet. Though she didn't like thinking too closely about the mines. The knowledge that parts of the mountain supporting the vast palace were hollowed out into tunnels and chambers far beneath her feet made her feel odd. Like she was back on a ship or the navire, unsure of her footing.

The dance floor was pale wood inlaid with silver, the patterns more sinuous than those on the walls. It would have been helpful if they'd formed the patterns of the Andalyssian set dances. She'd studied them on the journey, and they had seemed straightforward, but there hadn't been much room to practice on board the navire. As much as she liked to dance, the added complication of worrying about tripping over her feet trying to get the steps right while making appropriate conversation in Andalyssian seemed likely to turn it into a chore rather than a pleasure.

The rest of the room was furnished with low padded couches and benches and chairs, all covered with white velvet. Silver-legged glass tables sat between them, holding candles in glass lanterns. The flickering candlelight reflected and danced over the room, and the air carried the now familiar incense scent of the court. Above the room, vast chandeliers glittered, but the points of light within them were earth lamps, too steady to be flames.

The court congregated in small groups. She didn't see any pattern to the gatherings. No clear-cut territorial divide between the houses. Some groups wore predominantly the colors of one house, but others were more mixed, and she didn't yet know enough about the various alliances between the sixteen noble houses, let alone the lesser ones, to understand the politics at play.

The section of the room beyond the dance floor was the

domain of the royal family, the furniture more lavish, the servants more plentiful. Katiya, who wore a pink dress that seemed a well-judged way to avoid wearing either Surayov or Uleniska colors, stood with Mikvel and some of the other Surayovs. Irina stood with her sister, wearing a gown the color of sunlit seas. Their parents and several others in Uleniska blue and green rounded out the party.

The clothing was extravagant and less severe than the court robes. House embroidery edged hems, necklines, jacket cuffs, and lapels for the men, and most of the court still favored their house colors, but there was more variation in the ball gowns than in the formal robes they'd worn to the ceremony at the King's Hearth. The women's dresses had long sleeves and modest necklines. Helene hadn't been able to do much to raise the neckline of some of Chloe's gowns, but she'd added deep ruffled bands of beaded lace that reached her wrists to the formerly elbow-length sleeves. They would fall back when she danced but gave the illusion of length otherwise.

Chloe and Gilles joined Honore and Lucien, who were talking with a man in the night blue and red of House Petrov. House Petrov was deeply involved in the mines and had representatives at several of the earlier meetings, but Chloe didn't recognize him.

Before Honore could make introductions, the king led Katiya toward the dance floor and nearly everybody else hurried to form sets around them, leaving the Illvyans with no choice but to join in.

"How good is your memory?" Gilles asked as he led her to one of the sets forming farther down the room from the king. Good strategy for avoiding too much attention.

"As good as it's going to get for now. But I've always had a good memory for dances. How about you?"

"Your toes are safe with me, Lieutenant," he said.

"Let's hope so. I only brought three pairs of dancing slippers, and they have to last the month."

He laughed and swung her into place.

The music started, a swirl of strings and some sort of long pipe that pulsed low and deep, setting a steady rhythm that made her toes twitch. The next hour or so became a blur of dancing and laughing as she tried to cover her inevitable mistakes. Thankfully, most of them laughed with her.

The dances had begun with some slower choices, but the musicians quickened the pace with each set that passed until each dance was a whirl of spinning and changing partners and trying to catch her breath each time there was a minute's pause at the end of a song. At least the speed limited the need for conversation. Eventually the musicians came to a halt and stood for applause.

Mikvel led Katiya off the dance floor, and as soon as his feet were both clear of the inlaid wood, there was a mass exodus of people heading for the couches and reaching for glasses of campenois held at the ready by a legion of silver-and-white-clad servants.

Chloe tried not to gulp hers down too fast, wishing it was water rather than wine and that Andalyssians had the same fashion for fans as Illvyans. The room wasn't as hot as a ballroom in Lumia or even the palace in Kingswell, thank the goddess, but it was warm enough after dancing like a woman possessed for an hour. Her feet, in their new slippers, were already protesting. She was out of practice. Well, there would plenty of hot water to soak them in back in her room, and she knew which herbs she could add to ease the inevitable aches and pains. Maybe she should ask Irina for a tour of the stillroom to make sure there would be more available in the palace if she needed them. The supply she had brought with her might not last the month if all the dancing was going to as vigorous.

She looked around for Gilles as she sipped campenois. She'd changed partners so many times that she hadn't finished the dancing even in the same set as him. Thankfully, she hadn't yet had to dance with Lucien.

Before she spotted any of the Illvyans, Irina broke through the crowd, bearing her own glass. She grinned when she saw Chloe. "Tired already, Lady de Montesse?"

"Just resting a minute," Chloe said. "Those dances require some stamina."

"A good way of keeping warm on a cold winter night," Irina said, flashing a dimple.

Chloe could think of better ways. Mostly involving many layers of quilts and a good book in bed. Perhaps a companion, though that wasn't a subject to discuss with Irina, no matter how much her comment may have been a leading one. "Our nights aren't quite so cold in Illvya."

"The nights aren't so cold in most places," Irina agreed. "We're as cold as it gets. Well, other than the ice reaches, but nobody is dancing there, I think." She finished her wine and handed the glass to the nearest servant. "But I came to fetch you. Katiya has a favor to ask, my lady."

"Of course, Lady Irina," Chloe said, returning the formality. "I am happy to be of assistance to your sister."

Irina rolled her eyes. "I'm being polite. I was given strict instructions that you are Lady de Montesse at the evening celebrations, not Lieutenant de Montesse. Almost as though you are two people."

"Not two people, but two different roles, rather," Chloe said. "Lieutenant is the diplomat. Lady is the wedding guest. Well, as near as I can figure it. But they're both me, and I'd prefer that you called me Chloe."

"Let's wait until everyone has had a few more rounds of wine," Irina said. "Then all the eagle-eyed old biddies who are sticklers for protocol won't be watching me so closely. It's very dull, this business of being related to the near-queen. Bad enough growing up in one of the sixteen houses, but the royal family adds new layers of ridiculousness to the whole business."

"That has been my experience," Chloe agreed. "But you'll get used to it. And after the wedding, the fuss will die down. You'll be continuing your studies, won't you?"

"Yes," Irina said, not sounding enthusiastic. "For a while, at least."

Chloe was going to ask her what she meant, but they'd reached the royal party. Katiya stepped forward to take her hands and kiss her cheeks as Irina vanished back into the crowd.

Chloe managed a hasty curtsy in the king's direction when Katiya let her go.

"Good evening, Lady Katiya. That is a beautiful gown you're wearing."

Indeed, Katiya was glowing in a shade of pink light enough to echo the gleam of a pearl. Chloe didn't think she'd seen that precise shade before. It would be popular in Anglion, where the nobles were pearl-obsessed, believing, wrongly, that pearls repelled the sanctii they feared so much. They were learning differently now that they were ruled by a queen bonded to a sanctii, but she doubted they'd be giving up their jewels any time soon.

Andalyssians favored harder gems. Katiya was dripping in diamonds, the centerpiece of the collar she wore being a large stone nearly the same shade as her dress. Diamond clusters decorated her hair as well, set in delicate flower shapes placed to suggest a circlet...or perhaps a crown.

"Thank you. Yours is lovely also," Katiya said. "Perhaps after the wedding we will have a chance to discuss Illvyan fashion some more."

"I would be happy to, my lady," Chloe said. "Irina said you wanted to ask a favor?"

Katiya smiled. "I do. Speaking of Illvya, as it were, Mikvel and I thought it might be fun if you would teach us one of the Illvyan pair dances. What do you call them again?"

"A waltz?" Chloe half squeaked. Katiya wanted to waltz? The Andalyssian dances, fast as they were, did a good job of making sure the dance partners were rarely very close for long. And hands tended to clasp hands or shoulders or elbows, not waists as a waltz required. If Irina had been worried about using Chloe's name, what would her eagle-eyed biddies have to say about their king and his fiancée waltzing?

"That's it," Katiya said. "Will you?" She nodded at someone over Chloe's shoulder. "Lord Castaigne is right there. He seems to be a good dancer."

CHAPTER 18

Damn. Maybe Katiya wasn't out to cause a scandal but rather matchmaking. This was Andalyssia. In Andalyssia, women married. Chloe, as a widow, was an oddity. Irina's teasing about Lucien was just that, as far as Chloe could tell. But Katiya...well, she was more traditional, maybe. Or perhaps suffering from that peculiar state of being in love herself and therefore wanting everyone else to share her happiness. Whatever the reason, Chloe didn't want to add fuel to the fire by acting rattled by the idea of dancing with Lucien. "He's never trodden on my toes," she admitted. "Not that we've danced often." Not precisely true, unless she only counted her time in exile.

"He managed well in the sets," Katiya said. "As did you and the captain. It seems only fair that, after we've forced you to learn our dances, we let you try something more familiar." Her smile widened. "And here is Lord Castaigne now. Thank you, 'Rina," she said to her sister, who had joined them again.

Chloe set her teeth and turned to find Lucien standing behind her. She dipped a curtsy automatically. "Lord Castaigne."

He bowed in turn. "Lady de Montesse. Lady Katiya. I'm reliably informed my services are required?" He was smiling, but it was slightly wary to Chloe's eye.

"I want to learn how to waltz," Katiya said. "Would you and Chloe be so kind as to demonstrate? I understand our musicians know some suitable music."

They did? Chloe hid a sigh. Definitely planned, if Katiya had gone to the trouble of making sure the band could play Illvyan waltzes. And Mikvel would have to have agreed. As much as he adored Katiya, he wouldn't indulge her if there wasn't some benefit to the crown. So, matchmaking or politics? A way to show that the king and queen were forward-thinking? Or show that the Illvyans were scandalous and not to be trusted? Hopefully the former.

Chloe thought Lucien was no more pleased by the proposition than she was. But he, like her, was not letting that show. "Of course, Lady Katiya. Now?"

"While the court catches their breath, yes," Katiya said. "You'll have everybody's attention."

A muscle flickered in Lucien's jaw. No doubt he was analyzing the situation, too. But he merely bowed again, then offered Chloe his arm. "Shall we dance, then, Lady de Montesse?"

She forced a smile. "My pleasure, my lord."

The musicians, forewarned it seemed, were just taking their seats again as she and Lucien reached the center of the dance floor. The babble of conversation filling the room faded away. Not to the complete eerie silence that had greeted them in the King's Hearth, but they plainly had the court's attention.

"It seems we have become the evening's entertainment, my lord," she said, still smiling and pitching her voice in a low ballroom tone she knew wouldn't carry far.

"Then we shall put on a show, my lady," Lucien said. "I will try to keep this as short as possible, but I expect we won't get away with just one dance."

"I'm sure I'll survive," she said. "And we should start or

they'll think we're arguing. Are you going to give some instruction as we dance?"

He shook his head, a smile flashing briefly. "I don't feel like bellowing like a drill sergeant. Let them figure it out. It's not overly complicated, after all."

That was a matter of opinion. On the surface, a waltz was simple . An ability to keep to a count of three and follow one's partner were the main requirements. But there were a thousand tiny subtleties that could be communicated through the touch of a hand on one's waist or fingers or the precise distance held between the dancers' bodies. In the arms of the right man, a waltz could be a seduction. Indeed, the first dance she'd ever had with Charl had been a waltz. After that, she'd tumbled into love like a fool.

She was safe from that tonight. "Then let us get this over with. Unless you want me to lead?" It was an old joke that tipped off her tongue before she could stop it.

Lucien's eyes widened a fraction, but then he grinned. "Trust me, my lady. I'm more than capable of taking you where you need to go."

He nodded at the musicians and settled his hand on her waist, the clasp of it firm and familiar. Out of options, she placed her other hand in his and let him whirl her into motion.

It was strange at first, and awkward, as it had been back at Imogene's.

Not so much the shock of the unexpected but the fact that she was once again dancing with Lucien in a room full of people, drawing attention she didn't want. But to avoid fanning that attention into something worse, she needed to behave as she would with any other partner. So she smiled and looked into his eyes as though he was no different to any other man.

He smiled, too, the expression polite. But his eyes were less so. Before, when they'd danced, they'd talked and joked and laughed, and she'd never spent much time gazing into his eyes. Never noticed the gold flecks dancing amongst the green. Never noticed quite how thick his eyelashes were up close or that the outer rim of his pupil was circled with a green like the shadow beneath a moonlit leaf. A green so deep it might as well be black. A wild shade, capturing her attention.

Suddenly, there was no room, no other people. There was only the weight of his hand on her waist, so clear she fancied she felt each individual finger curled against her though the layers of fabric beneath them should make that impossible. His hand over hers was firm, his skin warm, and she swayed into his hold, moving a fraction closer unbidden.

His pupils flared, the green more intense. Her face was hot, and she knew she couldn't blame the dance. Nor was it responsible for the racing beat of her heart. No, something else drove her pulse and the sudden hum of heat over her skin. She wanted. Wanted in a way she hadn't for quite some time. In a way she couldn't want *him*.

Not Lucien. Not with all that lay between them.

She tried to pull away slightly, but he held her firm, as though he knew what she was thinking. *Please, Goddess,* she hoped he did not. He wouldn't use his power on her, couldn't if she wasn't speaking, but he knew her well, this man. Too well and not well enough. But he didn't let her go and he didn't let her falter, though she was suddenly afraid that the whirl of her feet and her mind might combine to send her stumbling.

He held her safe. Held her fast. While her world shattered and reformed and she fought for resolve.

Not this man.

Never him.

Her body might yearn, but she was not that young, foolish girl anymore, and he was the last man alive she would take into her bed, let alone her heart. Or so she told herself as they danced together as easily as if they shared a mind. Or a heart. Or a body.

Charl had been a good dancer. Lucien, tonight, was perfect.

But it was an illusion. One that had nothing to do with his magic and everything to do with reality. She would dance with him, but the music would stop and she would let go of his hand and step away. Would forget a moment of madness.

And lock away her heart and her treacherous body once more.

For the second waltz, some of the Andalyssians, including Katiya and Mikvel, joined them, and then for the third, the floor became crowded, which allowed her to regain some control of her senses.

At the end of the dance, Chloe made her excuses to Lucien and escaped into the crowd, wondering when the room had become so hot. She eyed the servants' trays, wanting something to clear her head, not cloud it faster. One man carried silver tumblers rather than wineglasses, and she worked her way toward him.

"What's in those?" she asked. When he smiled and told her it was snow-chilled mint tea, she grabbed one thankfully as the music began again.

When she turned back to watch the dancers, Irina had found her.

"That looks like fun," she said, watching her sister laughing as Mikvel waltzed her expertly around the room. Well enough, in fact, that it looked as though he'd been practicing.

"It can be," Chloe said. "You should try it."

"I avoid dancing. I'm clumsy."

Chloe narrowed her eyes. She hadn't seen Irina move anything less than gracefully. But she understood not wanting to draw attention.

"Are you sure you don't want to marry Lord Castaigne?" Irina asked.

Chloe almost choked on the tea. "Quite sure," she sputtered after regaining her breath.

Irina lifted a brow. "He was looking at you the way Misha looks at Katya."

The young king looked at his fiancée as though she was made of sunshine and everything that delighted him in the world. Smitten.

Lucien wasn't smitten. There'd been something in his eyes when they'd danced, but it wasn't adoration. No. It was more primitive than that, dark and heated. Something she wasn't ready to admit to herself, let alone discuss with a well-born Andalyssian virgin.

"It's the waltz," she said lightly. "You're supposed to gaze at each other while you dance it. He was merely being polite."

"Very polite," Irina said with a grin. "I'm in no hurry to get married, but when I do, I hope my husband has such good manners."

Chloe rolled her eyes. "Marriage takes more than good manners. So take your time and choose wisely."

"How old were you when you wed?" Irina asked.

"A little older than you are now." Too young, for all she'd felt certain of her choice and her wisdom back then. "If I had my time over, I'd wait a little longer."

"Did you make the wrong choice?"

That was a question she'd wrestled with for ten years. "I don't know. I loved my husband. I loved the life he represented. But in the end, it turned out I didn't know him. Or not all of him. I'm not sure you can ever fully know another person, of course. But Charl, well, he hid more than most, it seemed. And I didn't see it." None of them had. Until it was too late.

Irina wrinkled her nose. "Lord Castaigne is a Truth Seeker. They are supposed to be honorable men."

"They are. And he is. But I don't wish to be married again, and even if I did, he wouldn't be the man I would choose." She wished she knew exactly what Irina knew about her marriage. "But this is far too serious a topic. And I need more tea."

"They'll bring kafiet later," Irina said.

Chloe laughed. "I'll save the kafiet. The schedule for the next few days seems exhausting. How is your sister holding up? Weddings are stressful enough without all this." She waved a hand at the mass of people.

"She says she is well. She seems happy. But I think she will be happier after the ceremony. She likes other people to be the center of attention more than taking it for herself. She was quite shy when we were younger. Something she made herself overcome when she realized she might be queen someday, but she'd be perfectly happy to just marry Misha quietly and get on with things, I think."

"Well, only a few more days. Then they will get some time alone, yes?"

Irina nodded. "Two days after the wedding. On the third day, there will be a hunt and a picnic in the Senjo valley. Then more parties and ceremonies until the month is up, but not as many as this week." She blew out a breath. "Which is good. I'm behind in my studies."

"Will you stay at court?"

"Katya has asked me to, for the winter. Some of the houses return to their estates for the worst of the weather. But some stay here. The Ashmeisters remain. Winter is the time for planning and rest. I hope they'll let her and Misha be newlyweds awhile and not bother them. But I will keep Katya company if Misha gets too busy kinging."

"You're a good sister," Chloe said. "She'll need time to adjust. Being a queen is a lot of work as far as I can tell."

Irina laughed. "True."

They talked a while longer, and then Chloe rejoined the dances as they reverted to Andalyssian sets, mindful of why she was there. The hours passed quickly, and her feet were sore by the time the dancing ended.

She slipped away to the retiring room to ensure she didn't look too disheveled after the dancing. A few of the women had asked about her dress, seeming friendly, but there had been some disapproving looks, too. Aware she was under scrutiny, she had only had two glasses of campenois and avoided the kafiet, but that wouldn't stop people gossiping if her hair was falling down. But the damage looked minimal.

The retiring room was empty, so she took her time, savoring the peace as she smoothed flyaway hairs and inspected her dress for wrinkles or stains. The crowd in the ballroom had thinned out, but Honore had said they were to stay until Katiya and Mikvel departed. So far, those two had showed no signs of wanting to leave.

In Katiya's place, Chloe would be trying for as much rest as possible. But Katiya was young and in love, and at her age, Chloe had danced the night away without much thought of the morning.

The solitude was a relief after hours in the crowded ballroom, and she sniffed the bottles of scented toilet waters set on the counters as an excuse to delay her return. Most of the scents were spicy and rich, but there were a few lighter ones, including one that smelled like the mint of the kafiet combined with the freshness of a lemon. It smelled of warmth and light and sunny days in her parents' garden. A wave of homesickness caught her throat.

She'd wanted so badly to get away from Lumia. Now, suddenly, all she wanted was to be home again. Foolish. Deephilm was fascinating in its way, even though the newness of it all and the unrelenting schedule were overwhelming.

This was what she wanted. This was where she could do some good. If they could secure the mining agreements and determine if House Elannon were to be trusted, she would have served the empire. Done something useful.

One small step to right the wrongs of the past.

That thought made her freeze, the perfume's golden stopper in her hand.

Righting wrongs? Was that what was she doing? Which wrongs? Charl's treason? Her own wasted years?

She wasn't sure. Wasn't sure why the thought had even entered her mind other than she was tired, and in need of tea and sleep to offset the campenois and dancing and diplomacy.

It had a ring of truth to it though.

But getting to the bottom of half-buried motivations was hardly something she could do in a night. Not unless she wanted to ask Lucien to help her. To tell her if she was speaking the truth to herself. Which she most assuredly did not.

She put the crystal flask back on the table after one last sniff, patted her hair into place once more, and straightened her shoulders. Time enough for thinking later. Tonight she still had work to do.

But she'd barely stepped through the door when she almost bumped into Lady Cela coming in the other direction. Which led to an awkward flurry of apologies and sidestepping.

Lady Cela smiled at her, the expression too full of teeth. "Lady de Montesse, isn't it? Are you enjoying the ball?"

"I am," Chloe said. "His Majesty knows how to throw a good party."

"That he does," Lady Cela agreed. "But I'm sure it's nothing as grand as a ball back in Lumia."

"I wouldn't be so sure of that," Chloe demurred.

"Perhaps...." Lady Cela hesitated. "Would you wait for me? We could walk back to the ballroom together. I'd love to hear more of your country."

"Of course," Chloe said. She'd wanted an opportunity to get a better sense of the woman. No wasting this chance. Hopefully she'd find that her fears were unfounded. "I'll wait for you here."

Cela smiled her thanks and slipped into the retiring room.

Chloe, not wanting to loiter outside the door and risk a repeat of the near collision, moved a little way down the corridor to study the tapestry that covered a large part of the nearest stretch of wall. A forest scene, all tall tree trunks with angled branches and leaves in half a hundred shades of green. Beneath them grew plants that owed, she thought, more to the imagination of the embroiderer than reality. But amongst them were rabbits and foxes and deer. Birds perched in some of the branches, bright feathered and whimsical. She spotted two black birds she decided must be crows high in the branches of the tree closest to the center of the tapestry and smiled, stepping closer to study the detail.

Then jumped as a voice from behind her said, "Lady de Montesse?"

She whirled, one hand flying to her chest.

CHAPTER 19

The man who'd addressed her was medium height and older than Chloe. His hair was darker than most of the men she'd met in the palace, a sandy color she would have expected in Illvya, not Deephilm, and his eyes a middling green. His evening clothes were various shades of dark blue, including the embroidery, and she couldn't immediately recall any house that wore only blue. But at least it wasn't Elannon orange and green.

He flashed a nervous smile. "Forgive me, my lady. I didn't mean to startle you."

"I wasn't paying attention. Admiring the needlework." She didn't entirely relax, but he didn't seem to pose an immediate threat. And Lady Cela wasn't far away.

"It is beautiful," he agreed.

Please let him not be about to follow that with something predictable like "So are you." She was in no mood to deal with unwanted advances. She nodded, offering what she hoped was a polite but discouraging smile.

"The artisans who make them are following traditions that have existed here for many centuries," he continued.

Not the direction she'd expected him to take. But needlework was a preferable topic to seduction, so she nodded. "I hope

I might have time to meet some of them. Their traditions and techniques must be fascinating."

His smile widened. "Traditions are important. They are what make each land unique."

"Yes," she agreed, curious now despite her wariness. He had a point he was working up to, and she was keen to find out what it was.

"There is strength in difference." His expression had grown intent.

Her spine prickled. Maybe seduction would have been easier to deal with. This was sliding into politics. The kind she shouldn't try to deal with alone. Where was Lady Cela? "Strength comes from many places." There. A politely meaningless statement.

Her mystery man—damn, she should have asked for his name—seemed to take it as encouragement. "Strength, too, in ideals. In valuing the old ways. Your husband, I believe, valued these things."

Her husband? Definitely not a subject she wanted to discuss with a strange Andalyssian. Alone or otherwise. But she caught herself before she could do something that gave away the flare of alarm bumping up her pulse again. If he was interested in Charl's values, then he likely didn't have the empire's best interests in heart. In which case, it was her duty to find out more. So he could be stopped.

"He did," she said slowly. Honestly, she had no idea what Charl had truly valued. She'd never asked for the details of his confession. Didn't need to know more than "treason" and the fact that he had confessed. If he had harbored a desire for a particular outcome from his actions, if there had been a purpose to the plot he'd participated in, he'd never shared it with her. His trial had been short, and she hadn't attended, urged to stay away by both her family and his. There'd been no time after his execution and Lucien's warning to acquaint herself with the particulars of his crimes. "And he paid for those ideals."

"Yes. He was wronged. There are those who still share those ideals, my lady. Those who would offer your husband...sympathy. And his widow support," he said. "Support you were denied when it mattered."

Ah. Did he imagine she was a fellow conspirator? That she'd fled to avoid prosecution, not to avoid those who might worry Charl had told her too much? Not the first to make that mistake. Though, he would be the first, so far, who she had met who found that interpretation of her actions to be admirable. Which was, indeed, interesting.

"It was difficult," she murmured, trying to sound downcast. She needed to keep him talking. See if he said anything more to confirm her suspicions.

"I can imagine. But you have returned. And now that the emperor"—he said the word as though it was bitter in his mouth—"has offered you his protection, you can continue the fight."

"The fight?"

"To return things to the way they should be." He glanced around. "Many people share that aim."

"After so long?" She tried to sound encouraged by the thought rather than astounded that there were always men—and women, she supposed—foolish enough to throw themselves into idiocy. Did they truly think they could bring down the empire? Particularly when it continued to treat its citizens well and bring peace and prosperity? Or that it was wise to tell her so when they had no idea of her true motives? If Charl was convinced by men like this, then he truly had been an idiot.

And what did that make her?

"Always," he said. "The empire is not the natural order of things, and there are those who would see it come to an end."

Goddess. Who are these people? "I'm afraid, sir," she said, "that I know little of what Charl had planned." She knew nothing, in fact. She risked a quick glance back toward the retiring room. What was taking Cela so long? Had the woman fallen ill? Or—an unpleasant thought struck her—had she asked Chloe to wait for her so this meeting could occur and was taking her time to allow it to run its course?

"But you returned to Illvya. Why would you do that if you didn't want to see him avenged?"

She narrowly avoided blurting, "Because it's my home, you idiot." The man was flushed, and his face looked damp. Nervous, if she were any judge. And out of place. The jacket he wore was too simple compared to those worn by the male courtiers, the fit loose across the shoulders. Not his, she suspected. And, therefore, perhaps he wasn't a regular attendee at court. If she scared him off now, he might vanish. Leaving her none the wiser.

After all, she had no proof that Lady Cela asking her to wait wasn't just a coincidence. Nor could she discern truth from lie like Lucien.

"I—" She stopped. Decided it might be better to play things straight. Act nervous. She glanced around, shifting her weight. "I do not think this is a safe place to talk. Too many people in the palace for the wedding. Perhaps we could meet in the days after the ceremony? My schedule will be less full once the wedding itself is over. It would be easier for me to steal away for a few hours. Find out if our interests...align." Should she ask for his name, or would that just scare him off?

He looked somewhat relieved. "That can be arranged." He glanced around again, then nodded once. "I will be in touch, my lady." He sketched a rapid bow, turned, and hurried away, vanishing around a corner and out of sight.

Chloe was staring after him, wondering if she had imagined the entire encounter, when the door to the retiring room opened and Lady Cela stepped out.

"I'm sorry, Lady de Montesse," she said. "I had snagged my hem and wanted to catch it with a few stitches. I didn't intend to keep you waiting so long."

And that was a claim it would be difficult to disprove. Unless she wanted to demand that Cela turn up her skirt and show her the stitches. Which she did not. If Lady Cela was innocent, then no point making the woman think she had lost her senses. And, if she wasn't, then no need to give her any hint that she was alarmed by the encounter she'd just had.

"No matter," Chloe said. "I was enjoying the peace and quiet out here. And admiring the tapestries." She threw the last out in case Lady Cela might also confess a fervor for the maintenance of Andalyssian traditions and culture. But, instead, she barely glanced at them and then gestured toward the ballroom and smiled at Chloe.

"Let's walk back. But slowly. I have so many questions."

Chloe had a few of her own. But Cela's too-convenient timing had done nothing to ease her doubts about the woman. So she would hold her tongue and ask them elsewhere.

She answered Cela's questions, which seemed innocuous, as they walked back to the ballroom, then excused herself to look for Honore. But her search was cut short when the music started up again and she had to join the dancing once more.

Half a hundred questions of her own whirled around her mind for the few remaining sets. She searched the dancers for the man who'd approached her but didn't find him. Though one of her partners confirmed that none of the noble houses—vassal or otherwise—wore only dark blue. Which only added to the problem.

The last dance ended, and Mikvel and Katiya finally departed. Chloe stepped off the dance floor to find Lucien waiting. Which was convenient, as she had decided, after much debate with herself, that she should tell him rather than Honore about the man in the corridor. At least initially. After all, he was from the judiciary. Crimes against the emperor were his responsibility. Besides which, he knew more about what Charl had done and who else had been involved than anyone else on the mission.

"Lord Castaigne," she said, feigning a smile. "Come to escort me back to my quarters again?"

His brows flew upward, and she realized that, perhaps, that wasn't the best way to phrase that question. To the wrong man, it sounded rather like she might be issuing an invitation to something more than a late-night stroll through the palace corridors. Her cheeks went hot.

"There is something I need to discuss with you," she continued in a rush. "So, although I am in no need of an escort, perhaps we can walk together." She glanced around the rapidly emptying ballroom. No sight of Gilles, but Honore was talking with Roland. Their faces were both focused and intent, making her think they were probably discussing scheduling or some other administrative minutiae. Nothing requiring her presence. Her instructions had been to attend the ball. She had done that, and she had the sore feet to prove it. The invitation to treason was an unexpected addition.

But that was a burden to place in Lucien's hands rather than the colonel's. So better to make their getaway now.

"Shall we go?" she said to Lucien, who was regarding her with a slightly bemused expression.

"After you, my lady."

She said nothing until they had left the ballroom well behind them and reached a quieter part of the palace, headed for the guest quarters. There were more servants than the previous evening, but with the wedding growing ever closer, that was to be expected. They'd be working all hours of the day to ensure that all the guests were housed in perfect comfort, fed, and entertained.

For a moment she was, once again, very glad not to be Katiya, who would soon take on the job of managing the vast building for the rest of her life.

"Am I supposed to guess?" Lucien asked as they turned a corner.

"Guess?"

"What you wanted to talk about?"

Her encounter outside the retiring room. Her musings on Katiya's life had temporarily distracted her. She shivered as she remembered the fervent look on the stranger's face. "I think it's better discussed in private."

Lucien's brows lifted. Then he pointed at a door standing partially open a few feet down the hallway. The palace was dotted with small rooms used for meetings or gatherings of courtiers or to hide away from court life when one had had enough for a time. A palace was like a small town. People forced to live in close quarters who might not choose to do so otherwise. But small towns demanded less time given to games of status and protocol. Power and politics required time and effort and too much time in the company of others. Giving the courtiers space was important to prevent the inevitable frictions from boiling over into something more.

"Here?" she asked.

"Well, it's better than either of us being seen entering the other's bedroom at this hour, don't you think? Unless you have suddenly decided you no longer dislike me and were inviting me to...." He raised one brow.

Damn the man. Why did he have to look good arching a brow? And be so reasonable? "No. I haven't lost my mind," she said, the words a tad sharp. "But you're right. No point risking breaking some Andalyssian taboo and causing trouble. I just want to talk," she managed.

"Then after you, Lieutenant."

The lamps in the little room were alight, which seemed a waste, but at least that meant she wouldn't be alone in the dark with him.

Lucien closed the door and pressed his palm briefly to the wall. Magic shimmered around him, tolling through her, as a ward sparked to life.

The ease with which he raised the ward in a strange building was impressive. "Neatly done," she said, stepping closer to study the ward. Not a form she was familiar with, but it hummed with Lucien's magic. Deep and true and...intriguing. She stepped back hastily.

"Wards are part Air," he said. "I know we all learn them, but illusioners study them more than most. Plus, they come in handy in the judiciary. You don't want someone walking in and interrupting an interview with a suspect at the wrong time."

"No, I suppose not." It wouldn't be helpful to be interrupted when he was using his magic. Truth Seekers negated the need for harsher interrogation methods, but they were also bound by protocols on how they deployed their powers. Suspects were questioned by mundane means first, and he'd told her once that mood and atmosphere were important in encouraging them to talk.

The room held only two small sofas separated by a low table. Arranged for intimate conversations. The kind she had no desire to have with Lucien. She stayed standing.

So did he. "So, what did you want to discuss?"

"I left the ballroom to use the retiring room," she said. "A man approached me as I returned. He talked about Charl. About what he did. He seemed...sympathetic to his cause."

She had seen Lucien in official mode before. Not just during the mission but at various times at court back in Lumia. But she'd never seen him turn into a Truth Seeker before her eyes. His shoulders straightened, his face turned cool and his eyes intent. A hunter ready to lock in on prey. She didn't want to be the one he pursued with that look on his face.

"Who was it?" he demanded.

"I don't know," she said. "He didn't introduce himself. He wore dark blue. No house colors I recognized. I asked one of the Andalyssians whether any of the vassal houses wear that color, but he said no." She tried to recall the man's face, but the details had faded. "He was ordinary, I guess."

Lucien frowned. "You were always good with faces."

"I've met too many blond-haired green-eyed men in the last few days for one to stand out."

"Could he have been wearing an illusion?"

Damn. She hadn't thought of that. Hadn't even checked

whether he was using magic, too startled by the direction their conversation had taken. "I don't know," she said, inwardly cursing her lack of attention.

"Tell me what he said."

She recounted the conversation. "I wanted to leave him with the impression that I was open to further discussions. I didn't want to scare him off."

He smiled approvingly. Though there was a sharpness to it. Anticipating the pleasure of a successful catch. "Good. That was smart."

She let out a breath. He believed her. Trusted her. She had, she realized, been half afraid that he wouldn't. "He said he would contact me again."

His smile vanished. "How?"

"That much he didn't say. And he left before I could ask. I was going to ask his name, but I thought it might alarm him."

"Likely. Did anyone else see him?"

She shook her head. "No. Though...."

"Though, what?"

"One of the court ladies was in the retiring room. She asked me to wait for her. She was in there a long time. Long enough for him to appear, talk to me, and leave before she came out. It felt...a little convenient? But perhaps I'm jumping at shadows."

Lucien frowned again. "Who was she?"

"Lady Cela. I met her at the tscherov." It felt far longer ago than that.

"Anything unusual about her that you noticed then?"

"Only that she used orange and green in the tscherov she wove for Katiya."

"Wove? I thought the tscherov was a rite?"

"It is. But it involves the ladies weaving...well, bracelets braided from thread is the simplest explanation. There are different colors and patterns. It's all connected to houses and families and balance, of course. Each one slightly different."

"And Lady Cela's had Elannon colors?"

He hadn't missed the connection. "Yes. Irina said her grand-mother was an Elannon. She's Sejerin Silya's cousin."

"*Silya* is Elannon?"

"Perhaps. It would depend on who her mother married." She rubbed her forehead. Genealogy had never been her favorite part of court life, and she hadn't been studying Andalyssia long enough to even begin to scratch the surface of how their houses connected. "But Cela can't be considered to belong to House Elannon, can she? Katiya wouldn't be friendly with her if that were the case."

"The disgraced part of the house is trying to redeem itself. Being nice to the future queen would be part of that. Not to mention Mikvel needs to keep both sides happy for now."

"The tscherov is supposed to be for closer friends and family though. I got the feeling Katiya got to choose who was there. Sejerin Silya wasn't there. Just Sejerin Neni."

"Neni? I don't think I've met her."

"She was nice. Nothing like Silya. Didn't call me daughter of ravens for a start." She still had no idea what the seer had meant.

Lucien didn't smile. In fact he went still. "Silya was at the same meeting as me."

"With House Elannon?"

"Yes." He stared at her, face twisting as though considering what to say.

"And the king didn't tell you that she was related to them?"

"No."

"Perhaps the sejerin and svasyas are like the temple back home. Giving up allegiance to anyone but the goddess."

"You know as well as I that it doesn't really work like that in the bigger temples. Religion goes hand in hand with power. There are always those who look for advantage. I doubt it's any different here. A person's house and family are all part of the balance, after all." He blew out a breath. "Which makes me wonder why Mikvel didn't tell me about the relationship. Damn.

I thought he was being genuine in his desire for me to find the truth."

"Perhaps he is. Perhaps it didn't occur to him that you wouldn't know. You investigated House Elannon last time, after all."

"Perhaps," he agreed. "And maybe I did know once. She wouldn't have been a seer back then, maybe. Or not such a powerful one. Just a name on the list of women of the house." He rubbed his forehead. "This damn country is enough to addle anyone's brain."

"Some of them seem nice."

"I'm sure some of them are. But some of them are jostling for position. You're right to be wary of Lady Cela if she has a connection. House Elannon has a lot riding on my decision. Being reinstated to the council early would make life a lot easier for many of them. You should try to avoid Elannons if you can. Uli Elannon especially. He's the potential Ashmeister's uncle. He mentioned you today."

"Me?" Why was her name coming up in a discussion of an Andalyssian house?

"Yes. He was trying to make a point about treason. He used you to do it. Silya seemed on his side. And she mentioned that 'daughter of ravens' thing again. Said trouble followed you."

She shivered. The last thing she wanted was a seer weighing in on her fate. "I'm sure she was just being difficult."

"Maybe. But I don't like coincidence."

"You think Elannon was connected to what Charl did?"

"I don't know. But the trail out of Illvya cut off too neatly. We always suspected that meant another country was involved, but we had no proof. I still don't. But I want you to be careful. Don't go wandering around on your own."

"I hardly have time to bathe alone, let alone roam the corridors. And I'm not an idiot." His advice might be well-intentioned, but it still irritated her.

"I'm not suggesting you are. But this situation just became more complicated. So please, be careful."

"What if my mysterious stranger reappears?"

"Then you string him along, get away from him as soon as possible, and come find me."

"Just you? Not the colonel or the captain."

He rubbed a hand across his chin, which was starting to show a shadow of a beard. Testament to how late it was. "No. I'd rather not involve them. Not just yet. Until we know more, we can't approach Mikvel about it without risking making the situation worse. The more people we tell about this, the more chance whoever this is—whoever *they* are—will decide it's too risky and not approach you again. Or do something stupid. Let's keep this between you and me until after the wedding, at least. If they don't make contact again by then, we'll tell Honore and let her decide."

CHAPTER 20

"Chloe, you'll go with Major de Roche this morning," Honore said.

Chloe almost choked on her last bite of toast. Assigned to Lucien?

She looked to the top of the table. Lucien didn't look surprised. Had he requested her? Not something she could ask. Junior lieutenants went where sent.

She nodded at Honore, trying to look unconcerned.

As everyone was leaving the dining room, she worked her way to Lucien's side. "I thought you wanted me to avoid House Elannon?"

"I want you to avoid random encounters with them. This isn't a random encounter. You'll be with me."

Was he being protective of her or using her as bait? There wasn't time to ask any more questions. Lieutenant Plesse and one of the ensigns joined them, cutting off any chance of further discussion. Theo walked with her behind Lucien. If he was surprised at her inclusion, he was too professional to show it and just gave her a quick summary of the discussions the day before. He didn't mention that her name had come up, leaving her unsure if he was being discreet or whether Lucien had already told him she knew.

Based on Theo's briefing, she'd expected the meeting to be crowded. Instead, only Mikvel, Andrej Elannon, who wasn't much older than the king, and Niel Elannon, Andrej's Wardmeister, waited for them.

"My lord Truth Seeker," Andrej said as Lucien pulled out his chair. "Is there no way to make this process faster? I am willing to submit myself to your magic, if that would help."

Lucien took a moment to reply. "Thank you, my lord. But proving your own intent doesn't clear your house. It is, of course, a welcome step."

Andrej looked at the king. "Your Majesty, I would like to do this regardless. I don't want you to doubt me."

Mikvel nodded. "Lord Castaigne, would you indulge us in this? We appreciate that you still need to continue your investigation as agreed, but this would put our mind at ease."

Lucien stilled. For a moment, Chloe thought he would refuse. But then he nodded. "Very well, Your Majesty." He turned to face Andrej, took a breath. His magic swelled around her, the song of it near deafening. Yet still, somehow, calling her in.

Goddess. She'd forgotten what it was like to see him use his true power. It was awe inspiring and somewhat frightening, elevating her pulse even though she wasn't his target. He'd used it on her once to question her about Charl. She hoped he never had reason to turn it on her again. Everyone in the room was watching him as though an ice-wolf had suddenly appeared in their midst.

"My lord Elannon," he said, his voice rumbling with a power that felt impossible to resist. "Are you loyal to His Imperial Majesty Aristides Delmar de Lucien and your king, Mikvel Surayov?"

Andrej swallowed, as though his mouth was dry. But he met Lucien's gaze. "Yes. I am."

"Thank you, my lord," Lucien said. His magic disappeared, the absence of it like the silence after a thunderclap.

"Well?" the king asked.

"He is telling the truth, Your Majesty." Lucien smiled. "Which means we should proceed."

✧ ✧ ✧

The rest of the meeting moved quickly. Andrej and Niel helped Lucien compile a list of their family members, and Mikvel added other suggestions which Chloe and Theo dutifully noted down. Less than an hour had passed before the list was complete and King Mikvel concluded the meeting.

"What happens if you don't allow House Elannon to return?" she asked Lucien as they walked back across the palace.

"Hopefully, sanity prevails and they continue their work to deal with whatever lingering problems they have in their house, as they have for the last thirteen years, and wait another three years to try again."

"And if sanity doesn't prevail?"

"Then the king may have a fight on his hands if the other Ashmeisters or the church presses the point. That's harder to judge. I need to spend some time with the patrarch and the sejerin council to understand whether they are genuine in their religious objections or if it's all just politics. If they were truly devoted to balance, they would have elevated another house when Elannon was barred from the council."

She didn't envy him that task. She couldn't see Silya agreeing to him using his powers on her. "Is that a possibility?"

Lucien shrugged. "The patrarch at the time argued against it. Establishing a new house is a process of some length and expense, not to mention endless rituals. But my understanding is that it has happened a few times in their history. Not all their kings have been as lenient at the end of a rebellion as Aristides was."

"Why was he?" Aristides hadn't spared Charl. And the Ashmeister Elannon had come close to killing the empress and their unborn child. Charl had been discovered before he'd put anyone in danger. So why spare House Elannon?

Lucien half shrugged. "It wasn't the king who led the Elannon plot. He was trying not to punish the whole country for the crimes of a few. He has an empire to hold together, unlike a king who only has to manage one country. It's understandable."

"Did you agree with him?"

"It wasn't my place to agree or not," Lucien said. "It is my place to find the truth. But yes, I believe mercy is best, when it can be used. The Ashmeister was executed, as were his conspirators, but the damage after that was contained as much as possible."

She wondered if that was true. Supposedly she'd been spared any direct consequence from Charl's' crimes, but they had still thrown her life into chaos. How might a whole noble house react to their world being upended? And what might they do to regain that life?

Theo and the ensign had peeled off toward another meeting, leaving the two of them alone as they walked. "Why did you ask for me today?"

"I wanted to see if you recognized anybody in the meeting."

Neither Andrej nor Niel had been the man who'd spoken to her. Not unless they were master illusioners. They were both too tall—though a strong illusion might mask that. But nothing about them had reminded her of the man she'd spoken to. "No. I didn't."

He looked disappointed, though he should be relieved. So he was being protective. Which only confused her. "Perhaps we can shed some light as we meet with others from the house."

"You do think House Elannon are involved in this," she said.

"I don't know what to think. But I have learned to look for the most obvious answer first. Rule that out before proceeding to more complicated theories." He shook his head, as though trying to decide something, then came to a stop. "Regardless, that took less time than I expected. So you should take some time for yourself. I don't need you for the rest of the morning."

✧ ✧ ✧

Chloe left Lucien near the dining room, trying to ignore the fact that his dismissal had stung, and returned to her room, intending to read or maybe even snatch a nap. There would be another ball that evening, and a chance to catch an extra hour's sleep—or just some time alone—was an unexpected luxury. But she'd barely settled into a chair with one of her novels when Allita arrived.

"A message from the Lady Irina, Lieutenant," she said, handing an envelope to Chloe. "She asked me to wait to show you the way if you accept."

Chloe opened the note, curiosity warring with irritation at losing her free time. Another invitation. Just not one to yet another wedding ceremony. Instead, Irina was offering a tour of the palace's stillrooms. As tempting as the thought of two hours alone was, curiosity about how the Andalyssians used herbs and other medicinal elements with their magic won. She followed Allita into one of the servants' passages and then down quite a few flights of stairs, trying to ignore the curious looks of the servants they passed.

The games of politics and pageantry played out in the grander parts of the palace were where most people focused, but Chloe had always found the working parts of such places more interesting. As a child, she'd wandered the halls of the Academe, making friends with the cooks, the cleaning staff, the gardeners, and the Master of Ravens, of course. Far more interesting places for a child than libraries and classrooms.

Her fascination with those had grown, too, over the years, but her interest in how grand buildings were run had stood her in good stead when she'd taken over running the Matin household when her mother's illness had been at its worst, and when it came to managing the modest house she and Charl shared.

They'd only had a cook and a few servants, but it still took work to keep such a small household running. Her experience had come in useful again when she'd first won her job with Ginevra and then taken over the store entirely. She'd slanted the business slightly more to magical supplies, but supplies for earth witches, her primary customers, still leaned heavily toward the healing arts. She'd spent plenty of time with mostly herbs and other plants and ingredients to keep her company on long nights when she couldn't sleep or settle to reading.

When Allita opened a sturdy wooden door at the far end of a cool stone corridor and green-scented steam-tinged air wafted out, her heart twinged with sudden nostalgia. She had missed this. Herbcraft was as close to using her power as she'd been permitted in Kingswell. Maybe it was part of what she had been missing back in Lumia. But she'd chosen the corps.

But still, her earth magic sparked as she stepped into the long high-ceilinged room. Four long wooden tables—plain well-scrubbed wood—marched in a line down the center of the room. Rows of metal racks and wood shelves filled with neatly labeled jars and boxes lined the walls, along with several deep marble basins and counters and two small stoves. Empty containers nestled on shelves beneath the tables and bunches of drying herbs hung from wood racks above them. Though Chloe suspected there would be other drying rooms somewhere. This room was too cool and the air too damp from whatever was bubbling on the stove to be truly useful to dry herbs, and there were other ingredients that didn't like damp. There'd be a cool room, too. Though warmth was probably the harder thing to supply than cold in Andalyssia.

Irina stood at the second table, a practical dark gray linen apron tied over an equally sensible-looking dark blue gown. Katiya stood opposite her in a similar outfit.

Neither of them noticed Chloe, intent as they were on a complicated-looking setup of glass tubes and beakers connected to a hissing copper boiler. Some sort of distillation. Those were tricky things. She hung back by the door, not wanting to interrupt and potentially destroy hours or days of work. She was surprised to see Katiya. With only two days before the wedding, she would have expected the soon-to-be queen's days to be scheduled from dawn to dusk. But perhaps she had had an unexpected break in her schedule, too.

The sisters worked well together, obviously used to the task. But Irina took the lead. She mixed and sniffed and managed the brazier under the copper boiler with a confidence that reminded Chloe of Ginevra. Which suggested she had been underplaying her interests in the healing arts somewhat during their previous conversation.

Eventually Irina noticed her. "Chloe. You're here." She gestured with her free hand. "We'll be done shortly. Then I'll give you the tour."

"Don't rush. I'll just watch."

"Or come and help," Irina said. "You can assist Katya while I fetch more bottles."

Chloe didn't need a second invitation. She joined the sisters. Katiya bent down and pulled another apron from beneath the table and passed it over. As Chloe slipped it on and tied it around her waist, Irina peered at the pale yellow liquid beginning to drip into the second to last of a series of beakers.

"What are you making?" Chloe asked. She didn't recognize the precise shade of yellow, and the smell wasn't distinctive enough for her to identify.

"Sunwort and arnica," Irina said. "Good for bruises and

aches. We distill it, then make it into a salve. Though small amounts can be taken in tea or water for a headache. The kind that makes people sick with light or noise."

"Migraine," Chloe said. "Yes. I've not heard of sunwort though. The Anglions have something called redwort, but it's a stimulant. The Red Guard use it when they need to stay awake in battle." And others used it to ward off sleep as well. Though it only worked for a few days, and the crash that followed was swift, resulting in sleep that lasted as long as the waking period. Which limited its usefulness.

Katiya nodded. "That one is from the same family of plants. But it doesn't thrive in the mountains, so we don't grow it here. There's firewort, too. Which is rarer still."

"We don't mess with that one," Irina said. "Or if we did, Royve Ava would be supervising—she's the head healer here. The seers use firewort sometimes to aid their visions, but get the distillation or the dosage wrong and that will be the last vision you ever have." She adjusted the burner carefully.

"Poison?" Chloe asked. The Ashmeister Elannon had used poison against the empress. Not such a common weapon in Illvya—or Anglion—but not unheard of.

"Many things are poisons if used the wrong way," Katiya said.

Irina shrugged, grinning. "Poisons used to be something of a pastime here," she said. "Our ancestors had too much time on their hands during the long dark winters, or maybe just too much time in close quarters. Stabbing someone is not very subtle when you can't run away afterward. Poison is sneakier. But fire-wort was never a common one. It is deadly in small doses, and it is accessible because the seers use it, but it tends to tint things red. Harder to hide than some of the other common poisons. But these days we're very civilized." She glanced at her sister. "It's really only the king and his family who still have food tasters."

"And those are for show," Katiya said firmly. "Don't worry

about me. No one's used poison that we know of since—" She broke off, biting her lip.

The Ashmeister, presumably. Chloe decided to leave that subject alone. "Well, you seem good at this, Irina. Are you sure you—"

"I have to get the bottles," Irina said suddenly. She pointed at a valve on the boiler. "If the drip rate increases, turn this down slightly." She didn't wait for either of them to reply, just bustled off.

"Did I say something wrong?" Chloe asked as Irina vanished through a door at the far end of the room.

Katiya shook her head. "No. She is very good at this. She's always been interested in plants and healing. But it's not necessarily encouraged in the houses." She sighed. "And now, with her being my sister, I fear she won't be allowed to pursue the healer's path. A strong leaning for earth is one of the few times the svasyas will allow a step away from balance. Healers are valuable. But she will be the queen's sister, and that is even more valuable than healing skill to some. Someone will want to marry her. I'm doing what I can with Mikvel and our father to make sure she isn't rushed, but she will have to marry eventually. I think that's why she pretends she doesn't care. She would be a good healer. Perhaps a great one. But she won't get the chance to follow her heart. Between that and not being allowed to use her earth sense, it's been hard for her since she manifested."

Chloe bit her tongue. It would do little good to interfere. Irina's life was here, and it would still be safe and pleasant even if she married. If she was strong-willed enough, she would find a way to incorporate the things she loved into that life. And perhaps she would even find a husband who supported those interests.

Good men existed everywhere along with the bad ones.

But Katiya looked worried.

"It's difficult. But she is smart. She'll find a way," Chloe offered. "Perhaps she'll fall for a man with a scholarly bent of his own. You don't strike me as all warrior types." Andalyssians had to be smart to survive life in the mountains. The houses still had to make sure there was food and safety enough to go around through the winter months. The men they'd been dealing with in the negotiations mostly seemed intelligent and dedicated, with a few exceptions. But then Illvya and Anglion both had their share of men who'd rather bluster and posture than achieve any real good as well.

"I hope so," Katiya said. "I feel guilty that her choices are narrowed because of mine."

"I'm sure she wants you to be happy. And you love the king. You can't help that. Would she be happier if you didn't love him and were marrying him under duress?"

"No," Katiya said. "I guess not."

She looked up as the door reopened and Irina came back through carrying a basket of bottles. "Now, we will need to work fast."

Lucien watched the king's wedding ball growing wilder around him and wondered exactly how rowdy it would get. Perhaps this was a place for the Andalyssians to let off steam after the packed few days of pomp and spectacle that had prepared it.

Though he wasn't sure why they all didn't just want to be in bed as he did. He'd snatched a few hours here and there to meet with members of House Elannon, and so far, no one had sparked his suspicions. Other than those meetings, his days and nights had been crammed from dawn to near midnight with the various wedding rites and celebrations. He might have enjoyed it more had he been as young as the king and Katiya, but it had mostly made him feel old.

The wedding itself had been ceremony and ritual and spectacle, every second of it, he suspected, choreographed by the priests and seers who had appeared in multitudes.

The happiness of the bride and groom had been genuine though. He hadn't needed his magic to know the truth of the joy on their faces. From the looks that Sejerin Silya and the patrarch aimed in their direction occasionally, he suspected the smiles that kept creeping over Mikvel's and Katiya's faces weren't strictly in accordance with the rituals. But let the mystics be mystics. Weddings, even the weddings of kings, should be joyous affairs.

The ball was definitely joyful. Wine and spirits had flowed freely through dinner and continued to do so in the ballroom. In the last hour, servants had circulated with trays of kafiet. He had refused. The mood of the court might be one of wild celebration, but he wanted a clear head.

Chloe had accompanied him to some of his meetings with House Elannon in the last two days, but not all. She had her own wedding-related obligations to fulfill. They'd danced at the balls each night, but every time he'd asked if she had seen the man who had approached her, speaking Charl's name, she'd shaken her head. No further contact.

Which should have been a relief, but, in reality, it made a spot between his shoulder blades itch as though he was being watched. So he was watching, too, making sure she was safe. Tonight, at the largest ball of them all, that task was more difficult than usual. He took his turn at the dances, inviting a few of the Andalyssian women he'd gotten to know to dance with him. He'd even waltzed with Chloe again when Katiya and Mikvel had included a waltz in one of the sets.

She was, he thought, growing more comfortable with him. There'd been no tense wariness in her body under his hands, and he'd kept himself in check, determined to give her no reason to retreat from him once more and put her armor back in place.

Her gold-and-blue gown was one he rather thought he'd seen Imogene du Laq wear to the emperor's birthday ball the year before. Altered by an expert, as it looked as beautiful on Chloe as it had on the duquesse. It fit her like a glove above the waist before the skirts belled out in yards of fabric that floated and swirled around her as she danced, the silk shimmering. Her hair shimmered, too, braided and studded with sapphires and diamonds that possibly belonged to Imogene, too. Kind of her to help Chloe. It was a comfort to know she had powerful allies in Lumia. Doubtful that Chloe could have owned enough evening wear made to see her through the wedding, particularly when she'd had little time to prepare. But Imogene probably had entire houses filled with dresses. She was famously well-dressed. And famously cool to the new Marq of Castaigne.

Which he understood. Charl had cost Imogene her best friend for ten years, and he was the nearest person to blame.

She couldn't be outright rude to him. The du Laqs and de Roches had no true quarrels and shared some business interests. Jean-Paul still spoke to him civilly, but he tried to give Imogene the distance she seemed to desire. Which was a pity. Imogene was smart and witty, and he'd liked her when his friendship with Chloe and Charl had meant their paths crossed more often.

After the waltz came more dances. More watching to see whether anyone approached Chloe. The faces of the court had grown more familiar over the last few days. He didn't have names for all of them yet, but he was good at faces. Though "ordinary" as a description left something to be desired. He could draw a more detailed description of the man from her memory if she let him use his magic on her, but that was about as likely as him making it through the current dance without Irina interrogating him about life in Lumia.

He glanced over her shoulder, trying to spot where Chloe was.

"You do that a lot," Irina said.

He almost stumbled in the dance, dragged back from his thoughts. Right. The queen's little sister. He was supposed to be making conversation with her.

"Do what, my lady?" he asked. Irina, with her sharp green eyes, didn't seem to miss much.

"Watch Chloe."

This time he did stumble. Or at least came to a halt for a second before he forced himself into action again. "No, I don't."

"You do," Irina said. "You like her."

"She doesn't like me," he retorted before he could stop himself. Damn. He hadn't had kafiet, but he hadn't been able to entirely avoid the wine and campenois during dinner, and his tongue had gotten away from him.

"No, I don't think that's true," Irina said, her expression serious. "She's angry with you, I think, but that's not the same at disliking you. Did you do something wrong, my lord?"

"A long time ago," Lucien said. "We were friends before that. We are no longer."

Irina, cheeks flushed, said, "Friendships can be mended."

"I don't think this one can," he said, twirling her under his hand as the dance demanded. "What I did was necessary but unforgivable, I think."

"It's surprising what people can forgive when they care about someone," she said, coming back to his arms.

He frowned. Irina was not quite twenty-three. Too young to be dealing in forgiveness and wisdom in the middle of an increasingly drunken celebration of her sister's wedding. The dominas back in Lumia would probably have called her a viele ame, one wiser beyond their years. But wise or not, he wasn't going to tell her he had condemned Charl to death. Or encourage her matchmaking.

"I fear the wedding has turned your head, my lady. You are seeing potential romances where there are none."

"Who said anything about romance?" she shot back. "We were talking about friendship." She grinned at him. "Weren't we, my lord?"

Damn. Too sharp indeed. If she saw through him, then he needed to be more careful. "Let's just dance, my lady."

She snorted but didn't press. She did, however, wander in Chloe's direction after the dance finished. He made himself turn away. The last thing he needed was for Irina to tell Chloe he'd been watching her and for her to look across and find him doing just that.

Perhaps he was going to need some kafiet to make it through the night after all.

CHAPTER 21

The kafiet helped a little, though he had limited himself to two glasses. The clocks had traveled well past midnight and beyond by the time the king and queen retired for their wedding night and the court began to gradually disperse. Though some of them seemed intent on celebrating through the night.

He didn't intend to be among them. Nor did he think Chloe should be. He would see her safely back to her room, and then he would go to sleep and take up his dealings with House Elannon again in the morning.

Chloe, in her golden gown, was easy enough to find as the crowd thinned out. The look she gave him as he joined her was not entirely friendly. It was probably wrong-headed of him that he found her nearly irresistible regardless. Her cheeks flushed from the dancing, and her hair curled where it had come loose from its careful arrangement. It suited her, the not entirely buttoned down and in control look. He'd seen her downing kafiet with Irina earlier, but she didn't appear tipsy as she had been the first night he'd walked her back to her room. Or at least not enough to forget she didn't like him.

Damn it, what had Irina said to her?

"Lady de Montesse," he said. "Will you walk with me back to

quarters?" There. That sounded professional. They were the only two Illvyans left in the room. It had become a pattern of sorts. Honore tended to retire as early as possible after the king departed and the other senior nobles left, ending the prime opportunities for politicking.

He'd seen Gilles walking from the ballroom not long after Honore left. The captain had been talking with one of the Andalyssian women, and Lucien hoped the man was smart enough not to take things further. The Andalyssians were stricter about dalliances than Illvyans. Their daughters remained chaste until their weddings—though he suspected that, of course, some of them ignored that rule—and affairs were not common. Marriage vows were a rite of balance, and cheating approached blasphemy. The last thing they needed was a forced wedding to prevent a diplomatic incident. But Theisse was an experienced diplomat and knew enough, Lucien hoped, to keep himself out of trouble.

"I know the way, my lord," she said.

Ah. Definitely short with him. "I know. But we are both heading in that direction."

"Fine." Her hand flexed. Back in Illvya, she'd be snapping a fan at him in irritation. But they didn't use fans here. If a ballroom grew too hot, all they needed to do was throw open a window.

Her skirts swayed in a staccato rhythm as he followed her out of the room. Twitching like the tail of an annoyed cat. He, sensibly, kept quiet as he walked behind her. When they reached his room, he began to unlock his door. But before Chloe could continue down to her room, he asked, perhaps less sensibly, "Are you going to tell me what I've done to annoy you?"

Her eyes narrowed. "I'm not annoyed."

"That's a lie," he said.

"This is not a subject for discussion in the middle of a corridor."

He pushed his door open. "After you."

To his surprise, she marched inside. He followed warily, closing the door behind them and pressing his hand briefly to the wall to activate his wards. If he was going to be shouted at, he'd prefer everybody in the delegation didn't hear.

He turned back to face her. "Well?" A sensible man would back down from this discussion, send her back to her room. But it seemed he wasn't feeling sensible. Something about her anger was sparking his own frustration with the situation.

"Irina said you were watching me. Again."

"I was watching you," he said. "You are very beautiful in that gown."

That was deliberately provoking. It seemed to work.

"You're not supposed to be watching me," she hissed.

"Actually I am. A traitor approached you. If he does so again, I want to know about it."

"If he sees you lurking about staring at me, he's hardly going to do that, is he?"

"I guess we'll find out. Because I'm not going to stop watching."

"You should."

"But I won't."

"I'm telling you not to. I don't like it."

"That's a lie," he said, tongue flying ahead of him again. Stupid. But apparently some of that reckless mood of the ball had rubbed off on him. "You do like it," he continued before she could protest. "You wouldn't be so angry about it if you didn't."

Her eyes flared wide. "How do you know that? You said you wouldn't use your powers on me. Was that another lie? Well, I'm not sure what your powers told you. I don't like you. I *hate* you."

The anger roiled through him. Goddess damn her. She would keep pushing until one of them broke. "You can hate me, *Madame* de Montesse."

The words were wielded like a weapon. A reminder that he knew exactly who she had been. Who he suspected she still was.

The wife of a traitor. Whose memory held her as fast as steel chains might. Trapped in the past that hadn't let her go.

"You can hate me, but I'll be damned if you will stand there and insult me. I do not misuse my powers, and I keep my oaths. I have never lied to you."

"The oh so mighty Lord Truth Seeker. And his oh so mighty truth. To be held to at the expense of all else. Even his best friend's life."

"Yes," he agreed bluntly. "Because I am loyal. But he was the one who threw his life away. His death is not my fault. Charl was the one who broke his oaths. To his emperor. To his country. To you. To all of us. You should hate *him*." He virtually snarled the last word.

She went pale then, as though he'd slapped her. "He's not here to hate," she said, the pain in the words cracking him in half as she turned and ran from the room.

He swore as the slam of the door came. Swore viciously and repeatedly and then, unable to stop it at the last, stalked over to the bed and yelled, "*Fuck!*" so loud it nearly echoed off the stones.

Fuck Andalyssia and its fucking mountain of a city.

Fuck them all.

Fuck Chloe and her insistence on blaming him for everything Charl had done.

Though, he realized as he sank onto the mattress with a groan and buried his face in his hands for a moment, he hadn't told the truth tonight. He had lied to her. Many, many times. Every time he clamped his teeth to hold back the words he wanted to say. To tell her to throw over his idiot best friend and take him instead.

He'd never spoken them. He'd told them both that he was delighted for them.

He'd tried his best to be.

But it had been a lie.

Would continue to be a lie between them, it seemed.

He straightened and dragged his hands through his hair. He hadn't meant to upset her. Hadn't meant to hurt her. He should find her and apologize. Or try to. She would, most likely, slam another door in his face. Really, he wouldn't blame her.

So. He would go. Try to apologize. Be more discreet in his mission to make sure she was safe. And then they would try, once more, to keep things civil until they returned home.

✧ ✧ ✧

Chloe knew who it was when the knock came at her door.

For a moment, she contemplated not answering. But she'd been unfair to Lucien. She owed him an apology.

She wasn't entirely sure why she felt that way. Surely she owed him nothing? Perhaps. But nor should she hurt him. It wouldn't bring Charl back. And at this point, it seemed it would just make things harder.

Goddess. She had no idea what she wanted to do with him. He'd told the truth, even if he had only guessed at it. She did like his eyes on her. Or she had tonight. Every glimpse of him catching her gaze across the ballroom had made her skin hot and her dress feel too tight. When they'd waltzed, she hadn't wanted him to let go of her. In fact, she'd wanted him to pull her closer.

Infuriating man.

She climbed off the bed she'd flung herself down on and crossed to the door, opening it carefully to avoid any noise. "What do you want?"

"I came to apologize. Let me in."

She wasn't sure why she stepped back, why she did as he commanded.

Why she felt suddenly adrift.

He stepped into the room, and her heart began to pound.

He opened his mouth, and she knew that if he spoke—if he

said sorry or he took it back—if he said he didn't think she was beautiful, or said he wouldn't watch her anymore, then she was going to come apart.

She'd have to kill him, or...

"Impossible," she muttered, then stepped forward and pulled his head down to hers, pressing her lips to his as though she was drowning and he was the only source of air in the world.

Maybe he was. Or something more potent still.

Because at the first taste of him, something wild roared through her veins and burned every ounce of sense and self-preservation away to ash.

He pulled her closer with one hand, fingers gripping tight. The other hand slapped against the wall, sparking a ward to life with a thrust of power that probably wasn't particularly subtle.

She didn't care about subtle. She wanted him.

She was going to damn well have him.

Somehow they moved across the room, until his legs hit the bed and he tumbled backward, pulling her with him. She landed atop warm, hard male and nearly purred with the pleasure of it as their kiss grew more frantic. They kissed and rolled, and for a time, she wasn't sure which way was up or down or even who she was anymore.

Until she found herself on top of him, half kneeling, staring down at him as both of them gasped for breath. Did she look as shocked and lust drunk as he did? She suspected she did.

Good.

He reached for her, and she held up a hand. He froze obediently, which made her smile. "No," she said. "My way."

"Whatever the hell way you want," he breathed and raised his hands to grip the iron bed frame. Maybe he only meant to prove that he would behave himself. But there was something nearly irresistible about the thought of him beneath her, at her mercy. She undid his cravat with a few fast tugs and, when he made no move to object, tied his hands in place.

His eyes were wide, pupils blown so that all she would have

been able to see, had there been more light than the fire, would have been a thin rim of that wild wicked green. That window into the true heart of the man. The one he kept hidden beneath the layers of truth and duty and control.

She pressed her hips down harder, felt him there, hard beneath her. Let the sensation run through her. But it wasn't enough. She fumbled with her skirts, pulling the ridiculous lengths of fabric out of the way so she could get to his breeches. Get her hands on what she wanted. His cock was hot under her fingers as she freed it and positioned herself to slide against the length of him.

He felt so good, the jolt of pleasure so fierce, that she tipped her head back, closing her eyes to chase the feeling.

"Open your eyes," he said, the words rough and heavy. His heart was pounding under her hands, the beat vibrating up through her skin, joining the shivers of light and power. She pressed deeper against him, and he hissed.

"Goddess damn it, Chloe," he growled. "You can hate me, you can use me if you want. But you will open your eyes. No pretending it's somebody else inside you."

Her eyes flew open. "That wasn't—"

"I don't care about was or wasn't," he said. "But you will look at me while you fuck me."

His fingers tightened around the length of material stretched between his wrists and the bed frame. The muscles in his throat were tense, his pupils wild and dark and dangerous. He was hot and heavy between her legs, and all she had to do was move a little and he would be inside her.

She did hate him. Or she should. She was trying to remember why. Or why she should care if she did. "You said you wouldn't use your powers on me."

"I'm not," he groaned, hips pressing upward. "Chloe...."

She hated him, but her body didn't hate the sound of her name on his lips when he said it like that.

Like a prayer and a curse all in one. Like he might die if she didn't grant him what he wanted. Her body wanted back, and she lifted her hips and found him and slid back down, letting him fill her as she stared down at him.

The noise he made was hungry, and his fingers twitched again. If his voice could make her forget herself, make her want him so badly, what might his hands do if she set him free? Let him take off her dress and his clothes. Let him touch her all over. Let him kiss her again.

But no. That way was madness. She wanted sex. Wanted pleasure. For some insane reason, she wanted it with him, but it had to be only that and nothing more. So. He wanted her to see him. She would give him that while she took what she wanted.

A roll of her hips to lift her up and slide her back down. Another noise from his throat and then her name breathed like an invocation.

She moved again and again, watching him all the way, falling down into the depths of that wild green gaze. There was nothing else. His eyes and the feel of him inside her and the frantic need that drove her faster and harder against him, the pleasure true and deep and overwhelming. Sweeping her away. Sweeping the past that lay between them away. Sweeping all before it, to let her be free.

Lucien moved with her, raced with her toward oblivion. Until both of them reached the edge, and she broke over him with his name on her lips and he came with a shout.

When she came back to herself, she was slumped on his chest, sweaty and satisfied, a pleasant ache that started to turn to hunger again as she lifted her head.

Lucien was watching her again. And she liked the look on his face.

"Had enough?" he asked, one brow arching at her.

She could lie. Send him away. Or she could tell the truth. That she wanted him again.

"No," she breathed and reached to untie his hands.

✧ ✧ ✧

When she woke, glowing stars danced around the room above her. She blinked, entirely uncertain where she was or what was happening, until she registered the weight of another on the mattress behind her.

Lucien.

Goddess. The things they had done.

Her face went hot at the memories. Worse, her body sparked back to life, hungry for more.

"I know you're awake," he said.

She resisted the urge to pull the covers over her head and hide. She had slept with Lucien. Though, to be honest, until they'd both collapsed, panting and exhausted, there'd been little sleep involved.

Willing herself to be calm, she rolled to face him. He was sitting up, propped against several pillows. His cravat still dangled from the bed frame, and she pretended the sight didn't make her hungrier still for him. He held one hand out, palm up, and the stars streamed upward from it, filling the room with the night sky as they danced.

"What are you doing?"

"It's an illusion," he said. "I'm not just a Truth Seeker, after all."

"I know that." She waved a hand at the stars. They were heart-stoppingly beautiful. Almost as heart-stoppingly beautiful as the sight of him naked and draped in her rumpled sheets.

"I do this when I'm happy. I don't get much chance to just play with illusions these days."

He was happy?

Why? He had to know what was coming next. She would send him back to his own bed and try to forget this had ever happened. But she couldn't quite open her mouth to send him away just yet. Not when he made stars dance for her.

He'd made stars dance for her in other ways, too. He'd taken her at her word when she'd said she hadn't had enough. Had freed his hands with a quick tug, then scooped her up and carried her over to the fireplace. He'd had her there on the rug, and bent over the table, and back in the bed before he was done. And she'd loved it. Had demanded more each step of the way. She was honest enough to admit that. He had known exactly how to light her body on fire.

Which seemed unreasonably unfair.

Goddess. Why him?

"You need to go," she managed, clinging to sanity and the last shreds of dignity. "It will be light soon. No one can see you leaving my room."

He shrugged, and the lights died. Their loss made her heart clench.

"This doesn't change anything," she said as he climbed out of bed and found his clothes.

"You still hate me, you mean?" he said. "Well, if that's what you do with men you hate, then I'm happy to be hated."

She threw a pillow at him. He caught it and laughed. Then busied himself tugging on his boots while she pulled the covers around her shoulders, aware that she was still naked while he was not. When he was dressed, he straightened. Tossed the pillow back to her.

"Let me know if you need to hate me again," he said. "I'm more than happy to be of service." Then he walked out the door and left her lying in the dark.

✧ ✧ ✧

Three days after the wedding, Chloe found herself gathered with half the court, Lucien, Honore, Gilles, and Theo for the traditional post-wedding hunt. Chloe hadn't ridden regularly for years and had tried to wriggle out of the event, but she lacked a decent excuse, and Irina, who had appeared at her door the first evening following the wedding with a tea she insisted would be good for a hangover, had promised her a quiet horse.

How Irina had known Chloe was pretending to have a hangover to avoid dealing with Lucien was a mystery she hadn't tried too hard to solve. Either Allita had talked or Giane had gone seeking advice from the healers after Chloe had lied to her about being ill. Either way, it didn't matter. She'd avoided Lucien for the first day after their—

No, she didn't want to think about it.

Every time she thought about it, she felt him again. Tasted his mouth on hers, knew the bite of his fingers, the rush of pleasure as he moved beneath her or above her or behind.

Thinking about it was a very bad idea.

Though, when one hid in one's room, pretending to have the mother of all headaches, to avoid seeing the man one was trying not to think about, it left little else to do but think about him.

The second day, which was also a day devoid of any official events or diplomatic duties, she'd accepted an invitation from Irina to work in the stillrooms. Irina had only inquired how she was feeling, not teased her any more about Lucien as she had at the ball, and then put her to work. Chloe suspected she was working off some emotions of her own now that her sister truly had married the king and her new status had become irrefutable.

It had been a peaceful day, but now, on this third day, when the newlyweds would rejoin the court for the start of the month of festivities leading up to Katiya's coronation, it was back to work.

She stroked the nose of the dun gelding one of the stable hands had led over to her. He seemed friendly enough, accepting her patting with half-closed eyes. His name, she'd been informed, was Spetya. Near enough to "sleepyhead." That was hopefully a good sign that Irina had kept her promise.

"He likes peppermints," Irina said, appearing out of the crowd, as she had a habit of doing. "They all do. The Herdmeister uses them in training." She fished in the pockets of the long jacket she wore over breeches and extracted a waxed paper bag. "Don't give him too many, but a few now will help you make friends."

"Thank you." Chloe extracted one sweet and offered it to the horse. He lipped it out of her hand and snorted appreciatively. Shoving the bag into her own pocket, she smiled at Irina. "Any other tips?"

"Stay near the back if you don't actually want to hunt. If something happens and you get separated, stay with your horse. They know their way back here. Or even to the city if worse comes to worse."

"I hope so, because I doubt I would." The day's quarry was apparently some breed of fierce wild pig that lived in one of the forest valleys. Which meant riding down off the mountain behind the city on what had to be some hair-raising paths. The fact that the Andalyssian women rode astride, in trousers, when they didn't wear them any other time was proof enough that the riding would be precarious. Maybe it wasn't too late to fake another headache?

"Also, keep your cloak on. You'll feel too warm sometimes, but the weather turns fast. You don't want to be fumbling in saddlebags for your cloak if a storm brews." As if to demonstrate her point, Irina fiddled with the ties of her own dark blue cloak, which matched her riding outfit, testing the security of the knot.

Chloe wore her black corps cloak, though her breeches were civilian brown wool and the longer jacket a darker green. The Andalyssians probably would be appalled if they knew it had been cut down from one of Jean-Paul's castoffs, but it had been the quickest way to provide her with a habit suitable for the northerner's sensibilities.

She stayed talking with Irina until everyone began to mount. The dun wasn't a large horse, so she managed that part easily enough, though it wasn't her most graceful moment. If riding was going to be a regular part of her diplomatic duties, she would have to ask Imogene to ride with her sometimes once they were back in Lumia to sharpen her skills.

As she settled into the saddle, gathering the reins, she spotted Lucien's blond head near the front of the assembled riders. His horse—a long-legged gray—sidled in place, though he seemed to keep it under control easily enough, laughing at something the man next to him said. As though he felt her watching, he turned in the saddle, and their eyes met.

She couldn't look away. She wanted to, but the wave of wanting that swept over her as his eyes found hers froze her in place. The movement of the hunt saved her when Spetya started following the other horses and forced her to look ahead.

The ride down the mountain took even more concentration than she'd anticipated. Spetya gave her no trouble, but the road was terrifyingly narrow in parts and the drop off the mountain dizzying. It was a little like being on the navire again, seeing the ground recede and the next flat patch of land appear far below. Not a pleasant sensation. Though it didn't seem to worry any of the courtiers. They made small talk, calling good-naturedly back and forth as they rode. Most of the gentle teasing focused on the king and his new queen. Mikvel and Katiya seemed to take it in stride, which made her think it was all part of the ritual of the wedding.

It took nearly two hours to descend to the plateau where the actual hunt would take place. Grassy fields gave way to a dense forest of tall trees. Riding in forests, she recalled, wasn't often much easier than riding along hills. Given she had no desire to kill a pig, wild or not, the hunt seemed more another test to endure.

But first, lunch. On the very edges of the plateau, several large tents waited for them, along with a small army of servants to take care of horses and serve refreshments before they were all ushered into the tents to eat. Even so far from the city, fresh flowers festooned the tables and ceilings and ornate earth lamps provided light, reminding her that this was part of the wedding rituals despite the facade of a country picnic.

Sure enough, there were speeches and toasts and many, many courses, ending with a cake almost as large as the one served at the ball. The servants must have been up before dawn to have everything ready. The thought of riding or walking the mountain road in the dark made her feel vaguely ill, and she ate sparingly, not wanting to ride on a stuffed stomach. She did, however, sneak a few pieces of the toffee-and-nut confection they served with dessert into her pocket. That seemed easy enough to eat on horseback if she got hungry later on.

There was, thankfully, no sign of kafiet. There was plenty of tea, and some of it, she suspected, was laced with something alcoholic, as the men who drank it grew rowdier. But hers seemed unadulterated. It was warming and refreshing, but when she stood by Spetya, ready to remount, and realized she had already grown slightly stiff after the morning's riding, she wished she'd chosen something stronger.

CHAPTER 22

Lucien watched Chloe wince slightly, then mask the expression as she remounted. But there wasn't much he could do to ease her if she was sore, and after the last two days of her making every effort to avoid him completely, he doubted she'd appreciate any offer of help.

Charl had liked to ride, and Chloe had seemed to enjoy it when she rode with them, but riding the parks of the city or the de Montesse or de Roche estates was very different to the mountain terrain they were traversing. The forest would be easier, of course, but things could get wild in a hunt, and the valley ran back into the mountains on all sides.

He'd refused the Ilvsoir-laced tea, wanting to keep his wits about him. He'd hunted wild pigs before. Nasty beasts. Capable of injuring or even killing a horse or a man. He'd leave that part to the Andalyssians and try to stay back and observe. But he still had to take one of the long spears the servants were handing up to the riders and settle it into the niche formed in the saddle and harness straps to hold it in place. Most of the women didn't take one, Chloe included. Katiya did, positioning it in her saddle with practiced ease.

A fact to note. She had played the sweet and amenable

fiancée most of the time leading up to the wedding, but now that she was queen, perhaps she was going to let a little more of the spine he'd sensed beneath the smiles out. Which was good. She was a queen. She needed to rule. To be ruthless when required.

Chloe would make a good queen. She'd never had a problem standing up for herself.

The hunt moved off again. The morning's sunshine had vanished, leaving them with skies much the color of his horse, the clouds low but fast moving. Storms rolled in quickly here in the mountains. The summer storms he'd witnessed during his first visit has demonstrated that, though thankfully he'd only seen them from the inside of the palace.

The others were still talking calmly as they rode toward the trees. Still, he reined in his horse, moving farther back in the pack to be closer to where Chloe rode with the women. Honore, Theo, and the others were all good riders from what he'd seen so far. They could take care of themselves.

The riders had barely made it past the tree line into the dappled light of the forest when the first boar lunged out onto the trail, startling the lead horses. The riders split quickly, one group, including the king and queen, giving chase as the boar plunged away into the undergrowth. Lucien's horse snorted and danced in place, but he held him in check.

To his left, another series of crashing snorts heralded the arrival of another boar. The creature was large, mottled brown, and displeased to discover humans and horses in its territory. It charged at the nearest horses, and another chase began.

Two boars so close together suggested there were beaters in the forest, chasing the animals back toward the hunt. The pigs he'd hunted before had been shyer than these, though perhaps that was from living somewhere less wild.

He followed the rest of the hunt deeper into the woods, twisting in his saddle to check on Chloe. She was near the front of the remaining women, watching what was happening ahead. He turned back before she saw him. As he did so, he thought he heard thunder rumbling across the sky, but with the sound of the cheers and yells of the riders pursuing the two boars in the distance and twenty-odd horses moving around him, it was hard to be sure.

Neither of the first two groups had returned by the time a third boar stumbled onto the path about one hundred feet ahead of them. It turned on its heels and bolted. The riders around him surged forward. He didn't check the reins fast enough, and the gray got away from him, pounding after the others.

Thunder cracked above his head, loud enough to be clear this time, and he fought his horse back under control, trying to turn and loop back around, unwilling to leave Chloe alone in a storm. As he struggled with the horse, spooking now at the storm, and looked for a safe way back through the denser undergrowth off the path, Chloe passed him, leaning low over her horse's neck, smiling as she galloped with the others.

Fuck. She was caught up in the hunt. He'd thought she'd have the sense to stay back.

He urged his gray back onto the path but ended up with several horses between him and Chloe. Heedless, he threw his magic toward her, setting the illusion of a tiny star on the brass buckle at the rear of her saddle. The forest had been dark to begin with, and with a storm gathering, the light was fading quickly. The horses were running faster than was sensible. He could sense the strain in the gray, the nerves twitching beneath his skin. The horse tossed his head as the thunder crashed right above them, the noise like the sky roaring fury.

Lightning arced down through the trees, striking one just ahead of Chloe. For a minute, chaos reigned as horses reared and twisted and bolted in several directions. The flaring light dazzled him, turning the tree—which thankfully didn't fall or burst into flames—into pinwheels of light, and it took time to blink the spots away while wrestling the gray so it didn't bolt, too. When his eyes cleared, there was no sign of Chloe amongst the riders still in sight. His stomach coiled with fear. Where *was* she?

He cast his sense wider, seeking his illusion.

There. Off to the right. A tiny pulse of familiar magic.

He pushed harder and saw a flare of what he thought was his flame between the trees.

Chloe. Disappearing rapidly deeper into the forest. She must have lost control of her horse.

He kicked the gray into motion, aiming it in the direction she'd taken, just as the heavens opened and rain poured down as though someone had turned the sky into a waterfall. Madness to keep riding, but he wasn't going to let Chloe vanish into the forest and the storm, never to be seen again.

He cast another illusion, this time over every piece of tack the gray wore, lighting it up, to give himself a chance of seeing where they were headed as he tried to keep his senses tuned to the illusion on Chloe's saddle. It didn't help much. The rain blinded him, and the thunder, deafening now, made it impossible to hear anything else.

His horse ran like there was an army of rogue sanctii at its heels. Lucien had no idea how it managed to keep its feet and not throw him tumbling to the ground as they pelted after Chloe. At some point, a branch whipped his cheek with enough force to make him rock back in the saddle, but his face was too cold to really register the pain. He just crouched lower and held on, all the focus he could spare on his magic.

He had no idea how long the nightmare ride lasted, but eventually they broke through the trees and back onto a plateau. Though not, he thought, the one they'd entered from.

The rain was worse in the open, and lightning split the sky, making him too aware that out there, away from the trees, he was probably the tallest thing around. But the light let him catch a glimpse of Chloe and what he thought were mountains rising up ahead. Which brought to mind the map he'd studied before the hunt and the horrifying remembrance that, if he was right and they'd come out at the far end of the forest, the plateau ended in a cliff a hundred feet or so high. But he couldn't see to know if he was right, and all he could do was spur his horse on. The gray was beginning to flag, but he was bigger and stronger than Chloe's horse, so they had a chance to catch her.

He had to catch her. The thought of her plunging over a cliff....

No. He wouldn't lose her.

He sent his power ahead, reaching desperately. The tiny light of his illusion flared. Then, to his horror, he saw it arc upward before plummeting down and winking out of sight.

The cliff.

Fuck.

He dragged his own horse to a halt that was more skid than stop and threw himself off, running forward, uttering every prayer he could think of. The lightning came again, and he saw a lump of black on the ground.

Please, Goddess, let it be her.

His boots squelched and slipped over mud, but he reached her before his heart stopped entirely from the fear.

"Chloe!" He called her name as thunder boomed again, but she didn't stir. He dropped to his knees, feeling frantically for a pulse. If he hadn't already been on his knees, the relief he felt when he found it would have driven him there.

Focus. He could react later.

Right now, he had to worry about her. He knew basic first aid from his army training, and he cautiously felt his way along her limbs, searching for injuries. He found no immediate signs of broken bones, and she was breathing steadily. Trying to slow his own racing heart, he rolled her gently to one side. Mud splattered over half her face, and a long length of pale skin showed through a tear in her jacket sleeve. He summoned illusion again to give him more light and realized she'd cut her arm badly, either in the fall or in her madcap ride through the forest. Blood welled in the wound, enough of it to remain despite the pouring rain. He pulled his cravat free and bound up the wound, hoping like hell the downpour had kept it free of too much mud. He was no bloody healer to keep an infection at bay.

The rain eased somewhat as he finished checking Chloe over, but there was no sign of the storm abating, and black clouds still blocked the sun. Night fell early in Andalyssia. Chloe showed no sign of waking yet, and he didn't want to move her until he had a plan. He piled his own cloak on top of hers and looked around for his horse. It was cantering back the way they'd come, almost invisible in the dim light.

Fuck.

He gritted his teeth against the urge to roar with frustration. He needed to stay calm. He couldn't catch a horse on foot. It was gone, and with it any chance of finding the rest of the hunt quickly. So he needed another plan.

First, get his bearings. He stood, summoning another light to his hand. It didn't take much to see that Chloe lay maybe twenty feet from the edge of the cliff. His stomach swooped greasily when he realized how close she'd come to going over. He made himself walk to the edge, moving slowly and finally kneeling to peer over.

He could just make out a dark mass far below. Choe's horse.

Nothing he could do for it. There was no way it could have survived the fall.

He edged backward, then jogged back to Chloe. Just in time to see her eyes open.

"Don't move," he said, putting a hand on her shoulder.

She blinked up at him, looking bewildered. "Ow. Lucien? What?"

"Your horse bolted in the storm," he said. "You fell. Which is just as well, as it kept going, and there's a cliff about twenty feet that way." Not the most tactful way to tell her, perhaps, but he needed something to shock her into functioning.

His memory of the map was that the forest was several miles wide, and if they'd come out the other side—the wrong side— then they could be miles from any of the others. With the storm still active, night closing in, and the temperature falling fast, he wasn't counting on anyone coming to find them. The Andalyssians would prioritize getting the king and queen back to safety, and even if Honore protested—which she would—they would probably overrule her. The colonel lacked the knowledge of the terrain to search on her own. Theisse might send his sanctii to look for them, but again, the terrain played against them. Sanctii could find their own mage at any distance, but there was a limit to their ability to find others they were familiar with. He didn't know how far it stretched in strange territory.

He turned his attention back to Chloe as she made another pained sound. "What hurts?"

Chloe frowned. "Everything?"

That was probably true. "All right, what hurts *most?*"

"My arm." She winced and twisted her head to look at it. "And my side."

"Not your head?" She must have hit it to be knocked out after the fall. Or maybe she'd fainted.

"Not much," she said. "Not as much as my arm."

"You have a nasty cut," he said. "I've bandaged it. Right now, we need to figure some way to get out of the rain. The cold is a bigger risk than anything else. Do you think you can stand?" She was an earth witch. She'd have had training in healing. Which meant she was in a better place to judge her condition than he was.

"I think so," she said, grimacing. "Do you have your horse?"

"No. He ran off when I dismounted. Clearly Andalyssians don't train their horses to stay if they lose their riders."

"We need some of Jean Paul's warhorses. Those will stand through anything," she said, her voice shaky.

Goddess damn it, he needed to get her somewhere safe.

"Yes, well, perhaps we should suggest it to King Mikvel when we get back." If they got back. Not that he'd say that to Chloe. And it would bloody well be "*when*" if he had anything to do with it. "I think our best bet is heading back toward the mountain."

The left side of the plateau ended in steeply rising ground. "The edge of the trees is too far for you to walk. But if we climb a little, there should be some shelter. Rocks. Or a cave, maybe."

"If only one of us had earth sense," she muttered. "Let me up."

"Earth sense? Like the miners?" There'd been discussions of how the miners were planning on opening new shafts during some of the treaty discussions. The Andalyssians had mentioned earth sense, but he hadn't really paid attention to how it worked.

"Yes. Irina has it."

"Earth magic?"

"I think so." She pushed herself into a sitting position. "Ow. *Ow.* Ow. And bloody ow. You're going to have to help me stand." Her uninjured arm reached for him.

He took her good arm and pulled her gently to her feet, tucking her in against him. His cloak threatened to fall off her shoulders. He caught it, pulling it around both of them. They were both comprehensively soaked, but wet wool was still some protection against the elements. Chloe leaned into him for a moment, then straightened.

"Maybe I could try to find a cave," she said. "I mean, I understand the theory. They use the magic to follow the shape of what's beneath the earth. I should be able to tell solid rock from a gap, at least. How hard can it be?"

"Given it seems to be an unusual talent, perhaps harder than you think." And magic took energy. Energy she didn't have to spare.

"Yes, but they don't train people in earth the way we do. If those with earth sense are stronger in earth than usual—and men strong in earth are rarer anyway—then maybe what's difficult for them wouldn't be for me."

He couldn't think of a counterargument. Chloe was a strong witch. Granted, she'd spent ten years in exile not using much magic, but that didn't mean the power wasn't there.

"Let's get closer, and then you can try. No use wearing your self out." He didn't want her to carry her or, worse, have to leave her while he looked for shelter. The wild pigs weren't the only creatures in the forest, and while he hoped most of them would be sheltering from the storm, he didn't want to leave her alone.

"All right." Lightning flashed above them. "Can you do your sparkly light thing, at least? It's getting dark fast."

"Yes, I can do my sparkly light thing," he said, then did just that, conjuring the illusion to give them some light.

They moved slowly. He didn't want to hurry her despite his better instincts, but his memory of the map proved correct and they only walked what he judged to be a few hundred feet before the grass started to slope upward and peter out into stone. There was a boulder about ten feet past that point, and he led them around to the sheltered side. Out of the wind, it was slightly less cold. But not warm. They needed proper shelter or they would both freeze to death.

"This is probably as good a place as any to try," he said to Chloe, who was breathing hard despite the short distance.

She nodded and closed her eyes. He saw the gleam of magic surround her, but he had no idea what she was doing. So he shut up and let her do it.

She stood there for a long time, and he was beginning to think it wasn't going to work when her eyes snapped open and she grinned triumphantly at him. She lifted her uninjured arm and pointed farther up the slope.

"Up there. There's a gap in the rock. A hole. A cave, unless I'm doing this completely wrong."

"I'm sure you're not," he said with more confidence than he felt. Her breathing was fast again, and she slumped against the stone, as though the magic had taken more out of her than she'd expected. "So we should get going."

She winced at the suggestion but just nodded and took his arm again.

It wasn't far, though the journey up the sloping rocks, trying his best to support Chloe, seemed to take forever before they found the small entrance in the stone. The cave wasn't very big, stank like several large animals had met their untimely ends there, and was cold as hell. But it was empty, and mostly dry, and that was all that mattered. Chloe stood shivering beneath his arm and not entirely steady on her feet as he surveyed it. Finding the cave had clearly drained her. And with the bloodstain on the cravat he'd wrapped around her arm still spreading, she didn't have energy to spare.

Goddess damn it.

They needed warmth or they still might freeze to death, cave or no cave.

"Come away from the entrance," he said gently. "The wind won't reach us farther in." There was another near deafening clap of thunder as he spoke. Chloe flinched and moved deeper into the cave.

He listened to the storm a moment longer before he followed. The thunder showed no signs of easing, and the rain was still heavy, though not quite the torrent it had been earlier. Bad enough though. No one would be searching for them in this weather, not with night falling.

So, no rescue until morning, most likely. They only had an hour or so of light left, if he was judging the time correctly. No way to tell if he was.

"Right. We need to figure out how to stay warm," he said. He eyed her mud-stained, sodden cloak. His own wasn't much better. The wool might dry off some with a fire, but they wouldn't be warm enough to help them much if they weren't fully dry.

"I know a warming ch-charm," Chloe said, teeth chattering. "How about you?"

He shrugged, trying to seem unconcerned. "You know me, terrible at most magic other than illusions. And an illusion of fire won't help. It might keep animals out, of course, once it's dark, and it will give us some light, but it's not going to keep us warm." He grimaced. It was the problem with his talent. Too much of it channeled to illusion at the cost of all else. He remembered Charl once drunkenly teasing him that the truth wouldn't keep him warm at night. It seemed he would be proven right. "The question is, can you keep it going? You're hurt."

"I know," she said sharply. "But we have to do something. Unless you have matches and tinder somewhere handy." She swept her good hand around as she studied the cave. "There's enough leaves and branches here to burn for an hour or so, perhaps, but not longer than that. Anything outside will be too wet."

He thought fleetingly of his horse. The Andalyssians had made a point of telling them that there were matches and rations in their saddlebags. But that was no use when Chloe's horse was at the bottom of a cliff and his own had hopefully either found shelter or was on its way home to Deephilm. He hadn't remembered in his frantic need to reach Chloe when he'd spotted her lying so still and then the horse had been gone.

Which was the kind of mistake his squad sergeant in his basic army training would have had his guts for. They'd covered basic survival skills. He just had to remember what they were.

"All right," he said, coming to a decision. "I can spark a fire, at least, and we'll burn what we can for as long as it lasts. That will warm us up some, and we might be able to dry off the cloaks and our clothes enough to use them for sleeping. How wet are you?"

"Wet enough," she said. "Not entirely soaked through, maybe. Though my feet are frozen. I think water got into my boots when I fell."

"Right. Well, once the fire is going, you can take them off, and we'll see if we can dry your stockings out, too." Frostbite affected extremities first. It might not be actually snowing outside, but the air was frigid, and there'd been snow on some of the rocks they'd passed despite the rain. "You sit by the back wall, rest a while. I can make a fire."

She didn't argue, which made him think she was hurting more than she was letting on.

Goddess. Don't let her die.

It didn't take long to sort the few leaves and twigs and branches into piles. There weren't that many of them. The thickest branch was a few inches thick. If it was a slow-burning wood, it might last a few hours. But it snapped easily under his foot, and he suspected it was going to burn fast. He'd have to keep the fire small. Hopefully, the wind would draw some of the smoke out of the entrance, but a roaring blaze would simply fill the cave up with smoke and suffocate them. Not to mention use up their scant supply of wood too fast. So, big enough to keep them alive, small enough not to kill them. He made a pile of leaves and small twigs and sparked a flame to life, guarding it from the wind as he coaxed the fire into something that might survive any stray gusts of wind.

By the time he'd finished, Chloe had closed her eyes, and he wondered if she'd fallen asleep. The healers would probably tell him to keep her awake if she'd been knocked out. But surely she needed the rest? He rolled a large stone from the back of the cave over to the fire to give her something to rest against and she didn't stir, but she opened her eyes when he crouched in front of her and touched her knee.

"Come closer to the fire," he said, offering her a hand.

She took it, smiling weakly, wincing as her injured arm moved. He put his arm around her waist carefully and helped her back over to the fire, easing her cloak off and draping it on another rock next to his. Maybe, just maybe, there was a little steam rising from it.

He scooted back over to the fire, fed it a small branch, and eased down next to Chloe, taking the side closer to the entrance to block more of the wind from her. She was still shivering. Too soon to coax her into taking off her shoes or any other layers. The hem of her trousers and her jacket were soaked. Thank the goddess the Andalyssians had the sense to realize that riding sidesaddle in the mountains was too dangerous. If Chloe had been hooked into a sidesaddle, she could well be at the bottom of the cliff with her horse. Though the extra layers of petticoats and things women wore under their habits might have been useful to either keep them warm or keep the fire going longer.

"Say something or I'm going to fall asleep," Chloe said. "Ginevra would tell me it's a bad idea to sleep much after hitting one's head."

"Ginevra?" he said.

"She owned the store in Anglion before me. Good earth witch. Taught me a lot." She stretched her good hand toward the fire.

"She'd be useful about now."

"Yes. If she was still alive."

He winced. "I'm sorry. I didn't know."

"Why would you? We haven't exactly spoken much about my time there."

"Do you want to talk about it now?"

"Not particularly." She slanted a glance at him that he couldn't entirely interpret.

"You're the one who wanted to make conversation," he countered. "But I won't pry. Anglion aside, did this Ginevra teach you anything that might be helpful in this situation?"

"I'm thinking about that," she said. "Food isn't an immediate problem. Water more so. There's plenty of rain but nothing to catch it in."

He shifted, then remembered the kafiet flask. Sure enough, it was still tucked in his inner pocket. He pulled it free. "I have this." He regarded the flask. "It's not big, but it will do, I guess."

"It's not the best shape to catch rain."

"There was snow in places. It should be clean enough. And easier to scoop up."

"What's in there now?" she asked, nodding at the flask.

"Kafiet." He frowned. "In basic training, they said alcohol and cold don't mix. Or alcohol and head wounds."

She snorted. "Maybe not. But one mouthful each before you pour it out might warm us up a little. I'll risk it if you will."

"One mouthful only," he said and passed her the flask.

She unscrewed the cap, took a careful swig, and handed it back.

He took one swig, then poured the rest carefully into the fire. The alcohol flared fiercely, and the air filled with the scent of burning mint for a minute. Which was an improvement over long-dead animal. "Stay here. I'll fill it."

It didn't take long, which was good, because the air beyond the cave chilled him immediately. The flask held maybe two cups of liquid and only a handful or so of snow. He set it at the edge of the fire and tried to thaw out without taking up too much of the heat as he calculated how long the snow might take to melt. Chloe needed water to counteract the blood loss.

She shifted beside him, moving stiffly and supporting her injured arm.

Right. That was the next priority. See what could be done for her injuries. "You're an earth witch. Can you stop the bleeding?" he asked.

Her mouth flattened. "It's complicated. It takes a lot of energy to work on yourself. With the right herbs and things to use, it would be easier. Right now, I'm not sure I wouldn't just pass out."

He swore under his breath. "Well, let's keep thinking. We have an hour or so before it gets dark and the fire goes out. I'd prefer not to die on the side of an Andalyssian mountain."

That earned him a flash of a smile. "Me, too."

"Maybe the Andalyssians are right after all," he said glumly, staring into the sparking fire. "We should be more balanced in our magic. That way I could help you."

"Power," she muttered. Then frowned. Then went still, eyes widening.

"Chloe? What is it?"

"I'm having what might be a very bad idea," she muttered.

"Let's assume in this situation there are no bad ideas. Well, no ideas too bad to suggest. We can figure out whether or not they're useful after you tell me."

"You have power," she said. "I can do the magic we need, but right now, I don't have the power."

"Well, I'd share if I could...." He trailed off as he realized what she was suggesting. "An augmentier? Is that what you're thinking of?" A bond between mages. Not something illusioners bothered much with, but water mages did it with their sanctii, and some of the other magics used them, too. In Anglion they used marriage bonds to lock away some of their women's power, siphoning it to their husbands. "Aren't those kind of complicated?"

"They can't be that hard. Sophie and Cameron did it by accident." She blushed, and he wondered if perhaps the rumors about exactly how the Queen of Anglion and her consort came to be bonded were true. "I know the theory. They teach it to water mages. And earth witches for bonding petty fams."

He suspected bonding another human's magic might be more complicated than binding a raven. Though, admittedly, not as difficult as binding an infinitely powerful sanctii. Pity she'd never done that. If she had a sanctii, they'd be far safer. It couldn't transport them back to the palace, but it could let the others know where they were and fetch more wood and water. "Have you ever had to form a bond?" he asked.

"No. But it doesn't have to be perfect. Just last through the night. If I can access your power, I can stop the bleeding and, I'm guessing, keep a warming charm going well enough to stop us freezing to death." She squinted at him. "It's worth a try, isn't it?"

It said something about how bad their situation was that she was suggesting it. She'd had sex with him, but he didn't think she'd particularly changed her mind about him. She certainly hadn't yet sought out a repeat encounter. "What if something goes wrong? How do we know we can undo it?"

"Sophie once told me Elarus offered to break the bond between her and Cameron. I know quite a few sanctii. I'm sure one of them will help if we can't work it out ourselves."

He didn't particularly like the idea, but she was right. It was better than dying. "What do we need to do?"

"The basic version takes blood." She lifted her injured arm. "I have plenty of that right now. Do you have a knife?"

"Yes." He never hunted without a spare tucked into a sheath in his boot. Knives were handy things. He pulled his free. "Should have kept some of that kafiet to pour over it. Isn't that what you do?"

"Shove the blade into the fire for a bit, then wipe it off in the snow," Chloe suggested. "That should be clean enough. I don't have any virulent diseases that I'm aware of, and I assume you don't either."

"No," he agreed. Unless extreme idiocy was one. "All right." He followed her suggestion, and by the time he'd cooled the knife outside, he was shivering again. Chloe, on the other hand, had a tiny bit more color in her cheeks after the kafiet.

"So, what do we need to do?"

"Share blood and touch the ley line. And then I will try to hook my power into yours. There are words for the ritual, but Madame Simsa used to say they were more for show and focus when a mage is bonding with another mage. It's not like a sanctii, where you're warding yourself as well." She straightened her shoulders and held out her injured arm. "Unwrap the bandage, then cut your hand and put it over the gash. That should work."

"That's going to hurt you," he objected.

"Dying will hurt more. Or frostbite. I'm fond of my fingers and toes, Lucien. And Irina will be very upset if I let your ruin your looks by losing half your nose." She smiled, but the expression was shaky. If she was willing to put up with the pain, then he had to try. Share his power with her. Keep them both alive and deal with the consequences when they were safely back in Deephilm.

He passed the knife to Chloe. "Hold this while I deal with the bandage."

She nodded and looked away as he unwound the cravat, hissing a breath out as he got to the final layer. The cravat was unpleasantly damp with blood, but he couldn't throw it on the fire, despite his instinct to do just that. He could assess if they could spare something else to wrap it after they tried the bond.

At least there was still blood in the wound. It glistened in the firelight, and he swallowed hard. "Give me the knife."

He sliced across the meaty part of his palm under his thumb before he could stop and think. Blood welled, and he clamped his hand as gently as possible around Chloe's arm.

"Ow. Goddess damn it," she muttered. "All right, Truth Seeker. Grab that damn ley line fast. This hurts." She stared at him, focused but shivering. She was watching, he realized, for his magic.

He sent his power down, through the rock. The ley lines here were deep. He found one and pulled magic as hard as he dared, watching Chloe.

There was a sudden flare of color around her, brilliant sparks of gold that nearly blinded him. She reached for his other hand and wound her fingers through his.

"Now," she said. "Let me in."

Her eyes were wide, the pupils dark as they had been above him and beneath him and beside him in her bed. Her magic engulfed him, and something within him leaped toward it, willing to take whatever part of her she might offer him. He was dimly aware that she was saying something as magic spiraled around him and through him, unlike anything he'd felt before, surging like a forest blaze for a moment, like the rush of sex, before it quieted to another shower of sparks and then settled to a glow that surrounded both of them.

A sound like a faint chime of bells sang through the air. "Do you hear something?" he said.

Chloe was staring at him, eyes even wider, but her cheeks were flushed, and she looked far more alert than she had a few minutes ago.

"The magic," she said absently. Then her mouth dropped open. "You hear that? But you don't hear magic, do you?"

"No." He shook his head, the song distracting him. "I see sparks."

She laughed then, a gurgle of pleased satisfaction. "I think it worked."

Relief swept through him. They were going to survive. She would be safe.

"Good," he managed. "Then we should get to work getting you patched up."

CHAPTER 23

Chloe watched Lucien in the firelight as he reached for the bloodied bandage. The surge of shared power had left her giddy and somewhat breathless. Enough to make her forget for a moment how much her arm hurt. But now that the initial rush was fading, the ache was pushing back.

Lucien glowed, brighter than usual. If she kept using her mage sight to watch him, she wouldn't need the firelight. He'd always been loud to her, the song of his magic insistent if she let it steal her focus. Not quite this bright though.

Dazzling. Not just the glow around him but the sense of his power rolling through her. Tangible, even if she closed her eyes. With them open, a cord of light linked the two of them and offered that power to her. She tugged at it gently, just to experiment, and was rewarded with a rush of magic. Not quite the same as tapping a ley line, though more focused. Regardless, it was enough to strengthen her, a buzz of energy she sorely needed filling her veins.

But she couldn't drain him. No. She needed his strength to keep them warm through the night. So she would use his power to do the minimum to heal her arm, the slash marring one of his cheeks that he hadn't even acknowledged, and save the rest for the warming charm. The other aches and bruises making themselves known would have to wait. The healers at the palace could take care of those.

She shifted in place, wincing. A sharp pain in her side made her suspect she had cracked a rib. But it could just be bruising. There was no reason for her to be doing anything in the next twelve hours before daylight that should stress a minor crack further. It would be uncomfortable, but she could manage. At least she was no longer cold. The rush of magic had chased away the chill that the fire had barely lifted.

She turned her attention to her arm. The cut was jagged and deeper near her elbow. A thin trickle of blood still welled to the surface. Hopefully she could stop that and boost her body's will to heal now that she had power to burn. A distracting amount. If Lucien walked around with as much power as she was sensing through the bond all the time, she had no idea how he focused minute to minute.

But she would focus now. Closing her eyes, she tugged on the bond, drawing a thread of power, trying to feel the injury. Feel the path of the blood in her veins and where that path was broken. A true healer would perhaps be able to heal the wound entirely, but she lacked the training. Even if she had the necessary skill, performing that level of magic on herself would be risky.

So, stop the bleeding, send the suggestion of healing through her flesh, and that would hold her until morning.

It didn't take long.

Opening her eyes, she flexed her hand gingerly. The ache was still there, but dull and distant. As long as she didn't do anything too vigorous, it would be bearable until they could get back to the palace. Where, between the Andalyssian healers and the earth witches on the mission, the job could be finished. Hopefully without a scar. Otherwise, she might have to cover it with a tattoo.

The thought drew a soft giggle to her lips. The rush of power had left her giddy again. Almost as though she'd downed the rest of the kafiet Lucien had poured away.

"How does it feel?" Lucien asked.

"Well enough," she said. "You can bandage it again."

"Good." He set to work doing just that, mouth turned down in concentration. Did that mean he didn't feel as power-addled as she did? Maybe not, if he was used to having so much magic at his command all the time. But she was no slouch at magic either. Or at least she hadn't been. Maybe it was because she was still out of practice that it felt so strong. Or maybe the added weight of his illusion talent had thrown her off-kilter. Still, she didn't need to use much magic to close the cut on his face or start a warming charm. "Your cheek. Let me deal with that."

Lucien touched his face but shook his head. "No. It's fine. Don't waste your power."

She doubted it would do any good to argue. "Then I should start on the warming charm."

That earned her another headshake. "We have enough wood to last a little longer. Rest a little."

"I feel fine," she protested. Stretching the truth somewhat, but he didn't need to know that. "I don't need to exert much effort to dry the cloaks. You can bring them over to me. Better to do it now, in case the bond doesn't hold." It seemed unlikely, but she was swimming out of her depth with the augmentier. A small miracle it had worked at all.

She thought he would argue, but after a moment, he merely shrugged. "All right. You know more about such things than I do. Sit still," he said and hauled himself to his feet.

It didn't take long to dry the cloaks. When she was done, her stomach rumbled as Lucien moved them away again so she could work the charm on their clothes next. It had been a long time since luncheon. It felt like a lifetime. And longer still until breakfast, she expected.

"I don't suppose you can illusion up dinner?" she asked with a wry smile.

"No. Water is going to have to—" He stopped, then shook his head. "No, wait. I have these." He pulled out a small waxed paper bag from another inner pocket. She was going to need to make sure her clothes had more pockets from now on. And carry matches and whatever else she could think of to stash within them in case of disaster. "Mints," he said triumphantly. "They gave them to me for the horse. Not much, but it's a bit of sugar, at least."

She'd forgotten the mints. "I have some, too." She reached into her own pocket and felt for the bag. And the napkin she'd shoved in there at lunch with the nut confection. She pulled that out. It was sadly squashed and broken into small pieces, but it would be edible. Barely a few mouthfuls shared between the two of them, but as Lucien had said, something was better than nothing. She offered it to him. "Let's have this now. Save the mints for morning. Though I think I fed half of mine to the hor—" She broke off suddenly, remembering Spetya was dead. That he'd run over the edge of cliff. And she could have gone with him. Embarrassingly, she broke into sobs.

Lucien was back at her side in an instant and wrapped his arms gently around her. "Shhh. It's just the shock of it all. You're safe here. It's all going to be well." He let her cry on him, rubbing her back gently and whispering nonsense into her ear until she regained control of herself and pushed back, scrubbing at her eyes.

"I'm sorry, I don't know what came over me."

"It's perfectly normal after a scare," he said. "Today has been enough to test anyone."

"I'm not the crying sort." Crying was a luxury she'd learned not to indulge in very often.

"I know," he said. "But I think you can make allowances for yourself. It's bad enough to fall off a horse at the best of times, let alone in the middle of a storm. Though I'm glad you did."

She frowned, trying to remember the moment. It was foggy.

But she remembered the sensation of sliding. "I'm not sure I fell, exactly. The saddle slipped, I think."

His gaze sharpened. "That shouldn't happen."

"No. But maybe I'm confused. It happened fast."

"There was no sign of your saddle, so it didn't come off entirely."

She shrugged, then shivered. "Maybe I did fall. There was lightning. The horse shied. And then...that's all I remember."

He reached around her and picked up the napkin he'd abandoned. "Don't worry about it. Eat. That will make you feel better. Then maybe you can try to teach me the warming charm. You made my shirt soggy again."

He smiled as he spoke, but it wasn't a bad idea. If they were sharing power through the bond, he should be able to use some of her earth magic to work a charm. She took a few of the smaller pieces and nibbled. Lucien watched her, then ate, too.

He tried to make her take more, but she insisted that he have the larger share. He was bigger than her. Once they'd made sure they'd eaten all the crumbs—which, sadly, didn't take long—she climbed off his lap and tried to teach him the warming charm.

He got the hang of it fast, and his delight in mastering such a small magic made her smile. They practiced while the fire continued to burn, drying out their boots a little and her stockings. When Lucien put the last branch on the fire, the sliver of sky visible through the cave's entrance was black.

"We'd better get organized," he said. "The temperature will keep falling. And I don't want anything joining us for the night." He looked toward the entrance and raised a hand. A perfect semblance of a roaring fire blazed to life, lighting the cave better than the actual flames.

The ease with which he wielded illusion always startled her. If he hadn't been a Truth Seeker, he would have been, no doubt, highly sought after. Pity it gave off no warmth. "Could you add a warmth charm to an illusion?" she asked.

His brows lifted. "Perhaps. But not tonight. I don't want to waste any effort." He looked around the cave. "I'm thinking if we put my clothes down as a base layer and then use yours and the cloaks on top, we should be able to stay warm enough if we take turns sleeping and using the charm."

"You want us to take our clothes off?" she squeaked. "Lucien, it's freezing."

He nodded. "I know. But the army trained us to survive in odd conditions. Skin to skin is warmer than clothes."

"You snuggled up with your fellow soldiers?" It was an amusing thought.

"One fellow soldier. When faced with the choice of freezing or not. It wasn't my best night's sleep ever, but it was effective. Hairy though." He smiled. "You at least smell better."

That made her laugh. "I wouldn't be so sure of that after today." She suspected she smelled of mud and horse and damp wool and fear sweat. And smoke. Not that she should care what Lucien thought she smelled of. Even so, the thought of sleeping beside him skin to skin made her nervous. The night after the wedding had been a moment of insanity. Never to be repeated. But if that were true, then she shouldn't feel awkward about doing as he suggested. But the bump in her pulse wasn't just embarrassment.

"Your virtue is safe with me," Lucien said. "I'm suggesting this to get us through the night, not to get you back into my bed. A damp and smelly cave is hardly arousing."

Somehow she didn't think he was being entirely truthful. And that he, like her, wasn't entirely unaffected by his proposal. But she trusted him to keep his word.

"All right," she agreed. "Where exactly did you have in mind?"

It didn't take long to rearrange things as he suggested. He moved all the stones to the other side of the fire and then shifted to a spot several feet away from the flames, out of reach of any dying sparks but close enough to maybe benefit from whatever heat the embers gave off. He stripped down to his drawers without any hint of embarrassment, arranged his clothes on the floor, and turned his back while she slipped out of her clothes and added them to the makeshift pallet. She left her underwear on. Her corset, she suspected, would keep her sore rib more comfortable than not, and it and her other underthings were hardly going to add much to the pile of clothes beneath them. A corset, in fact, would only be uncomfortable to lie on.

They settled awkwardly on the pile of clothing and pulled the cloaks over them. At first she tried to keep some distance between them, but he put an arm around her waist and pulled her back against him gently. "Skin to skin is the point, Chloe," he said. "Now, you should sleep. I'll wake you in a few hours."

Warmth crept through her, and the faint hum of him filled her ears as he used the warming charm to make things comfortable. She was still all too aware that beneath the few layers of linen and cotton and wool, she rested on hard stone, but the chill of it receded enough to let her relax. And then, while she was still wondering how she would make it through the night with Lucien wrapped around her, she fell asleep.

"Your turn, Lieutenant."

Lucien's hand shook her gently, and Chloe opened her eyes, confused as to why he was waking her. It all came rushing back as he yawned and pulled the cloak higher around them.

The cave. The *accident*. She wasn't cold, though her face felt chilled. All she wanted to do was close her eyes again and fall back into sleep. But she sucked in a lungful of cold air instead. She had to wake up so Lucien could sleep.

"All right, I'm awake." She reached for the bond, let the magic rise through her to chase sleep away, and started the warming charm. "You can let go now. Rest."

"You're sure? I can do a few more hours." He yawned again, belying his words.

"You need to rest," she said firmly. "We may yet have to walk back to Deephilm." Goddess, she hoped not. Finding their way might not be a problem once it was light, but it was a long way to walk. Especially when the weather could turn savage so fast. But that was a problem for the morning. And to get to the morning, they had to survive the night. "Rest," she repeated.

"All right. Good night."

She felt it when he let go of the charm, the hum of his power fading. His breathing slowed and deepened, the warmth of him solid at her back, and she peeked through the bond to make sure he was truly asleep. Difficult not to wriggle closer still and soak up his heat, but she was warm enough with the charm and the weight of the cloaks above them. Between that and not wanting to complicate things, it was better to stay where she was. But lying there with him in the dark, staring at the illusion of fire he'd built at the cave's mouth, her thoughts whirled.

Lucien had saved her life today. None of the Andalyssians had come after her—or, if they had, they'd turned back as the storm had worsened. Only Lucien had thrown himself into peril. He could have been hurt, or worse, but he hadn't cared. He'd come after her. Without him, she probably wouldn't have woken up from her fall, freezing to death in the snow and rain.

A difficult thing to come to weigh. Especially considering what happened after the wedding.

She wanted to hate him. If for no other reason than loyalty to Charl seeming to dictate that she should. But he'd been right in the words he'd thrown at her. Charl was the one who'd forsaken them. So what loyalty did she owe his memory? He had shown her none with his recklessness. But Lucien...Lucien had protected her without hesitation. He'd done it the night he'd warned her after Charl's death, too. It could have cost him his career if his actions had displeased the emperor.

But what would people think if she became...friends again

with the man who'd condemned her husband? There would be gossip and worse. Near certainty that there would be some all too ready to think that perhaps they'd been together before Charl had fallen.

She wasn't sure she could bear it. Bad enough to be a traitor's widow. But to let people think she had betrayed him first? They would say she had driven him to his bad choices, perhaps. Easier to blame her. She was still here to blame. And what would Charl's family say? She didn't know how things were between them and Lucien now.

Simpler to remain at a distance. But simple didn't always consider emotion. She couldn't ignore the fact that the weight of him at her back and the warmth of his body and the knowledge that he would charge into a storm to save her made her feel...safe. Protected. In a way she hadn't for a very long time. A strange sensation to have lying in a cave in the Andalyssian wilderness, hoping not to freeze to death. But she knew it to be truth.

So what did that mean? What should she do?

Not something she would solve tonight. She tried to tame her thoughts and the heart that beat a little too fast with him beside her, even now in these ridiculous circumstances, back to something calmer. Focus on breath and just appreciating the presence of someone next to her in the dark. It had been a long time since she'd spent a whole night with a man. Not since...Samuel.

Ah, Samuel. Captain Jensen.

There was a memory to distract her.

The man who'd spirited her away from Lumia into exile all those years ago.

She still counted herself fortunate that it had been his ship she'd stumbled across on her flight from the city. He'd charged her a pretty penny, of course, but he hadn't robbed her, nor slit her throat and dropped her over the side of his ship after taking her money. And the advice he'd given her about what to say to the temple in Kingswell to claim asylum had worked.

She hadn't expected to see him again but a month or so after she'd finished her "supervised" stay in the temple, where they'd drilled her into her head that water magic was heresy and an abomination and made her take oaths never to practice it again, he'd stepped out of one of the Portholme laneways to join her on her walk home to the tiny room she could barely afford on the equally tiny wage she'd been making working in the kitchen of an inn.

Checking up on her, he'd said, and then he'd dropped a hint that Ginevra Talbot might be looking for an extra pair of hands. That had proved true, too. The next time she'd run into Samuel, her room had been less tiny, and she had begun to feel as though a life in Anglion might be possible. That time he'd looked her up and down, declared she was looking like she'd found a good mooring, waltzed her off to dinner, and charmed her into bed, telling her that she wasn't going to shed the sadness of whatever man was ghosting her memories alone.

She'd been part guilty, part relieved, to discover the next morning that he'd been right again, in a way. She hadn't forgotten Charl, but she had been reminded that her life wasn't over, too.

After that, Samuel had turned up every month or two. And most times, she let him into her bed, needing the fun and the forgetting he offered. Their liaison lasted, on and off, for nearly two years. At which point, Ginevra had died of an attack of the heart, and Chloe had made an offer to her son to take over the store. To her surprise, he had accepted.

Samuel appeared the night she'd first opened her doors as Madame Montesse's Magical Supplies. He'd brought flowers and wine. She'd made him dinner, let him make her laugh. She'd grown fond of him. He'd taken her to bed. And then he'd told her it would be the last time. She'd protested, but he'd been firm.

"Chloe, sweet," he'd said, sounding resolute but regretful, "you are a delight and nothing less. But you've had trouble enough due to men, and even if I were not too old for you, some of what I do is risky. And some of it just plain illegal. And I won't be another anchor around you, pulling you down to disaster if something goes wrong. You don't need me." And that had been that. He'd assured her she could call on him if she ever needed and instructed her how to do just that, but he'd never turned up on her doorstep again.

After that, her bed had been largely empty. There'd been a few nights where she'd gone to an inn on the far side of the city, hidden her hair with dye, and bedded some passing-through man with kind eyes or a ready wit to ease the loneliness, but none of them had ever stuck past the next morning.

So she'd been alone a long time. And Samuel had been right. She hadn't needed a man. Men were trouble and anchors and disaster. The fact that her stupid, foolish heart had decided to race for Lucien, of all people, was only proof that she was also a disaster when it came to romance.

So she would ignore her racing heart. And hope it was only the aftermath of nearly dying that made Lucien suddenly feel more like home than anybody else. And she would be perfectly fine.

She hoped. Her arm throbbed suddenly, and she shifted, easing herself into another position with a sigh.

"Chloe?" Lucien said sleepily. "Is something wrong?"

"No. Go back to sleep. Everything's fine."

His arm tightened around her, but he didn't speak again. She lay in the dark, listening to him breathing, and tried not to think about the morning.

"Well, this is unfortunate."

Chloe startled awake. That had sounded like Honore. But why would Honore be in the cave? In the cave where, Chloe realized as her head cleared, she was wrapped around Lucien, her face pressed into his neck and her injured arm laid across his chest. Naked Lucien. Or so it would appear to anyone who couldn't see what they had on under the cloak. Admittedly it wasn't much, but....

"Lieutenant, you appear to be out of uniform."

Definitely Honore. She cracked an eye open, turning her head.

Damn. Not just Honore. The colonel wasn't the only one staring down at the two of them. Behind her stood Gilles, Sejerin Silya, Mikvel, Irina, for some reason, and Roland. Honore looked exasperated. Sejerin Silya looked outraged. Mikvel looked mostly...resigned. Roland, she couldn't read, and Irina and Captain Theisse were struggling not to smile.

"The storm," she said, moving away from Lucien and elbowing him under the covers. Honestly, the man slept like the dead. "We were soaked...."

"Unholy," Sejerin Silya hissed. "Lust and worse."

Worse? Lust seemed unlikely enough in a freezing mountain cave in the middle of a storm. What did the woman imagine they'd been doing that was even more ambitiously depraved? She opened her mouth to object.

"Wha—" Lucien bolted upright. His hair stood half on end, and stubble lined his jaw. But his expression rapidly snapped from sleepy to cautious as he saw they were no longer alone. "A rescue party, I see."

"Yes," Honore said briskly. "Captain Theisse sent Caesarus to see if he could find you once the storm broke. But it was dark, and all he could tell us was you were in a cave at the far end of the plateau. We left this morning before dawn. Irina was kind enough to come along to lend her earth sense to try and determine which 'cave' it was that you might be in. The sejerin thought you might need medical aid. And here we are."

Chloe hid a wince. They had all made that ride back down the mountain in the dark to come looking for them. Though if Caesarus had found them, why hadn't the sanctii made himself known?

"The balance is broken," Silya said, glaring.

Her scowl suggested she'd far rather toss them over the edge of a cliff than heal them. Did the sejerin work as healers? Chloe had no idea. But she had a sinking feeling that the seer was here for entirely different reasons.

"Heathen foreigners." She glared up at Mikvel. "Your wedding rituals cannot be completed with the balance broken."

Honestly? Wasn't the balance already broken with House Elannon?

The king's brows rose. But it seemed he wasn't prepared to argue the point here in the cave. "I think we can discuss the ramifications of what has happened here when we get back to Deephilm. Lady de Montesse looks like she is hurt. Irina, Sejerin, perhaps you can see if you can provide her with some ease for the journey. And check that bruise on Lord Castaigne's face as well. Perhaps after he is dressed. After they're both dressed," he added. "We can wait outside."

Beside him, Irina rolled her eyes, but she followed when they all disappeared back out the cave entrance, leaving Chloe staring at Lucien.

"Well," he said. "This is...unexpected."

"What did she mean, 'The balance is broken'?" Chloe said. "She can't seriously think we were out here on a jaunt to find a place to...."

"Fuck?" Lucien suggested. "I don't know. I don't know what her game is at this point. I think we should do as Mikvel suggested. Get dressed and sort this out back at the palace. Saner heads will prevail once everyone is warm and comfortable again."

She wished she believed he was right.

✧ ✧ ✧

They emerged from the cave in short order. Dressing didn't take long, and the remnants of the fire were cold and dead. Not that the cave had anything in it left to burn.

Honore stood talking with Mikvel while Captain Theisse and Roland saw to the horses. One of them was the gray Lucien had ridden yesterday, and relief flashed over his face when he realized the horse had made it safely home.

"My lady, may I ask if we need to look for Spetya?" Roland asked. "He didn't return with Graimm here."

She swallowed, sadness for her horse mingling again with the mix of terror and relief that she hadn't gone with him. "I'm sorry, Wardmeister. He bolted in the storm. He went over the cliff. I am fortunate that I fell or I would have gone with him. I don't remember it all, but I think there was a lightning strike quite close. He was terrified."

Roland looked briefly sad. "Ah. Thank you, my lady. That is unfortunate, but the weather here can be deadly."

"Was the storm yesterday unexpected?" Lucien asked, staring at Sejerin Silya. Guidance on the weather was one of the talents the seers claimed.

"Balance broken," she said and clamped her lips shut, seeming to think that was enough of an explanation. It seemed a convenient excuse to cover the fact that the sejerin had gotten the weather wrong or perhaps decided not to tell the truth about it for reasons of their own. That seemed a risky game. It could have been anyone in the party who'd been injured. Even Mikvel.

Had they wanted something to happen to the king? Or maybe to her? She wished she knew what was going on in Deephilm.

"It came faster than anyone anticipated," Mikvel said. "It happens sometimes. I certainly wouldn't have risked the hunt if

I had thought it would happen yesterday. So, my apologies." He looked up at the skies, which were clear and sunny, though it was cold. "We should make our way back. But first tea, and Irina can see to you both. Then we'll be underway."

And so they were. They drank tea, ate rolls stuffed with cheese and ham, and then Chloe let Irina inspect and clean her arm before she rebandaged it.

"I will do something to block the pain," Irina said with a glance under her eyelashes at Sejerin Silya, who was standing apart from the others, looking like she wanted to blast the mountain into rubble. She hadn't offered to help Irina. "One of the more senior healers should look at it for anything more complicated. I don't want to trap any potential source of infection. Though it looks like you did something already. How, exactly?"

"I used some of Lucien's power," Chloe admitted. "I used an augmentier."

"A what?" Irina frowned. "Oh. A bond. Shards. Is that what that is?" She gestured vaguely at Chloe's side.

"You can see it?" Chloe asked. Sure enough, there was, now that she was paying attention, still a thread of light snaking between her and Lucien, and the song of him played in her head once more. More familiar than it should be.

"I see something," Irina said quietly with another glance at the seer.

"Is the bond what she's so upset about?" Chloe said.

"Maybe. Being found naked with a man you're not married to is generally not acceptable around here either."

"Is she going to try to use this to make trouble? Honestly, we needed to stay warm. We would have frozen to death."

Irina shrugged. "I don't know. Hopefully Misha can talk her round." She grimaced slightly. "You're lucky, being a foreigner. If it were me they'd found in a cave with a man who was not my husband, then he would become my husband in short order if he wanted to live."

Well, that was plainly ridiculous. But she wasn't going to argue the point out here in the wilderness with her arm smarting and the seer glaring at her. So she just thanked Irina and turned her attention to staying on the bay mare Roland had brought for her. Lucien looked rather like he wanted to grab her off the saddle and put her up in front of him. But she shook her head at him when he approached. Better they keep their distance.

The ride back was long and uncomfortable despite Irina's work on her arm. It didn't hurt much, but the rest of her felt like she'd, well, stampeded through a storm, fallen off a horse, and then spent the night sleeping on rocks. It took all her attention to stay awake and in the saddle, and she would have killed for some kafiet to numb the pain by the time they rode into the stable yard at the palace and Captain Theisse helped her down from the horse. She swayed slightly, and he grabbed her before Lucien could.

She kept hold of the captain's arm as they walked slowly back inside. There were far too many curious looks on the faces of the courtiers they passed, even though they were hastily swept away and turned into bows or curtsies as the king and the seer walked by. When they reached one of the intersections in the corridors that would lead back to the Illvyans' quarters, Mikvel said, "I suggest we meet again this afternoon. The two of you need to bathe and rest and let the healers—"

"Balance must be attended," Silya said, cutting him off. "Coddle them later. We need to address this. Now."

CHAPTER 24

The king pressed a finger to his forehead, sighing as though it pained him. Lucien sympathized. Sejerin Silya was enough to give anyone a headache.

"Very well. We will go to the Copper Chamber and discuss this further. Irina, go and fetch Royve Ava, please. There's no reason Lady de Montesse should remain in pain while we talk. Colonel Brodier, if you want someone from your own party to attend to her as well, feel free to send for them."

He turned on his heel and started walking.

"Good luck," Irina mouthed at Chloe before she headed back the way they'd come.

Lucien moved up to stand next to Captain Theisse as they followed the king. Chloe stuck close to Honore, avoiding him.

The Copper Chamber was aptly named, the metal gleaming from candlesticks and lanterns and copper gilt—if that was the right word—on the flowers embroidered on the autumn-shaded tapestries on the walls. An oval table in a burnished red-brown wood was surrounded by eight chairs finished in coppery silks. Mikvel sat at one end, and Silya took the chair next to him.

Chloe sank into one of the chairs farthest from the seer with a grateful sigh. She was too pale, and he bit down the immediate instinct to request that she be allowed to rest before this nonsense continued.

Best to get it over with. Still, sensible or not, he sat beside her, leaving Honore and Captain Theisse to bridge the gap in the center.

No one spoke immediately. It was protocol to let Mikvel go first, but Lucien was ready to ignore protocol if it would speed up proceedings.

"They should marry," Sejerin Silya said abruptly.

Apparently she wasn't going to worry about protocol either. Lucien clenched his jaw against the desire to ask her if she had lost her mind. "I beg your pardon?"

"Marriage would restore the balance," she said as though she was saying something perfectly sensible.

Maybe he had hit his head after all. Maybe he was back in the cave, still dreaming.

"You can't be serious," Chloe said, outrage clear in her tone. "We were merely trying to survive the night."

Mikvel laid one of his hands flat on the table, nodding. "Silya, these are not Andalyssians. They are not bound by our customs."

Relief swept through Lucien's gut. Good, someone was going to be sensible.

"But you are, Your Majesty," Silya said. "You took an oath to maintain the balance. We already have the difficulty from the council being incomplete for so long. Now you have another transgression. One which took place during your wedding hunt. Perhaps the goddess sent the storm to show her displeasure."

If she had, wouldn't that mean she had no issue with Chloe and him spending the night in a cave? Lucien's fingers flexed and he gripped his hands under the table, fighting to stay calm. His gut told him the sejerin was lying. But to try to use his power on her would be a flagrant breach of protocol. It would only make things worse.

"That's superstition and foolishness," Mikvel said, squaring his shoulders. "Seers don't always get the forecasts right. This is merely one of those times."

"Perhaps. But if the balance is skewed, the land is cursed."

"That is also superstition and nonsense," Mikvel said, his voice firm. "Curses don't exist."

Silya scowled. "You know nothing of the old times. Of what can be done when power is used wildly and with no regard for the balance."

Like Illvyans did?

"This is not the old times, Sejerin."

"You do not hear the land protest the balance broken as I do," she retorted. "Do not be so sure."

Mikvel looked pained all over again. "Nevertheless, we are discussing what has happened today. Not old magic and mysteries."

"Mysteries that keep your land safe, Your Majesty. You would be wise to remember it."

"Sejerin, do not forget yourself," Roland said.

Silya shot him a look.

"You both know the queen cannot be crowned if the sejerin and the priests do not confirm the balance," Silya continued, sounding slyly triumphant.

"Are you saying you won't?" Mikvel said flatly. "We are working to rectify the issue with House Elannon. This seems minor compared to that."

"I'm not saying we won't. I'm saying we could not." Silya looked too smug at the thought.

Lucien's heart sank. She clearly thought she had something over Mikvel here. Something the king might bow to rather than risk a scandal. But why was she forcing his hand? What was she gaining? Or, if not her, whoever it was whose interests she had in mind. "The balance is broken when propriety is so clearly ignored. Not to mention that...wrongdoing between them." She gestured at the space between them.

"Wrongdoing?" Chloe said indignantly. "Do you mean the bond? We needed that to stay alive."

Mikvel winced. "Lady de Montesse. In Andalyssia, bonds are uncommon magic. And they are never shared between unmarried members of the opposite sex. They are rarely used outside the priesthood or the seers, in fact. I understand that you were in need, but—"

"Forbidden," Silya finished. "Balance broken must be restored. It is the king's to uphold, and he cannot hold his oath and let this pass. It would leave him unworthy in the eyes of many."

Fuck. Lucien resisted the urge to rub his suddenly throbbing head.

Honore cleared her throat. "Your Majesty, may I be granted a few minutes with my officers?" She managed a smile. "This is...a complicated situation, but I'm sure we can come to a resolution."

"What if we just leave?" Chloe said. "You could say I needed medical attention. Send us back down to Elenia. No one needs to know what happened."

"The balance knows," the seer said.

Mikvel looked pained again. "That is true. But it's also true that we have need of the Lord Truth Seeker's services to finish this business with House Elannon. There can be no treaties or otherwise until we have determined the truth at the heart of them."

In other words, no slinking away and pretending none of this ever happened.

"We understand, Your Majesty," Honore said. "But again, I think it would be best if the four of us spoke alone."

Mikvel nodded. "Of course, Colonel. Come, Sejerin, we will find tea elsewhere. You must be tired after all that riding. I certainly am."

For a moment, Lucien though Silya was going to refuse, but

she seemed to remember that she was talking with the king and rose from her chair to accompany him.

"Would you ward the room please, Gilles?" Honore said to Captain Theisse. "We need privacy for this discussion."

Gilles pushed his chair back and crossed to the door. He turned the key and then pressed his hands to the wood. Light shimmered over all the copper as he placed a ward.

"We don't need privacy," Lucien said, "We need everyone to take a breath and regain the sanity that seems to have been lost."

"We need this mission to succeed and not end in flames and another diplomatic disaster. That would not please His Imperial Majesty," Honore said sharply.

"You think we should just play along?" Lucien asked. Honore was the last person he expected to lose her head.

"Yes," Honore said.

Beside him, Chloe choked.

"Get married," Honore said. "What does it matter? You can get a divorce when we return to Lumia. Aristides will grant it. Get married, behave yourselves, and we'll finish the mission and all go home. Consider it an order."

His temper snapped. "I think, Colonel," he growled, "that you have forgotten something here. I am the Marq of Castaigne. And I'm not under your command in that capacity. Nor in my role as Truth Seeker. You can't order me to do anything. We didn't do anything wrong. We were trying to stay alive. We can dissolve the bond, and they have no real cause to make a fuss. They're trying to embarrass us."

"And they're succeeding. I know it's not your fault, Lucien, but you've broken the rules. You knew what this place is like." She cast a glance at Chloe. "And you should know better, too, Chloe, after spending so much time in Anglion. Andalyssia may seem backward to us, but their customs are theirs. They honor them. It's our job to honor them, too, while we're here."

"But we didn't do anything," Chloe protested.

"Really?" Honore arched an eyebrow. "I have it on good

authority that there was a ward around your room for half the night after the wedding, Lieutenant. Were you worried about snoring too loudly and waking Giane?"

Chloe flushed.

Lucien lifted his chin. "They don't know about that."

"It was, in fact, an Andalyssian who asked me about the noisy ward, Lucien." Her tone was nearly colder than the air in the cave had been. He'd never seen Honore furious before. "So, you're mistaken. They had no proof, perhaps, that anything they consider untoward happened, but now they do."

"Goddess bite me," he snarled. "Hypocritical idiots. Are you telling me you think none of the court ever break their marriage vows? Chloe is a widow, not some blushing eighteen-year-old virgin. This is—"

"We should do it," Chloe said.

✧ ✧ ✧

Did she really just say that? Chloe stared at Lucien, not quite believing the words that had just escaped her lips. Lucien stared back, his expression indicating he thought she'd lost her senses.

"Did you hit your head after all?" he said in a strangled tone.

Chloe narrowed her eyes. "Did you hit yours?" She turned to Honore. "Lucien and I need to talk. Alone."

Captain Theisse grimaced. "If everybody keeps leaving, we're all going to end up standing outside in the hallway. I can't imagine that will improve the sejerin's mood any."

"It won't take long," Chloe said. At least, she hoped not. Lucien was angry, and it might take longer than she thought to make him see sense. She wasn't sure she was seeing sense herself. Her stomach churned.

"See that it doesn't," Honore said. "Gilles, let's wait outside."

Chloe had to fight the urge to follow them out the door and

then just keep running until she was safely off the damned mountain. "You should redo the wards," she said, trying to sound calm.

Lucien rose, stalked to the nearest bare patch of wall, and slapped his hand against it. The echo of the ward rang though her like a bell.

"That's hardly disproving their theory about who put the ward around my room the other night."

He swore under his breath, striding back to the table.

Her pulse was racing in her ears, her stomach rolling with the panicked sense that she had landed in a mess there was no good way out of. If there was no resolution, if she was disgraced on this mission, that would be the end of her chance at a career.

She made herself breathe more slowly. One of them had to be sensible. Apparently it was her. After all, she had the most to lose here. "Honore is right," she said. "Aristides would grant you a divorce. Or us, I suppose. I'm hardly the right wife for the Marq of Castaigne, and he'll see your hand was forced. We can return home, tell nobody, get divorced, and go our separate ways again."

His eyes blazed. "It's not that simple."

"Why not?"

"For a start, what if the emperor doesn't grant me a divorce?"

"That's hardly likely. Not if you explain things to him. Presumably the two of you are on good terms. You are the Marq of Castaigne. You were raised to deal with politics. This is politics. Play the game, my lord." True, it was somewhat unusual for nobles to get divorced, but that was because their marriages were carefully considered in the first place and made for reasons often more practical than passionate, both parties clear-eyed about what they were doing. But it happened from time to time. And when it did, everyone moved on eventually.

"Marriage isn't a game." His voice rumbled, and she didn't need the bond to know he was deadly serious. "It's a vow. I do not take any vow I make lightly, Chloe."

Was that what was making him stubborn about this? His bone-deep desire to keep his word? To stay true to the promises he made to his wife?

A shiver ran down her spine. What would it be like to have those promises honored? She hadn't planned on marrying again. Her aversion to making those vows was different to his. He believed in them. Wanted to honor them. She wasn't sure she *could* believe again. "In this case, it's politics. And I won't hold it against you."

"I'd bloody well hold it against me." His fingers drummed the table, restless, sunlight glinting off his signet rings.

She had to make him understand. "That's easy for you to say."

He stilled. "What does that mean?"

"It means that you are not the one who will come off worse out of this. You are, as mentioned, the Marq of Castaigne. A Truth Seeker. If you cause a scandal on a diplomatic mission, it will be a minor drama in your life. Gossip for a few weeks at best. But it won't be minor for me, Lucien. If they send me home from this mission, I won't get another chance. I'll be discharged. I don't want to be a scandal again. Or lose everything again. I can't. I *won't*."

He winced. "Chloe—"

"No. I lost Charl. Had my life upended. I paid a price for what he did. I'm not losing everything again for something that's not my fault. Can't you do this for me? We were friends once. You care about me. Or so you say. If you do, then do this. You can make this right. Make sure I don't lose my chance. And when we get home, it will be undone, and we will both be happy."

He was silent, eyes searching hers, every line of his body tense. Then he sighed. "All right. You're right. For you, I will do this."

Something in those words tolled in her chest. He was telling the truth. That it was for her. Impulsively, she leaned forward and kissed his cheek. "Thank you."

She pulled back. He opened his mouth, then snapped it shut again.

"Lucien?" she said. "Was there something you wanted to say?"

"No," he said. "It's fine. Things are settled."

This time the bell in her chest gave more of a dull thud. Like a cracked note. "That's a lie. What's wrong?"

His head snapped up. "What do you mean, that's a lie?"

"I mean you're not telling me the truth. I can—" She stopped, startled. "I can feel it."

Shock flared his own eyes wide. "You can access my power through the bond. Goddess. That's...strange."

Strange was one word for it. Fascinating might be a better one. "It's not all the time. That's the first time I felt it. Maybe it's just with you. We should test it. Tell me something. Something from when I was away. A truth and a lie. Let's see if I can tell."

He shook his power. "This power isn't a toy."

"I know that. I've known you for a long time, Lucien. Do you think I don't know the rules you live by? But we might as well find out how this works."

"I'm not entirely sure that's a good idea."

That was true. "Why?"

"Because my power is rare. If people find out you can...co-opt a Truth Seeker's power with a bond, then I can see several ways that might go badly for Truth Seekers."

She hadn't thought of that. He had a point. "True. But we don't need to tell anyone. In fact, maybe it might come in useful. We still have my mysterious traitor to deal with."

"If you use this power to catch him out, you'd need to explain how in court," Lucien said. "Please don't. Besides, it's not so simple as you think. The truth...can be dangerous. Painful. Trust me on this. It's tempting, I know. But using that power carelessly never ends well. Besides, if our bond is part of what is breaking Sejerin Silya's precious balance, I expect her next demand will be that we dissolve it."

"The king said married people share them." The denial was instinctive.

"He said it was unusual. And this bond has served its purpose. We survived. If you want me to marry you to make sure this situation is dealt with, then you have to be prepared to do the rest. Deal with the bond as well."

She hadn't thought of that. But he was right. Even though a part of her flinched away from the thought. It seemed it hadn't taken very long for her to get used to the feel of Lucien beside her. Or his power, at least. That song of him in her head was...comforting. Like the presence of an old friend.

Goddess, what did that mean? Maybe he was right. They should dissolve the bond as they would dissolve the marriage when they got home. Make the cut clean and keep emotions out of it before anyone got hurt.

"Whatever it takes," Chloe said. "I want my second chance, Lucien. I want my life. I earned it. I don't want to let an accident ruin me again. So. We should let them back in and tell them that we will marry."

Lucien looked less than enthusiastic, but he had given her his word. He stood, crossed to the door, and took down the ward.

"Well?" Honore asked after everyone was seated again at the table. Irina had returned with a tall, rangy blonde woman who Chloe assumed was Royve Ava. The healer ignored everyone and came over to her, gesturing for her to raise her arm. She held it out obediently and watched Lucien instead of the bandage being unwound yet again. She'd caught a glimpse of the wound when Irina cleaned it earlier, and, while she wasn't generally squeamish, it was always different when it was her own flesh and blood. Irina gave her a sideways look and rolled her eyes toward the sejerin as if asking what was going on, but she didn't ask outright.

"We will do as the sejerin has requested," Lucien said.

The king looked relieved. The seer more triumphant. What exactly was she up to? She shouldn't want to disrupt the negotiations if she truly wanted balance restored. Unless she had another game to play. Was she trying to help House Elannon? Or did her allegiance fall elsewhere?

Silya rapped the table. "Good. We should proceed with haste. Restore the balance."

"No," Ava said bluntly. She spoke at the same time as the king. Royve Ava gestured at Mikvel, her focus still mostly on Chloe's arm. "My apologies, Your Majesty. Please continue."

"I would hear your reason first, Royve," Mikvel said.

The healer lifted her gaze. Her green eyes were steady and undisturbed by the glare Silya directed at her. "Lady de Montesse's arm needs attention. After which she will need to rest. She and Lord Castaigne both need sleep and food and warmth to recover after a night in the mountains. There is no balance in rushing them into sickness, Your Majesty. They will be well enough in the morning for things to proceed."

The king nodded. "Thank you, Royve. I agree. Sejerin, they have agreed to hold to our customs. Which means we must hold to them, too. They must wed according to the rites. There is perhaps not time for a tscherov and such, and, of course, they are far from home. But the priests must be informed and the marriage marks exchanged, at least. You wish to uphold balance, so we must do things properly. Lord Castaigne and his betrothed will rest today. Tomorrow we will do the pre-wedding ceremonies and then the wedding the day after. The queen and I aren't due to complete another ritual until the day after that. All will be back in balance and satisfied. Does anyone have anything else to say?"

Irina, who was holding Ava's bag of supplies for her, said, "We could organize a tscherov. Katiya and I, some of the others, and the Illvyan women. If you can spare my sister for a few hours tomorrow. The lieutenant has been very kind to both of us. Katiya will want to celebrate with her."

Chloe didn't know whether that was true—or, indeed, if there was much to truly celebrate—or whether Irina was testing her new brother-in-law to see how far he was willing to indulge her. But she didn't care if it would buy her a little more time to understand what she'd just agreed to do.

Mikvel nodded and waved a hand. "Talk to Katiya. Lord Castaigne and I have other business to discuss."

More meetings with Elannon, Chloe thought. Which she would not be part of.

CHAPTER 25

Chloe had barely finished bathing the next morning when Allita knocked on the bathroom door.

"Come in." She eased herself into a robe. Her rib was still slightly sore. Soaking in the warm water helped, but she'd need more of Allita's assistance than usual to dress to avoid straining them more than necessary. And because she had no idea where most of her wardrobe was.

She'd been moved to a new room in the royal family's wing after the meeting with the king yesterday. Katiya had said it would make it easier for the wedding celebrations to be held and for Chloe to relax, but she suspected the real reason was to remove any chance that she and Lucien would break any more rules and upset the seers more before they could be safely married.

Married. Goddess. She stared at her reflection in the mirror, still not quite believing it.

Allita slipped through the door bearing a bowl holding a glass container of some sort of salve and some linen cloths. "Royve Ava sent this for your arm, my lady. Do you want me to apply it for you?"

"No, thank you. I think I can manage, if you just open the

jar." The healer had closed the wound on her arm, but the scar was still fresh and tender.

Allita nodded, put the jar down on the counter, and opened it before bustling back out into the bedroom. Chloe applied the salve to her scar cautiously. It was an odd shade of green but smelled pleasant enough, and the ache under the skin eased as she rubbed it in.

When she was finished, she scowled again at her reflection. What had she gotten herself into? She hadn't been allowed to talk to Lucien again yet. Once she and Lucien had announced they were willing to marry, Irina, Katiya, and Royve Ava had brought her to this room, the healer had worked on her arm some more, and then plied her with food and several cups of herbal tea that had sent her to sleep.

She'd woken when Honore arrived to check on her. Not the most comfortable conversation. Honore had delivered a gentle but clear lecture on all the ways Chloe had been foolish in sleeping with Lucien and then by getting caught with him in the cave. Not to mention forming a bond with him. She couldn't argue with the former part and had bitten her tongue about the latter. She understood Honore was duty bound, as her superior officer, to tell a junior when they had screwed things up, but the storm and what came after were not Chloe's fault, and the bond had been necessary.

Just as marrying Lucien was necessary if she wanted to survive this mission with her chance at a career as a diplomat intact. At least Honore hadn't discharged her on the spot.

After the colonel left, there'd been another round of healing and then more tea. She'd barely stirred until morning when Allita, who'd apparently been assigned with her in her new quarters, had woken her.

There was no point scowling. She'd made her choices. Now she had to make the best of them. Even if that meant spending the day with Irina and Katiya and playing the radiant bride-to-be instead of doing any actual work.

She left the bathroom to find Allita laying out clothes she didn't recognize on the bed. "Where did these come from?"

Allita turned with a smile. "My lady, Her Majesty thought you might like to wear something traditional for the day. She sent these."

A simple white gown and one of the long vests the Andalyssians wore lay on the covers. The vest was blue, its embroidery gold, similar to the colors in the gown that she'd worn to the wedding ball. Du Laq colors. Well, better that than de Montesse colors. Those would hardly be appropriate when she was about to marry Charl's best friend.

She didn't want to think about what Charl would think. He was dead. Imogene, on the other hand...well, after she stopped laughing, she might be sympathetic, but the laughter would come first. Rightly so. It was ridiculous. Chloe had survived ten years in Anglion without falling foul of any rules, but a week in Andalyssia and she was a ruined woman unless she married the man most of Lumia assumed was her mortal enemy.

Which he had been. But now...now she didn't know what Lucien was to her. Temporary husband. Lover for a night. Those were not things that usually went along with being mortal enemies.

Not to mention he'd saved her life. And had only agreed to this marriage to save her from the consequences. Hard to believe she should still hate him after that. It took effort to hold on to her anger. And she was tired of it. Tired of nursing old wounds and wishing she could fix old mistakes. Especially when it seemed she was still adding new ones to her tally.

So yes, Imogene would laugh and then stand beside her as she divorced her second husband. One step up from widowhood, she supposed. But two marriages and no husbands to show for it before her thirty-fifth birthday felt careless. And really, this entire business had only reinforced her resolve not to try for a third.

But first, she had to marry the second.

She stroked a finger over an embroidered flower. "Of course I'll wear them. That was very kind of Her Majesty. Will you do my hair in an Andalyssian style?" If she was going through with this, she might as well look the part. Maybe it would make it easier to continue down this path if she did.

"Of course, my lady." Allita lifted a small fabric pouch from beside the dress. "This came for you, too. From Lord Castaigne."

"It did?" She took the pouch, trying to hide her surprise. She hadn't expected anything from Lucien. Maybe a note. But the pouch was too heavy for just a note. She untied the laces that held it closed and tipped it upside down. A familiar gold ring fell out into her hand along with a folded sheet of paper. She put the note aside and stared at the ring.

Lucien's signet ring. Not the one he had inherited from his father and now wore as Marq. This was a smaller one that he wore on the little finger of his right hand. A gift from his grandfather for his Ascension. She didn't think she'd ever seen his hands without it, even though he wasn't a man who wore much in the way of jewels. And now he was giving it to her?

"A betrothal ring, my lady?" Allita peered at it. "Is that the customary style in Illvya? It looks like very good gold," she added, as though worried Chloe might take her comment the wrong way.

"It is the custom to have a betrothal ring, yes," Chloe said, still staring down at the ring. Why had he sent her this? To keep up appearances? That would be like him. Not wanting her to have to answer questions. Though, honestly, she was far more likely to get questions about why they were marrying so quickly than why she didn't have a betrothal ring.

Charl had given her a diamond. A family ring she'd left behind when she went to Anglion. She'd taken her wedding band. It had been proof of her widowhood in those early days. Eventually she'd stopped wearing it, and no one seemed to notice. She'd never quite been able to bring herself to sell it.

Charl had commissioned it himself, so it was hers free and clear. Along with the memories it carried.

It was hidden in one of her dresser drawers in her bedroom back in Lumia.

And now, for a time at least, she would wear a new ring. Make new complicated memories of it and a man. Hopefully less tragic ones.

She slipped the ring on. It fit, more or less, and she curled her fingers closed to admire it in the light. It was, as Allita had said, good gold, the band gleaming in the sunshine. The face of the signet was etched with the tower of the Castaigne family, three stars arching above it.

What would Lucien's family say if they knew what he was about to do? Goddess. She hoped Aristides would cooperate with a quick and quiet divorce when they returned. She didn't need more disapproving in-laws to deal with.

"It suits you," Allita declared. "But we must make haste. You are due to speak with the patrarch and Sejerin Silya in an hour, and then Lady Irina will take charge of the rest of the day."

The patrarch wasn't as intimidating as she had feared. The priest kept his questions brief and seemed satisfied when she said she was marrying Lucien of her own free will. She resisted the urge to look at Silya as she answered, afraid she wouldn't be able to resist rolling her eyes. But the patrarch took her answer at face value and didn't offer any objections to the wedding occurring the next day. Of course, that might have been the presence of the queen, Honore, and Irina who'd accompanied her. A reminder that whatever the goddess and the balance might think about things, the more earthly powers in the kingdom wanted the marriage to be done with quickly so they could all return to more pressing matters.

The patrarch and two of the svasyas performed a blessing rite, speaking seer tongue. Chloe risked a tiny thread of magic to see if she could see their magic, but despite a faint glow around the three men, she couldn't really tell what the purpose of the magic they used was. She decided to take it as goodwill and leave it at that.

After the priests stepped back from the small altar fire, Silya took a turn. Chloe kept her eyes downcast to avoid more disapproval from the seer, though she didn't entirely let go of her magic. Silya's part of the rite didn't seem to take long and ended with her proclaiming, "The balance will be restored."

The words rang true. She'd forgotten about that, that she had a taste of Lucien's power. She kept her face still, not wanting to give herself away. He'd told her not to use the power, but she hadn't actually been trying to. So, at least, Silya believed what she was saying. Did that mean her concern was genuine? Though belief in the balance and Chloe and Lucien providing an opportunity for her to interfere with the negotiations weren't necessarily mutually exclusive.

Chloe let go of her thread of magic again, feeling slightly guilty. Lucien had told her not to use the power. Hopefully he couldn't feel that she had. But still, unlike him, she'd sworn no oaths not to use it, and, frankly, when there were unknown people trying to manipulate her and him, she was going to use all means at her disposal to try and resist them.

The small party Katiya and Irina arranged was far more enjoyable than the rites before it. Chloe even forgot for a time why exactly it was happening and relaxed. The Andalyssian women invited were mostly Uleniskas, Katiya and Irina's mother and aunt and a few cousins. Along with the other Illvyan women. Lady Cela wasn't included, to Chloe's relief. Honore stayed for a time before leaving for yet another meeting, but Giane and the others stayed.

They ate and played silly games and drank wine and admired Chloe's dress and the ring on her hand. There wasn't a tscherov as such, though Katiya and Irina had both produced one of the woven bands and slipped them over Chloe's wrists. Katiya's was white and silver and then paler versions of the colors of the balance. Icy green and blue and blossom pink and yellow. Irina's was bolder—she'd woven black and a red similar to Chloe's hair with emerald green, then silver, blue, and gold.

"Like your dress at the wedding," she said, running her finger along the band.

The wave and swirl design was lovely and Chloe smiled at Irina. The party and the tscherov may have been frivolous, but they were a comfort. A reminder she had made friends here, even if there were some amongst the court who didn't wish her well.

After a few hours, Sejerin Neni arrived, accompanying a young woman dressed in indigo blue who carried a square basket covered with a cloth of the same color.

Irina's face lit at the sight of the two of them, and she went to greet them, hurrying them back over to Chloe and Katiya.

"Chloe, this is Mila. She's the Tintzmach. Come to do your marriage marks."

"Oh," Chloe said, blinking. She'd forgotten those. Part of Mikvel's reasoning for at least a short delay, that she and Lucien needed the marks. "Here?"

"No, there's a smaller room next door. We thought you'd be more comfortable with that given you don't know us well. You can have company with you—Lieutenant Giane, perhaps, or one of us if you'd like, or just you and Mila," Katiya said. "And remember, this is just indigo. No needles." She touched her own chest as though seeking the mark over her own heart. "It doesn't hurt, I promise."

Chloe nodded. It wasn't pain she was worried about. Well, not the kind of pain Katiya was trying to reassure her about. A few symbols drawn with dye weren't going to harm her.

Getting through this marriage and a divorce would likely do some damage. But she had pushed Lucien into this, so there was no point in borrowing trouble against the future, as Madame Simsa would say. She wasn't a seer—Andalyssian or Illvyan—and she didn't know what would come. She just had to handle the present.

"Maybe you could come with me? Tell me how this is all supposed to work," she said to Katiya. "After all, you've just gone through it yourself." She didn't want to mess part of the ceremony up and make things worse. Sejerin Neni wasn't as intimidating as Silya, but she seemed less friendly than she had at Katiya's tscherov. What did the seers see when they looked at her that worried them?

Hopefully nothing after tomorrow.

The smaller parlor was warm, the fire burning steadily.

The Tintzmach busied herself laying the indigo cloth over the white one laid on the tiny table and setting out her supplies. No needles, as promised. Just a jar of pigment, a couple of bottles, several delicate brushes, sheets of paper, and a pencil.

"Now, my lady," she said in a surprisingly deep voice, "if you come and sit here with me, we can discuss the design."

"Discuss?" Chloe said, looking to Katiya.

"You get to choose," Katiya said with an encouraging smile.

"There aren't particular runes or something I should choose?"

"No, we keep those for seers and priests. For weddings, it is the intention that matters, not so much the symbols. The marks are there to remind you of the intention behind your wedding vows." The sejerin looked meaningfully at Chloe.

"I see," Chloe said. What was the symbol for "I intend this to be temporary"? Not a question to ask aloud. So she took the seat that Mila had indicated. "But what kind of thing do people usually choose?"

"For nobles, usually the choice is between the common symbols of the two houses," Katiya said. "One each for the husband and the wife. Some add additional elements if they wish to include something personally meaningful."

"What is yours?" Chloe asked, then shook her head. "Sorry, was that rude? To ask? You don't need to answer me."

"No," Katiya said. "Not rude. Though most people probably wouldn't ask the queen. Mine is Misha's mountain and a deer. The deer is one of the symbols of my family. And I added a ring of starflowers. The first flowers Misha ever gave me. He picked them out of my mother's garden on a visit to our family home. He got in trouble for it, but I thought it was very kind. I believe I was six and he was eight." Her smile was both nostalgic and pleased.

The smile of a woman well satisfied with her love. It was a long time since Chloe had seen anything close to that look on her own face, let alone felt the emotion.

"Take your time," Sejerin Neni said. "I appreciate that it is unlikely you will get the tattoos. You'll be home in Illvya before there's time for that, but it's still important that these symbols mean something to you."

Chloe was tempted to ask what Lucien had chosen. But that seemed like cheating. She looked down at her hands, toyed with the ring on her finger. The light through the window caught the engraving. She held it up. "Lord Castaigne's family have this on their banners. A tower—well, a castle, really, and the stars. Would those be appropriate?" She pulled the ring off and passed it to Mila, pointing at the signet.

Mila held the ring up to inspect it. "Yes. That's a good choice. And for yourself?"

She didn't really have a family symbol. Henri, though he was respected and influential due to his position and his magic, wasn't from a noble family. The de Montesse arms, well, they weren't appropriate to carry in a new marriage, no matter how temporary it may be. It occurred to her then that she would be leaving that name in truth. She would be Lady Castaigne. For a short time, the Marquesse of Castaigne. A true lady. It seemed ridiculous. And ridiculous to try and choose something that would have any chance of representing all the complications of this wedding. Or her feelings for Lucien.

So maybe she should just pick something that felt like her. "A raven," she said suddenly. "That's the symbol of the Academe. And magic in Lumia. That will do."

Ravens were smart and tough. Survivors. And they had wings to fly away if they chose. She didn't want a tame, tethered bird. She'd been tethered to Charl and then tethered to Anglion. She might be bonded to Lucien now, but she didn't intend for anyone or anything to truly chain her down again. Which perhaps was an entirely inappropriate thought for a symbol that was supposed to represent her commitment to marriage. But it felt right for her commitment to her. To the person she wanted to be. "A raven in flight," she said firmly.

Mila's eyebrows lifted, one side of her mouth quirking.

"Is that wrong?" Chloe asked. "Inappropriate?"

Mila shook her head. "No, my lady. It's just that it is almost exactly what Lord Castaigne chose."

It was? Lucien had chosen a raven to represent her?

Neni finally smiled. "A good sign, at least. The two of you must be well suited."

Mila began to sketch, her hand moving quickly and without hesitation. She held up the drawing. "Something like this?"

Chloe blinked at the image. It wasn't large, only a few inches high and wide, but it was striking. A tower ringed with stars and a raven stylized but unmistakable above the stones. For the way Mila had drawn the wings, it could be either taking off or preparing to land. Free to stay or go. She smiled. "That's perfect."

"Very well. I will mix the dye if you'll unbutton your dress."

Mila handed several more indigo cloths to Katiya. "Your Majesty, perhaps you can show Lady De Montesse how to drape these?"

The Andalyssian dress had buttons down the bodice. It was a looser style than worn in Lumia, less structured. It was actually quite comfortable, the layers fine light wools and silks. Even the vest wasn't as difficult to manage as she had thought it might be. And the button front made sense for the purpose of the day. It allowed her to ease the dress away from her shoulder and bare the patch of skin above her right breast. Katiya tucked the indigo cloths into the top of her corset and around the shoulder.

"To catch any drips," she said. "I always thought they should just make us wear indigo dresses for the ceremony, but apparently white is more bridal."

Chloe grinned at that. Katiya had a practical streak underneath the well-bred lady. Another good quality in a queen. Queen Sophia had it, too. The ability to think clearly and make sensible decisions was useful for someone with power.

Mila wiped a cloth dipped in what smelled like some form of alcohol across Chloe's skin. It didn't take long to dry.

"Hold still, my lady." She set to work with her brushes. The indigo dye smelled earthy and rich, not unpleasant but strong. But it didn't take Mila much longer to complete her work than it had for her to draw the sketch. The Tintzmach clearly was very good at her job.

Katiya handed Chloe a small gold-set mirror as Mila straightened. "Take a look." The deep blue was very dark against her skin, but it was a perfect reproduction of the sketch Mila had drawn. She had a sudden flash of a similar image decorating the hard planes of Lucien's chest, and her mouth turned dry.

"It needs to dry for a few minutes, my lady. Then you can go. It will wear away naturally over the next month or two, but it won't be troubled by water or soap. So you don't need to make any allowances."

"Thank you." Chloe watched as Mila packed up her supplies again and left with the sejerin. She looked at the mark again in the mirror. Her fingers strayed upward, itching to touch, but she restrained herself.

"It looks good," Katiya said. "Those two symbols work well together."

Was that a hint that she thought Chloe and Lucien were a good match? But Katiya knew the truth of the situation. As Chloe did. This wasn't a real marriage, just a convenient way to avoid trouble.

But still, marriage. She fanned herself with the mirror, suddenly overly warm.

"It should be dry enough now," Katiya said. Then she frowned. "Do you feel unwell?"

"It's just a little warm," Chloe said. "And all of this...the last few days have been—"

"Why don't you go out in the garden, get some fresh air?" Katiya gestured toward the windows. "There's a door there, so you don't have to go through the other room. I can stay in here a while longer, and they'll all just think you're still drying off. No one will notice if you take some time to yourself."

"Cool air sounds nice," Chloe said. "I won't take too long."

Katiya just smiled and waved her toward the door. Perhaps she also wanted some time alone. Queens, from what Chloe had seen, didn't get much of that. Always surrounded by servants and ladies-in-waiting and courtiers and such.

The air outside was cold but refreshing. The garden stretched in both directions along the terrace, green with shrubs and beds of hardy plants, and dotted with a few small clusters of trees showing signs of autumn. Not many flowers so high in the mountains and closing in on winter, but the effect was still pretty, all the shades of green soothing. She walked away from the door, turning right so as to be out of view of the others waiting in the outer room, and took a path that wound through the beds until it reached the high wall of the section. An iron gate set in the stone gave her a view into the next part of the terrace, which seemed to be another garden. Just as empty as this one.

Which made sense. The terrace ran along the royal wing. No one would be allowed in without permission. Safe enough to venture a little farther. There would be guards somewhere at the perimeter, but she couldn't see any yet, and she wasn't ready to go back inside. Curious, she pushed the gate's handle. Not locked. She pulled it open and slipped through.

On the other side, the garden was planted to appear wilder. Taller shrubs and more trees, softening the hard stone of the palace wall and the outer wall. Curious, she walked to the edge wall. There were small gaps in the stone, and, stretching up on her toes, she could just look down on the four terraces below, alternating bands of greenery and paving. Only the lowest level, which sat just inside the wall separating the palace from the town, showed any signs of life, with guards and servants and courtiers going about their business. None of them looked up, and she doubted they could have seen her if they did. The gardens were designed to give the royal family some privacy.

Deephilm didn't have space for the kind of large parklands that surrounded the palaces in Lumia and Kingswell. It would be claustrophobic in winter when the weather prevented travel through the mountains and passes to anywhere that offered more space. The terraced gardens were a clever solution to provide some outdoor spaces to everyone who lived in the palace.

She was almost halfway to the next wall across the terrace when a man stepped out from a shaded group of trees.

The man from the party. She stopped, wary.

"Lady de Montesse."

"Yes?" How had he gotten into this section of the garden?

Think. Last time she had been too startled to look for magic. This time she knew better. She drew a trickle of power, just enough to let her see the glow around him and hear an odd dissonance in the air.

Not like any other magic she'd heard.

So, he was using magic. To disguise himself? That would require a strong illusion. The kind an Andalyssian shouldn't be able to wield. The kind she couldn't necessarily break. She'd never been good with illusion. And while she might have access to Lucien's power, she didn't know how to use it. The sense of truth she'd gotten from him the day before had been more instinctive. Maybe she could use that.

"My lady, I need to speak with you again." He sounded hurried, not quite desperate but eager in the wrong sort of way. The strange note of his magic grew sharper.

Her back crawled, and it was an effort not to step back and put more distance between them. But Lucien had said to keep him talking should he appear again. To find out more. If she let him see she was scared, he might vanish again.

"I'm listening. But I don't have long. The others I'm with will come to look for me." There. That let him know she wasn't alone, at least. There was no sign of a weapon, but that was one of the problems with Andalyssian robes. Difficult to see what lay beneath them. The stranger's clothes were relatively plain again, still in shades of deep blues. Who was he?

He frowned at that. "It's true, then? You are here in the royal wing before you marry Lord Castaigne?"

Who had told him that? To get to this part of the palace, he had connections to the court, but she still didn't think he was an actual courtier. A poor relation or a member of a lesser house, perhaps? Perhaps one that wanted to replace Elannon? "I am to marry Lord Castaigne tomorrow, yes."

He looked somewhat horrified, eyes widening. "My lady. You cannot. Not Lord Castaigne. He killed your husband. He is a dangerous man."

That rang true. He believed it. So, how best to play this? Act the reluctant bride, caught up in things beyond her control? That may well string him along. "I do not have any choice in the matter. Your sejerin declare it necessary for balance."

He scowled. "Balance. They are playing games. Rushing to restore Elannon. It is not the true way."

That rang true, too. "You don't think they should be restored? Why?"

"They are a failed house. They should be replaced."

Failed? Why? Because they had been disgraced, or because the Ashmeister had failed to kill the empress and bring about whatever he wanted to achieve through her death? War? Chaos? She didn't know.

Lucien might. She really needed to talk to him.

"Well, regardless, I have to marry Lord Castaigne."

"We could help you."

She doubted she wanted any kind of help he could offer. "We? Who is we? Can't you at least tell me your name?"

A violent head shake. "It is not safe, my lady. Not yet." His face cleared. "You could come with me. We could get you out of the kingdom. You could return to Illvya."

Maybe she was a better actress than she thought if she'd convinced him she'd take up such an offer from a complete stranger with a taste for treason. Or maybe he was growing more desperate. Which meant she needed to find a way to get away from him before he did something to convince her.

"No." She moved back a half step. Not enough to alarm him but enough that she was out of reach. "They would only come looking for me. That would only harm the cause." She needed to make sure he still believed she was sympathetic to his cause.

"But Lord Castaigne...my lady, he is working for Elannon. And the emperor who should not be."

He stepped toward her, one hand outstretched. She stepped back again, not wanting him to touch her, as the grating hum of his magic flared again, making her want to shake her head to clear it.

From behind her came a scrape of metal and the sound of voices. She glanced over her shoulder and saw a pair of palace guards walking through the gate she'd come through.

"The guard," she hissed at him. "You shouldn't be seen."

His hand stretched closer as though he was considering grabbing her and taking her with him. But then he stepped back, his magic screeched for an instant, and her senses blurred.

When the feeling left her, he was gone.

CHAPTER 26

The rest of the afternoon lasted an eternity, as she smiled and tried to act as though nothing alarming had happened. Irina and Katiya seemed determined not to leave her alone for an instant, giving her no chance to send a note to Lucien, and she smiled and pretended to pay attention until they finally took her back to her room after a long dinner.

After they left, she pressed her ear to the door, listening to their voices grow faint before she turned to write Lucien a note. The difficulty was how to phrase it so as not to give things away should it be read in transit. Eventually she limited herself to a comment that she had seen someone who had asked after their mutual friend again and buried it in innocuous pre-wedding nonsense before she sealed it with the signet and sent Allita to take it to Lucien.

While she waited for Allita to return, she changed into her night things—it was easier to get out of Andalyssian clothing without assistance than Illyvan—and lay down on the covers, wondering how she was going to fall asleep.

Tomorrow she'd be married again.

To Lucien.

It seemed impossible.

She closed her eyes, determined to at least rest if she couldn't sleep.

"Chloe." A man's voice.

Lucien.

Her eyes flew open, and she struggled to sit. The lamps in the room were still alight, as was the fire. But she'd clearly fallen asleep. Because Lucien was sitting in a chair by her bed.

"What are you doing here?" she asked in a furious whisper. "You're not supposed to see me."

"I bribed someone to tell me where they were hiding you," Lucien said. "Told them I wanted to arrange a surprise for you. Apparently gold and grand romantic gestures are effective."

"People could see you."

He lifted a brow, smiling. "One day you'll remember that I'm an illusioner. We're sneaky."

He was the very definition of not sneaky. Too honorable to sneak. Except when it came to seeing her, it seemed. The thought set up a small, pleased glow in her stomach that she didn't want to think too hard about.

"Also, we're good at concealment illusions," he continued. "And most Andalyssians aren't good at seeing through them. So here we are. You didn't think I'd want to talk to you after that note?"

"I thought you'd wait until after the wedding." She glanced across the room to the clock set on the mantel above the fireplace. After midnight. At least he'd waited long enough that the hallways of the palace should be relatively empty.

"You seemed upset. Tell me what happened. Was it the same man as before?"

Upset? How had he known that? She'd been careful to keep any hint of alarm out of the message.

There was no time to waste. She needed to tell him what happened and then send him on his way. "I think so. I was in the garden in the royal wing, and he found me," she admitted. "I think he was using an illusion of some kind, but the magic felt...odd. But I don't see any other way he could have gotten into that part of the terraces. So some Andalyssians, at least, must be good at illusions."

"Or they have help from someone who is," Lucien said.

"Perhaps. He was using some magic, at least. And whoever he is, and whatever magic he has, he wasn't pleased that we are marrying. Told me I was making a mistake to ally myself with the wrong side, that you were dangerous."

"Me?"

"I don't think he's on the side of House Elannon. He didn't seem to want them restored. He seemed to think you were going to clear them—so maybe that is useful information. Maybe they are sincere if there are others who want to stop them. I tried to convince him I'm still sympathetic to their cause, but I'm not sure he was satisfied. He seemed...anxious. A guard patrol interrupted us, and he vanished."

"What do you mean, vanished?"

"Another illusion, perhaps. His magic felt very strange." She clasped her hands around her knees, remembering the look on the man's face before he'd run, his hand reaching for her, and shivered. But she didn't tell Lucien how scared she'd been in that instant. Of being taken. Forced to go somewhere against her will.

But she didn't need to. He moved to the bed and reached for her hand. She let him take it, allowing herself the comfort. With him, with the sense of the bond between them clear, there was safety and comfort. And, as the awareness of his fingers on her skin flared, something more.

"No one is going to hurt you, Chloe. You can trust me on that. I'll talk to Honore in the morning. We need to be on alert if these people are growing reckless. There will be sanctii watching you when you're not with me. It's a pity you don't have one of your own, but there's not much we can do about that. After the wedding, we'll talk to Mikvel. Trust me. I won't let anything happen to you."

He couldn't guarantee that, of course, but she knew he would do as much as humanly possible to keep his word. If he said he would do something, it got done. He'd always been that way. "Thank you."

"It would be helpful," he said with another smile, "if you locked your door."

"I was expecting Allita back," she said. "And I didn't intend to fall asleep. I didn't think I'd be *able* to sleep."

"So excited by the prospect of marrying me that you can't sleep. Just as it should be." He smiled, but something lurked in the depths of his eyes that told her he didn't find it entirely amusing.

"I'm sorry," she said. "This is not how you hoped your marriage would be, I'm sure."

Did his fingers tighten fractionally on hers?

"Not entirely, no," he said. "I had rather expected my family would be in attendance, and that there'd be a wedding night, at least."

His thumb stroked over her knuckles. Paused on the signet ring. The caress shivered over her skin. And she knew she wanted him again.

"We could have that," she said softly.

His thumb went still, all of him tensing. "Sorry?"

"A wedding night. Or nights, I guess. I mean, they're going to expect us to sleep in the same room together. And we were...compatible the other night."

"If that's what you call merely compatible, Chloe, then I pity the men who you've actually had a good time with," he said, his voice roughened.

She rolled her eyes. "Don't fish for compliments, my lord."

"But you so rarely give them. Makes the angling worth it." He smiled again, and for a moment, it felt like tumbling back through time. Like they were best friends once more. "But go on. We're compatible, we will be sharing a room. You're proposing that we take advantage while we can?"

Heat choked her throat. "Yes. Clearly there is something between us. Which is unfortunate given what else lies in our past. You know as well as I do what that history means."

"I do," he said, though she wondered if it were more question than acknowledgment.

Safer to believe it was the latter. "But we are not in Lumia. And the Andalyssians will regard us as married."

"We will, in fact, *be* married," he pointed out. "Or else I let someone paint me with dye for no good reason."

He was right. They would be married. But she couldn't let herself believe it. Or it might become too hard later, when they divorced. So she ignored that part. And ignored the insane urge to demand that he remove his jacket and shirt and show her the marks on his chest. But she twined her fingers more tightly through his. "We can have a wedding night. After all, you're doing this to save my career. I owe you." Easier, perhaps, to let herself believe she was doing this for him rather than to indulge her own desire.

His brows drew down. "You don't owe me anything. Definitely not sex. You can invite me into your bed because you want me there, regardless of how you might feel about me otherwise. I am happy to be of service, as I said before. But I don't need you to fuck me out of obligation. If I wanted that, I could have married one of any number of Illvyan aristos who only wanted my title years ago."

Her stomach tightened at the thought that he might have married while she was away. "That's not what I meant, exactly. But is that why you're not married? You want a love match?"

He looked away with a shrug. And she was tempted to use his power to see if his answer, whatever it was to be, was true. But no. She'd told him never to use his power on her. She might have accidentally used the thread of it she'd gained already, but she wouldn't turn it against him.

"Talk to me," she said softly and touched his face, turning him back to her.

His eyes held hers for a long moment, and she thought he was going to refuse.

"When I was younger, I thought so," he said eventually. "Truth be told, my career leaves little time for romance. And there seemed no particular hurry until my father died and the title became mine."

"Then you will be searching for love again?" she asked. "After, I mean?" She didn't know why she was asking. Or what she wanted his answer to be. Her blood rushed loud in her ears as those green eyes locked with hers again.

"This is a peculiar conversation to have with the woman who is marrying me tomorrow," he said, mouth quirking. "Perhaps we should worry about that instead of you thinking about my next wedding already."

She laughed, relieved. There was no good answer he could have given her. And she was scared to know which option she would find worse, him moving on after they divorced or him giving up on love as she had. "True, my lord."

"Perhaps you could call me Lucien?" he asked. "At least when we're alone."

"All right. Lucien." The syllables slipped too easily off her tongue, though they still felt somewhat strange. Like turning back the clock to the time when uttering his name had been easy, as had their friendship. Not so easy now. Or simple.

He half smiled, then leaned forward and kissed her fast. "Stop thinking so hard. And get some sleep." He let go of her hand and climbed off the bed.

How did one simple kiss make her heart pound? She wanted another, despite knowing it to be foolish. Didn't want him to leave. "You could help me sleep."

"Oh no, that would lead to more of that trouble you're worried about." He shook his head. "Good night, Chloe. I'll see you in the morning."

"White is traditional," Katiya said uncertainly.

The queen was perched on the end of Chloe's bed, looking very regal in silver and white, her hair braided and held in place with a white gold and diamond circlet. Irina, also already dressed, was examining the jewels Katiya had arrived with in case Chloe needed a larger selection than she had brought with her.

"I'm a widow. I've done this before. I'm definitely not a virgin," Chloe said. "White would be redundant." She'd worn it for the ceremonies and festivities yesterday, and that had been fun, but today she wanted to be Illvyan. She'd worn a white—well, palest cream—gown to marry Charl. She hadn't been a virgin then either, but she'd liked the color with her hair, and it went well with the de Montesse family colors. But she saw no reason to do so again.

Besides, if she wanted to wear an Illvyan gown, it had to be one she had brought with her. Imogene's taste, like hers, rarely ran to pale, and most of the dresses reflected that. The gold-and-blue gown she'd worn to Katiya's wedding was the most beautiful, but also too formal for a small hasty wedding.

Lucien had put his foot down about that. The court wouldn't attend the ceremony. Only the king, Katiya, Irina, and Roland. And as many priests and seers as deemed necessary. Nobody else. Mikvel had agreed but insisted they should have a larger reception in the evening for the court to celebrate their nuptials.

But it wouldn't be anywhere as grand as one of his and Katiya's balls. So, she could wear any of gowns she hadn't already worn to one of the royal wedding celebrations.

She considered her choices again. Allita had produced several carved wooden racks and draped the options over them. The silver brocade might pass for white. But it wasn't her favorite, and silver had never been her color.

So, instead, she reached for one of the few gowns that Helene's seamstresses had made for her. Heavy silk in her favorite deep shade of pink. Cut simply—there hadn't been time for anything too elaborate—with a modest neckline and long sleeves, it was still Illvyan but wouldn't ruffle any feathers. Helene had cleverly trimmed it with lace dyed the same shade, the motifs cut out and sewn to the fabric in a manner that resembled Andalyssian embroidery. "This one."

Katiya looked unsure but didn't argue. Irina just smiled and held up a circlet of ruby and diamond stars. "You should wear this, then. It complements the silk, and the stars match your betrothal ring."

And the mark on her skin. Lucien's mark. Part of her wanted to refuse, but another part knew he would like it.

She nodded.

Irina smiled. "There's a necklace, too."

"Just the circlet. Let's keep things simple."

Her dress and jewels might be simple, but Chloe's emotions as she walked to the chapel were complicated. She was nervous. Which made no sense. This wasn't an actual marriage. Or, rather, not one that was going to last.

But apparently her stomach didn't recognize that. It fluttered with butterflies. A sensation she hadn't felt in a while. Anticipation. Of having Lucien in her bed again. Possibly not a frame of mind that Sejerin Silya would approve of. Chloe wasn't sure she approved of it herself. But she couldn't change it.

"Are you ready?" Irina asked as they reached the doors where Gilles waited to escort her into the chapel.

"As I'll ever be," she replied, taking a deep breath. Too late to do anything else now.

Captain Theisse stepped forward. "You look lovely, Lieutenant," he said.

She smiled at him, appreciating his avoidance of her last name. Charl's last name. Soon not to be hers anymore. Once Lucien divorced her, she would return to using Matin. He would find that true love he sought eventually, and whoever he married next wouldn't appreciate another Lady Castaigne running around. Besides which, would she even be Lady Castaigne after their marriage was dissolved? Charl had died. Divorce was different.

And this, she suspected, was another train of thought that Lucien would gently suggest was strange to be having just as she was preparing to go and make vows in front of the goddess, the balance, and who knew what other deities might care to look in that she was pledging herself to him forever. She took another breath, trying to steady her thoughts, and made herself smile Gilles.

"Thank you," she said and tucked her arm through his as the doors opened.

The ceremony was straightforward. Not as long or elaborate as the king's and without the interludes of massed choruses singing strange Andalyssian harmonies to echo round the stone arches. But, having attended that, she at least understood what to expect and what to say. She stood with Lucien and followed instructions to face various directions and be anointed with substances representing earth, water, blood, and air by the svasyas. The words and movements came by rote, her focus more on Lucien than what was going on around them.

Solid and strong and familiar to anchor her through this very strange day. At various stages of the ceremony, the hum of his song through the bond grew louder, as though he was perhaps watching the ceremony to see what magic was being used. No one had yet told them they needed to dissolve it, and she was glad. She wasn't ready to give it up, the comfort that came from feeling him near.

The only real surprise came when he produced another ring at the end of the ceremony. Katiya had shown her a selection of gold bands earlier that morning and told her to pick one to give to him. They were, the queen claimed, his size. Chloe hadn't argued, and Katiya had waved away her request to pay for it.

She wouldn't have been able to afford the ring that Lucien offered her. A band of rubies near the shade of her dress, set off with a black diamond in the center. The stones sparkled in the light. Expensive. Too expensive. But she could hardly mount an argument at the altar, so she just held out her hand and let him slip it into place as she recited the final vows obediently.

He smiled as he did so, something gleaming at her from those wild green eyes that made her think his mind was more focused on events after the wedding, too. Then he leaned forward and kissed her. Not as fierce as the night before. Not as unrestrained as the night they'd shared. But the hunger beneath it thrummed at her through the bond, and she was glad that his hands had gone around her waist as her knees wobbled and the world faded around her until he pulled away and the witnesses began to clap.

She didn't get any time alone with Lucien after the ceremony. Mikvel had promised the reception he'd planned would not be too extravagant, but she realized, as the hours passed and she began to grow more eager to have Lucien to herself once more, that they hadn't placed any limits on him as to time. That had been a mistake. They should have known by now that the Andalyssians liked long meals. And liked them more followed by dancing and free-flowing wine.

By the time Lucien led her onto the dance floor for their first dance, it was already late.

"How much longer, do you think?" she hissed through her smile as Lucien swung her into the rhythm of the waltz. As always, dancing with him was easy, and a pleasure now that she had let go of her anger, but while it was delightful, she also wanted it to be over.

"Some time, I'd imagine," Lucien replied. "After all, they haven't even brought out the kafiet yet."

Goddess. Kafiet. There'd been multiple rounds of the cursed stuff at Mikvel and Katiya's wedding. She wanted a clear head tonight. To be in command of her senses when she finally got Lucien alone. After all, she had learned that he was very good at making all of them happy.

"Remind me never to let an Andalyssian plan a party for me again," she said.

"I will," he said. "Of course, that requires that you'll still be talking to me after we return to Lumia and—"

"I'm sure I will," she cut him off. It seemed wrong to speak of divorce while dancing at their wedding. She didn't want to think much at all. Surely she deserved a night of frivolity where she could just pretend she was dancing with a lover and forget all the ways in which the coming days and weeks and months were going to be hard?

She reached for the bond, wanting distraction. They hadn't spent much time together yet since they'd formed it, and she was still curious about what exactly it could do. But what answered her wasn't the spark of magic but rather a sense of hunger and heat. Of wanting. The same need driving her impatience for the reception to be done with. But it wasn't hers. It was his. And the strength of it made her giddy, heating her cheeks.

Lucien raised a brow. "Would you care to share whatever thought crossed your mind just then?"

"Perhaps later," she said, batting her eyelashes.

He grinned, but then his gaze lifted, his eyes scanning the crowd as they waltzed.

Looking for the man from the garden.

"I doubt he will be here this evening," she said. "Just enjoy the dance. Leave the watching to Honore and the others."

Honore had come to her rooms while she'd been eating breakfast, wanting to know more of Chloe's encounter in the garden. There hadn't been much time to spare, but she'd promised the sanctii would be watching. Chloe lacked the talent that some water mages had that allowed them to sense the presence of a sanctii even when they were invisible, but it was comforting to know they were looking out for her.

Lucien didn't immediately look back, but when he did, he was smiling again. "My apologies. But I said I'd keep you safe."

"And I have perfect faith that you will," she said, meaning it. "But this is, as we discussed, your wedding night. As your bride, I feel obligated to make sure you enjoy it."

His grin widened, pupils flaring, and she knew she had captured his attention once more. A renewed pulse of heat came through the bond. "I have perfect faith that you will," he said and whirled her into the next dance.

There was more dancing. More wine. More Andalyssians whose names she came close to forgetting as her body grew more tightly focused on Lucien. They were standing talking with Theo, Giane, Mikvel, and Katiya when servants finally began appearing with trays of kafiet. At Mikvel's wedding, no one had drunk until the bride and groom did, and they had been served last. She watched as everyone took the tiny glasses, the kafiet gleaming pale green as it always did. Lucien took his before the male servant offered her the very last glass.

She took it, held it as Mikvel made the toast. Smiled at his gentle joke that earned laughter from the crowd. Went to lift it to her lips, eyes locked on Lucien's. But as he began to tip his back, she saw the servant still standing close, his expression intent. Alarm flared as a faint odd chord of magic sounded. As Lucien began to swallow, she saw a flash of red at the heart of the kafiet. A color that shouldn't be there.

Without thinking, she threw up a hand, pulling wildly on the bond. Her magic cracked through the room and the glasses all shattered, triggering shouts and cries of alarm.

She stood panting, almost reeling in the aftershock, eyes fixed on Lucien. Time enough to worry if she'd hurt anyone once she knew he was all right. That she'd been fast enough.

A tiny streak of blood appeared on his cheek, above the place where he'd been bruised by the branch back in the forest. He lifted his free hand to touch it, frowning. Said, "Chloe, what—" and then toppled over.

CHAPTER 27

"Lucien!" Chloe lunged forward but couldn't catch him as he crumpled. The court had erupted into panic, but she didn't care, dropping to her knees beside Lucien, searching frantically for a pulse.

There.

Too weak, but there.

Tightening her grip on his wrist, she reached for the ley line, sending a flood of magic into him, trying to give him strength.

Irina appeared on Lucien's other side, crouching carefully. Her face was pale, but her voice stayed steady as her eyes scanned Lucien's body. "What happened?"

"There was something in the glass," Chloe said, still pouring magic into him. "A flash of red."

Irina's eyes widened. She uncurled Lucien's hand, still wrapped around the base of his kafiet glass, pulled it free, and sniffed it cautiously. "Firewort," she said. "I think." She turned and snapped orders at the nearest servant to fetch her bags and the healers. Then she looked past Chloe to Mikvel, green eyes blazing.

"Poison," she said. "We need water for everyone. They

should wash their hands. Clean any wounds carefully. Anyone who has kafiet near a cut should leave it alone and stay still until the healers can clean them up."

Mikvel nodded and turned on his heel, bellowing orders of his own.

Katiya came over to stand by Chloe. "What can I do?"

"Are you hurt?" Irina asked, eyes going up to her sister. For the first time, she looked alarmed. "Did you get cut?"

"No."

"Then see what you can do to help others."

"No, wait," Chloe said. "The servant. The one who brought the tray to us. Do you know who that was?"

Katiya shook her head. "I don't think I noticed."

"Find him," Chloe snarled. She stared down at Lucien, his face too pale. She could barely hear anything over the deafening panicked thump of her heartbeat in her ears. But she could feel him through the bond. He was alive. She had to make sure he stayed that way.

"Chloe," Irina snapped. "Pay attention. Keep feeding him your strength. We have treatments. They can work."

"Can work" wasn't "will work." Irina had told her that firewort could be deadly. For a moment, she thought she might faint. But no. Lucien needed her.

Irina glanced past Chloe. "Colonel, if you have any healers, you should send for them, too. They can help the royves."

"They could help you." Honore's voice was calm and crisp. Her colonel voice.

Irina shook her head. "They don't know how to deal with firewort. Royve Ava will ask for help if we need it. Chloe is lending him her strength through their bond. No one else will be able to do more." She looked back at Chloe. "Don't let him go."

Lucien. Her stomach roiled, but she did as asked. Fed him power and waited for the healers to come.

It didn't take them long, and the panic in the ballroom

subsided as they set to work. Ava joined Irina and Chloe, crouching beside Lucien.

"Firewort, I think." Irina nodded at the glass she'd laid carefully by Lucien's side. "In the kafiet. He must have already sipped some of it before Chloe broke the glasses," Irina said and looked at Chloe. "That was a neat trick, by the way. If all the kafiet is tainted, you saved a lot of lives tonight."

"The kafiet looked wrong," Chloe said. "I saw red in his glass."

The royve gave her an odd look. She pulled a cloth from her pocket and lifted the glass, sniffing it as warily as Irina had. "You are right, Irina. It's faint, but it's there." She cocked her head at Chloe. "I will worry later about how you know what color firewort is." She wrapped up the glass in the cloth and put it back down next to the bag she'd arrived with, placing a hand on Lucien's chest, over his heart. Just below where the marriage mark Chloe hadn't yet seen would be.

"Irina, there is patyiet in my bag. Mix a grain with a spoonful and put it on his tongue." She glanced up at Chloe. "I know Silya doesn't approve of this bond you formed, but it's just as well you did. It might just be what keeps him alive."

Lucien.

Goddess. Someone had tried to kill him. Maybe tried to kill both of them.

Her fear started to fade. What flared up to fill the void it left in its wake was anger.

Mikvel knelt beside Chloe. "Lady Castaigne, how can we help you?"

She managed not to snarl with an effort. Angering the king wouldn't do any good. "Find who did this." The words were still too sharp, but it was the best she could do. At least the king hadn't been harmed. "Start with the servant. He used magic, just before. It felt strange." She cast a wild glance around the room, searching for that face again. The healers were moving between people sitting and lying on the ground, bandaging cuts and performing other tasks. Some of the courtiers looked as though they had passed out as well. "Why are those people unconscious? Did they all drink firewort?" she asked Ava.

The healer shook her head. "Everyone is alive. Firewort would have killed some of them. My guess is that the other glasses were dosed randomly with other substances. It would have made it harder to single out what happened to your husband if you had not acted so swiftly, my lady."

"So whoever did this knows healing. Or has access to a healer willing to help them. Or—" Her eyes narrowed. "Irina, you said the seers are the ones who use firewort." She turned to Mikvel. "Where's Sejerin Silya?"

"Right here." The sejerin's voice came from behind her. Chloe twisted but didn't let go of Lucien's wrist. It was easier to feed him power while touching him.

The seer looked unexpectedly rattled.

"No seer did this, Lady Castaigne. I give you my word. Your husband's powers are not in accordance with our beliefs, but we wish him no harm."

The words rang in the way Chloe was coming to recognize as truth. Which meant Silya believed what she was saying. So it seemed forcing a marriage might be acceptable to her, but an outright attack was not. But believing something was true did not make it so.

"You are related to House Elannon, are you not?" Chloe said, and Silya frowned. Perhaps wondering how Chloe knew.

"Elannon used poison against the empress," Chloe continued.

"House Elannon wishes to be restored. Attacking the man who has the power to decide whether that will happen would be foolish," Silya said. "And though I am no longer House Elannon, I can tell you I believe them to be sincere in the changes they have made."

Truth again. Not helpful when she couldn't tell anybody that she knew it was truth. She doubted the seers would take the news that she shared a little of Lucien's power now very well. They already disliked the bond.

Silya had turned her attention to Royve Ava. "Did you use patyiet?"

Ava nodded. "Yes. Which is why he is still alive. That and the bond he shares with Lady Castaigne, I think." She lifted her chin defiantly, as though expecting Silya to argue that point. Chloe didn't care though. She doubted anyone in Andalyssia was strong enough to break the bond against her will. And she believed Ava. Lucien needed the bond, so she would fight anyone who tried to take it from her.

"If not House Elannon," Mikvel said, "then who?"

Chloe studied Mikvel's grave expression. They hadn't yet told him about the man who'd approached her. But she didn't care about protocol anymore. "I've been approached twice by a man who was trying to determine if I shared my late husband's politics, Your Majesty. I don't know where he was from, and I haven't seen him elsewhere in the court or we would have told you sooner, but the second time we met, he used magic that felt similar to what I felt from the servant just before Lucien collapsed."

"A servant used magic?" Silya said. "That's impossible."

"I know what I felt," Chloe snapped.

"Then it was not a servant," Mikvel said. "Not one who would be serving drinks tonight, anyway. We do not employ those with magic as a rule. There are exceptions for the healers and some of the guard, but otherwise, no."

"Then it was someone pretending to be a servant. I suspect he used an illusion in the garden."

Silya hissed. Chloe held up a hand. "There's no time for lectures about balance, Sejerin. I know that such an illusion isn't Andalyssian magic, but this man was Andalyssian. And he did not seem to favor House Elannon being restored. He didn't like the idea of Lucien and me marrying either, presumably because of Lucien's role with Elannon. So I suggest, Your Majesty, that you look hard at those houses—or vassals or whomever—that will benefit if Elannon falls."

Mikvel's brows drew down. "I need to know more."

"Colonel Brodier can fill you in. She knows everything I do. You need to clean your house, Your Majesty. Or the emperor will do it for you."

"Chloe!" Honore snapped. "My apologies, Your Majesty. The lieutenant is upset."

"Maybe I am. But that doesn't make what I said wrong. Aristides is very fond of Lucien. Lucien's father named him for the emperor, after all. Their families have been close for centuries. Even without Lucien being one of his lords and one of his Truth Seekers, the emperor wouldn't have taken this well." She looked back at Mikvel. "Think of Anglion, my lord. The emperor does not interfere in local politics if it does not disrupt the empire. But someone in Anglion began to plot, and that plot stretched to Illvya, and now Anglion has a new queen."

The king's eyes had turned icy. But he was not, Chloe thought, angry at her. "The emperor has no need to doubt my loyalty. I will deal with this."

"Good," Chloe said. She focused back on Honore. "Is the navire at Haalbrod?"

Honore frowned. "It should be. It will be due to leave in the morning if they have kept to the schedule."

"Send a sanctii," Chloe said. "Tell them to wait." It would be too dangerous to try and take Lucien off the mountain in darkness. They would have to go in the morning.

"Why?" Mikvel asked.

"Because I will need it. I'm sorry, Your Majesty, but someone tried just tried to kill my husband. I'm taking him home. Lumia's healers are stronger than yours."

"Lumia's healer's don't deal with firewort," Ava said.

"Well, you and Irina can explain to me what they—and I—need to do to deal with the firewort," Chloe said. "We can keep him alive if you tell me how."

"It may be wiser to stay," Mikvel said.

"Your court is not safe right now, Your Majesty. I am not going to give anybody the opportunity to try to finish what they started."

Honore said, "We need Lucien to complete his investigation of House Elannon."

She shook her head. "Colonel, you are forgetting one point."

"Which is?"

"That I am now the Marquesse of Castaigne. I outrank you. And I'm taking my husband home. If you think the emperor would prefer to risk one of his lords, not to mention his best Truth Seeker, then you can argue with me about it when you return to Lumia. You can stay here and continue the mining negotiations, but I will be leaving in the morning with my husband. I will take some of the blood and water mages with me to help the navire team. I'm sure the Elenian ambassador can send you more soldiers to make up the numbers temporarily. Just as I am sure the emperor will arrange for another Truth Seeker to join you as fast as humanly possible to finish dealing with House Elannon. But I will not let Lucien die because he did not receive the best care possible. I am taking my husband home."

Lucien survived the night, though he didn't wake despite her magic and the best efforts of the healers. Irina and Ava had attended him through the night, and Katiya had stayed to keep them company, organizing tea and food and whatever supplies the royve called for. But Lucien remained stubbornly unconscious, his pulse still weakened.

As the sun crept over the horizon, the frown Ava had worn half the night deepened. "If it was just firewort, then he should have roused by now. The patyiet should have staved off the worst of the hurt. But he is...out of balance, and I cannot determine the cause yet."

She and Irina exchanged a glance.

"What?" Chloe said from her chair beside his bed. Despite the power she was channeling from the ley line, she was beginning to feel fatigue shadowing her senses.

"If he were Andalyssian, some might say he'd been cursed," Irina said. "The old stories talk about magic being pulled out of shape. Out of balance."

"Curses are superstition," Ava said firmly. "And old stories are just that."

"Silya said something about curses," Chloe said. She rubbed the hand not holding Lucien's over her forehead. "When we returned from the hunt. The man who approached me, his magic did feel strange. It sounded out of tune."

"Unbalanced," Ava said. "It would be for an Andalyssian, if he was using a strong illusion." She frowned down at Lucien. "But Lord Castaigne feels unbalanced to me anyway. His talent for illusion warps the rest. I don't think I could tell if something had been done to him. Do you sense anything different?"

Chloe shook her head. "Not that I've noticed. His magic is fainter, perhaps, but that's because he's unconscious."

"Good," Ava said. "Though that doesn't necessarily help us. The fact remains that he is still sleeping. You were right, Chloe. He needs more help than we can give."

Which only strengthened her resolve to take him home. Ava and Irina understood firewort, but they didn't understand Illvyan mages. She needed Illvyan healers. "The healers at the main temple in Lumia are the best in the empire. If anyone can figure this out, they can." She glanced down at Lucien, willing him to wake through the bond. So far her efforts had been as ineffectual as the healer's. He remained stubbornly asleep, his skin paler than it should be and his pulse still skittering where it should be steady.

"Perhaps Irina can accompany me down to Haalbrod. She can tell me more about what I need to know about treating him." She trusted Irina, and she doubted the king would want to be without his chief healer with others in the court still being treated for their symptoms. There'd been a stream of healers knocking on the door during the night to consult with Ava about the others who'd been impacted by the kafiet. Not in the same way as Lucien, Ava had been right about that, but still sick enough to concern the healers.

"I could come, too," Ava offered.

"You are needed here," Chloe said firmly. "Irina will be enough. Once Lucien is safely on board the navire, she can return. Now, let's get my husband home."

The journey out of the Eissgora to Haalbrod was like a fever dream. Or a nightmare. The carriages the king provided were more comfortable than the charguerres and the horses nimbler than fer-taureau, but the road was still difficult and the journey too slow. They'd fashioned a stretcher for Lucien, which swayed with the rhythm of the horses. He didn't rouse for any of it, but every jolt and shudder of the carriage around her was an echo of the shuddering beat of his heart, reminding her they were losing time with every second.

Though he seemed to be holding steady, there was no improvement. Her fatigue grew stronger, forcing her to pull more power to stave it off. But she had redwort tea in her medicine case. That would keep her awake for several days if necessary. Long enough to get back to Lumia. The navire wouldn't need to land as often as it had on the journey to Andalyssia. There would be no mail to deliver, no diplomatic duties to attend. They would stop once to take on a new mage team. The journey should take only three days, according to Gilles's calculations.

She could last that long. She *would* last that long.

She'd lost a husband to politics once before. She wasn't about to lose a second, no matter how they'd come to be married. Back in Deephilm, they would be hunting for answers. Mikvel had come to see them off but had told her that, so far, they hadn't found the man who'd served Lucien. Though how he could be sure without a Truth Seeker was a point she'd been too tired to raise. Time enough to untangle the mess once Lucien was safe.

Irina fed her cups of tea and recited a steady stream of alarming Andalyssian poison lore at her as they descended the mountain. It would have been useful, Chloe thought vaguely at one point, if Irina were a sanctii. Then she could have dumped it all straight into her head, like a reveilé.

But she wasn't, so Chloe did her best to pay attention.

By the time they reached Haalbrod, the sun was low in the sky. The yard where the navire had landed was a swirl of torches and braziers, black-clad Imperial soldiers and mages swarming around the carriages.

Chloe hugged Irina goodbye, then focused solely on the passage of Lucien's stretcher up onto the navire and down into one of the cabins.

She organized her bags and the various herbs and medicines Ava and Irina had provided, finding safe places for them between checking on Lucien every few minutes. She only registered the sensation of the navire lifting into the air when her link to the ley lines began to stretch and she had to focus harder to reach them.

After that, the world reduced to just Lucien and keeping him alive.

Several hours passed before there was a knock on the door. "Come in."

Giane entered, carrying a tray of food that she set on the table. She and Theo were amongst the mages sent to fly the navire back to Lumia. "I brought food," she said. "You need to eat. Also, we have a problem."

"Unless we're about to crash, problems can wait," Chloe said. Her stomach growled at the smell of the food, but she kept her attention on Lucien.

"This one is important," Giane said, grimacing. She turned back to the door. "You might as well get in here."

Chloe looked up, wondering who she was talking to. Her mouth dropped open as Irina stepped through the narrow doorway.

"Bloody hell. What are you doing here?"

"She stowed away," Giane said, glaring at Irina. "So, it seems we've kidnapped an Andalyssian princess on top of everything else. This is going to be an issue."

"I'm not a princess," Irina said, squaring her shoulders and matching Giane's glare.

"You're the queen's little sister, and that's close enough, my lady," Giane said. "What were you thinking?"

Quite possibly that here was a chance to get away from Andalyssia. One Irina had seized. Chloe wasn't sure whether she felt admiration or irritation.

"Lady Castaigne will need my help," Irina said, lifting her chin in a manner reminiscent of both Imogene and Sophie. She might not be a true princess, but apparently she could do haughty with aplomb. "None of you know Andalyssian herb lore. And most of you have to help fly this thing, from what I understand." She swept a hand around the cabin. "Chloe can't stay awake for three days. She probably thinks she can, but if she takes redwort to do it and gets it wrong, then that could be very bad for Lord Castaigne. I might be a problem, Lieutenant, but I imagine a dead marq would be a bigger one."

Giane opened her mouth, but Chloe cut her off. "She's right, Giane. And we're not turning back to take her home. Nor are we going to leave her at the next stop. She needs a chaperone and an escort back to Andalyssia, and we can't spare anyone. She's here. We'll deal with the rest in Lumia."

CHAPTER 28

By the time the navire settled in Lumia, Chloe was near delirious with exhaustion. But she fought it back with sheer will. She would sleep when Lucien was safe. When he was smiling at her once more.

She wasn't ready to let him go.

When she saw Imogene standing on the dock, she almost burst into tears of relief but bit them back as she descended from the navire. Imogene hurried over to her, slipping her arm through hers to offer support as a team of ensigns carried Lucien's stretcher off the navire, Irina supervising. The girl had been goddess sent. She hadn't slept much either, staying by Chloe's side and working with her tirelessly to make sure she stayed strong enough to keep Lucien alive. As far as Chloe was concerned, if Irina wanted to stay in Lumia, then Chloe would damned well make sure she could. She and Lucien both owed her.

"Who's that?" Imogene asked. "She's not Illvyan."

"She's the queen's younger sister, Irina. And what she's doing here is too long a story." Chloe leaned into Imogene, willing herself to stay upright.

"Darling, you're shaking," Imogene said, "Do you need a

healer?"

Chloe shook her head. "I'm all right. I just need to get Lucien to the temple. And then I need to speak with the emperor."

To her credit, Imogene didn't bat an eye, or ask any of the ten thousand questions she must have wanted to ask. "Of course. The fer-taureau is waiting. And we have an escort through the streets. But you need to rest. You aren't any use to him if you collapse."

"I can't rest yet." She hadn't slept. "Our bond might be what is keeping him alive."

"Your bond?" Imogene's brows flew up. Then her eyes narrowed as she looked from Chloe to Lucien's stretcher. "So I see. This is going to be an interesting story once you have time to tell. I have to admit, you returning from Andalyssia married to Lucien de Roche was not a possibility that entered my head."

Chloe nodded. "Mine either. And I'll tell you all about it. But first the temple."

The next few hours moved quickly. The healers at the temple took charge of Lucien, even Domina Francis herself coming to the hospital wing of the building to assist. The dominas questioned Chloe and Irina about firewort and everything they had done, including the bond. Then shooed them both outside the room after assuring Chloe the bond wouldn't be affected by a distance of twenty feet or so.

They sat with Imogene, waiting. The urge to force her way back into the room crawled under Chloe's skin. Being unable to touch Lucien after the near constant contact of the last few days felt wrong. Irrational or not, she wanted to be with him.

Strange. A little over two weeks ago, she'd still hated him.

Now she didn't know what she would do if he died. Other than, perhaps, burn the world down around those who had hurt him.

After an eternity, Domina Francis reemerged from the room. She was smiling, and Chloe's heart started pounding. "Is he awake?"

"No, child. But he has improved. I think he will rest a little longer, but I expect he will wake in the next day or so." Domina Francis had eyes as green as any Andalyssian, but her hair was blazing red streaked with silver, a sign of her strength in earth. Her words tolled through Chloe, and she knew they were true. "You and the Lady Irina did well. But now both of you need to rest. Then we will see how to proceed with your husband once he awakens and we can assess him. Whatever he was given, it was strong. He may need to recuperate for some time."

"But he won't die?" She sounded like a child asking to be reassured that there was no monster under the bed, voice quivering.

"No, he will be well," the domina said, voice pitched to a soothing tone. "And you must rest. Your bond will give him strength, but not if you make yourself unwell through worry and exhaustion."

"I—" The urge to lie down and sleep was overwhelming. But she wasn't done yet. "I need to talk to the emperor."

"You need to rest. Aristides will wait." The domina's tone was steely. She turned her attention to Imogene. "Your Grace, perhaps you can tell His Imperial Majesty that Lady Castaigne needs to recover from her journey before she speaks with him?"

"Of course," Imogene said. She squeezed Chloe's hand. "Domina Francis is right. Aristides will wait. I will go to him, and your fellow lieutenants can brief him on anything urgent. I'm guessing sending another Truth Seeker to Andalyssia might be one of those things."

Chloe nodded. "But not until I can speak with them. Giane and Theo don't know everything that has happened."

Imogene smiled. "All right. Now go see your husband. Then

sleep. We'll wake you when you're needed."

"I can see him?" Chloe asked.

"Of course," Domina Francis said. "We've made up a bed for you next to his. I thought you would want to stay close." She smiled at Irina. "We'll make up a room for you, child. Then, after you have slept, I think we may have things to talk about."

Irina's smile at that was somewhat triumphant. But Chloe would worry about her later. Now, she wanted Lucien.

Domina Francis walked with her back into the room, shooed the other healers out, and told Chloe they would check back regularly. Then she left the room, closing the door softly.

Lucien was still sleeping, but there was, she thought, more color in his face. And her sense of him through the bond felt more solid.

She sat on the bed beside him, laid her hand on his chest so she could feel his heart beating, then leaned down to kiss him, willing him to hear her. "Keep breathing. Wake up. I need you. And we have traitors to hunt."

THE END

Chloe and Lucien return in
THE TRAITOR'S GAME

Join my VIP reader's list and get an EXCLUSIVE short story
featuring Chloe and Imogene
CLICK HERE (or scan the QR code below)

A NOTE FROM M.J.

I hope you loved reading THE EXILE'S CURSE.

The Daughter of Ravens series continues Chloe's story in The Traitor's Game. You can also read Courting The Witch, a prequel novella featuring Imogene and Jean-Paul.

As an indie author, it really helps me when readers get the word out about my books, so if you enjoyed the book, please consider leaving a review at the store where you purchased it and tell your friends! If you want to stay up to date with all my news, find out about new releases and sales, then please sign up to my newsletter using the QR code below and get an exclusive short story!

ABOUT THE AUTHOR

M.J. Scott is an unrepentant bookworm. Luckily she grew up in a family that fed her a properly varied diet of books and these days is surrounded by people who are understanding of her story addiction. When not wrestling one of her own stories to the ground, she can generally be found reading someone else's. Her other distractions include yarn, cat butlering, dark chocolate and watercolor. To keep in touch, find out about new releases and other news (and receive an exclusive freebie) sign up to her newsletter at www.mjscott.net. She also writes contemporary romance as Melanie Scott and Emma Douglas.

You can keep in touch with M.J. on:

Instagram @melwrites
Facebook AuthorMJScott
Pinterest @mel_writes
TikTok @mjscottwrites

Or email her at mel@mjscott.net

ALSO BY M.J. SCOTT

Romantic fantasy

The Four Arts series

The Shattered Court

The Forbidden Heir

The Unbound Queen

Courting The Witch (Prequel novella)

The Daughter of Ravens series

The Traitor's Game

The Rebel's Prize

The Half-Light City series

Shadow Kin

Blood Kin

Iron Kin

Fire Kin

Urban fantasy

The Techwitch series

Wicked Games Wicked Words Wicked Nights

Wicked Dreams Wicked Ways

The Wild Side series

The Wolf Within The Dark Side

Bring On The Night

The Day You Went Away (free prequel short story)

ACKNOWLEDGMENTS

This book was pure fun to write so maybe I should thank Chloe and Lucien for behaving. But thank you to everyone who has been reading my books and telling me you enjoy them.

Thank you to Deranged Doctor for the gorgeous cover art! And Etheric Designs for bringing my tower and stars to life.

Big hugs and thanks as always to my Mum, the Lulus, Sarah, the Office gang and everyone else who's been sharing these weird times with me. Smooches.